Grandmaster of Demonic Cultivation
MO DAO ZU SHI

1

墨香銅臭

Grandmaster of Demonic Cultivation
MO DAO ZU SHI

1

WRITTEN BY
Mo Xiang Tong Xiu

TRANSLATED BY
Suika & Pengie (EDITOR)

COVER ILLUSTRATION BY
Jin Fang

BONUS ILLUSTRATION BY
moo

INTERIOR ILLUSTRATIONS BY
Marina Privalova

Seven Seas

Seven Seas Entertainment

GRANDMASTER OF DEMONIC CULTIVATION: MO DAO ZU SHI VOL. 1

Published originally under the title of 《魔道祖师》
(Mo Dao Zu Shi)
Author ©墨香铜臭 (Mo Xiang Tong Xiu)
English edition rights under license granted by 北京晋江原创网络科技有限公司
(Beijing Jinjiang Original Network Technology Co., Ltd.)
English edition copyright © 2021 Seven Seas Entertainment, LLC
Arranged through JS Agency Co., Ltd
All rights reserved

《魔道祖师》(Mo Dao Zu Shi) Volume 1
All rights reserved
Illustrations granted under license granted by Istari Comics Publishing
Interior Illustrations by Marina Privalova
US English translation copyright © Seven Seas Entertainment, LLC

Cover Illustration by Jin Fang
Bonus Color Illustration by moo

No portion of this book may be reproduced or transmitted in any form without written permission from the copyright holders. This is a work of fiction. Names, characters, places, and incidents are the products of the author's imagination or are used fictitiously. Any resemblance to actual events, locales, or persons, living or dead, is entirely coincidental. Any information or opinions expressed by the creators of this book belong to those individual creators and do not necessarily reflect the views of Seven Seas Entertainment or its employees.

Seven Seas press and purchase enquiries can be sent to Marketing Manager Lianne Sentar at press@gomanga.com. Information regarding the distribution and purchase of digital editions is available from Digital Manager CK Russell at digital@gomanga.com.

Seven Seas and the Seven Seas logo are trademarks of
Seven Seas Entertainment. All rights reserved.

Follow Seven Seas Entertainment online at
sevenseasentertainment.com.

TRANSLATION: Suika
EDITOR: Pengie
INTERIOR LAYOUT & DESIGN: Clay Gardner
PROOFREADER: Jade Gardner, Ember Valmore
COPY EDITOR: Dawn Crane
IN-HOUSE EDITOR: Tamasha
BRAND MANAGER: Lissa Pattillo
PRINT MANAGER: Rhiannon Rasmussen-Silverstein
MANAGING EDITOR: Julie Davis
ASSOCIATE PUBLISHER: Adam Arnold
PUBLISHER: Jason DeAngelis

ISBN: 978-1-64827-919-5
Printed in Canada
First Printing: December 2021
10 9 8 7 6 5 4 3 2 1

GRANDMASTER OF DEMONIC CULTIVATION

CONTENTS

CHAPTER 1: Reincarnation — 9
(CONTAINS WEB SERIALIZATION CHAPTER 1)

CHAPTER 2: The Intractable — 13
(CONTAINS WEB SERIALIZATION CHAPTERS 2-5)

CHAPTER 3: The Prideful — 59
(CONTAINS WEB SERIALIZATION CHAPTERS 6-10)

CHAPTER 4: The Elegant Flirt — 119
(CONTAINS WEB SERIALIZATION CHAPTERS 11-18)

CHAPTER 5: The Sunny Pair — 205
(CONTAINS WEB SERIALIZATION CHAPTERS 19-22)

CHAPTER 6: The Malevolent — 243
(CONTAINS WEB SERIALIZATION CHAPTERS 23-27)

CHAPTER 7: The Morning Dew — 287
(CONTAINS WEB SERIALIZATION CHAPTERS 28-32)

APPENDIX: Character & Name Guide — 353

Glossary — 377

Contents based on the Pinsin Publishing print edition originally released 2016

1
Reincarnation

"**R**EJOICE, Wei Wuxian is dead!"

It hadn't been a day since the Siege of the Burial Mound, and the news had already flown across the entire cultivation world as if it had sprouted wings. The speed was only comparable to how fast the flames of war had spread back then, if not faster.

Suddenly everyone, whether they were prominent clans or rogue cultivators, was discussing this operation of vanquishment that had been led by the four great clans and attended by hundreds of sects both big and small.

"Fantastic, fantastic indeed! Who was the hero who killed the Yiling Patriarch?"

"Who else could it be? Ain't it his shidi, the little sect leader Jiang Cheng? The four major clans fronted the attack: the Jiang Clan of Yunmeng, the Jin Clan of Lanling, the Lan Clan of Gusu, and the Nie Clan of Qinghe. Crushing family for the greater good, they destroyed Wei Wuxian's good ol' lair, the Burial Mound."

"I must say, well done."

Someone immediately clapped and exclaimed in agreement, "That's right, well done! If it wasn't for the Jiang Clan of Yunmeng, who took him in and raised him, then Wei Wuxian would've been a no-name street rat in the countryside—never mind becoming anything else! The former Jiang sect leader raised him like his own son, eh? But look at him: publicly defecting from the clan, making himself an enemy of the world. He's embarrassed the Jiang Clan of Yunmeng utterly and almost doomed them to the same fate of extermination. What do you call a traitor? Him!"

"I can't believe Jiang Cheng allowed that guy to run amok for so long. If it were me, I wouldn't have just stabbed him when he first defected, I would've cleaned house! He wouldn't even have gotten the chance to do all those crazy things. What does a childhood friendship matter when facing people like him?"

"That's not what I heard, though? Didn't Wei Ying's[1] demonic cultivation backfire, causing him to be ripped apart and devoured by the ghosts under his command? I heard he was chewed to pieces while still alive."

"Ha ha ha ha! That's what you call karma. I've wanted to say this for a long time now, but those ghost generals he raised were like a pack of unleashed mad dogs, biting people everywhere. And in the end, he got bit to death himself. Well deserved!"

"Be that as it may, if the little Jiang sect leader hadn't been the one to plan this siege based on the Yiling Patriarch's weaknesses, then success would've been difficult to guarantee. Don't forget what Wei Wuxian had in his clutches, or how over three thousand renowned cultivators were all completely annihilated that night."

"Wasn't it five thousand?"

"Three thousand, five thousand, they're all the same. Five thousand is more believable."

"He really is completely mad…"

"He destroyed the Yin Tiger Tally before he died, so he gets at

---

[1] Wei Wuxian's birth name is Wei Ying. See Characters and Name Guide for more information.

least some credit for that. If that evil thing was left to cause harm in the world, his sins would only deepen."

The moment the Yin Tiger Tally was mentioned, there was suddenly silence, as if everyone was wary of something. A moment later, someone sighed.

"Man…speaking of that Wei Wuxian. He used to be a young master in an extremely affluent and distinguished cultivation sect back then. It wasn't like he had no accomplishments. He gained great success in his youth. How glorious and unbridled he was… How did he end up on this path…?"

The subject changed, and voices were raised again in heated discussion.

"It's obvious from this case that the path of cultivation must always follow the righteous way. The demonic path is only glorious for the moment. You think it looks so glamorous? Heh, look where that got him."

"Death without a corpse!" a voice replied forcefully.

"It's not all because of the cultivation path. At the end of the day, it's still because Wei Wuxian was someone of bad character. He roused the wrath of the heavens and the grudges of men. You know what they say: What goes around comes around; the heavens are watching…"

……

After Wei Wuxian's death, judgment of his character was no longer refutable. The discussions were mostly the same, and any small voice of dissent was immediately squashed.

However, gloom still firmly enveloped everyone's minds.

Although the Yiling Patriarch, Wei Wuxian, had died at the Burial Mound, the remnants of his soul couldn't be summoned.

Perhaps his soul had also been ripped apart and devoured by the millions of ghosts. Or perhaps it had escaped.

The former would naturally be a joyous occasion for the entire world. However, the Yiling Patriarch had the ability to topple the earth and move mountains and seas—at least, that was what the legends said. It would be no great task for him to resist soul-summoning if he desired it. If his spirit returned in the future…if he took over a body and was reincarnated, then the cultivation world—the entire mortal world, in fact—would be cursed to face even greater vengeance, sinking into an endless storm of darkness and blood.

And so, when the hundred and twenty stone beasts required to seal a mountain were set down at the peak of the Burial Mound, every major clan began conducting frequent soul-summoning rituals. They also strictly monitored for cases of possession, sought far and wide for abnormal occurrences, and heightened their security to the max.

In the first year, all was peaceful.

In the second year, all was peaceful.

In the third year, all was peaceful.

……

In the thirteenth year, all was still peaceful.

Thus, more and more people finally came to believe that perhaps Wei Wuxian had not been that amazing after all. Maybe he really had perished.

Even though he had once turned the world upside down, there had at last come a day when he was the one overturned.

No one could be worshiped on the divine altar forever. Legends were merely legends.

2
The Intractable

WEI WUXIAN had only just opened his eyes when someone kicked him.

A voice thundered in his ears: "PLAYING DEAD?"

He almost coughed up blood from the kick. His head hit the ground, and with his face turned up, he thought hazily, *You've got nerve, daring to kick me, the patriarch.*

Wei Wuxian had already lost count of the number of years it'd been since he last heard a live person speak, never mind such awful caterwauling. He was dizzy, and the cracked voice of a young man was rattling between his ears.

"Think for a moment *whose* land you're living on, *whose* rice you're eating, and *whose* money you're spending! So what if I took a few things of yours? They should've been mine in the first place!"

Soon after, there was the clamoring noise of chests and cabinets alike being ransacked. It was a good moment before Wei Wuxian's eyes could focus. A dim ceiling came into view, as did an unfortunate-looking face with a greedy glare. That face was spraying spittle all over him.

"And you dare go tattle on me!! You think I'm actually afraid of you tattling?! Do you *actually* think anyone in this house would take your side?!"

Two large men who looked like servants came over. "Young master, everything's smashed!"

"So fast?" the quacking youth questioned.

"There wasn't much stuff in this broken shack anyway," the servant replied.

The quacking youth was extremely pleased. He turned to Wei Wuxian, pointing so hard at the man that he was practically jabbing his finger up his nose and into his brain.

"Go and tell on me, I dare you. Who are you playing dead for? As if anyone would actually give a crap about all this junk and wastepaper. I've smashed everything; let's see what else you've got to go tattle on me with! Think you're all that just because you went to a cultivation sect for a few years? Well, didn't you get kicked out like a stray dog anyway?!"

Presently half dead, Wei Wuxian thought to himself, *It's not pretend. I've actually been dead for many years.*

Who was this?

Where was this??

When had he ever done something like forcibly possess the body of another???

After having kicked the man, ransacked the house, and spent all his temper, the quacking youth strutted out the door along with his two servants, slamming the door behind him.

He ordered in a loud voice, "Keep proper watch, don't let him come out to embarrass people!"

The servants outside the door all heeded. Once the man had gone, silence settled both inside and out of the house. Wei Wuxian wanted to sit up, but his limbs would not obey him, so he lay back down and flipped over. His head continued to spin as he looked at his strange surroundings and the mess on the floor.

Next to him was a copper mirror that had been tossed onto the ground, and Wei Wuxian snatched it up. A dreadfully pale face

CHAPTER 2: THE INTRACTABLE

appeared in the mirror. Two large blots of red were smeared unevenly on each cheek; if he were to stick out a long and vividly red tongue, then he'd be the very picture of a hanged ghost.

Wei Wuxian tossed the mirror aside, a little disgusted. He wiped his face and found his hand smeared with white powder.

Fortunately, it wasn't that this body had been born strange, but rather, the penchant of the previous owner. A full-grown man with a face heavily caked in makeup, and sloppily applied at that...

This shocked some energy back into Wei Wuxian, who was finally able to sit up. Only then did he notice the circle of a spell array beneath him. The array was scarlet and crooked, seemingly hand-drawn using blood as the medium. It was still damp, emitting a metallic stench. There were warped and crazed spells drawn within the array that had been somewhat smudged by his body, but the remaining shapes and characters were gruesome in their evil intent. Wei Wuxian had been called by titles such as the Supreme Evil Lord, the Grandmaster of Demonic Cultivation, and whatnot for years, so naturally, he was very familiar with obviously devious arrays such as these.

It wasn't that he had robbed anyone of their body—he had been offered one!

The nature of this "sacrificial ritual" was a type of curse. The caster was to harm themselves with a weapon, making cuts on their body and using their own blood to draw the array and write the spells within. They would then sit in the center of the circle and give up their mortal body to evil spirits, using the annihilation of their soul as the price to summon a nefarious, malicious ghost. This was all done in order to request the fulfillment of a wish. Thus, it was the opposite of "possession."

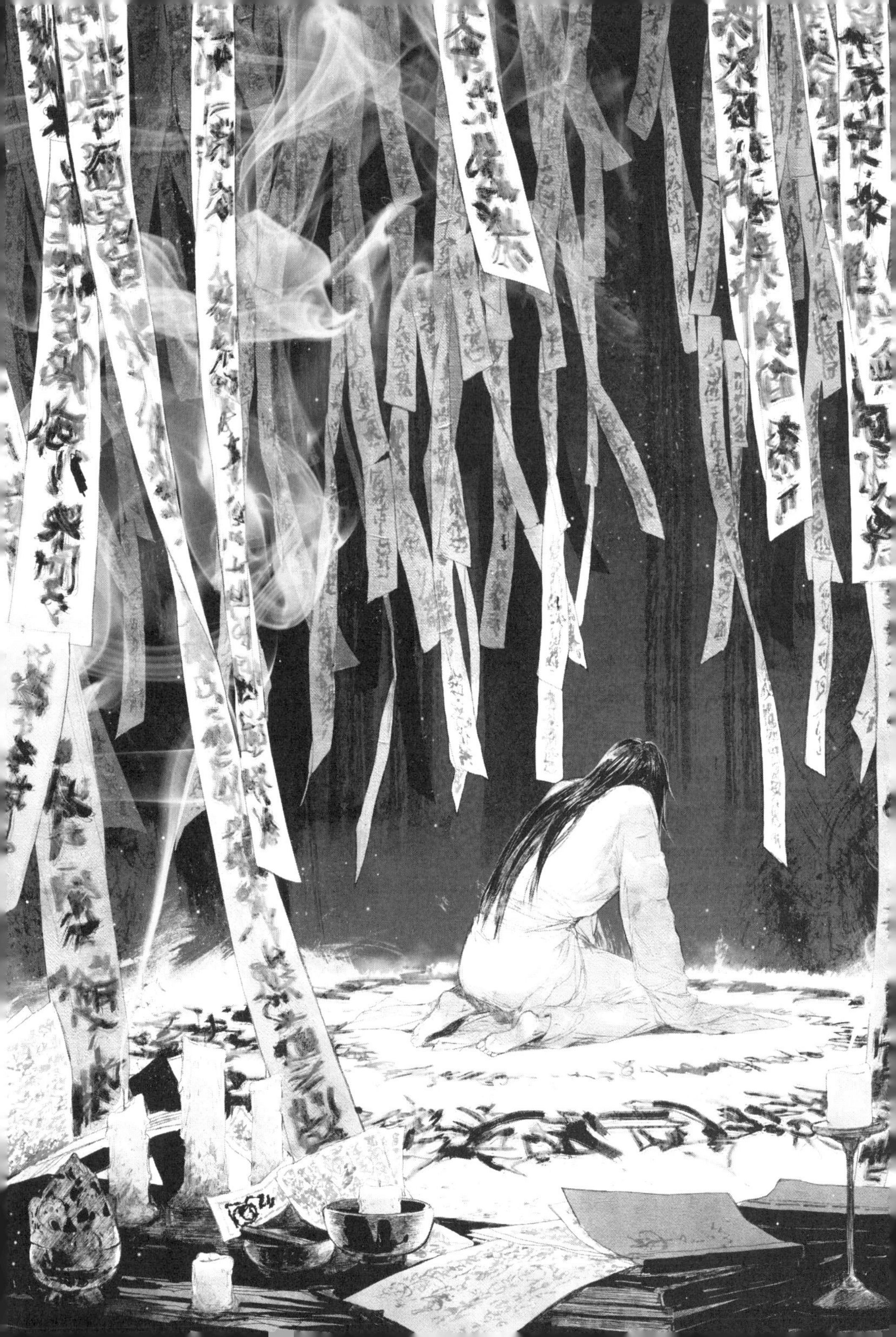

While both were forbidden magics of ill repute, the difference was that the former was much less popular than the latter. After all, few wishes were so strongly desired as to make someone willingly sacrifice everything they had. This was why the technique had been nearly lost after centuries of disuse. The examples recorded in ancient books had only a handful of cases that were backed by reliable evidence, and every single one of them had been for revenge. Every malicious ghost summoned by the ritual had fulfilled the caster's wishes perfectly, in cruel and bloody ways.

Wei Wuxian refused to accept this.

Since when was he categorized as a "nefarious, malicious ghost"?

While he'd had a fairly poor reputation and died an extremely tragic death, he didn't haunt the living, for one, and he'd never sought vengeance, for two. He could swear there was not a single wandering ghost in this world who was more decent and honest than he!

But the tough thing was, the Sacrificial Ritual followed the will of the caster first and foremost. So it didn't matter how much he objected… He was already inside this body, which was a silent acknowledgement that both parties had formed a contract. He had to fulfill the wish of the caster, or the curse would rebound, destroying the possessor's primordial spirit and extinguishing it forever.

Wei Wuxian yanked his sash loose and raised his arms to inspect them. Sure enough, both of his wrists had been slashed with a sharp tool, leaving them covered in crisscrossing lacerations. The bleeding had already stopped, but Wei Wuxian knew these were not normal injuries. If he didn't fulfill the caster's wish, then these wounds would be unable to heal, and they would worsen the longer this dragged on. If the deadline for fulfillment was missed, then he who had accepted this vessel would be ripped apart in both body and soul alike.

He triple-checked that there was no mistake and cried *This is ridiculous!* mentally ten times before finally rising to his feet with difficulty, supporting himself against the wall.

This house certainly was big, but it was empty and shabby. The bedding was emitting a sour smell—who knew how many days had gone by since it was last changed. There was a bamboo basket for trash in the corner that had been kicked over earlier, and both trash and wastepaper were strewn across the floor. Wei Wuxian noticed there seemed to be ink marks on the crumpled papers, so he picked one up in passing. He opened it to take a look, and sure enough, it was covered in words. He quickly went around to collect all the balls of paper.

These were probably written by the owner of this body to vent his frustrations. Some of the sentences were incoherent and disordered, but the anxiety and nervousness were abundantly clear. Wei Wuxian patiently examined each sheet, and the more he looked, the more he felt something was amiss.

Through some guesswork, he figured out a few things. First, the owner of this body was named Mo Xuanyu, and this place was called the Mo Estate.

Mo Xuanyu's grandfather on his mother's side was from a rich family in this area. The family wasn't large, and the man was not fated for a son. After years of trying, he still only had two daughters. The name of the second daughter wasn't mentioned, but either way, the eldest daughter was born of the lawful wife. Thus, they were looking for a husband to marry into their family name. Although the second daughter was exceptional in appearance, she was born of a servant, which was why the Mo family had originally planned to marry her out without giving much thought to the groom. Who would've thought she was fated for a fortuitous encounter?

CHAPTER 2: THE INTRACTABLE

When she was sixteen, the head of a prominent clan was passing by and fell in love with her at first sight. The two made the Mo Manor the site of their rendezvous, and a year later, the second daughter gave birth to a son. This was Mo Xuanyu.

The inhabitants of the Mo Estate would normally have held such an event in contempt, but people at the time worshiped cultivators. In the eyes of the mundane folk, cultivation clans that pursued immortality were loved by the heavens, mysterious and noble. Furthermore, that prominent clan leader would financially support this new outer family branch of his every so often. So naturally, these circumstances were special. Not only did the Mo family consider this an honor, but others were extremely envious too.

However, the good days did not last. That wandering clan leader was only hungry for the novelty of fresh meat, and he was over it after two years, coming to visit less and less frequently. After Mo Xuanyu turned four, the man never appeared again.

In those passing years, the Mo Estate's opinion changed again. The contempt and mockery returned, now with added disdain and pity. Second Lady Mo refused to accept this, believing firmly that the prominent clan leader would not turn a blind eye to his own son. And sure enough, when Mo Xuanyu turned fourteen, that clan leader sent over a grand party to officially take him back.

Second Lady Mo's head was held high again. Although she could not go with them, this event swept away all the grievances she had. Feeling proud and elevated, she proclaimed proudly to everyone she saw that her son would definitely become a leader of cultivation sects in the future—rise to the top and bring glory to the ancestors. Thus, the people of the Mo Estate changed their opinion for the third time.

However, Mo Xuanyu was driven out before he managed to cultivate acclaim and succeed his father. And driven out in the most shameful way: Mo Xuanyu was a cut-sleeve, a male homosexual, and he was so audacious as to harass his fellow peers. With this scandal exposed, and the fact that he possessed only average talent and no real achievements in cultivation, the sect had no reason to keep him.

Adding frost to snow, something had upset Mo Xuanyu. When he returned home, it was as a madman. His mental state had been upended, as if he had been scared silly.

Having read to this point, Wei Wuxian's brow twitched a couple times.

The cut-sleeve matter aside, the man was a lunatic too. No wonder he had smeared enough powder on his face to look like a hanged ghost. No wonder no one thought it strange that there was such a large, bloody spell array on the ground. Mo Xuanyu could probably smear blood all over this house, from the floor tiles up the walls and to the ceiling, and no one would think it weird. Because everyone knew he was crazy!

After Mo Xuanyu returned to his old home, he was bombarded with ridicule. This time, it seemed, the situation was unsalvageable. Unable to take this blow, Second Lady Mo was choked to death by her own unappeasable outrage.

At this time, Mo Xuanyu's grandfather had already passed, and the one managing the household was First Lady Mo. This Madam Mo had never been able to stand her little sister, and she scorned that sister's bastard son. She had a single son herself by the name of Mo Ziyuan—the one who had just ransacked Mo Xuanyu's house. When Mo Xuanyu first left with such impressive fanfare, First Lady Mo had felt they now possessed something of a family tie to that prominent cultivation sect and had hoped the cultivator envoys would bring Mo Ziyuan along with them too. Of course, she had been rejected, or rather, ignored.

Duh. This wasn't like selling cabbage in the markets: buy one, get one free!

Who knew where this family got its confidence? But they all possessed a bizarre idea: they firmly believed that Mo Ziyuan had potential, that he had talent, and that if he were the one who had gone with the cultivators, then he would have been recognized for his worth for sure, unlike his failure of a cousin. Although Mo Ziyuan had been young when Mo Xuanyu left, he had been repeatedly indoctrinated to believe this nonsense without a single doubt. Thus, he caught Mo Xuanyu every other day to humiliate him, cursing him for having robbed him of his path to cultivation. Yet he remained enamored with the talismans, the pills, and the little spiritual devices that had been brought back from the cultivation sect and would take them all for himself, breaking them as he willed. While Mo Xuanyu was often in the throes of madness, he knew when he was being humiliated. He tried his best to endure it, time and time again, but Mo Ziyuan's behavior only worsened, practically emptying the entire house. At last, Mo Xuanyu had enough. He finally stammered a complaint to his uncle and aunt, which was why Mo Ziyuan had come knocking today, looking for trouble.

The words on the paper were tiny and cramped. Wei Wuxian's eyes were sore from reading all this, and he thought to himself, *What kind of hellish life was he fucking living?* No wonder Mo Xuanyu had preferred to end it, offering his body to summon malicious ghosts to avenge himself.

After his eyeballs started feeling better, it became his head's turn to ache. Technically, the caster of the array had to mentally recite their wish. As the evil spirit summoned, Wei Wuxian should have been able to hear the details of his request. However, this forbidden magic had probably been secretly copied off a book with missing pages; it was incomplete, and Mo Xuanyu had missed that step. Although Wei Wuxian could guess that he most likely sought vengeance against the Mo family, how exactly did he want it done? To what extent? Take back what was taken? Beat up the family?

Or...wipe them out entirely?

It was most likely wiping out the family, eh! After all, anyone who had been in the cultivation world would know the words most often used to describe Wei Wuxian: treacherous, mad. Was there anyone who better fit the description of "fiendish"? Since the man had dared to summon him by name, his wish was definitely not something easily granted.

Wei Wuxian said helplessly, "But you've got the wrong person..."

At first, he wanted to wash his face and gaze with reverence upon the dead countenance that had once belonged to its former owner. However, there was no water inside this house, not even drinking water. What's more, Wei Wuxian figured the only container around was for lavatory purposes and *not* for washing up.

He tried pushing the door, but it was barred from the outside, probably to prevent him from running amok. There was not a single thing that could allow him the slightest bit of joy in being reincarnated!

He might as well meditate for a while and get used to the new body.

An entire day passed this way. When he opened his eyes once more, there was sunlight seeping into the house through the cracks of the window. Although he could get up and walk, his head was still spinning, and it didn't appear to be getting better. Wei Wuxian was puzzled.

This Mo Xuanyu's cultivated spiritual power is so minuscule, it might be completely overlooked. There's no reason why I can't manipulate this body. So why is it so difficult to use?

CHAPTER 2: THE INTRACTABLE

It wasn't until a strange noise sounded from his stomach that he realized it had nothing to do with spiritual power; it was simply that this body, not trained for fasting, was hungry. If he delayed seeking food any longer, he might just become the first malicious ghost in history to die of hunger immediately after being summoned.

Wei Wuxian took a deep breath and raised his foot. But just as he was about to kick the door open, there was suddenly the sound of footfalls on the other side, drawing near. Someone gave the door a kick, which was followed by an annoyed call:

"Meal time!"

While those were the words, it didn't appear the door was going to open at all. Wei Wuxian looked down just in time to see a small bowl be heavily set down before a small slat at the bottom of the door.

The servant outside then added, "Hurry up! What's the holdup? Put the bowl out when you're done!"

The slat was smaller than a dog flap, not large enough to allow people to go in and out, but bowls could be passed through. There were two dishes and one bowl of rice that looked awfully disgusting. Wei Wuxian bitterly stirred the chopsticks that were stabbed into the rice.

The Yiling Patriarch had returned to life—only to be kicked down and yelled at. The first meal to welcome him back was cold leftovers. Who would believe him if he told them? What had happened to his bloody reign? His absolute massacres? His unadulterated annihilation of the sects? Truly, out of the mountains a tiger can be bullied by a dog, in shallow waters a dragon can be mocked by a shrimp, and a plucked phoenix is lower than a chicken. Stripped of their privileges, the strong will be belittled by the weak.

Just then, the voice of the servant outside the door was heard once more. But this time, it was a laugh that sounded as if it came from a completely different person.

"A-Ding! Come over here."

A delicate and frail feminine voice answered from a distance, "A-Tong, did you come to deliver food for that person in there again?"

A-Tong clicked his tongue. "Why else would I come to this miserable courtyard?!"

A-Ding's voice was at the door, much closer now. "You only make deliveries once a day, and no one scolds you even if you slack off every now and then, so why are you frowning at being so free? Look at me, so busy with errands that I can't even go out to play."

A-Tong complained, "It's not like delivering meals is the only thing I do! And you still dare go out right now? There are so many walking corpses roaming about that every household has their doors firmly shut."

Wei Wuxian was crouched down by the door, pushing around the contents of the bowl in his hand with two chopsticks of different lengths, listening as he ate.

Seemed like things hadn't been peaceful here at the Mo Estate. Walking corpses, as per their name, were the walking dead: reanimated corpses that were low-level and commonplace. Their eyes were usually glazed, their movements sluggish. They were fairly harmless. Nonetheless, that was enough to terrify average folks, and their putrid smell alone was enough to make one fill a pot with puke.

However, to Wei Wuxian, they were the easiest to manipulate and the most obedient of puppets. In fact, it even felt somewhat endearing to suddenly hear about them.

A-Tong appeared to have winked. "You have to take me along if you want to go out, so I can protect you…"

A-Ding cut him off dismissively. "You? Protect me? Please. Can you actually fight those creatures off?"

"If I can't fight them off, then no one can," A-Tong grumbled.

A-Ding laughed. "How do you know if other people can't fight them off? Let me tell you, delegates from a cultivation sect have already arrived at our Mo Manor today. I hear they're from an incredibly prominent clan! The madam is receiving them in the main hall right this minute. Everyone in town has gathered to watch, they're all so curious. You hear that noise? They might order me around again in a bit. I don't have time to play with you."

Wei Wuxian listened intently. Sure enough, there was the faint sound of commotion. After a moment's contemplation, he got up and kicked the bar locking the door, which broke with a crack.

The two servants flirting with each other screamed in surprise when the door was suddenly flung open. Wei Wuxian tossed the bowl and chopsticks aside as he stalked out, but the sunlight blinded him. The glare also caused a small, pinching pain on his skin, so he raised his hand to his brows and closed his eyes for a moment.

A-Tong had screamed louder than A-Ding a moment ago, but when he looked closer, he realized it was that lunatic everyone could bully. His courage returned. Feeling he must regain the dignity he'd just lost, he jumped over and waved, shooing Wei Wuxian like one would a dog.

He yelled, "Get outta here! Shoo! Go back in! What're you doing outside?!"

Not even beggars or flies could have received more unsightly treatment. This was probably how these servants had treated Mo Xuanyu in the past, and they grew ever more impertinent when he didn't retaliate.

Wei Wuxian gave A-Tong a light kick, sending him tumbling, and laughed. "Who are you trying to humiliate, huh?"

With that, he headed east, following the noise. Both the east hall and the east courtyard were crowded with people, and just as Wei Wuxian stepped into the yard, he heard a woman whose voice rose louder than the others.

"...We have a junior at home who also had an affinity for cultivation once..."

That must have been Madam Mo, who was trying to build connections with cultivation clans again. Wei Wuxian didn't bother waiting for her to finish before he languidly squeezed through the crowd, entering the main hall. He waved enthusiastically.

"HERE, HERE, OVER HERE!"

In the main seat of the hall sat a middle-aged woman, well maintained and sumptuously dressed. This was Madam Mo. The one sitting below was her husband, who had married into the family, and across from him were several white-clad youths with swords on their backs. When a disheveled, unkempt weirdo suddenly emerged from the crowd, conversation came to an abrupt stop.

However, Wei Wuxian seemed to take no notice of the frozen atmosphere. He said unabashedly, "Who called me just now? The one with an affinity for cultivation, isn't that me?"

There was too much powder on his face, and it cracked when he smiled, flaking as it fluttered off. One of the white-clad youths snorted, almost laughing out loud, but he restrained himself when another youth who appeared to be the leader of the bunch shot him a disapproving look.

Wei Wuxian snuck a glimpse at them and was somewhat taken aback. At first, he had thought "an incredibly prominent clan" was but the exaggerated praise of an unlearned servant. But the people here really were cultivation disciples worth their name. Who would've thought?

Graceful-sleeved and light, airily sashed, these youths were exceptionally pleasing to the eyes, transcendent and poised. Judging by their uniforms alone, it was obvious they came from the Lan Clan of Gusu. They were disciples with blood ties to the Lan family as well, since every single one of them had a two-centimeter-wide white ribbon patterned with rolling clouds tied around their foreheads.

"Elegance and Righteousness" was the motto of the Lan Clan of Gusu, and this forehead ribbon symbolized self-restraint. The rolling clouds were the Lan family's insignia, and guest cultivators, or sect disciples of outside families affiliated with the prominent clan, were only allowed to wear ribbons without the pattern. Wei Wuxian always cringed every time he spotted someone from the Lan family. He'd often complained under his breath in his previous life that their uniforms looked like funeral clothes, so he knew he wasn't mistaken now.

It had been a long time since Madam Mo had seen this nephew of hers, and it took a while before she was able to recover from her shock. After realizing who this heavily powdered person was, she was furious. But she couldn't lose her composure, so she hissed at her husband.

"Who let him out? Get him out of here!"

Her husband responded with an apologetic smile and got up with a glum look, ready to seize Wei Wuxian. All of a sudden, Wei Wuxian dropped down without warning and latched firmly onto the ground, immovable no matter how he was pulled or dragged. Not even the servants who were called in to help could do anything. If not for the outsiders who were present, they would've started to kick him already.

Madam Mo's face was growing darker and darker, and the husband was drenched in sweat as well.

He yelled, "You damn lunatic! If you don't go back right now… Be careful or I'll put you in your place!"

Although everyone from the Mo Estate knew there was a young master in the Mo family who had gone mad, Mo Xuanyu had withdrawn into that gloomy house of his for many years, afraid to see anyone. Now that they saw how both his appearance and his actions resembled those of a raging monster, they started to whisper among themselves, excited to watch this spectacle unfold.

Wei Wuxian spoke up, "I can go back if you want." He pointed at Mo Ziyuan. "But you have to make him return everything he stole from me first."

Mo Ziyuan never thought this lunatic would have the gall. He'd taught the guy a lesson just a day ago, only to have him turn around and expose him here today.

His face changed colors as he exclaimed, "YOU'RE LYING! Since when have I ever stolen anything of yours? Why would I need to steal any of your stuff?!"

"Right, right, right," Wei Wuxian agreed. "You didn't steal, you snatched!"

Madam Mo could now tell that Mo Xuanyu had obviously come prepared. His mind was perfectly clear, and he was bent on humiliating them.

Shocked and livid, she accused him sharply. "You fully intend to wreak havoc here today, isn't that right?!"

Wei Wuxian looked confused. "He stole my stuff, snatched it from me, even. Is asking for it all back considered 'wreaking havoc'?"

Mo Ziyuan grew agitated, raising his leg to kick Wei Wuxian before Madam Mo could answer. However, one of the sword-carrying

CHAPTER 2: THE INTRACTABLE

white-clad youths moved his fingers slightly, and Mo Ziyuan immediately lost his balance. The kick brushed past Wei Wuxian, missing the mark, and the boy tripped over himself. However, Wei Wuxian still tumbled and rolled as if he really had been kicked. He even ripped open his robes, revealing on his chest the footprint left behind by Mo Ziyuan's kicks the day before.

The villagers of the Mo Estate were enjoying the show immensely. Excitement filled the crowd. There was no way Mo Xuanyu could have kicked himself to create that footprint, and no matter what, he was still a member of the Mo family. What a vicious household. The boy hadn't been this crazy when he first returned, so it was probably the family's doing. Either way, it wasn't like they were the ones being beaten, so as long as there was a show to watch, all the better. This spectacle was truly more interesting than the arrival of the cultivators!

With so many eyes watching, the youth couldn't be beaten and he couldn't be kicked out. Madam Mo had no choice but to forcibly smooth the whole debacle over with fury thick in her throat.

She said impassively, "What 'steal'? What 'snatch'? Such ugly accusations. We are family; it's nothing but borrowing. A-Yuan is your younger brother,[2] so what if he takes a few things of yours? As an elder brother, will you be this stingy? Throwing a childish tantrum and embarrassing everyone over such a small matter—it's not like he wasn't going to return your things."

The white-clad youths stared at each other in dismay, and one of them almost choked on his tea. The disciples who grew up with the Lan Clan of Gusu were raised in refined elegance, so they had probably never encountered such a farce, nor heard such *brilliance*. Today's events were probably widening their horizons.

---

2   Cousins are still referred to as brothers or sisters in familial address.

Wei Wuxian laughed maniacally in his mind and extended his hand.

"Give them back, then."

Of course, Mo Ziyuan couldn't return anything. All the items were long since tossed out or torn apart, and even if he could have returned them, he wouldn't have done so willingly. Red in the face, he cried out in protest.

"*MOM!*" He scowled at her. "Are you going to let him insult me like this?!"

Madam Mo glowered at him, signaling him not to make this scene any worse than it was. Unexpectedly, Wei Wuxian spoke up again.

"While we're on the topic, not only should he not have stolen my stuff, he shouldn't have done so in the middle of the night. Everyone knows I like men. Even if he has no shame, *I* know not to make myself suspicious."

Madam Mo drew in a sharp breath and yelled, "What are you spewing in front of the village folks?! How shameless! A-Yuan is your little cousin!"

When it came to outrageous behavior, Wei Wuxian was an expert. In the past, he'd had to maintain some form of decorum so people couldn't accuse him of having a poor upbringing, but now he was a lunatic anyway, so what did he care for shame? He could go wild and cut loose to his heart's content.

He stiffened his neck and said outright: "He knew he was my little cousin, but he still didn't observe propriety and keep his distance, so who is the more shameless one here?! I don't care if you don't care about your reputation, but I still care about mine!! I STILL GOTTA FIND A GOOD MAN!!!"

Mo Ziyuan roared, raising a chair to hurl it Wei Wuxian's way.

CHAPTER 2: THE INTRACTABLE

Seeing that he'd finally snapped, Wei Wuxian quickly scrambled up to go hide. That chair broke into pieces upon impact with the ground. The spectators crowding in and out of the east hall were waiting with unconcealed delight to watch the Mo family be disgraced, but they all quickly dispersed once things got violent, afraid they might be injured.

Wei Wuxian ducked toward the youths from the Lan family, who were completely dumbfounded by what was unfolding, crying as he did so.

"You see! You see!! He's hitting me even though he stole my stuff—how heartless!"

Mo Ziyuan chased him over, ready to lunge, but the leader of the youths stopped him. "This... Gongzi, we can talk this out."

Seeing that the youth intended to protect the lunatic, Madam Mo grew apprehensive. She forced a smile. "This young man is my younger sister's son. He's a little...unstable *here*. Everyone at the Mo Estate knows he's crazy. He's always saying strange things, so don't take him seriously. Esteemed cultivators, you mustn't—"

Before she could finish, Wei Wuxian poked his head out from behind the youth. "Who said I can't be taken seriously? From now on, if anyone tries to steal my stuff, I'm gonna chop off an arm for every time they do. Just try me!"

Mo Ziyuan was being held back by his father at first, but when he heard this, his anger flared up again. Wei Wuxian darted out the door like a fish, taunting him with a *la-la-la* as he went.

The youth quickly blocked the door right after and changed the topic, assuming a serious face to talk business. "Um... Then we will be borrowing your esteemed west courtyard for tonight. Please remember exactly what I said earlier. Lock all doors and shut all windows tight after dusk. Do not come out for any activities, especially not near the west courtyard."

Madam Mo was shaking with rage, but it wouldn't have been courteous to push the youth aside, despite him blocking her. So, she could only reply, "Yes, yes, thank you, thank you…"

Mo Ziyuan was in a state of disbelief. "MOM! Are you gonna let that lunatic get away with slandering me in public?! Didn't you say yourself that he was only a mere—"

"Shut your mouth!" Madam Mo cut him off sharply. "Can you not wait until we're back inside?!"

Mo Ziyuan had never suffered such a wrong before, nor had he ever been humiliated this way. He had especially never been scolded by his mother like this.

He cried furiously, "That lunatic is dead!!"

After Wei Wuxian was done letting loose, he went out the main entrance of the manor and strolled around the Mo Estate to show his face, scaring innumerous passersby and enjoying himself while he was at it. He began to understand the joy of being a madman and was even starting to be pleased with the hanged ghost makeup, not wanting to wash it off.

It's not like there's water around anyway, so I'll let it be.

He fixed his hair and glanced at his wrist. There was no indication the cuts were fading or healing at all, which meant the trifling revenge of venting anger on Mo Xuanyu's behalf was far from enough.

Did he really have to slaughter the entire Mo family?

…To be honest, that wouldn't have been anything difficult to do.

Wei Wuxian pondered this as he sauntered back to the Mo Manor. As he snuck past the west courtyard with small, quick steps, he noticed the Lan disciples on top of the rooftops and wall eaves, gathered in somber discussion. He snuck back again with those small, quick steps and looked up, watching them intently.

CHAPTER 2: THE INTRACTABLE

While the Lan Clan of Gusu was a major part of the coalition that had come to besiege him in the past, those juniors hadn't yet been born at the time, or if they had, would've been only a few years old. So that event had nothing to do with them. Wei Wuxian stood there and observed, wanting to see how they planned on handling the situation. As he looked on, he suddenly felt something amiss.

Why did those black flags being flown on the rooftops and wall eaves look so familiar?

The flag was called a spirit-attraction flag. If it was stuck on a living person, then it would attract every dark spirit, every vengeful ghost, every fierce corpse, and all such manner of evil to attack said person. Since wearing a flag was akin to becoming a live target, the flag was also called a target flag. It could also be stuck on buildings, but said building had to have living persons within, and the range of the target would increase to include all people within the building. Since yin energy swirled around the area where these flags were planted like a black whirlwind, they were also known as black wind flags. Those youths were setting up the flag formation and had told others not to go near, so they had to intend to lure the walking corpses here to capture them all at once.

As for why the flags looked familiar…how could they not? The creator of the spirit-attraction flag was this very Yiling Patriarch!

It appeared that, despite how the cultivation world had demanded Wei Wuxian's demise, they nevertheless had no qualms about making use of his inventions.

One of the disciples on the rooftops noticed him watching and chided him. "Go back, this is not a place you should be."

Though he was being ordered to shoo, it was done with good intentions, and the tone of voice employed was also greatly different from that of those Mo servants. While the youth was off his guard, Wei Wuxian hopped up and plucked a flag.

Greatly alarmed, that disciple jumped down the wall to chase after him. "Don't touch that, it's not for you!"

Wei Wuxian hollered as he ran, looking completely like a lunatic; his hair flying loose and disheveled, arms waving and legs skipping. "Finders keepers! I want this! Mine!"

That disciple quickly caught up with him and grabbed his arm. "Give it back! Or else I'll hit you!"

Wei Wuxian clutched the flag tightly, refusing to let go. The leader of the group that was setting up the flag formation was alerted by the commotion and also came fluttering down from the eaves.

"Jingyi, let it go. Retrieve the flag nicely; there is no need to start a dispute."

"Sizhui, I didn't hit him for real!" Lan Jingyi complained. "Look at him, he's messed up the flag formation!"

During their push and pull, Wei Wuxian had swiftly finished inspecting the spirit-attraction flag. The drawn patterns were correct, and none of the spells were missing either. There were no mistakes, so no mishaps would occur if the flags were used. The only issue was that the person who'd drawn the flag was not very experienced, so the spell could only attract any evil and walking corpses within a two and a half radius at most. But that would be enough.

Lan Sizhui turned to him with a smile. "Mo-gongzi, it is getting late, and we will be starting to catch walking corpses here soon. It is dangerous at night. You'd best hurry back to your chambers."

Wei Wuxian sized up this youth. The boy was gentle in disposition, refined and elegant, noble in his bearing with a light grin curving the corners of his lips. This was a good sprout very worthy of encouragement, and Wei Wuxian mentally gave him a nod of approval. The child had set up the flag formation in a proper and orderly manner, and his upbringing really was quite commendable as well. Wei Wuxian wondered who among that terrifying group full of uptight sticks-in-the-mud known as the Lan Clan had managed to raise such a junior.

Lan Sizhui added, "This flag—"

Before he could finish, Wei Wuxian tossed the spirit-attraction flag onto the ground and humphed. "What's so good about this crappy flag? I can draw better!"

He then took off right after. The juniors who were on the rooftop, watching the show, burst out laughing at his shameless declaration so riotously that they almost fell off the roof. Lan Jingyi also laughed in exasperation, then picked up the flag on the ground, dusting it off.

"What a lunatic!"

"Don't say that," Lan Sizhui chided him. "Let's go back and help now."

As for Wei Wuxian, he wandered idly about for a while. It wasn't until after dark that he returned to Mo Xuanyu's little courtyard. The door latch was snapped, without anyone to clean up the mess. He ignored it and picked a somewhat clean spot in the room before sitting down and continuing to meditate.

Yet unexpectedly, it hadn't reached the morning hours when a noisy commotion outside pulled him out of his meditative state. A clamor of footsteps mixed with wailing and screaming was rapidly approaching, and Wei Wuxian heard these cries repeated:

"…Break in and drag him out!"

"Report him to the authorities!"

"Who cares about the authorities, just beat him to death!"

He opened his eyes just as a number of servants charged in. The entire courtyard was lit up as bright as day, and someone was shouting:

"Drag that murdering lunatic to the main hall and make him pay with his life!!"

Wei Wuxian's first thought was: *Did something go wrong with those youths' flag formation?*

The smallest carelessness in the usage of his inventions could cause disaster, which was why he had earlier purposely gone to verify whether the spirit-attraction flag was properly drawn. Thus, when those large hands came to drag him out the door, Wei Wuxian lay there limply, allowing himself to be dragged out. It saved him the trouble anyway. He was dragged to the east hall, where it was as lively as could be; surprisingly, there were no fewer townspeople gathered than there had been during the day. Many of the servants and close family relations had come, some still dressed in inner robes, not having had time to coif their hair, panic painted on each of their faces. Lady Mo sat slumped in her seat as if she had only just awoken from having fainted. There were traces of tears on the sides of her cheeks, the rims of her eyes still wet. However, the moment Wei Wuxian was dragged in, her tears instantly transformed into a baleful glare.

On the ground, there lay something that resembled the form of a human. The body was covered by a white sheet, and only its head was exposed. Lan Sizhui and those youths were bent down over it, inspecting the body solemnly and whispering to each other. Their words filtered into Wei Wuxian's ears:

"...It hasn't been one incense time since he was discovered?"

"Right after subduing the walking corpses, we were rushing to the east courtyard, and the dead body was lying there in the corridor."

CHAPTER 2: THE INTRACTABLE

This body was Mo Ziyuan. Wei Wuxian swept a glance over him, then took another look in spite of himself.

This corpse looked like Mo Ziyuan, but at the same time not. While the facial features were clearly that of his cheap little cousin, the cheeks were deeply sunken, the eyeballs bulging, and the skin wrinkled. It was as if he had aged twenty years compared to the previous Mo Ziyuan, who had been in the prime of his youth. It also almost seemed as if he had been sucked dry of his blood and flesh. He looked like a mere sack of bones dressed in an extremely thin veil of skin. If it could have been said that the Mo Ziyuan from before was simply ugly, then his corpse now was old *and* ugly.

Wei Wuxian was just taking a detailed look when Madam Mo suddenly came charging over. Something shining flashed in her hand. She was holding a dagger! Moving as fast as his eyes saw, Lan Sizhui knocked it out of her hand, but before he could say anything, Madam Mo was already screaming at him.

"My son died a tragic death—I need to avenge him!! What're you stopping me for?!"

Wei Wuxian once again ducked behind Lan Sizhui and shot back, "What does your son's tragic death have to do with me?"

Lan Sizhui had watched Wei Wuxian make a scene during the day, then later heard plenty of exaggerated rumors about this illegitimate son from the others. He felt great pity for this mentally ill person and couldn't help but try and speak up for the man.

"Madam Mo, the state of your son's corpse is clearly the work of evil. Its blood, flesh, and spirit have been completely sucked out. He could not be the culprit."

Madam Mo's chest heaved. "What do you know?! This lunatic's father is a cultivator, so he must've learned plenty of evil magic!"

Lan Sizhui looked back and took a glance at the seemingly half-witted Wei Wuxian. "Madam, there is no evidence, so it is still best…"

"THE EVIDENCE IS ON MY SON'S BODY!" Madam Mo pointed at the corpse on the ground. "Take a look yourselves!! A-Yuan's dead body has already told me who his murderer is!"

Without waiting for the others to make a move, Wei Wuxian raced to pull back the sheet from head to toe. Mo Ziyuan's corpse had something missing.

His left arm, from the shoulder down, had vanished as if it had sprouted wings!

Madam Mo added, "You see that? You all heard him today, right? What this lunatic said? That if A-Yuan touched his things again, he would chop off A-Yuan's arm!"

After her hysterics had settled, she covered her face and sobbed.

"…My poor A-Yuan never touched anything of this lunatic's. Not only was he slandered, he was killed by this maniac…"

Maniac!

It was so endearing. How many years had it been since he'd heard himself described as such? Wei Wuxian pointed at himself, but he didn't have the words to rebuke that particular statement. He didn't know, either, whether he really was mental, or if Madam Mo was the one who was ill. After all, he had boasted about slaughtering entire sects, laying waste to millions, making blood flow like rivers, and other such things when he was younger. But that was all talk, most of the time. If he really could do all that, he would've tyrannized the world already. Madam Mo wasn't trying to avenge her son at all. She was only looking for someone to vent her anger on.

Wei Wuxian didn't want to bother with her. After a moment of thought, he reached into Mo Ziyuan's robes and searched, finally

CHAPTER 2: THE INTRACTABLE

digging something out. When he unfolded that something, it was a spirit-attraction flag.

In that instant, it dawned on him. He muttered under his breath, "Mo Ziyuan brought this on himself!"

When Lan Sizhui and the others saw the item taken out of Mo Ziyuan's robes, they also understood what had happened. Thinking back to the farce that had taken place during the day, it wasn't hard to deduce what had transpired. Earlier, Mo Ziyuan had lost considerable face due to Mo Xuanyu's hysterics, filling him with hatred. He'd had a mind to settle scores, but Mo Xuanyu had gone out frolicking, nowhere to be found. So Mo Ziyuan intended to wait until nighttime to teach Mo Xuanyu an underhanded lesson.

Yet when night came and he snuck out the door, as he passed by the west courtyard, he saw the spirit-attraction flags planted atop the wall eaves. While there were strict instructions against outings at night—and that the west courtyard was forbidden and that those black flags were not to be touched under any circumstances—Mo Ziyuan thought that was the cultivators purposely scaring people off because they were afraid of others stealing their precious spiritual weapons. He was unaware of just how dangerous and ominous the effects of the spirit-attraction flag were, and that once held, a flag would make the bearer a living target. Mo Ziyuan's hands had never been clean. He'd grown addicted to stealing the talismans and spiritual tools belonging to his crazy older cousin. When he saw the magical objects, he couldn't help but feel the itch to take them for himself, no matter the cost. Thus, while the owners of the flags were subduing walking corpses in the west courtyard, he secretly plucked one away.

The flag formation utilized six spirit-attraction flags, five of which were set up in the west courtyard using those youths from the Lan family as bait. However, they themselves were protected by the countless spiritual tools carried on their persons. Although Mo Ziyuan had only stolen the one flag, he didn't have any protective tools on him. Go after the weakest, as they say. Naturally, the evil spirits were lured to him. If it had only been walking corpses, then it wouldn't have been a big deal. At most, he'd have been bitten a couple times. It wouldn't have resulted in his death. There would still have been a chance to save him. Yet it just so happened that this spirit-attraction flag had unintentionally summoned something more terrifying than walking corpses. And it was precisely this unknown evil spirit that had killed Mo Ziyuan and robbed him of an arm!

Wei Wuxian raised his wrist. Sure enough, a cut on his left arm had healed. It seemed the sacrificial ritual had acknowledged Mo Ziyuan's death as his doing. After all, the spirit-attraction flag was Wei Wuxian's invention, so he'd hit the mark out of pure luck.

Madam Mo was perfectly aware of her son's little flaws, but she would never admit Mo Ziyuan had caused his own death. Anxious and aggravated, she picked up a teacup and hurled it at Wei Wuxian's face.

"If you hadn't made a scene and framed him in front of so many people yesterday, would he have gone out in the middle of the night?! It's all your fault, you bastard!!"

Wei Wuxian was already prepared and sidestepped to dodge the attack. Madam Mo then screamed at Lan Sizhui.

"AND YOU! You bunch of useless fools!! What cultivators are you, what evil can you exorcise?! You can't even protect a child! A-Yuan is so young!!"

Those youths were still green and only had so much experience under their belt. They hadn't detected anything unusual in this area, which was why they'd never thought there'd be such a ferocious evil.

At first, they'd been quite sorry because they felt themselves lacking, but after Madam Mo's indiscriminate tongue-lashing, they were growing upset. After all, they came from a distinguished clan. No one had ever dared treat them this way. The teachings of the Lan Clan of Gusu were extremely strict: they forbade raising a hand against normal folk, and not even rudeness was allowed. Even though they were irritated, they had to force it down, causing dark expressions to cloud their faces.

Wei Wuxian couldn't take it anymore. He thought, *After so many years, the Lan Family still acts this way. What's the use of all that self-restraint unless you're looking to suffocate yourselves? Watch me!*

He spat loudly. "Who do you think you're yelling at? Do you really take them to be your servants? They came all this way to exorcise evil for free, and now they *owe* you? How old is your son again? At least seventeen, right? A 'child' still? How old do you have to be to understand human words? Did they not instruct us again and again yesterday *not* to go near the west courtyard, *not* to touch anything in the formation? Your son snuck out in the middle of the night to dally about—is that my fault? Or is it his fault?"

Lan Jingyi and the others let out a breath, no longer looking as upset. Madam Mo was both extremely sad and resentful, and her mind was filled with nothing but thoughts of death. More specifically, it wasn't thoughts of herself dying to accompany her son, but rather thoughts of having everyone in this world die, especially the ones currently in front of her.

Whenever something happened, she'd always order her husband around, so she shoved him. "Call everyone in! Call everyone in here!"

However, her husband was in a daze. Perhaps the shock of the death of his only son was too great, but he shoved her back. Knocked down to the ground so abruptly, Madam Mo was stunned.

If this had been before, Madam Mo needn't have pushed him; as long as she raised her voice a tiny bit, he'd do whatever she said. Yet today he dared fight back!

The servants were all terrified by her expression, and a trembling A-Ding helped her stand. Madam Mo grabbed her heart, and said with a shaking voice, "You...you...YOU GET LOST TOO!"

Her husband seemed not to have heard. A-Ding shot A-Tong a number of looks, and A-Tong quickly dragged his master out. It was chaos within the east hall. Seeing how the family was finally quieting down, Wei Wuxian went to inspect the corpse further. However, he had barely glanced at it before another high-pitched scream pierced through the door.

The crowd inside the hall poured out and were greeted with the sight of two bodies spasming on the ground in the east courtyard. One was a slumped A-Tong, alive. The other was collapsed on the ground, its body wrinkled and withered as if its blood and flesh had been completely sucked dry. Its left arm was already gone, and there was no blood flowing from the wound. The state of this corpse was exactly the same as Mo Ziyuan's.

Madam Mo had just shaken off A-Ding's supporting hand, but when she saw that corpse lying on the ground, she was stunned in place. At last exhausted of the energy to throw more fits, she fainted. Wei Wuxian happened to be standing near her, so he caught her and passed her to A-Ding as she came running over. He then took a glance at his right hand. A cut there was gone as well.

Madam Mo's husband had only stepped out onto the threshold of the hall. He hadn't even entered the yard before he died tragically on the spot. Everything had happened within an instant.

Lan Sizhui, Lan Jingyi, and the others paled, but Lan Sizhui was the first to compose himself. He questioned the slumped A-Tong.

CHAPTER 2: THE INTRACTABLE

"Did you see what it was?"

A-Tong was thoroughly horrified, his teeth clenched so hard that he couldn't utter a word for the moment, only shaking his head. Lan Sizhui, burning with impatience, instructed his peers to bring the boy inside before he turned to Lan Jingyi.

"Did you fire the signal?"

"I did," Lan Jingyi replied. "But if there are no seniors nearby who can come to offer assistance, our people will probably take at least an hour before they can make it here. What do we do? We don't even know what it is right now."

It was, of course, impossible for them to leave. If a clan's disciples only cared about escape when running into evil spirits, then not only would they embarrass the clan, but they themselves would be too ashamed to go out again. The terrified folks of the Mo household could not leave with them either. The evil spirit was most likely among them, so it would have been useless even if they fled.

Lan Sizhui clenched his teeth. "Stay on guard until help arrives!"

Since the distress signal was already fired, other cultivators would soon come to their aid. In order to avoid adding to the present trouble, by all accounts, Wei Wuxian should have retreated. Best if whoever came was no one he knew. If it was someone he had crossed paths with before, or had fought with, then it was hard to tell what would happen.

With the sacrificial ritual's curse on him, he could not leave the Mo Estate yet. Besides, if the summoned creature could take two lives within such a short span of time, then it was abnormally ferocious. If Wei Wuxian dropped everything and left, then by the time reinforcements arrived, the entire Mo Estate would have its streets filled with corpses missing their left arms. And surely, some of those corpses would include the familial disciples of the Lan Clan of Gusu.

After a moment's deliberation, Wei Wuxian said to himself, *Let's end this quickly.*

Those youths were fledglings, each of them looking nervous. Despite that, they still scrupulously took their places to protect the Mo Manor and stuck talismans inside and outside of the hall. The servant A-Tong had already been carried inside, and Lan Sizhui checked his pulse with his left hand while his right massaged Madam Mo's back. He couldn't treat both at once and was in a sorry dilemma when suddenly, A-Tong crawled up from the ground.

A-Ding exclaimed, "A-Tong, you're awake!"

Before any delight could cross her face, A-Tong raised his left hand and seized his own neck.

Seeing this, Lan Sizhui targeted several of A-Tong's acupoints with a triple tap of his hand apiece. Wei Wuxian knew that while the Lan clan appeared gentle on the surface, their arm strength was not gentle in the least. Using that method, anyone could be rendered thoroughly unable to move. However, A-Tong appeared not to have felt a thing. His left hand gripped harder and harder, his face scrunching more and more with pain. Lan Jingyi went over to pull at his left hand, but it was like trying to break off a chunk of iron: immovable. Moments later, *crack.* A-Tong's head drooped down, and only then did the hand let go. But his neck was already broken.

He had actually strangled himself before the eyes of all!

Seeing this, A-Ding's voice trembled. "...A *ghost*! There's an invisible ghost here, and it made A-Tong strangle himself!"

Her voice was shrill and sad, raising hairs on everyone's necks. They all believed her. Wei Wuxian determined it to be the exact opposite, however. This wasn't a malicious ghost.

He had seen the talismans those youths had chosen, and they were the spirit-repelling type. They had plastered the entire east hall with them, airtight. If this really were a malicious spirit, then those talismans would have immediately burned with green flames when it entered the east hall. Things would not be as quiet as they were now.

It wasn't that this group of youths was slow to react; it was that the intruder was truly ferocious in nature. The cultivation sects had strict criteria for determining whether something was a "malicious ghost": one was considered such if it killed once a month for up to three months consecutively. This was a criterion Wei Wuxian himself had set, and it was probably still in use now. Dealing with this type was his specialty, and based on what he'd seen, killing once every seven days would make this creature a malicious ghost that caused particularly frequent mischief. However, this thing had just killed three times in a row, and in a short time span too. Even accomplished cultivators would have been hard-pressed to come up with a counter strategy, never mind these novice juniors.

Just as he was thinking this, the firelight flashed. A blast of sinister wind whipped by, and every lantern and every candle in the entire courtyard, including the east hall, was extinguished.

Screams erupted the instant the lights went out. The men and women pushed and shoved, falling and fleeing.

Lan Jingyi shouted, "Stay where you are—don't run! We'll arrest whoever runs!!"

Those were not words spoken without reason—wreaking havoc in the dark and taking advantage of confusion was the nature of evil spirits. The more the people screamed and ran amok, the easier it would be to attract trouble unknowingly. It was extremely dangerous to be left alone or to lose one's head at a time like this. And yet it could not be helped that everyone was scared out of their wits, so how could they possibly pay attention to and heed any instructions? It didn't take long before the east hall fell quiet, with only the sound of light breaths and faint sniffling. Most had probably left.

In the darkness, a firelight suddenly flared. It was Lan Sizhui, who had lit an illumination talisman.

The flames of the illumination talisman could not be extinguished by the sinister wind that carried evil, and he used this talisman to relight the candles anew while the rest of the youths went around to console the others. Under the light, Wei Wuxian took a nonchalant glance at his wrists. Another cut had healed.

It was then that he suddenly realized the number of cuts were wrong.

There had been two cuts on his left wrist and two on his right. One cut healed after Mo Ziyuan's death, another cut healed after the death of Mo Ziyuan's father, and then a third after the death of the servant A-Tong. Tallying that up, there should have been three healed cuts, leaving only the cut with the deepest wound and the deepest hatred.

But now there was nothing on his wrists. Not a single cut was left.

Wei Wuxian trusted that Madam Mo was most definitely among those whom Mo Xuanyu wished to seek revenge upon. The longest and the deepest gash was likely for her, yet it had surprisingly vanished.

Was it Mo Xuanyu who had suddenly let it go and abandoned his hatred? That was impossible. His soul had been sacrificed as the price for summoning Wei Wuxian. In order for the cut to heal, Madam Mo had to die. Unless…

He slowly moved his gaze from his wrist to Madam Mo, who had recently roused and was surrounded by the crowd. Her face was white as a sheet.

CHAPTER 2: THE INTRACTABLE

...Unless she was already dead.

Wei Wuxian was sure something had already possessed Madam Mo. If that thing was not a spirit, then what could it be?

Suddenly, A-Ding cried, "Hand...hand, A-Tong's left arm!"

Lan Sizhui moved the illumination talisman over A-Tong's corpse. Sure enough, his left arm had also vanished.

The left arm!

In that flash of a second, everything was clear. The creature causing mischief and the vanishing left arms formed a connection that clicked in Wei Wuxian's mind. He suddenly snorted and burst out laughing.

Lan Jingyi huffed. "That dummy, how can he laugh at a time like this?!" But then he realized that, given the man was a dummy, what was the point of bothering with him in the first place?

However, Wei Wuxian grabbed Lan Jingyi's sleeve and shook his head. "No, no!"

Lan Jingyi irritably tried to pull his sleeve back. "No what? Not a dummy? Stop playing around! No one's got time for you."

Wei Wuxian pointed at Father Mo's and A-Tong's corpses on the ground. "That's not them."

Lan Sizhui stopped Lan Jingyi, who was about to blow up. He asked, "You said 'that's not them.' What do you mean?"

Wei Wuxian replied solemnly, "This isn't Mo Ziyuan's dad, and that's not A-Tong either."

With his face smeared in makeup, the more solemn he was, the more it felt like he really was mentally ill. However, under the haunting candlelight, his words were surprisingly hair-raising. Lan Sizhui was stunned for a moment, then questioned him in spite of himself.

"Why is that?"

Wei Wuxian said smugly, "Because of the hand! They're not left-handed, they always beat me with their right hands. I know that much at least."

Lan Jingyi lost his patience and spat, "What are you so smug for? Look at that pleased face!"

Lan Sizhui, however, had broken out in a cold sweat from the shock. Thinking back, A-Tong had strangled himself using his left hand, and when Madam Mo's husband pushed his wife down, he had also used his left hand.

But during the day, when Mo Xuanyu had been causing a ruckus in the east hall, those two had been busy trying to chase him out using their habitual right hands. Surely they couldn't both have turned into left-handers all of a sudden right before their deaths.

Although the cause was presently unknown, in order to investigate what was causing mischief, they had to start with those "left arms." Having come to this conclusion, Lan Sizhui sent a bewildered look at Wei Wuxian. Despite himself, he thought, *For him to suddenly say something like that, really…doesn't seem like a coincidence.*

Wei Wuxian only continued to laugh cheekily, knowing that the hint had been too conspicuous, but there was no other way.

Thankfully, Lan Sizhui didn't dig into it, thinking, *Either way, since this Mo-gongzi was willing to call attention to it for me, it most likely wasn't done out of ill intent.* He moved his gaze from Wei Wuxian, swept it over A-Ding, who had fainted from weeping, and landed his eyes on Madam Mo.

His eyes traveled down from her face to her hands. Her arms were hanging by her sides, mostly hidden in the sleeves, revealing only the tips of her fingers. The fingers of her right hand were snow white and slim—truly the hand of a woman who lived in privilege, without the hardship of labor.

However, the fingers of her left hand were longer and thicker than those of the right. The knuckles were curled, filled with strength.

How was that the hand of a woman? It was clearly the hand of a man!

"Hold her down!!" Lan Sizhui shouted.

The youths had already twisted Madam Mo's arm back in a hold. With a "Forgive me," Lan Sizhui pulled out a talisman. He was ready to slap it down when Madam Mo's left arm twisted at an impossible angle, aiming for his throat.

The only way for a living human to twist their arm that way would be if their bones were broken. The hand's movement was fast, and it would have seized his neck had it not been for Lan Jingyi tackling Lan Sizhui with a loud "gah!" and blocking the attack for him.

There was a flash of firelight. That hand had only just grabbed Lan Jingyi's shoulder when green flames flared to life at the same spot. It instantly loosened its grip. Having escaped death, Lan Sizhui was just about to thank Lan Jingyi for coming to his rescue when he saw that half of Lan Jingyi's uniform had been burned to ashes, making him look incredibly unkempt.

Flustered and enraged, Lan Jingyi stripped off the unburnt half of his uniform as he looked back and yelled, "Why did you kick me?! Stupid lunatic, did you want me killed?!"

Wei Wuxian scurried away, hugging his head. "It wasn't me!"

It was most certainly he who had kicked Lan Jingyi. The outer robe of the Lan family's uniform was tightly embroidered with spells and incantations inside its lining to provide protection. However, the effect would have been nullified after one use when encountering a formidable creature such as this. Under these dire circumstances, Wei Wuxian could only give Lan Jingyi a kick to make him use his body to shield Lan Sizhui's neck.

Lan Jingyi was going to yell some more, but Madam Mo collapsed to the ground. The flesh and blood of her face had been drained so utterly that only a layer of skin pressed against her skull remained. The man's arm that did not belong to her fell off of her left shoulder, yet its fingers could still move as it willed. It was as if it were stretching, the pulsing of its veins clearly visible.

That thing was the evil that had been summoned by the spirit-attraction flag.

Dismemberment was a standard violent death. It was a little more dignified than the way Wei Wuxian had died, though not by much. Unlike being crushed to ashes, the limbs of a dismembered corpse retained a part of the grudges of the deceased. One would yearn to return to its body, yearn to die a complete corpse. Thus, it would also attempt to seek out the other parts of its body. Once found, the corpse would then perhaps rest in peace and satisfaction, or perhaps wreak greater havoc. If the rest of its original body wasn't found, however, a limb could only go for the second-best option.

What was the second-best option? Seek out the bodies of living humans and make do, just as this left arm had demonstrated: devour the left arm of the living, take its place, and suck out the living human's spirit, blood, and flesh. Then abandon the body to continue searching for the next host. This would continue until all parts of its original corpse were found.

Once this arm attached itself to a body, it was instant death for the host, though prior to their blood and flesh being completely eaten, the human could still move normally under the arm's control, as if still alive. After the arm had been summoned, the first vessel it found was Mo Ziyuan. The second vessel was Mo Ziyuan's father. When Madam Mo had told her husband to get lost, he'd acted out of character and pushed her. At first, Wei Wuxian had thought it was because the man was heartbroken because of his son's death and that he had also had enough of his wife's unreasonable behavior. In retrospect, that had not been the demeanor of a father who had just lost his son. That had not been the stupor of despair—it had been stillness. The stillness of the dead.

The third vessel was A-Tong, and the fourth was Madam Mo. The left arm took advantage of the chaos when the lights went out earlier to migrate to her body. And when Madam Mo was killed, the last cut on Wei Wuxian's wrist had also vanished with her demise.

Seeing how the talismans were useless but their clothes were not, all the Lan youths each stripped off their outer robes and threw them at the left arm, covering and wrapping it in layers upon layers of robes like a thick white cocoon. A moment later, this ball of white clothes ignited with a *WHOOSH*, the wicked green flames blazing to the skies. Though it worked for the time being, it would not last long. Once the uniforms were completely burnt, that arm would break free from their ashes. While no one was paying attention, Wei Wuxian ran straight for the west courtyard.

Over a dozen walking corpses those youths had captured were standing silently in the yard. A spell had been drawn upon the ground to seal them inside its boundary, and Wei Wuxian stomped on one of the characters, destroying the entire array. After two claps, the walking corpses jerked. Their white eyes opened abruptly, as if they had been shocked awake by an explosion of thunder.

"Wake up," Wei Wuxian said. "Time to get to work!"

He never needed any complicated spells or summoning incantations to control corpse puppets. The most straightforward command would suffice. The walking corpses at the very front quivered as they struggled to shuffle a few steps. Then, the moment they approached

Wei Wuxian, they fell face-first to the ground like living humans, as if their legs had grown weak from terror.

Not knowing whether to laugh or cry at this, Wei Wuxian clapped twice more, but much softer this time. However, these walking corpses had probably been born at the Mo Estate and had died here as well. They'd never seen the world. So while they instinctively obeyed the summoner's command, they were also terrified of the summoner for some reason, lying on the ground whimpering, too afraid to get up.

The crueler the evil spirit, the easier it was for Wei Wuxian to manipulate it. These walking corpses had never gone through his training, so they could not withstand his direct control. He had no materials at his disposal to immediately create a device that could ease their fear either, and nothing with which to improvise. As he watched the blazing green flames from the east courtyard gradually die down, an idea suddenly came to mind.

Why go out searching to find a cruel and vicious deceased, one steeped in extreme hatred?

The east hall already had one. More than one!

He darted back to the east courtyard. Lan Sizhui's first plan had come to an end, so he devised another. The youths all unsheathed their longswords, planting them in the ground to form a fence of blades. The ghost arm smashed about within the enclosure. It was taking all their energy just to hold the hilts in place and prevent them from being expelled by the force; no one had the time to pay attention to who was going in and out of the hall.

Wei Wuxian stepped into the east hall and yanked up the corpses of Madam Mo and Mo Ziyuan, one in each hand. In a low voice, he gave a command:

"Awake yet?"

CHAPTER 2: THE INTRACTABLE

At the sound of his voice, the souls returned!

An instant later, Madam Mo and Mo Ziyuan opened their white eyes and let out a shrill shriek unique to malicious ghosts at the moment of their resurrection.

Amidst the high and low shrieks, another corpse crawled to its feet in trepidation, calling out feebly with a voice that could not have been any softer. It was Madam Mo's husband.

The cries were loud enough, the hatred plentiful. Wei Wuxian was extremely pleased.

"Recognize that arm out there?"

He smiled.

"Tear it apart," he ordered.

The three members of the Mo family were like three blasts of black wind, blowing forth in an instant.

That left arm had broken a longsword. Just as it was about to break out of the pen, three left-armless fierce corpses came lunging at it.

Even aside from the fear of disobeying Wei Wuxian's command, these three carried an intense hatred for the creature that had killed them, and they unleashed all their fury upon that ghost arm. The one leading the attack was undoubtedly Madam Mo. Once reanimated, female corpses were often particularly ferocious. Her hair was flying wild, her white eyes crawling with red, and her nails had burst in length exponentially. She was foaming at the mouth, her shrill cries practically raising the roofs, completely crazed. Mo Ziyuan followed his mother closely, working in concert with her to both tear and bite at the left arm while his father trailed behind them, filling in the gaps between the other two's attacks.

The Lan youths who had been struggling to hang on earlier were all stunned. They had only ever heard of such fights between fierce corpses from sundry books and hearsay. This was the first time they had witnessed such a gory scene, and they gawked, unable to avert their eyes. They only had one thought in their minds: *This is so exciting!*

The three corpses and the one arm were in the throes of battle. Suddenly, Mo Ziyuan shrieked as he dodged; that arm had swiped at his abdomen, and several ropes of his intestines drooped from the tear. Madam Mo snarled incessantly at the sight of this. She pulled her son behind her to shield him while escalating her attacks, her nails slicing through air as sharply as blades made of iron and steel. However, Wei Wuxian could tell she was slowly losing against the arm.

Even three freshly dead fierce corpses working together could not subdue this one arm!

Wei Wuxian watched the battle closely. He curled his tongue slightly, holding a sharp whistle back between his lips as he hesitated to let it loose. If he whistled, he could evoke greater hatred within the controlled fierce corpses, and that would perhaps turn the tables. However, it would be difficult to ensure no one noticed that he was the instigator.

In the span of a second, that hand moved as fast as lightning, ruthless and precise as it snapped Madam Mo's neck. Seeing how the Mo family was being steadily beaten back, Wei Wuxian was just about to let loose the whistle he held under his tongue when—right then—two strums from a guqin sounded in the far distance.

The two notes were skillfully played, ethereal and clear, carrying with them the tinkling bleakness of windswept pines. The collection of demonic evils that were in the middle of a brawl all froze.

The youths of the Lan Clan of Gusu immediately beamed as if they had been resurrected. Lan Sizhui raised a hand to wipe away the blood on his face and then looked up, calling out in delight:

"Hanguang-jun!"

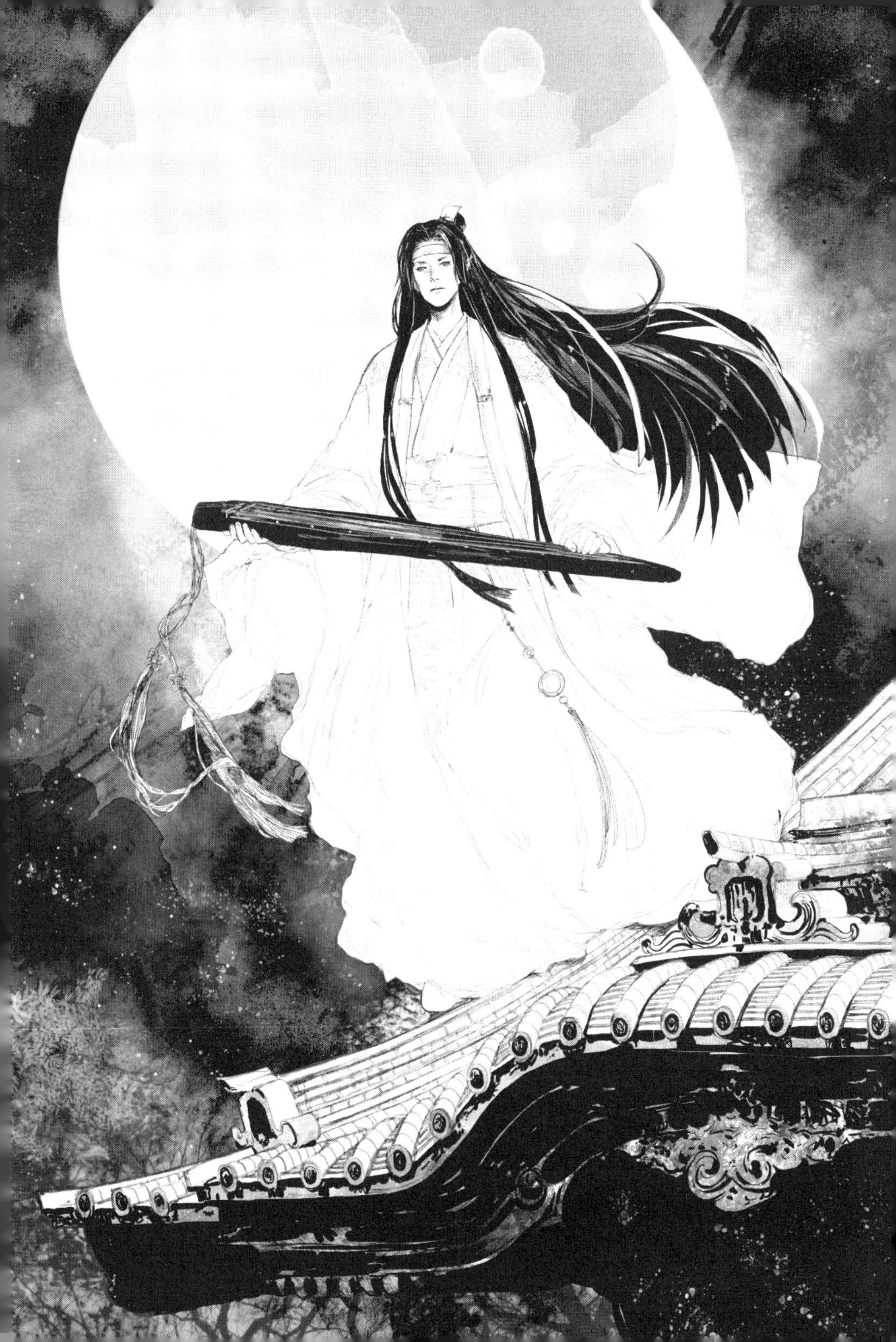

The moment he heard the cry of that sobriquet and the distant guqin, Wei Wuxian turned to leave.

Another strum. This time, the note was higher pitched, piercing through the sky like the austere harshness of winter's first approach. The three fierce corpses shrank back while covering one ear with their right hands at the same time. However, it was impossible to block out the Eradication Tone of the Lan Clan of Gusu in such a way. They only managed to back up a few steps before there was the faint sound of cracking in their skulls.

As for that left arm, after engaging in such a ferocious fight, hearing the sound of the strings now made it suddenly drop to the ground. Though its fingers still twitched, the arm was already lying limp and silent.

After a short silence, the group of youths couldn't help but erupt in loud cheers, the sound filled with the jubilation of having survived. They had endured a terrifying night, and now that help from the clan had finally arrived, they couldn't have cared less if they were harshly punished later for "disgracing the sect with a breach of etiquette."

While they waved toward the moon, Lan Sizhui suddenly noticed someone missing. He tugged at Lan Jingyi.

"Where is he?"

Lan Jingyi was busy being happy and replied, "Who? He who?"

"That Mo-gongzi," Lan Sizhui replied.

"Huh? Why are you looking for that lunatic? Who knows, maybe he was scared of getting beaten up by me and ran off somewhere."

"..."

Lan Sizhui knew that Lan Jingyi was unmindful and straightforward, never thinking deeply on things or harboring suspicion. He thought to himself, *I'll just wait until Hanguang-jun is down here, then report to him about that man and the incident.*

CHAPTER 2: THE INTRACTABLE

The Mo Estate slumbered soundly, though whether that peace was real or fake was difficult to tell. Even though there had been a bloody corpse fight in the Mo Manor's east and west courtyards, no one was getting up in the middle of the night to watch it. One had to pick and choose the right spectacle to watch, and a spectacle with such incessant screaming was best avoided.

Wei Wuxian rapidly destroyed any remaining evidence of the sacrificial ritual array, then ran out the door.

Of all people who could have come, it had to be the Lan family; of all people to come, it just *had* to be Lan Wangji!

This was someone with whom he had once crossed paths and fought, so he retreated in a hurry. Anxious to find a steed, as he passed by a courtyard, he noticed a spotted donkey tied next to a large millstone, chewing something in its mouth. It seemed a little surprised when it saw him come dashing over, giving him a side-eye like a person would. The instant Wei Wuxian met its eyes, he was immediately moved by the disdain in its gaze.

He went up to it, yanked off its rope, and started dragging it out. The spotted donkey loudly complained. Wei Wuxian cajoled as he dragged, coaxing it in every way possible to move it along. Stepping out in the lightening of dawn, they clattered onto the main road.

3
The Prideful

It didn't take long before Wei Wuxian discovered that he might have made a mistake: this spotted donkey that he'd stolen away with was way too hard to please.

It was a mere donkey, but all it would eat was fresh, tender grass that dripped with dew, and it would refuse to eat if the tip of the grass had yellowed even a little bit. When they passed by a farmhouse, Wei Wuxian stole a bit of straw to feed it; after only chewing a couple of bites, it spat it out in disgust, and the sound of it was louder and clearer than when a human spat. If it didn't eat well, then it would refuse to walk, throw tantrums, and kick its legs; Wei Wuxian himself was nearly walloped many times. On top of that, its braying cry was remarkably horrible.

As a steed or as a beloved pet, it was utterly useless!

Wei Wuxian couldn't help but miss his sword, which was most likely now hanging on some major clan leader's wall as a trophy.

Pulling and dragging the donkey for all he was worth, he traveled down the rambling road. He finally came to pass the large paddy field of a village. The sun was scorching. Next to the field ridge was a large locust tree, and the area beneath the tree was thick with green shade. There was also an old well, and the villagers had placed a bucket and a scoop next to it to provide relief to the thirst of passersby. When the spotted donkey reached this place, it refused to walk a step farther. Wei Wuxian hopped down and patted its esteemed derriere.

"Well, aren't you a pampered and noble little steed? And even harder to please than I am."

The donkey snorted at him.

As they mucked around, a group approached from the crisscrossing paths in the distance.

Those people carried handwoven bamboo baskets and wore cloth shirts and straw shoes. They exuded the rustic air of the country from head to toe. There was a round-faced young girl among them, somewhat delicately beautiful, but hardly notably so. Perhaps they had also trekked for too long under the scorching sun, as they also wanted to come over for a drink of water and to stand under the shade. However, when they saw a kicking and screaming spotted donkey tied to the tree, accompanied by a disheveled, loose-haired lunatic smeared with rouge and white powder, they didn't dare come over.

Wei Wuxian had always considered himself a man who cherished beauty, so when he noticed their hesitation, he moved from his spot to give them space and went to bother the spotted donkey. When that group saw he was harmless, they relaxed and walked over. Each of them was drenched in sweat and red in the face, fanning themselves and drawing water as they needed. The girl sat by the well, and, seeming to know that Wei Wuxian had purposely yielded space, she smiled softly at him.

One of the men was holding a compass in his hands, and he gazed far into the distance before looking back down, confused.

"How come the needle still won't move, even though we're almost at the foot of Mount Dafan?"

The carvings on that compass and its needle were both quite peculiar. It was no ordinary compass: a Compass of Ill Winds wasn't used to pathfind but rather to point out the whereabouts of nearby nefarious creatures. Wei Wuxian knew that this meant he had come across one of the small, downtrodden clans of the countryside. Outside of the elite, affluent clans, there were also quite a number of these small, independent clans. Wei Wuxian thought perhaps that they had traveled here from the countryside to seek refuge with a large clan with which they had some familial relation. Or maybe they were out here to go on a Night Hunt.

The middle-aged man who was the group's leader told the other man to go for his drink and commented, "Is that compass of yours broken? I'll give you a new one later. Mount Dafan is less than five kilometers away, so we can't rest for too long. We've traveled all this way. It won't be worth it if we slack off now and fall behind the others."

It was a Night Hunt, as expected. Many cultivation clans, in their appreciation for refined elegance, called the act of traveling the world to exorcise evil "hunting expeditions." And because said evils often appeared at night, such activities were thus called Night Hunts. There were numerous cultivation clans that had come and gone, and only a handful that had been able to make a name for themselves. If an ordinary clan—one without generations of accumulated reputation to stand on—wanted to join the higher ranks and become famous, wanted to gain prestige and respect among the cultivation world, then they had to show tangible achievements. Only when they hunted down ruthless monsters or disaster-bringing malicious fiends did their words gain any weight.

These Night Hunts had originally been Wei Wuxian's expertise, but he had been constantly on the move the past few days and had only managed to hunt down a handful of little devils from the few graves he'd broken into. He was in need of a band of tyrannical ghost generals to do his bidding, so he, too, decided to head to that

"Rice Mountain" to try his luck. If there was one that proved useful, he'd capture it for his own use.

That group had finished their break and was ready to be on their way as well. Before they left, the round-faced girl took out a half-green, barely red apple from the basket on her back and handed it to Wei Wuxian.

"For you."

Wei Wuxian extended his hand to receive it with a happy grin, but the spotted donkey raised its head and bared its teeth to bite for it, so Wei Wuxian quickly snatched it up instead. Seeing how the donkey drooled for the little apple, an idea came to him. Upon finding a long branch and some fishing thread, he dangled the apple in front of the donkey. The spotted donkey smelled the sweet fragrance of the apple and craved it. With its head raised, it chased after that apple that dangled just barely out of reach. It ended up becoming faster than all the renowned steeds Wei Wuxian had seen before, leaving them all in the dust!

The donkey ran without stopping, and Wei Wuxian arrived at Mount Dafan before dark. It was only when he reached the foot of the mountain that he learned the "fan" in "Dafan" did not mean "rice" but instead "Brahma." Seen from a distance, the shape of the mountain resembled that of a short, carefree, and content Buddha, hence its name. There was a small town at the foot of the mountain, and so it was called Fojiao Town, meaning "Buddha's Foot."

There were more cultivators gathered here than he imagined. It was an assembly of all sorts, a confusion of colors caused by the different uniforms of various clans and sects walking down the streets. For some reason, everyone appeared tense. Even at the sight of his wacky looks, no one seemed like they could spare a moment to mock him.

CHAPTER 3: THE PRIDEFUL

At the center of the long street, there were a bunch of cultivators gathered in a serious discussion. It sounded like they were having quite a difference of opinions; Wei Wuxian could hear them far down the street. It was all right at first, but it somehow grew more and more heated.

"…I do not believe there are soul-eating beasts or fiends at all. There was clearly no activity on any azimuth of the Compass of Ill Winds."

"If there aren't, then how did seven townspeople lose their souls? They couldn't possibly have all contracted the same disease? I've never heard of such an illness before!"

"Just because the Compass of Ill Winds doesn't show something doesn't mean it's not there! The most it can do is point in a general direction anyway. It's not accurate enough to be fully trusted. Maybe there's something nearby that's obstructing the needle?"

"Why don't you think about who invented the Compass of Ill Winds? I've never heard of anything that can interfere with the needle."

"What are you trying to say, huh? What are you implying? Of course I know the Compass of Ill Winds was created by Wei Ying, but it's not like his creations are perfect, so why are you stopping people from questioning it?"

"I didn't say you can't, and I didn't say his creations are perfect either! No need to slander!"

And so their argument swerved in a different direction. Wei Wuxian giggled and laughed as he rode past on his donkey. He wouldn't have thought that, after so many years, he still stood strong and unfailing as a topic in cultivators' verbal battles. He had a Wei of starting conflict, you might say. If there was ever a vote on who had the most enduring popularity amongst all the clans, then he was the sure winner.

In all fairness, that cultivator wasn't wrong. The Compass of Ill Winds that was in common use now was only an early version, so it was indeed not accurate enough. He had started on refining it, but it wasn't his fault that his good ol' lair had been toppled before that was done, so everyone would just have to deal with it and continue using the fallible first edition.

Anyway, creatures that consumed flesh were mostly low-level—walking corpses, for example. Only refined, high-level monsters or spirits could consume and digest souls. Seven souls had been eaten in one go too, so it was no wonder many clans had assembled here. Since this Night Hunt's prey was hardly insignificant in strength, it couldn't be helped that the Compass of Ill Winds would run into issues.

Wei Wuxian pulled on the reins and hopped off the donkey, then grabbed the apple that had been dangling in front of it this entire way and tugged it down to its mouth.

"One bite. Only one bite... Bah! Are you trying to eat my entire hand in one bite?!"

He took a couple of bites from the other side of the apple, then stuffed it back into the spotted donkey's mouth. As he was reflecting on how he'd fallen so low as to share a single apple with a donkey, someone suddenly bumped into his back. He turned his head and saw it was a girl. While she was the one who had bumped into him, she took no notice of him at all. Her eyes were unfocused as she gazed, fixated, in a certain direction with a smile on her face.

Wei Wuxian followed the azimuth of her gaze. In that direction was a dense mountaintop. It was Mount Dafan.

All of a sudden, without warning, the girl started dancing in front of him.

This dance was feral and threatening, her arms flailing. Wei Wuxian was taking great pleasure in watching the show, but just then, a woman came dashing over with her skirt lifted. She wailed as she hugged the girl.

"A-Yan, let's go back, let's go!"

A-Yan fought her off. The smile on her face, never having faded, carried a hair-raising sense of maternal affection, and she danced and pranced while that woman continued to chase after her around the streets, weeping as she went.

A street vendor on the side commented, "What a sin. A-Yan from Blacksmith Zheng's house escaped again."

"It's truly sad for her mom. A-Yan, A-Yan's husband, and her own husband as well... It's not right at all."

Wei Wuxian sauntered about, and from snatches of overheard conversation on the streets, sorted out the strange affair that had happened here.

There was an old graveyard on Mount Dafan, and most of the ancestral graves of Fojiao Town's people were located there. Sometimes, they also dug graves and placed wooden markers for unnamed corpses. Many months ago, there had been a stormy night where lightning crashed and thunder drummed, and after a night of being battered by torrential rain, a piece of land from the mountain slid and collapsed. This piece of land, more specifically, was the graveyard.

Many of the old graves were destroyed, and several coffins were expelled from the earth. Then lightning struck, sending the coffin lids flying and charring black both the corpses and their coffins.

The people of Fojiao Town felt very uneasy at all this. They prayed for good fortune and rebuilt the old graveyard in the hopes that would settle things. Despite their efforts, since then, cases of people losing their souls began to frequently crop up in Fojiao Town.

The first one was a deadbeat. This man was a penniless good-for-nothing, spending his days in idleness. But since he always loved catching birds up on the mountain, it just so happened that he got trapped on Mount Dafan the night of the landslide. He was scared half to death, but at least he was still alive.

The curious thing was that it didn't take long after his return for him to suddenly get married. The wedding was conducted with great fanfare, and he declared his intent to do good from that day onward, to accumulate good fortune, and to live the rest of his life in peace.

On his wedding night, he got blackout drunk and never got up after lying down in bed. The bride called to him, but he wouldn't respond. It was only after pushing him that she discovered the groom had an empty stare, his body cold. Aside from his breathing, he was no different than the dead. He lay like this, neither eating nor drinking, for many days, then was finally buried in peace. Pitiful was the bride who had only just been married, to be turned into a widow.

The second one was A-Yan from Blacksmith Zheng's family. The girl had just gotten engaged when, the very next day, her future husband was killed by a jackal while hunting on the mountain. After learning of this, she was struck by the same affliction as had descended upon that deadbeat. Fortunately, she recovered from the soulless disease on her own after some time. However, it also caused her to become deranged, giggling as she danced outside in front of others.

The third one was A-Yan's father, Blacksmith Zheng. To date, there had now been seven people who had fallen victim consecutively.

Wei Wuxian mulled this over. This was most likely a soul-eating fiend, not a soul-eating beast.

Even though the difference was but one word, they were completely distinct creatures. Fiends belonged to the ghost category, while beasts were of the monster category. In his opinion, all this might be the fault of the old graveyard that had collapsed from the tremors of the landslide. Once lightning struck open the coffins, any ancient fiends that were resting within would be unleashed. He'd be able to determine if this was really the case once he took a look at what the coffins were made of—and if there were any remnants of seal talismans. However, the people of Fojiao Town must surely have reburied the charred coffins a long time ago, and also reburied the corpses anew, so there definitely wouldn't be much evidence left.

He would have to take the trail that started from Fojiao Town in order to properly scale the mountain, so Wei Wuxian leisurely treaded up the hill on his donkey.

After a while, he ran into a few people descending the mountain with gloomy expressions. Some of them carried injuries on their faces, and they were talking all at once. They all jumped in surprise when they ran into this donkey-rider with a face caked in hanged ghost makeup under the darkening skies, and they cursed as they went around him to hurry down the hill. Wei Wuxian turned his head and wondered: Could it be that the prey was too difficult to handle, and they were going back empty-handed? He slapped the donkey's hip after a moment's thought and trotted up the mountain.

That group groused and complained after his departure:

"I've never met anyone so unreasonable!"

"Why would the clan leader of such a big clan come here just to fight us over a soul-eating fiend? He already killed plenty of those when he was younger, I'm sure!"

"What can you do? He's the sect leader. Of all the clans to offend, you don't offend the Jiang Clan, and of all the people to offend, you never offend Jiang Cheng. Let's just write it off as our bad luck, pack up, and get outta here."

A torch would be necessary to continue into the mountain forest if the sky got any darker. Wei Wuxian walked for a while and was quite surprised to not run into many cultivators. *Of all the clans that came, could it really be that half are arguing theory in Fojiao Town, while the other half are like that group from earlier? Trying, failing, and going back empty-handed?*

Suddenly, a cry for help came from ahead.

"SOMEBODY!"

"HELP!"

There were both male and female voices, their cries full of panic and helplessness. It didn't sound fake—even though nine times out of ten, cries for help in the wild were evil spirits out causing mischief, luring the ignorant into a trap. Wei Wuxian, however, was thrilled.

The eviler the better! It had better be evil enough!

He urged the donkey to run toward where the voices were coming from, but when he arrived, there was nothing in sight. When he looked up, rather than any evil spirits or monsters, he saw the independent countryside clan he had run into previously by the field ridge. They were hanging from a tree, caught in a massive, shimmering gold net.

That middle-aged man had led the group to patrol and scout the forest area at first, but they hadn't run into the prey they were hoping for. Instead, they stepped into the net trap some rich folk had set up and ended up hanging from the tree as they cried their grievances. They perked up when they saw someone had come but were immediately greatly disappointed to realize it was the lunatic. While the threads of this immortal-binding net were thin, the material was of the highest grade, durable and indestructible. Once caught, it didn't matter if you were a human or a god, a ghost or spirit—you'd be trapped a good while. Unless, that is, the net was cut with an immortal device of an even higher grade. It'd be pointless to expect this lunatic to help them down. He probably didn't even know what the net was.

CHAPTER 3: THE PRIDEFUL

Just as they were going to try to ask him to find help, there came the sound of agile steps crinkling leaves, approaching swiftly. From within the pitch-black woods there emerged a youth dressed in a light-colored jacket.

There was a vermillion mark dotted between the brows of this little young master, and his features were so fine they were almost harsh. He was extremely young—around the same age as Lan Sizhui, a mere adolescent. On his back, he carried a quiver of arrows and a longsword shimmering with gold, and in his hand, there was a longbow. The embroidery on his robes was indisputably exquisite, swirling together into extraordinary white peonies. The golden threads twinkled delicately in the night.

Wei Wuxian marveled inwardly. *Rich!*

This had to be a young master belonging to the Jin Clan of Lanling. Only this clan used the white peony as their insignia. By comparing themselves to the king of flowers, they implied they were kings among immortals. Dotting one's forehead with cinnabar symbolized the conviction to open the doors to wisdom, allowing the vermillion light of eternity to shine upon the world.

This little young master had been about to shoot, but when he saw the immortal-binding net had only captured humans, disappointment flashed on his face, and he lost his patience.

"It's you stupid idiots every time. Over four hundred immortal-binding nets, but it's always the same: before they manage to catch any prey, dozens of them get wrecked by you lot!"

The same thought was still foremost in Wei Wuxian's mind: *Rich!*

An immortal-binding net was already considerably expensive, and he'd still set up over four hundred of them in one go. As expected of the Jin Clan of Lanling—an even slightly smaller clan would have been reduced to poverty and ruin. However, to abuse the immortal-binding net like this to hunt indiscriminately was not a Night Hunt. This was clearly an act of driving others out in order to hoard the spoils. It appeared that the cultivators who retreated previously hadn't done so because the prey was difficult but because these prestigious sects weren't ones to be offended.

During the days he'd spent strolling along, and on account of his ravenous eavesdropping earlier in Fojiao Town, Wei Wuxian had heard plenty of gossip about the rises and falls within the cultivation world. As the final victor of the tangled war between cultivation clans that had spanned over a hundred years, the Jin Clan of Lanling now led the clans and sects; the head of their clan was even respectfully addressed as "Cultivation Chief." The Jin clan had always been haughty and enjoyed extravagance. In the span of years spent presiding high above the others, the clan had prospered and grown powerful, and their disciples were raised to dominate others without scruple. Inferior clans, no matter how much they were humiliated, had no choice but to swallow it down. Such a small cultivation house from the countryside could afford even less to offend them. This was why, although the boy's words were harsh and the people hanging in the net turned red in the face at the abuse, they still didn't dare argue back.

The middle-aged man said subserviently, "Will the young master grant us the favor of lowering us down?"

The youth was frustrated that his prey still hadn't shown itself, so this country bumpkin was a perfect secondary target for venting his anger. He crossed his arms.

"Stay hanging there so you don't wander around and hinder me again! Once I catch the soul-eating beast, I'll let you guys go, if I remember."

If they really hung from that tree the entire night, unable to move, there would be nothing they could do but have their souls sucked

CHAPTER 3: THE PRIDEFUL

out if the thing wandering Mount Dafan came upon them. The round-faced girl who had given Wei Wuxian an apple was terrified and wept out loud. Wei Wuxian was sitting cross-legged on the back of the spotted donkey, but when the donkey heard her crying, its long ears twitched.

Suddenly, it leapt forth. It even let out a long bray when it did, and if not for that uniquely horrible sound, it would've appeared irresistibly heroic. It wouldn't be idle flattery to call it a mighty young colt. Caught off guard, Wei Wuxian was thrown off its back and nearly broke his skull from the fall. The spotted donkey's broad head charged toward the youth, apparently convinced that it could send the boy flying with a headbutt. The youth's arrow was still nocked in his bow, so he was ready to shoot it down. Wei Wuxian didn't want to go find a new ride so soon, so he pulled at the reins with all his might.

That youth took a glance at him and briefly appeared stunned before his expression immediately turned into scorn. He pursed his lips.

"So, it's you."

That tone was two parts surprise and eight parts revulsion, making Wei Wuxian blink in confusion.

"What, you went crazy after getting kicked back to your old home? Look at that ghastly painted face, I can't believe they let you out!"

What was this incredible thing he'd just heard?!

Could it be...? Wei Wuxian slapped his own thigh. Could it be that Mo Xuanyu's father was not some random small-time clan leader but the infamous Jin Guangshan?!

Jin Guangshan had been the previous head of the Jin Clan of Lanling and had long since passed on. This was a character with a long story. He'd had a fiercely strict madam wife from an illustrious family and been notoriously afraid of her, but scared as he might've been, he still incessantly played around with other women. No matter how strict Madam Jin was, she couldn't follow him around twenty-four hours a day. He was relentless in his affairs, bedding women from distinguished ladies above to wild prostitutes below. And, while he loved womanizing and had a great number of illegitimate children, he was extremely fickle in love. Once he grew tired of a woman, she'd be cast from his mind without any thought to responsibility. Of his many illegitimate children, only one had been outstanding enough to be recognized and taken back, and that was the current family head of the Jin Clan of Lanling, Jin Guangyao.

Furthermore, even the way Jin Guangshan died was an embarrassment. Old, but fully confident he was still robust, he'd fooled around with a bunch of women at once in order to challenge himself. However, he unfortunately overestimated his vitality and died during the orgy. This was simply too embarrassing to speak of, so the Jin Clan of Lanling unanimously declared that the old sect leader had passed due to overexertion, and the rest of the clans, in tacit understanding, all pretended not to know the full truth of the statement. In any case, that was the real reason for his infamy.

Back during the Siege of the Burial Mound, Jin Guangshan's contributions to the effort had come second only to Jiang Cheng's. Now that Wei Wuxian had overtaken his illegitimate son's body, he really didn't know how this score should be settled.

The youth saw him zone out and grew annoyed. "Get outta here! Just seeing your face disgusts me. Damn cut-sleeve."

In terms of seniority, Mo Xuanyu might have been this boy's uncle or some other elder. And yet he had to suffer such humiliation from a junior. Even if it wasn't for himself, as he was currently in Mo Xuanyu's body, Wei Wuxian felt he had a responsibility to humiliate the boy back.

CHAPTER 3: THE PRIDEFUL

So, he countered, "Didn't your mother teach you any manners?"

Raging flames of fury flashed in the youth's eyes. He pulled the longsword from his back and glowered.

"What...did you say?"

The sword shimmered gold. It was clearly a rare, high-quality weapon that would be out of many clans' reach even if they hustled their entire lives. Wei Wuxian studied it, fixated, and felt the sword appeared rather familiar. But he'd seen plenty of high-quality swords that glowed golden, so he didn't think too deeply on it. He only twirled a small pouch in his hand.

This was a spirit-trapping pouch that he'd thrown together haphazardly a few days ago, using scraps of fabric he found. The youth lunged at him, brandishing his sword, and Wei Wuxian took a small piece of paper cut in the shape of a human from the pouch. He dodged the attack, then slapped the paper onto the other's back.

The youth was already swift, but Wei Wuxian had plenty of experience in tripping people and slapping talismans onto them, so he was faster. The youth felt his back go numb and heavy, then fell forward onto the ground involuntarily. The sword dropped to his side with a clang. He couldn't get up, no matter how hard he tried; it was as if Mount Tai was sitting on top of him. More specifically, it was a ghost that had died of gluttony that clung to his back, crushing the breath out of him. While the little ghost was weak, it could easily take care of a brat like this.

Wei Wuxian picked up that sword, weighed it in his hand, and then swung at the immortal-binding net, snapping it.

The cultivation family dropped to the ground in sorry confusion, then ran away in a hurry without a word. The round-faced girl seemed to want to express thanks, but her elder dragged her away, afraid that the young master Jin would hold an even deeper grudge should she say one more word.

The youth on the ground yelled angrily, "Damn cut-sleeve! Lookit you, going down the demonic path just because your spiritual power is too weak to cultivate into anything worthwhile. You watch yourself! Do you know who's here today?! I'm gonna…"

Wei Wuxian clutched his heart insincerely. "Ah! I'm so scared!"

The cultivation method he'd employed in the past was denounced by the public. It harmed the cultivator's constitution after prolonged practice, but it allowed for speedy success and was unrestricted by one's innate spiritual prowess and natural talent, which was why it was an extremely tempting path. There was never a shortage of people who craved shortcuts in their training, and so this youth also thought Mo Xuanyu had strayed from the right path after being driven out of the Jin Clan of Lanling. It was a perfectly logical suspicion, and it saved Wei Wuxian from further unnecessary trouble.

The youth tried to push off the ground but still couldn't get up after several attempts. His face was flushed, and he clenched his teeth.

"If you don't remove this thing, I'll tell my uncle, and you'll be dead!"

Wei Wuxian asked curiously, "Why is it your uncle and not your dad? Who's your uncle?"

There was suddenly a voice behind him, grave and intensely frigid.

"I am his uncle. Do you have any last words?"

At the sound of that voice, every drop of blood in Wei Wuxian's body seemed to surge to his head but then immediately drained away again. Thankfully, his face was already a mess of ghastly white, so it didn't look strange when he went a little paler.

A man in purple attire strode over. He was dressed in a narrow-sleeved light robe, with his hand resting on the hilt of his sword.

CHAPTER 3: THE PRIDEFUL

A silver bell dangled from his waist, yet there was no sound when he walked.

This young man had fine brows and almond eyes, with a chiseled handsomeness to his features. His eyes were deep and intense with a hint of aggression, his gaze like two streaks of cold lightning. He stopped and stood three meters away from Wei Wuxian. His expression was like that of a nocked arrow on a bow, ready to shoot, and even his composure was suffused with arrogant pride.

He furrowed his brows. "Jin Ling, why have you dawdled for so long? Do I need to come and invite you back? Look at the terrible state you're in. Get the hell up."

After the initial numbness in his brain had passed, Wei Wuxian quickly snapped out of it. He beckoned with his fingers inside his sleeve, withdrawing the paper doll. Jin Ling felt the weight disappear off his back and immediately scrambled up, grabbing his sword back and scurrying to Jiang Cheng's side.

He pointed at Wei Wuxian and yelled, "I'LL BREAK YOUR LEGS!"

When the two stood together, there was a vague resemblance in their looks, much like a pair of brothers. Jiang Cheng moved his finger, and the paper doll swiftly slipped from Wei Wuxian's fingers and flew into his hand. He took a glance at it, and a wave of resentment flared in his eyes. He clenched his fingers and the paper was set ablaze, the ghost shrieking as it was burned to ashes.

Jiang Cheng said darkly, "Break his legs? Haven't I told you that when you run into heretics, you should kill them outright and feed them to your dog?!"

Wei Wuxian hastily backed away, leaving the donkey behind too. No matter how much Jiang Cheng hated him, he had thought the feeling would've dispersed somewhat after so many years.

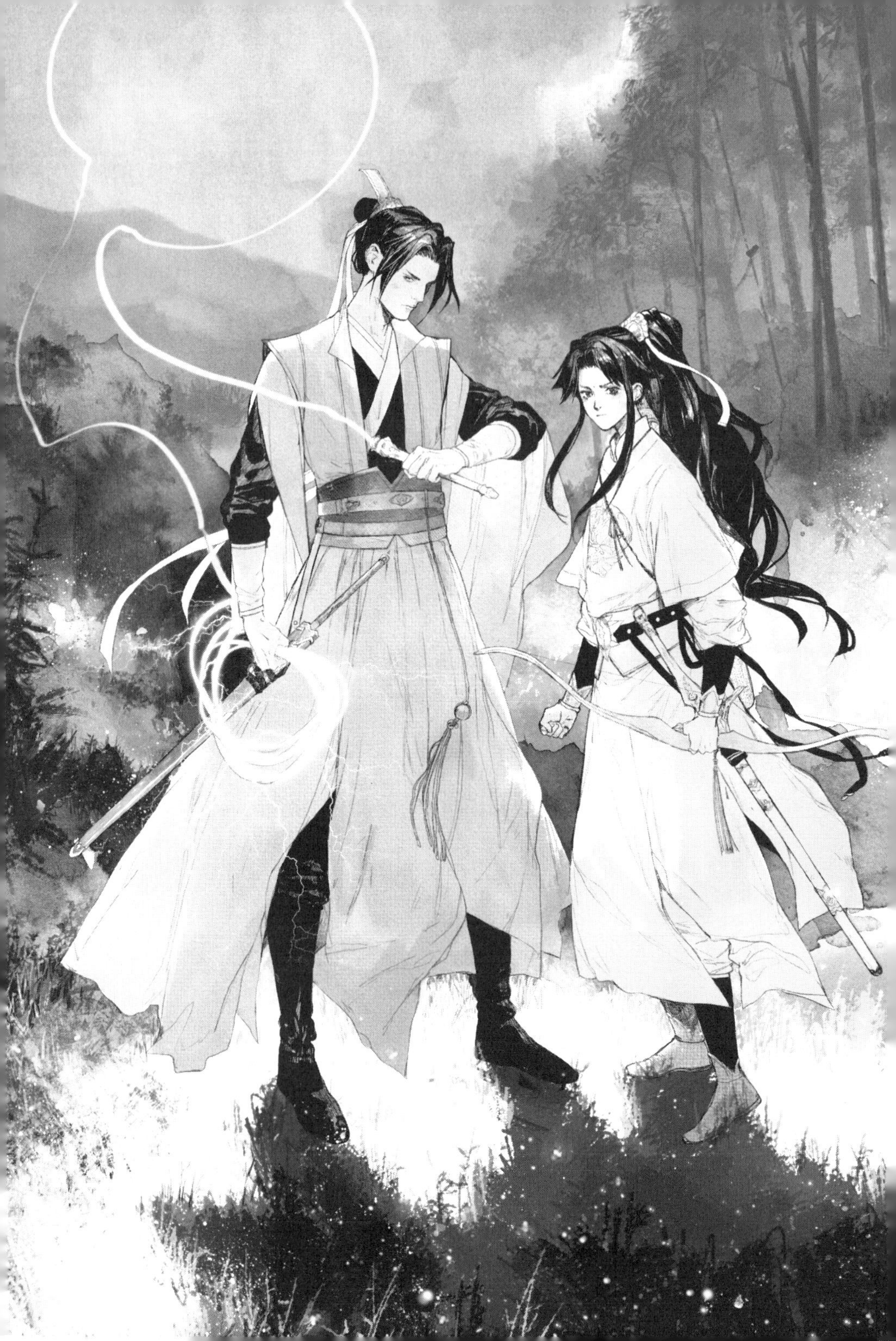

Who would've thought it wasn't that easy? Not only was the hate still there, but it had thickened with time, like a jug of aged wine. And that rage was taken out on every cultivator who imitated him!

There were people behind them standing guard, and this time, Jin Ling attacked with greater ferocity. Wei Wuxian slipped two fingers into the spirit-trapping pouch, but just as he was about to move, a streak of blue flashed. It was the glare of a sword clashing with Jin Ling's sword, and it shattered the golden shimmer of this high-quality blade in an instant.

It wasn't that the other sword was superior but rather that the difference in ability between the two wielders was too great. Wei Wuxian had had the timing figured out at first, but the radiance of this incoming sword disrupted his steps, and he stumbled, falling flat on the ground before a pair of snow-white boots. He froze for a moment, then slowly looked up.

The first thing that entered his vision was a long and slender blade, as crystalline as ice.

This sword was famous in the cultivation world, and Wei Wuxian had had the honor of experiencing its power directly on multiple occasions, both fighting alongside and against it. The hilt was forged from pure silver that was refined by a secret method, and the blade was extremely thin, clear, and transparent. It emanated the frigid air of ice and snow, yet it could cut through iron as if it were mud. Thus, while the sword appeared light, agile, and transcendentally airy, it was extremely heavy, and no ordinary person could possibly swing it.

It was the sword Bichen!

The blade reversed, and above Wei Wuxian's head there came the clang of the sword being sheathed. At the same time, Jiang Cheng's voice came from the distance.

"I was wondering who it was. So, it's Lan-er-gongzi."

The pair of white boots unhurriedly took three steps forward, walking around Wei Wuxian. Wei Wuxian looked up and got to his feet. When he brushed past the person, the two locked eyes for a brief second, seemingly accidentally.

The newcomer was cloaked in soft, white moonlight. He carried a seven-stringed guqin on his back. The body of the instrument was narrower than the usual standard and ebony-black in color, but soft in the luster of its wood. A cloud-patterned ribbon was fastened around this man's forehead.

The man was exceptional in both looks and elegance: his skin was fair, and his features were as refined as smoothed jade. The color of his eyes was abnormally light, almost like colored glaze, and it made his gaze appear overly cold. There was a frostiness to his expression, which was stern enough to appear stiff. Even when he saw Wei Wuxian's currently ridiculous-looking face, he appeared unperturbed.

From head to toe, he was scrupulous and immaculate, without a single foot placed incorrectly. Even so, two words still jumped out in Wei Wuxian's mind:

Funeral clothes!

Those were funeral clothes, and that couldn't be denied, no matter how much the other clans proclaimed the uniforms of the Lan Clan of Gusu to be the most pleasing to the eye and sang their exaggerated praises to the heavens. Furthermore, no matter how thoroughly Lan Wangji was praised as an unrivaled rare beauty, nothing could help the fact that he looked profoundly embittered, as if he had lost his wife.

In an unlucky year, enemies are bound to clash. Blessings never come in pairs, and misfortunes never come singly.

Lan Wangji stood unspeaking. He faced Jiang Cheng with quiet calm and met his eyes squarely. Jiang Cheng was exceptionally

CHAPTER 3: THE PRIDEFUL

handsome, but he was still a little inferior to the one standing before him and certainly the more impatient of the two. He quirked a brow.

"Hanguang-jun truly lives up to his reputation of appearing where there is chaos. What brings you here to the deep mountains today?"

Leaders of prominent cultivation clans did not normally care for these low-level evil spirits. However, Lan Wangji was an exception. He was never picky about his Night Hunt prey, nor would he refuse to appear if the nefarious creature wasn't tough enough or if it would not earn him any acclaim. He would attend as long as there was a plea for help, and it had always been that way, ever since he was young. Thus, "appearing where there is chaos" was how the people appraised Hanguang-jun's Night Hunt expeditions and praised his character. The way Jiang Cheng used the phrase was not complimentary, however, and the juniors attending behind Lan Wangji all felt a little uncomfortable with his tone.

Lan Jingyi was the blunt and outspoken sort. "Isn't Sect Leader Jiang here too?"

Jiang Cheng replied coldly, "Tsk. An elder is speaking, who are you to interrupt? The Lan Clan of Gusu pride themselves on being a clan of etiquette. This is what disciples are being taught?"

Lan Wangji, who didn't seem to want to exchange any words with him, sent Lan Sizhui a look. The latter understood: let the juniors speak to each other. And so, Lan Sizhui stepped forward and turned to Jin Ling to reply.

"Jin-gongzi, the Night Hunts have always been a fair competition among the clans. But Jin-gongzi has set up nets all over Mount Dafan and made it difficult for the cultivators of other houses to tread, for fear of falling into traps. Does this not violate the rules of Night Hunts?"

Jin Ling's cold expression was cast from the same mold as his uncle's. "What can I do if they step into traps due to their own stupidity? I must capture my prey; everything else can wait."

Lan Wangji wrinkled his brow. Jin Ling was about to say more when he suddenly realized he couldn't open his mouth, nor produce any sound from his throat. He paled in panic.

When Jiang Cheng saw that Jin Ling's lips were now glued together, unable to part, anger clouded his face and all previous forced civility went out the window.

"You, Lan! What's the meaning of this? It's not up to you to discipline Jin Ling. Release the spell!"

This silence spell was what the Lan clan used to punish its disciples. Wei Wuxian had fallen victim to this little trick on many occasions. While it was not complex magic by any stretch of the imagination, only those of the Lan family could undo the spell. If one attempted to speak by brute force, then either their lips would be torn to shreds by the effort or they'd lose their voice for days. The penitent one had to keep their mouth shut and self-reflect in silence until the punishment period was over.

Lan Sizhui said, "There is no need to be angry, Sect Leader Jiang. As long as he does not try to forcibly break the spell, it will be automatically undone in one incense time."[3]

Jiang Cheng had yet to reply when a man clad in the Jiang Clan's purple came rushing out of the woods. "Sect Leader!"

When he saw Lan Wangji standing there, however, he appeared hesitant.

Jiang Cheng said derisively, "Go ahead. What other bad news do you have to report?"

---

3   One incense time roughly equals thirty minutes. See the Glossary for more information.

The sect disciple said in a small voice, "Not long ago, a flying blue sword destroyed the immortal-binding nets you arranged."

Jiang Cheng shot Lan Wangji a look, anger clouding his expression once more. "How many?"

The sect disciple replied cautiously, "All of them."

Over four hundred!

Jiang Cheng seethed with anger.

He had never expected such bad luck in this expedition. He had originally come to assist Jin Ling: the boy was fifteen this year, the age to make his debut and fight for experience with the juniors from other clans. Jiang Cheng had reviewed the options carefully before deciding on Mount Dafan as the hunting ground. He had then set up nets everywhere and scared off all the other cultivators, making it so difficult for them to move that they'd be forced to back off—all so Jin Ling would emerge the winner without anyone fighting him for the title. While over four hundred immortal-binding nets were extremely expensive, the price was nothing to the Jiang Clan of Yunmeng. However, destroyed nets were a small matter compared to losing face. Lan Wangji's actions made Jiang Cheng boil with anger, and his fury spiraled higher and higher. He narrowed his eyes, and his left hand subconsciously stroked the ring on his right index finger.

This was a dangerous sign.

Everyone knew that ring was a formidable and deadly spiritual weapon. Once the Jiang Clan leader started fiddling with it, it signaled his intent to kill. However, Jiang Cheng didn't stroke it for long before he forced his hostility back down.

Although he was quite unhappy, as the leader of a sect, there was much to consider. He couldn't be as impulsive as that brat Jin Ling. Ever since the decline of the Nie Clan of Qinghe, of the current three great clans, the Jin Clan of Lanling and the Lan Clan of Gusu had always been close due to the strong personal friendship shared by their clan leaders. Jiang Cheng ruled the Jiang Clan of Yunmeng alone, so it could have been said that he was in a state of isolation. Hanguang-jun—Lan Wangji—was a distinguished cultivator of great prestige. In addition, his elder brother Zewu-jun—Lan Xichen—was the clan leader of the Lan Clan of Gusu, and the two brothers had always gotten along well. Overall, it was best if Jiang Cheng kept things peaceful instead of giving in to his violent urges.

Furthermore, Jiang Cheng's sword Sandu had never formally crossed with Lan Wangji's sword Bichen, so no one knew which was the better blade. Although he had on his hand the family heirloom ring Zidian, Lan Wangji's guqin (also named Wangji) was equally renowned. Jiang Cheng loathed being at a disadvantage in a fight, so unless victory was absolutely certain, attacking Lan Wangji was not within the realm of consideration.

Jiang Cheng slowly withdrew his left hand, which had been stroking the ring. It appeared that Lan Wangji had set his mind to interfere in this affair, so continuing to play the role of the villain would only cause trouble. He would simply have to remember this, for the time being.

After weighing his options, Jiang Cheng turned his head and saw that Jin Ling still had his hands covering his mouth angrily.

"Since Hanguang-jun wants to punish you, take the lesson this once. It's not easy for him, either, to manage the juniors from another clan."

His tone was sarcastic, but it was unclear to whom it was directed. Lan Wangji, who never responded to such provocation, ignored him.

Jiang Cheng turned, his voice scathing. "What are you standing around for? Waiting for the prey to run into your sword itself?

CHAPTER 3: THE PRIDEFUL

If you can't catch the creature here on Mount Dafan tonight, then you needn't come to me again in the future!"

Jin Ling shot Wei Wuxian a death glare but didn't dare to glare at Lan Wangji, who'd been the one to punish him into silence. He sheathed his sword and bowed to the two elders, then left with his bow in hand.

Lan Sizhui spoke up, "Sect Leader Jiang, the Lan Clan of Gusu will fully recompense all the immortal-binding nets that were destroyed."

Jiang Cheng sneered. "No need!"

Then he turned in the opposite direction and strode confidently down the mountain. The sect disciples behind him all quietly followed with long faces, knowing there'd be an inevitable round of punishment upon their return.

After they had gone, Lan Jingyi posed a general question: "Why is Sect Leader Jiang like that?!"

Then he remembered his Lan family upbringing and the rules against speaking behind another's back. He snuck a scared peek at Hanguang-jun before shrinking back and shutting up.

Lan Sizhui gave Wei Wuxian a light smile and said, "We meet again, Mo-gongzi."

Wei Wuxian forced a smile, but it was Lan Wangji who spoke instead, his order succinct and clear without any flowery language.

"Do your work."

Only then did the juniors remember why they were on Mount Dafan. They gathered themselves and respectfully awaited further instructions.

A moment later, Lan Wangji said, "Do your best, but do not overexert."

His voice was deep and captivating. If one stood close, it would make the heart flutter. The juniors acknowledged the order politely and headed deeper into the woods, not daring to stay longer. Wei Wuxian thought to himself that Jiang Cheng and Lan Zhan really were two completely different people. Even their methods of instructing juniors were irreconcilably opposed.

Just as he was thinking this, he suddenly saw Lan Wangji give him a nod, curt and almost imperceptible. It made him unconsciously pause.

Lan Wangji had been painfully serious ever since he was young. A principled perfectionist, always so stern and stiff, as if there had never been a time when he was lively. Back then, he'd been extremely against Wei Wuxian cultivating the demonic path. Lan Sizhui should have already informed Lan Wangji of his suspicious behavior at the Mo Estate, yet the man only nodded at him to give his regards. Wei Wuxian figured he was thanking him for helping the Lan juniors out, so he immediately returned the gesture without thinking. But when he looked up again, Lan Wangji was already gone.

He paused for a moment, then turned to descend the mountain.

It didn't matter what prey was on Mount Dafan. He couldn't pursue it anymore. Wei Wuxian could rob anyone, but not Jin Ling.

He couldn't believe that was Jin Ling.

There were so many disciples in the Jin Clan of Lanling that he'd genuinely never imagined he might run into Jin Ling. Had he known, he would never have mocked Jin Ling with that comment of his, *"Didn't your mother teach you any manners?"* If anyone else had said that to Jin Ling, Wei Wuxian would've taught that person what "a loose tongue spells trouble" meant. But the tongue that said it had been his own.

After a moment of standing in silence, Wei Wuxian raised his hand and slapped himself across the face.

That slap was hard and clear, stinging his right cheek. Suddenly, there was rustling in the bushes nearby, and when Wei Wuxian peered over, a spotted donkey emerged. He dropped his hand, and this time, the donkey voluntarily approached to rub against it. Wei Wuxian tugged at its long ear and smiled wryly.

"You wanted to save the damsel in distress but made me go act the hero instead."

The spotted donkey was whining in response when a wave of cultivators came from the distant end of the hill. After the four hundred-plus immortal-binding nets were slashed by Lan Wangji's flying sword, the hesitant cultivators that had lurked in Fojiao Town now swarmed up the mountain anew. They were all technically Jin Ling's competition, and Wei Wuxian pondered for a moment on whether to beat them back down. After a moment of thought, he silently moved off the path.

The group was composed of disciples from various clans, dressed in all sorts of different uniforms. They complained as they went.

"That Jin-gongzi! The Jin family and the Jiang family both, they all spoil him. So young and already so unreasonable and bossy! It'll be the end of the world if he takes over control of the Jin Clan of Lanling in the future. We'll be doomed!"

Wei Wuxian slowed his pace.

A softhearted girl cultivator sighed, "How can they not spoil and pamper him? Losing both his parents at such a young age…"

"Shimei, it doesn't work like that. So what if he lost both his parents? There are plenty of people in the world who've lost their parents. If everyone acted like him, it'd be terrible!"

"That being said, Wei Wuxian really went for it, didn't he? Jin Ling's mother was Jiang Cheng's blood sister, eh? And what's more, she was also the shijie who raised that Wei Wuxian."

"What an injustice for Jiang Yanli, too, to have raised such an ingrate. And Jin Zixuan was an even more tragic case. To meet such a horrible end just because of some quarrel with Wei Wuxian in the past…"

"Why did Wei Wuxian have quarrels with everyone…?"

"Ain't that just the question? Besides that pack of crazy dogs he kept, who have you ever heard of getting along well with him? He had enemies everywhere. The world despised him. Even Hanguang-jun couldn't stand the sight of him. They were always at complete odds with each other."

"Speaking of, thank goodness for Hanguang-jun today…"

After walking for a while, the sound of a trickling creek suddenly flowed into Wei Wuxian's ears.

This was something he hadn't heard on his way here. Only then did Wei Wuxian notice he had taken the wrong path down the mountain and forked off onto another road.

He led the donkey down to the side of the creek. The moon had risen, and the skies above the water were unconcealed by any branches or leaves. The creek was cracked with patches of frosty white. Reflected back at him, Wei Wuxian saw a face that distorted with the flow of the water.

He slapped the water viciously, shattering that absurd, laughable face. He raised his dripping palms and washed away the powder foundation with the creek water.

What the water now reflected was a young man. Incredibly handsome and poised, he was so pristine it was as if he had been washed by the moonlight above, with a beaming face and bright eyes, and lips that curved slightly upwards. But when he hung his head to stare at himself, the droplets clinging to his lashes fell relentlessly like tears.

This was a young, foreign face. This wasn't the Yiling Patriarch Wei Wuxian, who had once razed the earth and ravaged the world with bloody tempests.

He stared at that reflection for a long time before he wiped his face a few more times, rubbed his eyes, and sat down heavily by the creek.

It wasn't that he couldn't endure talk. After all, he was already well aware of the path he'd chosen back when he first made his decision. He had already cautioned himself to remember the motto of the Jiang Clan of Yunmeng: "Attempt the impossible."

He had truly thought his heart was made of stone. But humans were no stalks of grass, not unfeeling, and in the end, he was human after all.

The little spotted donkey seemed to know he wasn't in a good mood right now, and amazingly it did not bray impatiently, only swishing its tail while walking away after a moment of quiet. Wei Wuxian sat by the creek and didn't react. It looked back and kicked its hooves. Wei Wuxian still ignored it, so the spotted donkey returned in a huff and caught Wei Wuxian by the hem with its teeth, tugging and pulling.

It made no difference to Wei Wuxian whether he stayed or left, so since the donkey had gone as far as to bite him, he went with it. The spotted donkey led him to some trees and started circling around a piece of grass. A qiankun bag sat quietly there. Over it hung a broken golden net, so it must've been something an unlucky cultivator dropped when they tried to break free. Wei Wuxian picked up the bag and opened it. Inside was an assortment of items like a bottle gourd of medicinal wine, talismans, a little yao-reflecting mirror, and so on.

He rummaged through the bag for a bit and casually took out a handful of talismans. A ball of flames was suddenly ablaze in his hand.

What had just ignited was a yin-burning talisman. Like its name, it used yin energy as fuel and would automatically be ignited upon contact with yin energy. The greater the yin energy, the bigger the flames. It blazed the instant it was taken out of the bag, meaning there were spirits nearby.

The moment Wei Wuxian saw the firelight, he raised his guard and probed around for the direction with the torch raised. When he turned eastward, the fire died down; when he turned westward, the fire blazed. He had only taken a few steps in that direction when he saw a slumped form in white appear beneath a tree.

The talisman burned out, and remnant embers fell from his fingertips. An elder, with his back facing him, was grumbling under his breath.

Wei Wuxian slowly approached, and the words mumbled from the elder's lips became clearer.

"It hurts, it hurts."

"Where does it hurt?" Wei Wuxian asked.

"Head, the head. My head," that elder replied.

"Let me take a look," Wei Wuxian said.

He circled around to the elder's side and saw a large, bloody gaping hole on his forehead. This was a soul of the dead, probably killed by way of some weapon to the head. He was wearing funeral clothes, their material and cut both of high quality, meaning he had already been properly buried. This wasn't a soul of the living that a human had lost.

But a soul of the dead should never have appeared on Mount Dafan.

Wei Wuxian couldn't come up with a plausible explanation for this. Feeling uneasy, he hopped onto the back of the donkey, gave it a slap and a shout, and urged it to chase in the direction that Jin Ling and the others had approached the mountain.

CHAPTER 3: THE PRIDEFUL

There were a number of cultivators pacing near the old graveyard, intending to wait for a windfall. Someone had brazenly raised a spirit-attraction flag, only to summon a bunch of wailing souls.

Wei Wuxian pulled the reins, scanned the area, and asked loudly, "Excuse me, might I ask where the little gongzi of the Jin family and Lan family have gone?"

As expected, there were actually responses now that he'd washed his face. A cultivator answered, "They left this place and went to the Shrine of the Heavenly Maiden."

"The Shrine of the Heavenly Maiden?" Wei Wuxian asked.

The family of independent cultivators from the countryside had also snuck back up the mountain after hearing the immortal-binding nets had been destroyed and joined the night patrol. The middle-aged man saw that his clothes, along with that teeth-baring donkey, looked like those of that lunatic who had rescued them earlier. Feeling somewhat awkward at the realization, he pretended nothing was the matter, but the round-faced girl pointed the way.

"That way. It's a stone cave shrine on top of the mountain."

Wei Wuxian questioned, "Which deity is worshiped in that shrine?"

"I...I think it's a naturally formed stone statue of a Heavenly Maiden."

Wei Wuxian nodded. "Thank you."

Then he urgently dashed in the direction of the Shrine of the Heavenly Maiden.

The deadbeat's marriage, the coffins struck by lightning, the fiancé killed by jackals, the father and daughter who lost their souls consecutively, the extravagant funeral clothes... Bead by bead, everything was being threaded together to form a complete string. No wonder the Compass of Ill Winds couldn't point in the right direction, and the spirit-attraction flag was even more useless. They had all underestimated the creature on Mount Dafan.

Because it wasn't what they thought it was at all!

Meanwhile, Lan Sizhui and company had already moved on to the Shrine of the Heavenly Maiden in search of clues after coming up empty-handed when investigating the old graveyard.

In Mount Dafan, besides the ancestral graves belonging to the townspeople of Fojiao Town, there was also a Shrine of the Heavenly Maiden. It was neither Buddha nor bodhisattvas that were worshiped in the shrine but a "Dancing Heavenly Maiden."

Centuries ago, a hunter from Fojiao Town traveled deep into the mountains and discovered a strange rock within a cave. It was nearly three meters tall, naturally formed, and looked extraordinarily like a human with all of its limbs posed as if dancing. What was more incredible was that the five features of this stone statue's face were vaguely recognizable, resembling the smiling face of a woman.

The people of Fojiao Town were greatly amazed. They believed this was a divine rock forged by the gathering of spiritual qi between heaven and earth, and they fabricated many of its related myths themselves. There was one about an immortal lord who was secretly in love with Jiutian Xuannu and carved a statue in her image to alleviate the misery of longing. When the Xuannu discovered it, she was enraged, and the incomplete statue was never heard of again. There was also another where the Jade Emperor had a beloved daughter who passed early, and his longing for her manifested as this statue. There were all sorts of stories, and all were mind-boggling. Eventually, the townspeople began to truly believe these constructed myths they told each other. And so, the stone cave was renovated into a divine shrine, the stone platform carved into a divine altar, and the stone statue was thus worshiped as the "Dancing Heavenly Maiden" with year-round offerings.

The interior of the cave was as spacious as a double-entranced temple, and that statue of the Heavenly Maiden stood in its center. At first glance, it certainly did very much resemble a human. Even the waistline could be said to be wonderfully graceful. However, one began to notice how rudimentary it was upon closer examination. Nonetheless, that a naturally formed object could resemble a human to this degree was already quite the marvel.

Lan Jingyi raised the Compass of Ill Winds high up, then down low, yet the needle was unmoved. Upon the altar was a mess of candle wax residue and a thick layer of incense ash, and the smell of rotten sweetness wafted from the offering plates. The people of the Lan Clan of Gusu were all at least a little germophobic, so he fanned the air in front of his nose.

"I hear the locals say prayers made at the Shrine of the Heavenly Maiden are very effective, so why is it so run-down? Why isn't anybody clearing this place?"

Lan Sizhui replied, "Seven people consecutively lost their souls, and rumors say it's some fierce fiend that came out of the ancestral graves after lightning struck, so everyone is scared of coming up the mountain. Since the worshipers stopped coming, there's naturally no one to clean up either."

A disdainful voice sounded from outside the cave: "Nothing but a crappy hunk of rock. Who knows who bestowed it with its divinity and had the audacity to place it here for worship!"

Jin Ling entered with his hands folded behind his back. The silence spell hadn't lasted long, and his mouth could open once more. However, he had nothing good to say the moment said mouth opened. He humphed, peering at the statue of the Heavenly Maiden.

"These rural villagers. Instead of making a concerted effort on their own when there's trouble, all they do is pray to the divine. There are thousands of millions of people in the world, and the deities can barely take care of themselves, so why would they care about them?! Besides, it's just some nameless rogue deity. If it's so efficacious, then can I wish for the man-eating spirit on Mount Dafan to appear right now in front of me and have that wish be granted?"

A group of cultivators from small clans followed behind him, and at his words, they immediately agreed, laughing uproariously. The once-silent shrine grew noisy and crowded all of a sudden with the inpouring of people.

Lan Sizhui shook his head quietly and turned around, his eyes unconsciously sweeping past the face of the Heavenly Maiden. The visible but indistinct features seemed to be a compassionate, smiling face. But he felt an indescribable sense of familiarity with this smiling face, as if he had seen it somewhere before.

Where in the world had he seen it before?

Lan Sizhui felt this was something important. He unconsciously approached the altar, wanting to examine the face of the Heavenly Maiden in greater detail. Right then, someone suddenly bumped into him.

A cultivator who had been standing behind him suddenly collapsed noiselessly. The others were greatly alarmed, and everyone instantly raised their guard.

Jin Ling demanded cautiously, "What's wrong with him?"

Lan Sizhui bent down with his sword in hand to check. The cultivator was breathing just fine, as if he had merely fallen asleep all of a sudden, but he wouldn't wake no matter how he was slapped or called to. Lan Sizhui stood up.

"This is like…"

But before he could finish, the cave that had been dark was suddenly alight. Red light filled it, like a cataract of blood washing down the walls. The candles on the altar and in the corners of the stone cave all began to burn on their own.

Clangs resounded in the cave as those who had swords unsheathed them and those who had talismans pulled them out. Right then, someone outside the shrine suddenly rushed inside and splashed the Heavenly Maiden statue with his gourd of medicinal wine. The stone cave was instantly flooded with the thick, choking smell of alcohol. The newcomer took out a talisman and slashed it through the air, hurling it toward the statue. The altar was immediately set ablaze, illuminating the cave with the brightness of day.

Wei Wuxian tossed aside the qiankun bag he'd picked up, having used up everything that was inside it.

He shouted, "Everyone get out! Watch out for that soul-eating Heavenly Maiden!"

Someone cried out in alarm, "The Heavenly Maiden's changed pose!"

The divine statue had clearly had both arms raised earlier: one arm pointing to the sky and one foot lifted, her form graceful. Yet in that moment, amidst the vibrant reds and yellows of the blazing fire, it had dropped both arms and legs. This was absolutely the truth and not a trick of the eye!

In the next second, this divine statue raised one of its legs…and stepped out of the flames!

Wei Wuxian yelled, "RUN, RUN, RUN! Stop hacking at it! It's useless!"

Most of the cultivators paid him no mind. The soul-eating monster they'd been searching all over for had finally appeared, so how could they let it go?! However, even though there were so many spiritual swords attacking, so many talismans being thrown, and many other spiritual devices waving about, none of them stopped the statue from moving. It was nearly three meters high, and when it moved, it was like a towering giant, exceedingly imposing. It picked up two cultivators and raised them to its face. Its stone mouth seemed to open and close, and those two cultivators' swords dropped to the ground with a clang, their heads bowed. Obviously, they'd just had their souls sucked out.

None of the attacks were effective. Finally willing to listen to Wei Wuxian, the others swarmed out of the cave, fleeing for their lives in all directions. With so many people and so many faces, the higher Wei Wuxian's anxiety climbed, the harder it was for him to find Jin Ling. He rode the donkey out, searching as he dashed into a bamboo grove. When he looked back, he encountered the Lan juniors, who were also in flight.

Wei Wuxian called after them, "Children!"

"Who are you calling children?!" Lan Jingyi protested. "Do you know whose house we're from? Do you think you're our elder just because you washed your face?!"

"Okay, okay, okay, gege," Wei Wuxian acquiesced. "Set off a signal, call over that...that Hanguang-jun from your clan!"

The juniors nodded and searched their pockets as they ran. A moment later, Lan Sizhui admitted aloud:

"The signal flares...were all used up that night at the Mo Estate."

Wei Wuxian was shocked. "You guys didn't restock?!"

The signal flare was rarely ever used—maybe once every eight hundred years. Lan Sizhui replied, feeling ashamed, "We forgot."

"How could you forget?" Wei Wuxian tried to scare them. "If your Hanguang-jun finds out, you'll all be sorry!"

Lan Jingyi turned ashen-faced. "Oh no, we'll be punished to death by Hanguang-jun this time..."

CHAPTER 3: THE PRIDEFUL

"Good. Rightly deserved! You won't remember without punishment."

"Mo-gongzi, Mo-gongzi! How did you know that the creature eating souls wasn't a fiend or a beast, but that Heavenly Maiden statue?" Lan Sizhui asked.

Wei Wuxian searched for signs of Jin Ling as he ran. "How did I know? I saw."

Lan Jingyi caught up, and the two sandwiched him, one running on his left and one on his right.

"What did you see? We saw plenty too!"

"You saw, and then? What's around the old graveyard?"

"What else is there? Souls of the dead."

"Exactly, souls of the dead. So it couldn't be a soul-eating beast or fiend. That's obvious. If it were either one of those things, then would it leave all those dead souls floating around and not eat them up? No."

This time, there was more than one asking questions. "Why's that?"

"I gotta say, you Lans of Gusu..." Wei Wuxian couldn't resist anymore. "Can you focus less on memorizing cultivator etiquette, clan origin history, and all that stinking, long-winded nonsense? And teach more practical things instead? What's there not to understand? Souls of the dead are easier to absorb than souls of the living. The flesh of the living is like a protective screen, so in order to devour souls of the living, this screen must be removed. Just like..."

He took a glance at the spotted donkey that was panting and rolling its eyes back as it ran.

"Just like this: if there's an apple in front of you and another apple locked in a box, which one would you eat first? Of course, the one in front of you. That creature only devoured souls of the living, and it has a very particular way of doing so. Which means it's super picky, and quite powerful too."

Lan Jingyi was shocked. "Is that how it is? That makes a lot of sense, I think! Wait! So you're not actually crazy!"

Lan Sizhui explained as he ran, "We all thought the landslide and the lightning striking the coffins was how the lost souls came about, so naturally, we thought it would be a soul-eating fiend."

"Wrong," Wei Wuxian said.

"What's wrong?"

"The order is wrong and the cause is wrong. Let me ask you: between the landslide and the soul-eating business, which came first and which came after? Which is the cause, and which is the consequence?"

Lan Sizhui replied without hesitation, "The landslide happened first, the soul-eating came after. The former is the cause, the latter the consequence."

"Completely wrong," Wei Wuxian explained. "The soul-eating came first and the landslide after. The soul-eating was the cause, and the landslide was the consequence! The night of the landslide, there was a sudden thunderstorm, and lightning struck open a coffin. Remember that. The first to lose his soul, that deadbeat, was trapped on the mountain for a night, then got married a few days later."

"What's wrong with that?" Lan Jingyi asked.

"Everything!" Wei Wuxian replied. "An idle, penniless good-for-nothing—where did he get the money to host such a grand wedding?"

The boys couldn't answer. It was no wonder—the Lan Clan of Gusu had never been a family that needed to consider the question of wealth and poverty.

Wei Wuxian continued, "Have you seen all the souls of the dead floating around Mount Dafan? There's an old man who was killed by a brutal strike to the head. The craftsmanship and material of his funeral garb were both exceptional. To wear such extravagant funeral garb—there was no way his coffin was empty. There must've been some accompanying funerary items to keep his spirit at peace. The coffin that was struck open by lightning was probably his. The people who came to collect the corpse didn't discover any funerary items, so they must've been taken by that deadbeat, which would explain his sudden wealth. The deadbeat suddenly became rich and got married after the night of the landslide, so something strange must've happened that night. It was storming, and he was hiding from the rain in the mountains. Where on Mount Dafan is there shelter from the rain? The Shrine of the Heavenly Maiden. And usually, when people visit a shrine, they always do one thing."

"Make a wish?" Lan Sizhui said.

"Correct. For example, he might ask to get lucky, hit it rich, have the money to get married or something. The Heavenly Maiden fulfilled his wish and sent forth lightning that struck open the graves, showing him the wealth within the coffins. His wish was granted, and as its price, the Heavenly Maiden descended on his wedding night and sucked out his soul!"

"You're just guessing, right?" Lan Jingyi said.

"Yes. But if we pursue this train of thought, then everything can be explained," Wei Wuxian replied.

"How do you explain Miss A-Yan?" Lan Sizhui asked.

"Good question," Wei Wuxian said. "You must've asked around too, before you ascended the mountain. A-Yan had only just gotten engaged at that time. Every young girl who's just been betrothed must have the same wish."

Lan Jingyi didn't quite get it. "What wish?"

"Nothing more than 'I hope my husband will love and cherish me for the rest of his life, that he'll only love me,' or some such," Wei Wuxian said.

The youths were confused. "Can a wish like that be granted...?"

Wei Wuxian shrugged. "It's easy. As long as her husband's life ended soon after, then wouldn't he have loved only her for his entire life?"

Understanding dawned on Lan Jingyi, and he exclaimed in excitement, "Oh! *Oh!* So...so...so after Miss A-Yan became engaged, her husband was killed by a jackal in the mountains the very next day, and it's very possibly because Miss A-Yan went and made a wish at the Shrine of the Heavenly Maiden!"

Wei Wuxian struck the iron while it was hot. "Whether it was the jackal or something else that killed him is hard to say. A-Yan has another point of interest: of all the victims, why is she the only one whose soul has returned? How is she different from the others? The difference is that she has a family member who also lost his soul. In other words, there was a family member who replaced her! Blacksmith Zheng, A-Yan's father, loved his daughter. So when he saw that his daughter had lost her soul and no medication was working, under such dire circumstances, what was the only thing he could do?"

Lan Sizhui answered quickly this time. "He could only place his last hope in the heavens, so he also went to the Shrine of Heavenly Maiden to make a wish. The wish was 'I hope my daughter A-Yan's soul will return'!"

Wei Wuxian commended him. "That's why only A-Yan's soul returned and the reason why the third person to lose his soul was Blacksmith Zheng. And although A-Yan's soul was spat back out, it couldn't escape being damaged. Once the soul returned to its rightful place, A-Yan unconsciously began to imitate the dancing pose of the Heavenly Maiden, including the smile."

The commonality between those who had lost their souls was

clear: they had most likely all made a wish before the Heavenly Maiden statue, and the price for their wishes to come true was their souls.

This Heavenly Maiden statue had once been an ordinary rock, but it just so happened to resemble a person, so it had received centuries of worship that led it to gaining spiritual power. However, its greed was insatiable. One single, deviant whim gave it a mind to expedite the elevation of its spiritual powers by way of consuming souls. Offering the fulfillment of a wish in exchange for the devouring of a soul—it operated on the same terms as those wish-makers who offered their own souls up to be devoured. It was a fair trade, by all appearances. Everyone got what they wanted, which was why the needle of the Compass of Ill Winds did not move and the spirit-attraction flag summoned nothing. The treasured swords and talismans were all ineffective because the creature on Mount Dafan wasn't some nefarious being, but instead a god! This was a rogue god, raised up by centuries of worship, so to use devices made for attacking malicious spirits against it was the equivalent of attempting to extinguish fire with fire!

Lan Jingyi exclaimed loudly, "*Wait!* Just now, inside the shrine, someone else got their soul sucked out too, but we didn't hear his wish!"

Wei Wuxian's heart lurched, and he halted in his step. "Someone had their soul sucked inside the shrine? Tell me every detail of what happened there without leaving out a single thing."

Lan Sizhui quickly gave a clear account. When Wei Wuxian heard Jin Ling had said— "*If it's so efficacious, then can I wish for the man-eating spirit on Mount Dafan to appear right now in front of me and have that wish be granted?*"—he exclaimed aloud.

"Is that not a wish?! That was making a wish!"

The others who had agreed with Jin Ling were tacitly understood to have made the same wish. Since the soul-eating Heavenly Maiden was right before them at the time, the wish had already come true, so what followed had been a collection of payment owed!

All of a sudden, the spotted donkey came to a stop and started running in the opposite direction. Caught off guard, Wei Wuxian was once again thrown off its back, but he stubbornly grabbed onto the reins. However, from ahead of them in the shrubbery there came the crunching and slurping sound of something being eaten. An incomparably gigantic figure was hidden in the bushes, its massive head moving back and forth over the abdomen of a person on the ground. When it heard an approaching noise, its head shot up, meeting their eyes.

The soul-eating Heavenly Maiden's facial features had originally been unclear, the shapes of the eyes, nose, ears, and mouth rough. But after she'd devoured so many cultivators in one go, her five features were now distinct. It was now the face of a smiling woman. Copious blood dripped from her bottom lip as she gnawed vigorously upon the arm dangling from her mouth.

Everyone immediately followed the spotted donkey and bolted in the opposite direction.

Lan Sizhui cried despairingly, "That's not right! The Yiling Patriarch said the high-level ones only ate souls, and only the low-level ones ate flesh!"

Wei Wuxian replied helplessly, "What are you blindly believing in him for? Anything he came up with was utter bullshit! None of the rules are absolute! Just take her for a baby. When she didn't have teeth, she could only eat gruel and soup, but now that she's grown up, she wants to eat meat. Her spiritual powers just shot up—of course she'll want to try something new!"

The soul-eating Heavenly Maiden stood up. She was big and tall, and she moved all four of her limbs as she danced crazily, seeming jubilant. Suddenly, a piercing arrow came flying through the air and caught her right in the forehead, the arrowhead penetrating through to the back of her head.

Having heard the strum of the bowstring, Wei Wuxian gazed at where the sound came from. Jin Ling stood upon a tall hill nearby, already nocking the second arrow onto his bow and drawing the string. He let go, and another arrow pierced through her head, its impact so powerful that it forced the soul-eating Heavenly Maiden to stumble back.

Lan Sizhui yelled, "Jin-gongzi! Set off your signal flare!"

Jin Ling ignored him, determined to bring down this monster. Sullenly, he nocked three arrows onto the bow this time. The soul-eating Heavenly Maiden wasn't upset in the least, despite having been shot in the head twice. A smile still graced her face as she charged toward Jin Ling. Although she danced as she went, her speed was still terrifyingly fast, and half the distance was covered in an instant. Several cultivators popped out from the sides to fight her, impeding her from moving farther.

Every single arrow Jin Ling shot hit the mark, and he fired non-stop. It seemed as though he'd made up his mind to empty his quiver before going near the soul-eating Heavenly Maiden for close-range combat. His hands were steady and his aim was precise, but unfortunately, no spiritual devices would work on her!

Jiang Cheng and Lan Wangji were both waiting for news in Fojiao Town. Who knew if they would notice anything amiss and rush over? You needed water to extinguish fire. If spiritual devices wouldn't work, then how about demonic tricks?!

Wei Wuxian pulled out the sword hanging on Lan Sizhui's

waist, cut down a piece of thin bamboo, and swiftly made a flute. He placed it on his lips and sucked in a deep breath. A sharp flute note pierced through the night sky like a whistling arrow, shooting straight for the clouds.

He shouldn't have done this unless it was absolutely necessary. But with things as they were, he no longer cared what was summoned, as long as it was murderous enough and vengeful enough. As long as it could rip apart the soul-eating Heavenly Maiden, it was good enough!

Lan Sizhui was completely dumbfounded. Lan Jingyi, however, covered his ears and cried out in dismay.

"What are you doing playing a flute at a time like this?! It sounds horrible!"

Of the group of cultivators engaged in fighting the soul-eating Heavenly Maiden, several had already had their souls sucked away. Jin Ling drew his sword. He was less than six meters away from the soul-eating Heavenly Maiden, and his heart was pounding, hot blood surging to his brain.

If I don't take her head in one swing, then I will die here. If I die, I die!

Just then, clinking and clanking sounds resounded within the forest of Mount Dafan.

Clink clank, clink clank. Sometimes fast, sometimes slow, the noise came haltingly and reverberated in the deathly silent forest. It sounded like iron chains hitting each other, dragging on the ground. It was coming closer and closer, louder and louder.

For some reason, this sound was oppressively threatening. Even the soul-eating Heavenly Maiden stopped her dance, her arms raised in the air as she stared blankly at the deep darkness from whence the sound came.

CHAPTER 3: THE PRIDEFUL

Wei Wuxian put away the flute and stared intently in the same direction.

Although the ominous feeling was growing stronger and stronger, since this creature was willing to answer his summons, then at least it was one that would obey him.

The noise came to a sudden stop, and a silhouette materialized from the darkness.

After seeing the figure and its face clearly, many of the cultivators' faces contorted.

Even when facing the soul-eating Heavenly Maiden, who could suck away their soul at any time, they never shrank back, nor did they show any sign of fear. However, the sound of their screams was now filled with unconcealable terror.

"...The Ghost General, it's the Ghost General, it's Wen Ning!"

Like the Yiling Patriarch, the one known by the moniker "Ghost General" was infamous and widely known by all. And the two usually appeared together. There was only one man whom that name referred to: the number one fierce corpse under the control of Yiling Patriarch Wei Ying, the one who aided his tyrannical rule, fanned the flames of chaos, helped the villain in his evil, and caused havoc in the world. Wen Ning!

Wen Ning's head was slightly bowed, and his hands drooped by his sides like a marionette waiting for the orders from his puppeteer.

His face was pale and delicate, and as a matter of fact, he had a certain easy and somewhat melancholic handsomeness. However, there were no pupils in his eyes, only a field of deathly white. With this, plus the numerous black cracks crawling up his neck to his cheeks, that melancholia was transformed into a terrifying gloom. The hems of his long robes and sleeves were tattered and frayed, revealing wrists the same ghastly white as his face. A pair of iron shackles and chains were locked over them, same with the ankles. The clinking and clanking sound was created while he was dragging himself along, and when he stopped, everything returned to a deathly silence once more.

It wasn't hard to imagine why the cultivators present were all terrified. Wei Wuxian wasn't any calmer than the others, and the tempestuous waves in his heart had already surged past his head.

It wasn't that Wen Ning shouldn't have shown up here but rather that he shouldn't have appeared in this world at all. He should've been killed and reduced to ashes long before the Siege of the Burial Mounds!

When Jin Ling heard the others say Wen Ning's name, the sword he was pointing at the soul-eating Heavenly Maiden unconsciously changed directions. Taking advantage of him being distracted, the soul-eating Heavenly Maiden reached out her long arm in delight and picked him up.

Seeing how she had already opened her mouth wide and was nearing Jin Ling's face, Wei Wuxian no longer had time for his own shock. He raised the bamboo flute once more. His hands were trembling slightly, and the melody he played quivered with him. On top of that, because of how crudely made the flute was, the sound could almost be said to be raspy and awful.

Two notes were played, and Wen Ning began to move.

In the blink of an eye, he shifted and appeared before the soul-eating Heavenly Maiden. Wen Ning struck out with his palm, and the soul-eating Heavenly Maiden's neck made a cracking sound. Her body didn't move, but the slap turned her head all the way around. Her face was now facing the same direction as her back, but still that smile remained. Wen Ning struck again, barehanded, and cleanly chopped off the soul-eating Heavenly Maiden's right hand, which held Jin Ling in its clutches.

She looked down at the wrist that had been cut so cleanly. She didn't twist her own head back to the correct position but instead turned so her face and her back were facing Wen Ning. Wei Wuxian didn't dare slack off. He took a deep breath and bowed his head, directing Wen Ning to face battle. However, it wasn't long before he began to feel more and more apprehensive.

Low-level walking corpses could not think for themselves and required his orders as guidance. Even fierce corpses, stronger in attack, were often confused with no consciousness of their own. Wen Ning was different. He'd been refined by Wei Wuxian, and it wouldn't have been a lie to say he was the strongest fierce corpse in the world. One of a kind. He could think, he could ponder. Other than his lack of care for injuries, or for fire, cold, poison, and anything the living might fear, he was no different from the living.

But the Wen Ning in this moment clearly had no consciousness of his own!

Just as he was feeling bewildered by this, alarmed cries suddenly sounded from the field. It turned out Wen Ning had beaten down the soul-eating Heavenly Maiden, firmly pinning her on the ground before picking up a boulder taller than a man, raising it over the soul-eating Heavenly Maiden, and heavily bludgeoning her with it. The powerful blow struck the soul-eating Heavenly Maiden's body like lightning, forcefully crushing her into pieces!

Amidst the white debris of rocks strewn about, a glowing, snow-white pearl rolled forth. This was the core formed by the dozens of souls the soul-eating Heavenly Maiden had devoured, and if collected and carefully managed, the people whose souls had been devoured earlier could still be restored. However, no one had the

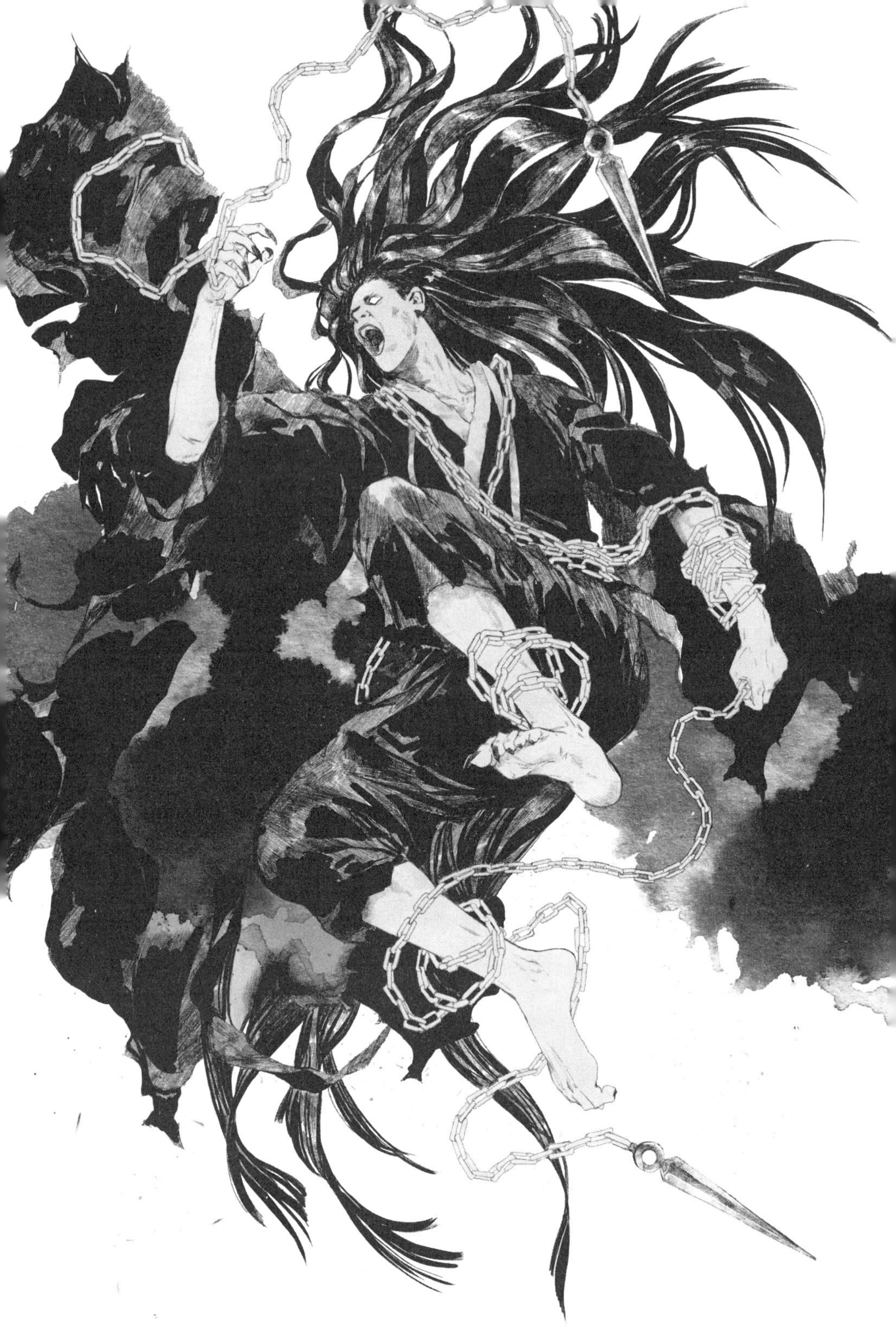

CHAPTER 3: THE PRIDEFUL

mind to pick up that pearl at the moment. All the swords that had been previously pointed at the soul-eating Heavenly Maiden earlier had all now turned Wen Ning's way.

One of the cultivators shouted at the top of his lungs, "SURROUND HIM!"

Some answered hesitantly, but there were more who were wavering, and some slowly backed away. That cultivator shouted again:

"Fellow cultivators, stop him and don't let him escape! It's Wen Ning we're talking about here!"

His words roused the crowd. As if a mere soul-eating monster could be compared to the Ghost General. Although it was unknown why he had come, killing a thousand soul-eating fiends could not compare to capturing one single Wen Ning! After all, with a bite harder and more fearsome than its bark, this was the most obedient mad dog of the Yiling Patriarch's. Catching him would make one's name soar across the cultivation world! The only reason they had rushed to attend the Night Hunt at Mount Dafan in the first place had been to fight over nefarious creatures and gain experience, so it couldn't be helped that there were those who stirred at this thought.

However, the older cultivators, who had personally witnessed the madness of Wen Ning in the past, still didn't dare to move recklessly, and so that man shouted again:

"What are you all afraid of? It's not like the Yiling Patriarch is here!"

That was true, when they thought about it. Yeah, what was there to be afraid of? Wen Ning's master had already been shredded to pieces!

With those words, the swords circling around Wen Ning abruptly closed in. With a swing of his arm, the heavy black chains swept the circle, knocking all the flying swords away. Then he took a step forward, seized the neck of the person closest to him, and lifted him easily off the ground. Wei Wuxian knew the melody he had played earlier was too urgent, too aggressive, and it had exacerbated Wen Ning's ferocity. He had to be neutralized, his emotions calmed, and so Wei Wuxian confidently played another tune.

This melody was one that came to his mind naturally, gentle and tranquil, a significant contrast to the strange, sharp sound from before. Wen Ning froze at the sound, then slowly turned toward where the flute was calling to him. Wei Wuxian remained still, meeting those pupilless eyes.

A moment later, Wen Ning let go, and the cultivator fell to the ground. He dropped both his arms and walked step by step toward Wei Wuxian.

His head was hung low as he dragged his chains across the ground, appearing somewhat dejected. Wei Wuxian backed away as he played the flute, luring him over, and they walked for a while like this, retreating into the forest. Suddenly, he smelled the refreshing scent of sandalwood.

He backed into someone and felt a sharp pain around his wrist, the sound of the flute abruptly stopping with it. *Oh no,* Wei Wuxian thought. When he turned around and looked, he was met squarely with Lan Wangji's eyes. Their color was so light, the man's gaze appeared frozen.

Not good. Lan Wangji had personally witnessed him play the flute to control corpses in the past.

Lan Wangji had Wei Wuxian firmly gripped in one hand, and Wen Ning stood woodenly not six meters away from them. He looked around sluggishly, as if searching for the sound of the flute that had vanished so suddenly. In the forest nearby, firelight and voices began to grow.

Wei Wuxian's mind spun rapidly, and he came to a decision right there: *So what if he's seen it before? There are millions out there who know how to play a flute, and the number of people who tried to learn the Yiling Patriarch's way of controlling corpses with flutes could form an entire sect on their own. I'll deny everything, even if it kills me!*

He resolutely ignored the hand gripping him, raised his arms, and continued playing the flute. This time, he played even more urgently, as if urging, as if reprimanding, his breath unsteady, the notes cracking, shrieking and sharp. He suddenly felt Lan Wangji grip harder. His wrist was going to snap from the force. Unable to withstand the pain, Wei Wuxian's fingers slackened, and the bamboo flute fell to the ground.

Thankfully, his orders were clear enough, and Wen Ning retreated rapidly, delving soundlessly into the hauntingly dark forest in an instant and vanishing without a trace. Wei Wuxian was afraid Lan Wangji would give chase to kill Wen Ning, so he reversed the hold and seized him back. Yet unexpectedly, Lan Wangji's eyes were locked firmly on him, and he'd never spared a single look Wen Ning's way. The two stood there thus, clutching each other, face-to-face as they stared at one another.

It was then that Jiang Cheng arrived.

He had forced himself to wait patiently for the conclusion of the hunt at Fojiao Town, yet he hadn't even finished a cup of tea before a sect disciple came rushing down the mountain in a panic, telling of the terrible and brutal creature on Mount Dafan. Greatly shaken, he charged back up the mountain, shouting:

"A-LING!"

Jin Ling had almost had his soul sucked away earlier, but he was safe and well now, and all in one piece. "Jiujiu!"

Seeing that nothing had happened to Jin Ling, Jiang Cheng was greatly relieved. However, that relief soon turned into a furious reprimand: "Do you not have a signal flare on you?! Don't you know to set one off when you run into those creatures?! What are you pretending to be so strong for? Get the hell over here!"

Jin Ling was angry at not having captured the soul-eating Heavenly Maiden as well, and he yelled back, "Weren't you the one who said I had to capture it at any cost?! That I couldn't go back to you until I caught it?!"

Jiang Cheng really wanted to slap this stinking brat back to his mother's womb. But he had indeed said those things, and he couldn't possibly eat his own words. He could only turn to the cultivators who had collapsed all over the ground and demand of them mockingly:

"So what was it, exactly, that has pulverized you all into such an honorable state?"

Among the cultivators dressed in a myriad of colors were a number of disciples from the Jiang Clan of Yunmeng in disguise, secretly assisting Jin Ling under Jiang Cheng's orders in the event he couldn't win this challenge. Truly, as the elder, he had gone through great pains regarding this outing.

One of the cultivators was still in a state of shock. "Sect…Sect Leader, it…it was Wen Ning…"

Jiang Cheng thought he might've heard wrong. "What did you say?"

"Wen Ning's back!" that man said.

In that split second, a mixture of shock, hatred, fury, and disbelief all assailed Jiang Cheng's face.

It took a while before he replied, coldly: "That creature was already reduced to ashes as a warning to all. How could he come back?"

"It really was Wen Ning!" the sect disciple exclaimed. "There was definitely no mistake! I definitely wasn't mistaken..."

He suddenly pointed over.

"...He was the one who summoned him!"

Wei Wuxian was still at a standstill with Lan Wangji, but in an instant, he became the focus of attention of everyone present. Jiang Cheng's lightning-cold eyes also slowly gazed in his direction.

A moment later, Jiang Cheng's lips pulled into a twisted smile. His left hand subconsciously began stroking that ring once more.

He said softly, "Excellent. Back, are you?"

He let go of his left hand, and a long whip dangled from it.

The whip was extremely thin. Just as the name Zidian implied, it was a long purple current of lightning, crackling like the dark thunder that crawled through stormy skies. He firmly gripped one end in his hand. When he brandished it, it was as if he had struck out with an incomparably swift thunderbolt!

Wei Wuxian hadn't yet made a move, but Lan Wangji had already taken out his guqin. Steadfast as he plucked the string, like a rock in a river rousing ripples, the sound undulated in the air. It clashed against the purple lightning, canceling the attack.

All previous considerations Jiang Cheng had had of "not recklessly engaging in a fight" and "not making enemies of the Lan" went out the window.

That night, in the skies above Mount Dafan's forests, there were at times bursts of purple light. At other times, it was as bright as day. There were at times the crashes of thunder, and at times the long wails of the guqin. The rest of the cultivators quickly retreated to a safe distance to watch from afar, scared witless but unable to move their eyes away. After all, it was rare to have the chance to see two distinguished cultivation leaders from prominent clans clash in combat, and they couldn't help but hope the fight turned even more aggressive, more intense. There was a certain current of unspeakable anticipation as they hoped the Lan and Jiang clans really would fall out. Things would be more interesting then. And, over on the other side, Wei Wuxian found his chance and bolted.

Everyone was astonished. Hadn't the whip been missing him because Lan Wangji had been blocking it for him? Was he not seeking his own death by running off now?!

Sure enough, it was as if Jiang Cheng had grown eyes on his back the moment he saw Wei Wuxian break out of Lan Wangji's area of protection. There was no way he'd miss such a good opportunity. He raised the whip and swung, and the purple lightning swam forth like a vicious dragon, striking him right in the heart of his back!

Wei Wuxian was almost sent flying by the whip's impact, but fortunately, the spotted donkey blocked him before he crashed directly into a tree. However, when the strike hit, both Lan Wangji and Jiang Cheng stopped in their tracks, dumbfounded.

Wei Wuxian rubbed at the small of his back and crawled to his feet with the support of the donkey, then hid behind it while he yelled.

"*Wow!* Must be nice, coming from such a powerful clan, eh? Beating whoever you want! Tsk, tsk, tsk!"

Lan Wangji commented, "..."

Jiang Cheng also commented, "..."

Shocked and outraged, Jiang Cheng commented further: "What's going on?!"

Zidian held a strange power: if used against an individual who was possessed, the body and the interloping soul would be separated, and said soul would be cast out of the flesh by the purple lightning without exception. However, this man still behaved and moved as normal after being whipped, lively and well. There was no other explanation aside from the conclusion that he was not possessed.

Wei Wuxian, however, thought: *Duh. Of course Zidian can't whip my soul out. I'm not possessed; I was offered a body. Forcibly offered a body!*

Jiang Cheng appeared shocked and confused, and was about to whip him again when Lan Jingyi protested:

"Sect Leader Jiang, isn't that enough? That's Zidian you're using!"

There was no such thing as an initial blunder that required a second attempt for a spiritual device on the level of Zidian. If a soul wasn't whipped out, then it was not whipped out. If the man wasn't possessed, then he was not possessed. Otherwise, it wouldn't live up to its name. That shout forced Jiang Cheng, who cherished his reputation, to cease his assault.

But if that wasn't Wei Wuxian, who else could summon Wen Ning?

Jiang Cheng couldn't accept it, no matter how he thought about it, and he pointed at Wei Wuxian with a dark face.

"Who exactly are you?!"

Just then, a nosy onlooker finally interrupted. He cleared his throat. "Sect Leader Jiang, you might not be aware of this because you don't pay attention to such matters, but this Mo Xuanyu is that Jin Clan of Lanling's...*ahem*, he is a former sect disciple of the Jin Clan. But because his spiritual power was weak and he wasn't serious in his training, in addition to that...harassment of his peers, he was kicked out of the Jin Clan of Lanling. There was also talk that he'd gone crazy? In my opinion, he was probably indignant at having failed in cultivating the orthodox path, and so he deviated. He might not be...possessed by the Yiling Patriarch."

"'That harassment'? What harassment?" Jiang Cheng demanded.

"That…*that* kind of harassment, you know…"

Someone couldn't hold back and said, "A cut-sleeve!"

Jiang Cheng's brows twitched. The look he gave Wei Wuxian was even more disgusted now. There was more to it, but no one dared say so in front of Jiang Cheng's face.

While his reputation wasn't great, it had to be admitted that before the Yiling Patriarch Wei Wuxian had defected from the Jiang Clan of Yunmeng, he had been well known to be a handsome man and a sophisticated gentleman well versed in the Six Arts. He had been ranked fourth in looks and character among the young masters of the prominent clans. "Charming and cheerfully handsome," the people had called him—and this hot-tempered Sect Leader Jiang had happened to be ranked fifth, defeated by one rank, so no one dared raise the subject with him. Wei Ying was frivolous and a flirt, and he'd loved ambiguously gallivanting about with beautiful women. Who knew how many lady cultivators had fallen victim to his rotten charms? And yet there was never any word of him liking men. Even if he were to possess another in order to avenge himself… based on Wei Ying's taste, he would never pick a gay, donkey-riding lunatic with his face painted like a hanged ghost!

Someone else grumbled, "They're not alike, no matter how you look at them…and that flute was played so awfully…he can't even learn that right; it's nothing but crude imitation."

Upon the battlefield back during the Sunshot Campaign, the sound of Yiling Patriarch's flute had pierced through the lasting night, and his ghost soldiers and ghost generals had been like an invincible army of millions, cutting down all who stood in their way. That flute was said to be like divine music, so how could it be compared to the sad moan horribly played by the abandoned son of the Jin Clan? Even if Wei Wuxian was an awful character, that wasn't how comparisons should be drawn. It was simply too insulting.

Wei Wuxian felt a little woeful. ...*Why don't* you *try not practicing for a dozen years, then make a crappy flute from some chopped sticks and play me a tune? I'll kneel if you can play it well!*

Jiang Cheng had determined this man to be Wei Wuxian earlier, and the cold blood in his veins boiled. But now, the Zidian in his hand was clearly telling him that no, it wasn't him. Zidian would never lie to him, nor would it ever make mistakes. He quickly calmed down to contemplate. This wasn't a big deal. He would find an excuse to take the man back with him, then use every means possible to beat a confession out of him. Something would be spilled—there was no fear regarding that. He refused to believe the man would give nothing away. In any event, it wasn't like he hadn't done similar things before.

Having come to this conclusion, he gave a hand signal. The disciples understood and approached in a circle. Wei Wuxian quickly led his donkey and hopped behind Lan Wangji's back, clutching his heart and gasping.

"Ah, what are they gonna do to me?!"

Lan Wangji cast him a glance, tolerant of his incredibly rude, noisy, and exaggerated antics.

Jiang Cheng saw he had no intention of moving aside and said, "Lan-er-gongzi, are you trying to make things difficult for me on purpose?"

Everyone in the cultivation world knew that this young clan leader of the Jiang family had developed a near-crazy obsession with taking precautions against Wei Wuxian—and that he would rather catch the wrong person than let anyone go. Anyone that was even remotely suspected of being possessed by Wei Wuxian would be taken back to the Jiang Clan of Yunmeng to undergo brutal torture. If he elected to apprehend someone and bring them back, they would be certain to lose half their life.

Lan Sizhui spoke up. "Sect Leader Jiang, the truth is before us. Mo-gongzi is not possessed, so why must you trouble an insignificant individual?"

Jiang Cheng said coldly, "Then I wonder why Lan-er-gongzi has been so determined to shield this insignificant individual since earlier?"

Wei Wuxian suddenly snorted and chuckled.

"Hey, Sect Leader Jiang," he said. "Um, it's troublesome that you keep clinging to me like this."

Jiang Cheng's brow twitched, instinctively sensing this person wasn't about to say anything pleasant.

Wei Wuxian continued, "Your kindness is too much, thank you. But you're also overthinking things. Even if I like men, I don't like *all* men, and I definitely don't just go home with any man who waves at me. I'm not interested in your type."

Wei Wuxian was trying to disgust him on purpose. Jiang Cheng hated losing; no matter how nonsensical the competition, if someone were to say he wasn't as good as so-and-so, he'd be so angry that he'd stop eating and drinking until he'd thought of a way to win against them. Sure enough, Jiang Cheng's face darkened.

"Oh? Then please enlighten me, what *is* your type?"

"What's my type?" Wei Wuxian replied. "Mmm, I quite like Hanguang-jun's type."

Lan Wangji, on the other hand, could never tolerate such frivolous and senseless jokes. Once he grew disgusted, he would definitely draw the line and keep his distance on his own. Disgusting both of them would be like killing two birds with one stone!

Yet unexpectedly, when Lan Wangji heard him, he turned around.

"As you say," he said expressionlessly.

"Hmm?" Wei Wuxian said.

Lan Wangji looked back. Without breaching etiquette, but allowing no room for discussion, he stated:

"I am taking this person back to the Lan Clan."

Wei Wuxian was briefly speechless.

"...Huh?"

4

The Elegant Flirt

THE LAN CLAN RESIDENCE was located deep within a mountain outside Gusu City.

Within the gardens of waterside pavilions, charmingly dispersed, there were long, endless stretches of black-roofed white walls shrouded in the mountainous mists year-round. To stand within them was akin to standing amidst a transcendent sea of clouds. Fog permeated the early morning, the first rays obscured in haze, complementing its name: the Cloud Recesses.

The mountain was as tranquil as the people were silent, and the mind was made to be still as water. The only sound to be heard was the tolling of the bell from a high tower. While this was no Buddhist monastery, it resonated with the vast emptiness that was whispered from the zen of Hanshan.

However, this stately meditative scene was abruptly pierced by a long wail. With their morning studies and sword practice interrupted thus, it sent a shudder through the clan disciples, both familial and sect alike. In spite of themselves, they looked to the main gate from whence the sound came.

Wei Wuxian was bawling in front of the main gate, clinging to the spotted donkey. Lan Jingyi was reprimanding him:

"What are you crying for?! You're the one who said you like Hanguang-jun. Now that we've brought you back, what's with the blubbering?!"

Wei Wuxian was miserable.

Ever since that night at Mount Dafan, he'd had no chance at all of resummoning Wen Ning—no chance to figure out why Wen Ning had lost his mental faculties, nor any chance to find out why he had reappeared in this world—before he'd been carried back here by Lan Wangji.

When he was younger, he and some disciples from other clans had been sent to the Lan family to study for three months, and he had personally experienced the dull dreariness that was the Lan Clan of Gusu. He still had lingering fears of the Wall of Discipline, which was densely engraved with over three thousand rules. Just now, as he was being dragged and hauled up the mountain, he had glanced at the stone wall again in passing. There had been a thousand more rules engraved since, so it was now over four thousand. Four thousand!

Lan Jingyi admonished him, "All right! Quiet down. Clamor is prohibited in the Cloud Recesses!"

It was precisely because he didn't want to enter the Cloud Recesses that he was making such an awful racket!

Once he was dragged in, it'd be difficult to get back out. Back when he'd attended school here, the visiting student disciples had each been given a jade travel token. Only with the token could one come and go freely—otherwise, the protective barrier surrounding the Cloud Recesses could not be crossed. Over a decade had passed since then, so security could have only grown tighter, not laxer.

Lan Wangji stood silently before the main gate, turning a deaf ear and watching on coolly. When Wei Wuxian's voice quieted a little, he said:

"Let him cry. Drag him inside once he is tired."

Wei Wuxian clung to the little spotted donkey and cried even harder. He knocked his head repeatedly against the creature. What misery! He had thought that after getting whipped by Zidian, he'd have been cleared of any suspicions. He'd been feeling light and airy, and his lips could never pass up an opportunity to tease, so he'd spoken offhandedly to disgust Lan Wangji. Who would've thought Lan Wangji didn't react to such things like he used to? What logic was this? Could it be that over the years, despite the heights he had reached in cultivation, he had only become that much pettier?

Wei Wuxian said, "I love men, you know. Your clan has so many beautiful men, I'm scared I won't be able to control myself."

Lan Sizhui reasoned with him. "Mo-gongzi, Hanguang-jun brought you here for your own good. Sect Leader Jiang wouldn't have stood down unless you came with us. Over the years, countless people have been arrested and taken to the Jiang Clan's Lotus Pier, and none were ever freed."

"That's right," Lan Jingyi said. "You've never seen Sect Leader Jiang's methods, have you? Super vicious…"

He stopped when he remembered the Lan Clan rule *"Do not speak behind another's back"* and snuck a peek at Lan Wangji. Only when he saw that Hanguang-jun had no intention of punishing him did he regain the courage to continue his grumblings.

"It's all the Yiling Patriarch's fault for starting the trend with his evil craft. There are way too many people playing around with that senseless cultivation method of his, and Sect Leader Jiang is such a paranoid person. Would it even be possible for him to catch them all? Why didn't he take a proper look before suspecting someone like you? Playing the flute like that…heh."

That "heh" said more than a thousand words. Wei Wuxian very much felt the need to explain himself.

"Um, actually, maybe you guys won't believe me, but I usually play the flute all right…"

Before he could finish, several white-clad cultivators stepped out from the grand entrance.

They were dressed in the Lan uniform, their simple robes flowing as light and white as snow. The one in the lead was tall and graceful in bearing. At his waist hung a sword, and also a xiao of white jade. When Lan Wangji saw him, he gave a light nod in respect, and the man returned the gesture. He then gazed toward Wei Wuxian and smiled.

"Wangji never brings guests home. And this is?"

As this man stood face to face with Lan Wangji, they appeared to be mirror reflections of each other, except for the color of their eyes. Lan Wangji's eyes were extremely light, as faint as tinted glass, while the other man's eyes were of a deeper, gentler hue.

This was the clan leader of the Lan Clan of Gusu, Lan Huan. His sobriquet was Zewu-jun, and his courtesy name Lan Xichen.

People were a product of their environment. The Lan Clan of Gusu had always been renowned as a family who consistently produced handsome men, and the Twin Jades born of the head household of this generation were especially striking. While these two brothers had not been born twins, their looks were very similar, and it was difficult to discern who was the superior in appearance. However, they were one color, two shades. Lan Xichen was warm and elegant, sincerely gentle. Lan Wangji was overly aloof and stern, completely unsociable, and kept others at arm's length. This was why, in the rankings for the looks and character of the clans' young masters, the former was ranked first and the latter second.

Lan Xichen was worthy of the title of sect leader. Even at the sight of Wei Wuxian clinging to a spotted donkey, he didn't appear

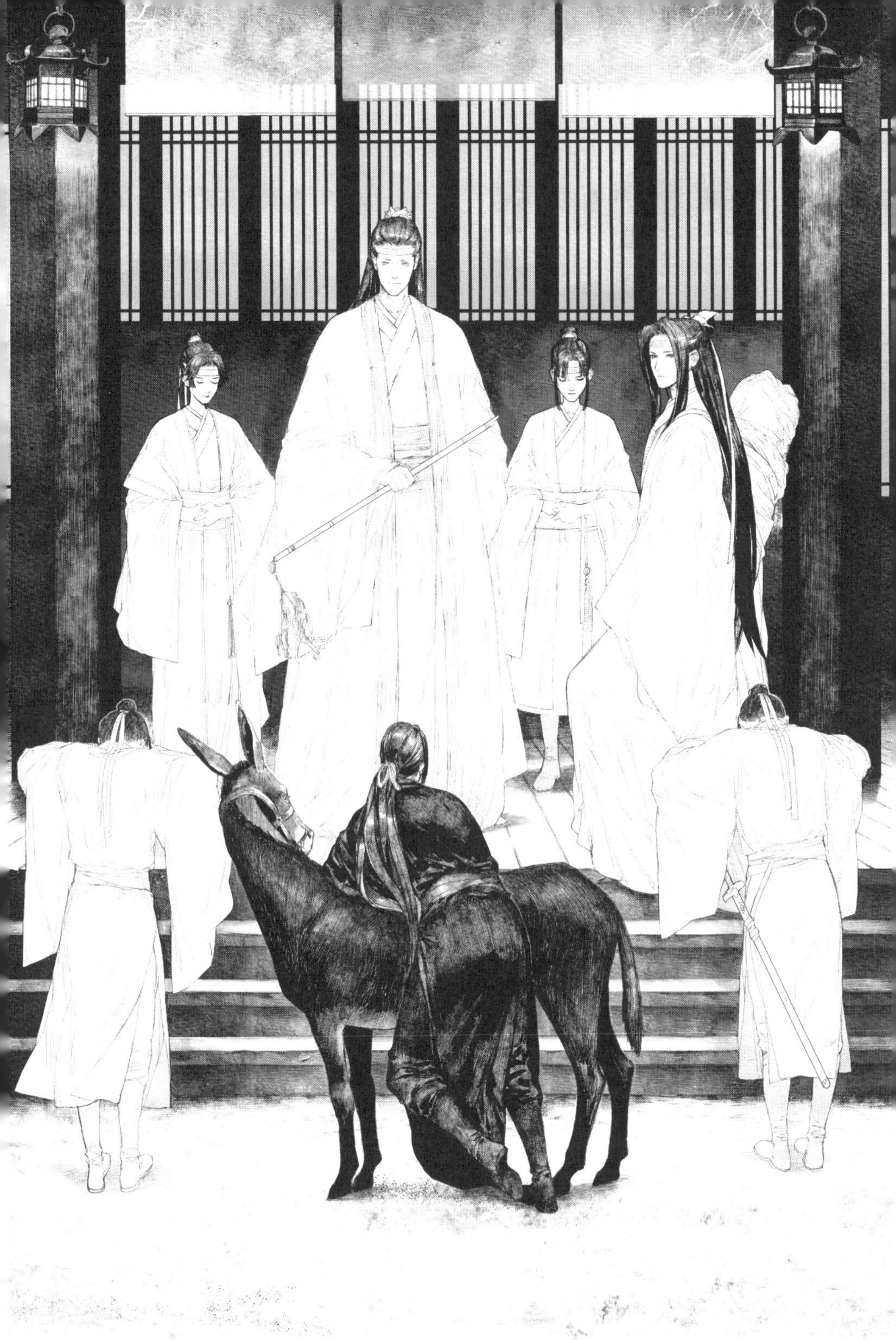

perturbed in the least. Grinning broadly, Wei Wuxian let go of the donkey and approached. The Lan Clan of Gusu placed extreme emphasis on seniority and social ranking, so all he had to do was spew sheer nonsense at Lan Xichen and he'd surely be beaten out of the Cloud Recesses. Yet unexpectedly, just when he was about to demonstrate what he was capable of, Lan Wangji cast him a glance and Wei Wuxian's upper and bottom lips became inseparable.

Lan Wangji turned his head and continued to exchange words with Lan Xichen in full seriousness. "Xiongzhang, you again take your leave to visit Lianfang-zun?"

Lan Xichen nodded. "To plan the next symposium at Golden Carp Tower."

Wei Wuxian couldn't open his mouth, so he returned to the spotted donkey to stew in bitterness.

Lianfang-zun, courtesy name Jin Guangyao, was the current clan leader of the Jin Clan of Lanling—and the only illegitimate son Jin Guangshan had ever recognized. Jin Guangyao was also Jin Ling's little uncle, being half-brothers with Jin Ling's father, Jin Zixuan.

Jin Guangyao was also the elder half-brother, born of another different mother, to Wei Wuxian's current identity, Mo Xuanyu. They were both illegitimate sons, yet the difference between them was night and day. Mo Xuanyu slept on the ground and ate leftovers at the Mo Manor while Jin Guangyao sat upon the highest seat of the cultivation world, with all those below at his beck and call. He could invite Lan Xichen for a visit if he so wished, could organize a symposium if he so wanted. However, it was no surprise that the two leaders of the Jin and Lan Clans shared such a close friendship. After all, they were known to be sworn brothers.

"Shufu has taken what you brought back from the Mo Estate for examination," Lan Xichen said.

Wei Wuxian's ears perked up at the mention of the Mo Estate, but then he felt his lips part. Lan Xichen had removed the silencing spell and turned to Lan Wangji.

"It is rare for you to bring anyone back home and also to appear so happy. Treat your guest well; do not be like this."

Happy? Wei Wuxian scrutinized Lan Wangji's face.

Exactly where did he see that?!

After watching Lan Xichen leave, Lan Wangji instructed, "Drag him inside."

And so Wei Wuxian was forcefully dragged into the place he'd sworn never to set foot in ever again.

In the past, those who came to visit the Lan clan had all been distinguished clan leaders or important figures. They had never received a guest like him, so the juniors jostled as they swarmed him, all finding this both refreshing and fun. If not for the strict clan rules, the trip definitely would have been full of merry laughter.

Lan Jingyi asked, "Hanguang-jun, where do we drag him to?"

"The Tranquility Room," Lan Wangji said.

"…The Tranquility Room?!"

The juniors all looked at each other in dismay, not daring to speak up. Wei Wuxian was left in the dark as to the meaning of their reaction, but the same thought had flashed through all the juniors' minds: *But that's the study and bedroom Hanguang-jun has never permitted others to enter…*

The interior of the Tranquility Room was minimalist, without any superfluous decoration. The folding screen was illustrated with paintings of the rolling, ever-changing clouds, done in the realist style of gongbi, and a guqin table was placed before the screen. In the corner there stood a three-footed incense table, and an incense burner of hollowed white jade was diffusing swirls of light smoke, filling the entire room with the fresh fragrance of sandalwood.

Lan Wangji went to discuss business with his uncle, and Wei Wuxian was pushed into this room. Lan Wangji had only just left when Wei Wuxian took the opportunity to slip out right after. He strolled around the Cloud Recesses and found that, just as he expected, even if he could scale the multi-meter-high white wall, without the jade travel token, he'd still get thrown down by the rebound of the barrier and immediately attract the attention of the nearby patrol.

And so, Wei Wuxian could only return to the Tranquility Room.

He never really got anxious when faced with problems, so he paced back and forth inside the Tranquility Room with his hands folded behind his back, confident he'd come up with a counter-solution sooner or later. The refreshing fragrance of sandalwood was cool and clean, ephemeral and alluring.

In his idleness, he mindlessly thought, *This is the scent that was on Lan Zhan. The fragrance probably sank into his clothes with all the time he spends in here, practicing his guqin or meditating.*

With this thought in mind, he couldn't help being drawn in closer to that incense table in the corner. As he moved, he felt a floorboard beneath his foot was conspicuously different from the others. Out of curiosity, Wei Wuxian bent down and started knocking about. He had done plenty of grave-digging and unearthing underground pits and holes in the past, so it didn't take long for him to come across a suspicious panel.

It was already shocking enough to Wei Wuxian to have discovered a secret compartment within Lan Wangji's room, but when he saw what was hidden, he became even more astonished. Once he lifted the wooden panel, an aromatic fragrance that was imperceptibly mixed with the sandalwood incense permeated the room. Seven to eight little round black jugs were revealed, all crammed into this tiny square cellar.

Lan Wangji had indeed changed: he was even hiding alcohol now!

Alcohol was prohibited at the Cloud Recesses. It was because of this very rule that the two of them had a little fight upon their first meeting, during which Lan Wangji spilled a jug of the Emperor's Smile that Wei Wuxian had brought back from Gusu City, which was nestled at the foot of the mountain.

After his return to Yunmeng from Gusu, Wei Wuxian never again got the chance to taste this famous and exclusive brew of Gusu. It was something that stayed on his mind for an entire lifetime. He always said he'd come back and try it if there was a chance, but that never panned out. As for the liquor hidden here, he didn't even need to open the jugs and test their taste; he knew by the fragrance alone that this was Emperor's Smile. He had never imagined that there'd come a day when Lan Wangji, someone who abided by the rules and never touched a drop of liquor, would have his secret booze cellar be exposed by Wei Wuxian. Truly, what goes around comes around.

Wei Wuxian sighed emotionally as he downed a full jug. He was a heavyweight when it came to tolerance and loved to drink, and since Lan Wangji owed him a jug of Emperor's Smile, he thought he should collect some interest after so many years. Thus, he drank another jug. Just as he was beginning to enjoy himself, an idea struck him: how hard could it be to acquire a jade travel token?

Within the borders of the Cloud Recesses, there was a cold spring with a myriad of special effects, serving the male disciples for cultivation purposes. Apparently, it had such effects as the calming of one's mind and the cooling of wicked inflammation.[4] Clothes were bound to come off when entering the cold spring, so what were the guys gonna do with that jade travel token? Dangle it from their mouths?

Wei Wuxian clapped and finished the last sip of the jug in his hand. He looked around but surprisingly did not find anywhere to toss the jugs. So, he filled the two empty vessels with water and sealed them like they had been before, then stuffed them back into the cellar and closed the floorboard. Having done the deed, he went out in search of a jade travel token.

Although the Cloud Recesses had been burned down once in the past, before the start of the Sunshot Campaign, its layout hadn't changed after the reconstruction. Wei Wuxian relied on his memories to navigate through the quiet, winding paths, and it didn't take long before he found the serene and secluded cold spring.

The sect disciple guarding the spring was standing quite a distance away. There was another designated area for the female cultivators, so they didn't use the facilities here, and there was never anyone in the Lan clan who dared do something as shameless as peeping. Thus, security wasn't strict and was extremely easy to deceive: perfect for Wei Wuxian to go be shameless himself. Just as luck would have it, a set of white robes were laying on top of a white rock behind a thicket of eupatorium grasses. Someone was already here.

This set of white robes was so neatly folded that it made one's hair stand on end. It was like a square piece of tofu; even the forehead ribbon was meticulously laid. When Wei Wuxian reached in to rummage for the jade travel token, he almost felt bad for messing it up. He casually cast a glance at the spring and suddenly couldn't look away.

---

4   *Wicked/evil fire is a cause of illness in traditional medicine, but also serves as slang for arousal.*

CHAPTER 4: THE ELEGANT FLIRT

The water of the cold spring was bone-bitingly freezing. Unlike hot springs, there was no steam to obscure vision, so he had a clear view of the upper back of the man in the spring. The man in the water was tall in build and fair of skin, his hair long and ink black, dripping and gathered to the side. The lines of muscle running down his back to his waist were smooth, graceful, and full of power. In short, a beauty.

However, Wei Wuxian was most definitely not someone unable to avert his gaze when stunned by a bathing beauty in the first place. And it wasn't as if he were actually into men, no matter how beautiful this man was. It was because there was genuinely something in particular on the man's back that he was unable to look away.

Dozens of crisscrossing scars.

Those were the type of marks left behind by a discipline whip. Among the cultivation clans, there was a type of discipline whip that was used to punish scion disciples of the head family. It was reserved for those who had committed the most grievous of mistakes, and after such punishment, the scars would never fade. While Wei Wuxian had never experienced this particular lashing himself, Jiang Cheng had. Wei Wuxian had wracked his brain to help him lighten that humiliating mark, but all efforts had been fruitless. Wei Wuxian would never mistake the sight of such a scar.

Usually, a couple of lashings from the discipline whip was already a severe lesson: enough to engrave it into one's memory forever, never to commit the same wrongs again. But there were, at minimum, thirty discipline whip scars on that man's back. What heinous crime had he committed to get whipped like this? And if it truly was so heinous, why hadn't he been executed outright to purge the sect of such corruption?

Just then, the man in the spring turned around. Below his collarbone, near the heart, was a conspicuous mark from a branding iron. When Wei Wuxian saw that brand, his surprise reached new heights.

The brand had stolen all of Wei Wuxian's attention, leaving none to spare a look at the man's face. It made him question whether his eyes were mistaken. Even his breathing quickened. Suddenly, white filled his vision, as if a curtain of snow had dropped. Immediately after, that snow curtain was slashed by the blue glare of a sword, which attacked with a frozen aura.

There was not a single person in the world who didn't recognize Hanguang-jun's famous sword, Bichen! Damn, this was Lan Wangji!

Wei Wuxian was no stranger to dodging swords and running for his life. He dropped efficiently to the ground and rolled away, just barely dodging. He even had the time to pluck a piece of stray grass from his hair as he fled from the cold spring. As he darted about like a headless fly, he ran into a few people on night patrol and was caught and scolded.

"What are you rushing around for?! The Cloud Recesses prohibits hurried walking!"

When Wei Wuxian saw it was Lan Jingyi and company, he was overjoyed. Thinking that this presented him with a perfect opportunity to get flogged off the mountain, he quickly offered himself up:

"I didn't see! I didn't see anything! I was definitely not here to peep at Hanguang-jun bathing!"

When the juniors heard, they were instantly shocked speechless by his audacity. Hanguang-jun was revered everywhere, considered a distinguished cultivator never to be profaned. Both juniors and disciples of the clan respected and admired him as if he were divine. To peep at Hanguang-jun bathing in the cold spring! Just the thought of doing such a thing was an irredeemable felony.

CHAPTER 4: THE ELEGANT FLIRT

Lan Sizhui was so stricken that even his voice changed. "What? Hanguang-jun? Hanguang-jun is in there?!"

Lan Jingyi seized him in outrage. "Damn cut-sleeve! Is...is...is that something you think you're allowed to peep at?!"

Wei Wuxian struck the iron while it was hot and confirmed his own crimes. "I saw neither hide nor hair of Hanguang-jun's naked body!"

Lan Jingyi exclaimed furiously, "You just gave yourself away! What are you sneaking around here for if you didn't peep? Look at you! Utterly shameless!"

Wei Wuxian covered his face. "C'mon, don't be so loud. The Cloud Recesses prohibits clamor."

Amidst this chaos, Lang Wangji emerged from the thickets of eupatorium grasses draped in a white robe with his hair long and flowing. While they were arguing, he had already re-dressed himself in a neat and tidy fashion, but Bichen was yet to be sheathed. The juniors hurriedly bowed.

Lan Jingyi quickly said, "Hanguang-jun, this Mo Xuanyu truly is despicable. You brought him back because of his assistance at the Mo Estate, but he...he..."

Wei Wuxian thought he'd surely crossed the line enough to get kicked out this time. But unexpectedly, Lan Wangji only cast a nonchalant glance his way. After a moment of silence, Bichen was sheathed with a resonant *sching*.

"Everyone dismissed."

Two simple words, yet spoken with extreme authority and without room for objection. The crowd immediately dispersed. As for Lan Wangji, he calmly and leisurely picked Wei Wuxian up by the back of his collar and dragged him all the way back to the Tranquility Room.

In Wei Wuxian's previous life, the two had been similar in stature, both slender in build and notably tall in height. Back then, Wei Wuxian had only been shorter than Lan Wangji by a tiny bit, and when they'd stood side by side, the difference had been barely noticeable. However, the situation had changed when he was roused back to life in this body. While he was still considerably taller than average folk, he was more than a full five centimeters shorter than Lan Wangji. Caught in his grip, he couldn't even struggle.

Wei Wuxian staggered, ready to scream, yet Lan Wangji coldly reprimanded him.

"Noisemakers will be silenced."

Throw him out of the mountain? Yes, please! Silence him? No, thank you. Wei Wuxian just couldn't figure it out. Since when had the Lan clan started tolerating such shameless crimes as peeping at their most distinguished cultivator in the bath? Was that even something that could become tolerable?!

Lan Wangji carried him into the Tranquility Room and went straight for the inner chamber, throwing him onto the bed with a thump. Wei Wuxian "aiyoh"-ed as he landed, and couldn't get up for a moment, squirming as he did. He had the thought to whine coquettishly to raise Lan Wangji's hackles, but when he looked up, Lan Wangji was looking commandingly down at him, standing there with Bichen in hand.

He was used to seeing Lan-er-gongzi with his hair and forehead ribbon fastened, orderly, and methodical, not a single piece out of place. The sight of him now—slightly loose black hair, thinly robed—was something he had never witnessed before, so Wei Wuxian couldn't help but take a look or two. In the midst of the dragging and throwing, Lan Wangji's tightly closed collar had also been tugged askew, revealing his defined collarbone as well as the dark red brand mark below.

At the sight of the brand mark, Wei Wuxian's attention was stolen again.

He'd had an identical mark on his body too, before he'd become the Yiling Patriarch. And the one on Lan Wangji now was no different from the one Wei Wuxian had had in his former life, in place or in shape. It was no wonder it looked familiar and not strange at all.

Speaking of, it wasn't only that brand mark that was strange. There were also the thirty-some lash marks from the discipline whip on Lan Wangji's back.

From a young age, Lan Wangji had made a name for himself. He was highly commended and the most orthodox of the distinguished orthodox cultivators—one of the Twin Jades in whom the Lan Clan of Gusu possessed intense pride. His every word and action were regarded by the elders as the benchmark for disciple excellence. So what unforgivable crime had he committed to garner such a severe punishment?

Over thirty discipline whip scars…was literally being lashed to death. And once the scars were on the body, they would remain for a lifetime. It was so the punished would forever remember their crimes, never to commit them again.

Following his gaze, Lan Wangji lowered his eyes and tugged at his collar, concealing his collarbone and hiding the scars. He was, once more, the cold-as-ice Hanguang-jun. Just then, the somber tolling of a bell sounded from the distance.

The rules of the Lan clan were strict, their daily routine rigid: rest at hai time, the beginning of night, and rise at mao time, the morning twilight. The toll of the bell served as a reminder. Lan

Wangji listened closely until the tolling ended, then turned to Wei Wuxian.

"You will sleep here."

He turned into the room next door without giving Wei Wuxian time to respond, leaving him sprawled on the bed, alone and confused.

It wasn't like he hadn't considered the idea that Lan Wangji had guessed who he really was…it was just that such suspicion made no sense from him. The Sacrificial Ritual was forbidden magic. Those who knew of it were extremely few in number to begin with. Over the years, any written knowledge passed down was, at best, fragmentary passages without any practical use. Practitioners of such magic dwindled more and more as time passed. Who knew where Mo Xuanyu had gotten his hands on those secret manuscripts in order to summon Wei Wuxian? There was no way Lan Wangji could have recognized him solely based on the bit he'd played on that crappy flute, could he?

Wei Wuxian didn't think he'd shared any sort of deeply consequential friendship with Lan Wangji in his past life. While they had been peers once, had had narrow escapes together and fought side by side, their meetings and partings had always been as swift as petals carried away by flowing water. Lan Wangji was a disciple of the Lan Clan of Gusu, and that predetermined him to be "elegant" and "righteous" without fault—completely incompatible with Wei Wuxian's personality. Wei Wuxian felt their relationship couldn't have been called *bad*, but he could hardly pretend that it had been *good*. He figured Lan Wangji's appraisal of him would be the same as that of the prevailing public opinion: wicked and unethical, with wanton indulgence for massacre, a disaster in the making sooner or later. After Wei Wuxian defected from the Jiang Clan of Yunmeng and became the Yiling Patriarch, he'd been in significant conflict with the Lan Clan of Gusu, especially in the months prior to his death. If Lan Wangji really was certain that he was Wei Wuxian, then they should surely have been brawling to the ends of the earth by now.

And yet he didn't know if he should lament the current state of things. In the past, Lan Wangji had been unable to tolerate a single thing he did. And now Wei Wuxian had done everything in his power to stir up trouble and the man had just endured it. Could it be that this was the result of years of great progress? Well then, congratulations?!

After taking a little while to despair and stare blankly at nothing, Wei Wuxian rolled off the bed and moved extremely quietly to the next room.

Lan Wangji was lying on the bed, seeming to be deep in slumber already. Wei Wuxian approached soundlessly.

He still hadn't given up. He was ready to feel up the man and see if he could fish out that jade travel token that had so stubbornly eluded his endless yearning. Yet unexpectedly, just as he reached out, Lan Wangji's long lashes quivered, and he opened his eyes.

At that moment, Wei Wuxian made a decision and threw himself onto the bed.

He remembered that Lan Wangji despised physical contact with others. Just a touch had sent him flying in the past. If the man could endure this as well, then he was definitely not Lan Wangji anymore. Frankly, he suspected Lan Wangji was also possessed!

Wei Wuxian straddled Lan Wangji, his legs spread wide and bent along the man's sides. His hands pushed against the wooden bed, trapping Lan Wangji between his arms as he slowly lowered his face. The distance between their faces narrowed, growing closer and closer, so close Wei Wuxian was practically suffocating before Lan Wangji finally spoke.

Lan Wangji said, after a moment of silence, "Get off."

"No," Wei Wuxian replied, thick-skinned even now.

A pair of light-colored eyes met Wei Wuxian's own gaze. They were barely inches apart.

Lan Wangji stared unflinchingly at him and repeated, "Get off."

"Nope," Wei Wuxian said. "You should've expected something like this would happen when you made me sleep here."

"Like this? Are you certain?" Lan Wangji questioned.

"…"

For some reason, Wei Wuxian felt this was a question he had to consider carefully before answering.

Just as he was about to curl his lips, he suddenly felt his waist go numb, his legs weakening. Then his entire person collapsed onto Lan Wangji's body.

That curve not yet formed on his lips froze as his head landed on the right side of Lan Wangji's chest. He was completely immobile. Lan Wangji's voice sounded from above. His voice was low and deep, his chest gently vibrating with the enunciation of his words.

"Stay like this tonight, then."

Wei Wuxian had never expected this to be his fate. He jerked, wanting to get up, but his lower body remained limp and powerless. That he could do nothing but remain stuck firmly onto the hard body of another man in such an embarrassing position…he was completely dumbstruck.

What happened to Lan Wangji after all these years? Why is he like this now?

Is this still the same Lan Wangji from the past?!

He's the one possessed, right?!?!

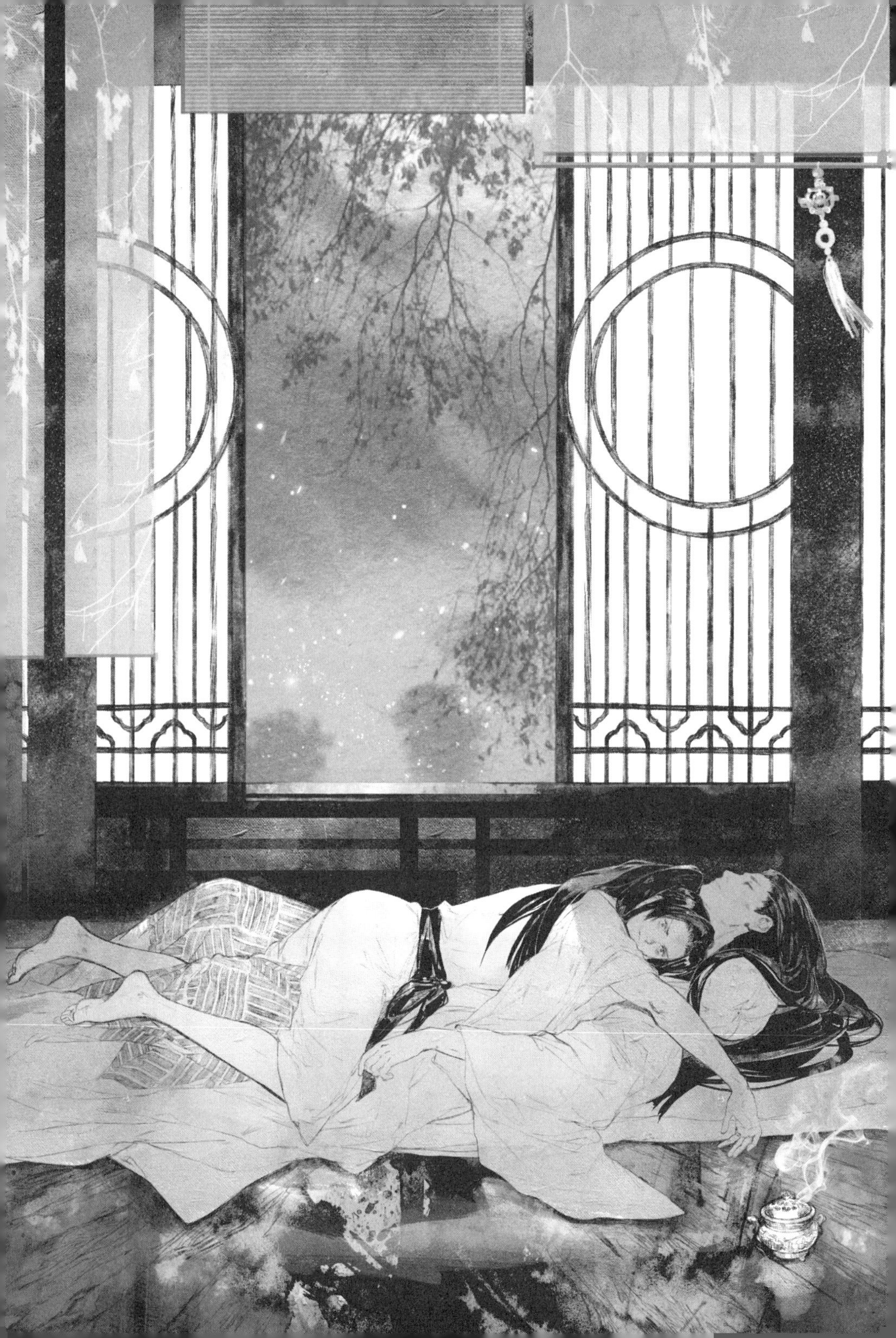

Just as he was embroiled in internal turmoil, Lan Wangji suddenly raised himself up a bit. Wei Wuxian perked up, thinking he'd finally had enough. Yet unexpectedly, Lan Wangji only gave a light wave of his hand.

And the candle was extinguished.

◇ ⟡ ◇

When Wei Wuxian reflected on it later, the start of his poor relationship with Lan Wangji could probably be traced back to the year when he was fifteen. That was when he and Jiang Cheng went to the Lan Clan of Gusu to study for three months.

There was a highly respected and reputable elder named Lan Qiren in the Lan Clan of Gusu. Among the distinguished clans, he was publicly recognized to have three major traits: pedantry, pertinacity, and proficiency in producing peerless pupils from his strict instruction. The first two items kept many at a respectful distance—indeed, even made some secretly abhor him—but the latter item made many others stop at nothing to finagle their children into his classes. Over the years, he had raised countless exceptional Lan disciples. Anyone educated under him for a couple of years, no matter how terrible they were going in, would appear decent coming out—or, at the very least, their poise and etiquette would see considerable improvement. Many parents wept streaming tears of excitement when they picked up their sons upon completion of their tenure.

To that, Wei Wuxian posed the question aloud, "Do I not appear decent enough already?"

With great foresight, Jiang Cheng replied, "You will definitely become a mark of shame on his teaching career."

CHAPTER 4: THE ELEGANT FLIRT

Aside from the Jiang Clan of Yunmeng, there were plenty of other young masters from other clans that year, all of whom were sent by parents who admired the reputation of the establishment. These young masters were all no more than fifteen or sixteen years of age. The prominent clans often dealt with one another, so while the students weren't necessarily already close, they knew each other's faces. Everyone knew that although Wei Wuxian wasn't surnamed Jiang, he was the clan's chief and eldest disciple. It was also known that he was the son of an old friend of Jiang Fengmian, the clan leader of the Jiang Clan of Yunmeng, and that Jiang Fengmian saw him as his own child. Young people often didn't care about backgrounds and blood as much as their elders, so they quickly mingled, calling each other gege and didi after only a few words had been exchanged.

Someone asked, "The Lotus Pier of the Jiang Clan must be so much more fun than this place, right?"

Wei Wuxian laughed. "Whether something's fun or not all depends on *how* you play. There's definitely not as many rules though, and no need to get up so early."

The rise at mao and rest at hai time routine of the Lan Clan of Gusu was not to be disrupted. Someone else asked, "When do you guys usually get up? What do you do every day?"

Jiang Cheng humphed. "Him? Rise at si, rest at chou, and he doesn't practice his sword or meditate when he gets up. Instead, he's off boating, swimming, picking lotus pods and hunting pheasants."

A boy exclaimed, "I'm going to school at Yunmeng next year! Don't anyone stop me!"

His spirits were immediately dampened by another. "No one's stopping you. Your older brother will break your legs, that's all."

That boy wilted instantly. This was the second young master of the Nie Clan of Qinghe, Nie Huaisang. His older brother Nie

Mingjue was a man who was swift and resolute in action, reputed for his might within the cultivation world. Although the brothers were not born of the same mother, they shared a close relationship. Nie Mingjue was extremely strict when it came to educating his little brother and was deeply concerned with his studies. This was why, although Nie Huaisang greatly admired his older brother, he also feared Nie Mingjue bringing up the subject of schooling the most.

"Gusu is actually pretty fun too," Wei Wuxian said.

"Wei-xiong, listen to my heartfelt advice," Nie Huaisang said. "The Cloud Recesses can't be compared to Lotus Pier. Now that you've come to Gusu, remember to never provoke a certain person."

"Who?" Wei Wuxian asked. "Lan Qiren?"

"Not that old man," Nie Huaisang replied. "The one you have to be careful of is his favorite disciple, Lan Zhan."

"Lan Zhan of the Twin Jades of Lan? Courtesy name Lan Wangji?" Wei Wuxian asked.

The current clan leader of the Lan Clan of Gusu had two sons, Lan Huan and Lan Zhan. Enjoying fame as the Twin Jades of Lan, they had been used since the age of fourteen by the elders of various clans as role models to compare their own disciples to. Standing squarely under the limelight thus, their names resounded like thunder in everyone's ears.

Nie Huaisang continued, "And that Lan Zhan, he's…sheesh. He's the same age as us, but he's not as lively as a boy should be. Stiff and strict. He's the same as his shufu, or worse."

"Oh," Wei Wuxian said. "Is he a pretty good-looking fellow?"

Jiang Cheng snickered. "Who among the Lans of Gusu is ugly? When it comes to enrollment, that clan rejects disciples who don't have proper facial features, you know. Find one with an average-looking face and show me."

"Particularly handsome," Wei Wuxian stressed and gestured to his head. "Dressed all in white with a forehead ribbon and a silver sword on his back. Very pretty, but all stiff in the face, like he's mourning at a funeral."

"…That's him!" Nie Huaisang confirmed. Then, after a pause, "But he's been training in seclusion and only just returned yesterday. When did you see him?"

"Last night."

"Last…last night?!" Jiang Cheng was stunned. "There's a curfew here at the Cloud Recesses—where did you see him? How come I didn't know?"

"Over there." Wei Wuxian pointed.

The place he pointed at was a high eave.

Everyone was speechless. Jiang Cheng's eyes were bulging, and he gritted his teeth.

"Causing trouble for me the moment you get here! What happened?"

Wei Wuxian grinned widely. "Nothing happened. Didn't we pass by that Emperor's Smile liquor store on the way over? Last night, I tossed and turned and finally couldn't hold it in anymore, so I went down the mountain to town and brought two jugs back. There's nowhere to drink that in Yunmeng, you know."

"Then where's the liquor?" Jiang Cheng demanded.

"Well, didn't I just hop over the eaves and get caught by him before I even got a leg on the other side?" Wei Wuxian replied.

"What luck, Wei-xiong," one of the boys said. "He was probably patrolling after coming out of seclusion, and you got caught by him red-handed."

"Those who return at night are not permitted to enter until the end of mao time, so why did he let you in?" Jiang Cheng questioned.

Wei Wuxian shrugged. "He didn't. He was demanding I remove the leg I'd put over. How could I do that, right? So up he came on the roof, airy and light, and demanded to know what was in my hand."

Jiang Cheng only felt his head throb. He had a bad feeling about this. "How did you answer?"

Wei Wuxian replied, "'It's Emperor's Smile! I'll share a jug with you, so pretend you never saw me, okay?'"

Jiang Cheng sighed. "…The Cloud Recesses prohibits liquor. Now you're doubly guilty."

"He told me the same thing too," Wei Wuxian said. "So I asked him: 'Why don't you tell me what your family *doesn't* prohibit?' He seemed a little angry and told me to go look at the Wall of Discipline at the front of the main gate. Honestly, over three thousand rules, written in ancient seal script no less—who's gonna read it? Did you? Did you? Either way, *I* didn't. What's there to be angry about?"

"That's right!"

The group felt the same way. They started complaining about the various outdated, unfathomable rules of the Cloud Recesses, deeply regretting they hadn't met each other sooner.

"Whose clan has over three thousand rules, without any repetitions? Never mind the *'killing prohibited, private fights prohibited, promiscuity prohibited, night outings prohibited, clamor prohibited.'* But I can't believe there's also *'laughing without reason prohibited,' 'improper sitting prohibited,' 'eating more than three bowls of rice prohibited'*…"

Wei Wuxian cut in quickly, "What? Private fights are forbidden too?"

Jiang Cheng said, "Yes. Please don't tell me you fought with him."

"I did," Wei Wuxian admitted. "And knocked over a jug of Emperor's Smile too."

The group slapped their thighs and exclaimed regretfully about what a shame that was.

The situation couldn't get worse either way, so Jiang Cheng changed focus. "Didn't you get two jugs? Where's the other one?"

"I drank it."

"Where'd you drink it?" Jiang Cheng asked.

"In front of his face. I said: 'All right, if the Cloud Recesses prohibits liquor, then I won't go in. I'll drink it on top of the wall. That's not breaking the rules, right?' And then I drank every last drop in front of him."

"...And then?"

"Wei-xiong..." Nie Huaisang was utterly shocked. "You're so arrogant."

Wei Wuxian arched his brows. "Lan Zhan's skills are pretty good."

"You're dead, Wei-xiong! Lan Zhan has never suffered such grief from anyone before. He's never gonna take his eyes off you now. You better watch out. Lan Zhan may be in the same classes as us, but he's in charge of punishment in the Lan clan!"

Wei Wuxian wasn't scared in the least. He waved dismissively. "What's there to be scared of? Didn't they say Lan Zhan is a child prodigy? If he's so precocious, then his shufu should've taught him everything by now, and he should be spending his days in secluded cultivation without any free time to keep eyes on me. I..."

Before he finished, the group rounded the corner of a garden-windowed wall and saw a white-clad youth sitting poised and proper within the Orchid Room. His long hair and forehead ribbon were fastened, and the air around him seemed to be shrouded with icy frost. He shot them a frigid look.

It was as if dozens of mouths had been suddenly struck by the silence spell. They quietly entered the Orchid Room, quietly picked out their seats, and quietly left alone any free seats around Lan Wangji.

Jiang Cheng tapped Wei Wuxian's shoulder and whispered, "His eyes are on you. Best of luck."

Wei Wuxian only needed to turn his neck to see Lan Wangji's side profile. Exceptionally handsome and refined, with long, delicate lashes, his posture was incomparably upright, eyes to the front. He wanted to start a conversation, but just then, Lan Qiren stepped into the Orchid Room.

Lan Qiren was tall and thin, his back as straight as a brush. Although he had a long black goatee, he was most definitely not old, and in line with the Lan Clan of Gusu's tradition of birthing beautiful men every generation, he was most definitely not ugly. Unfortunately, however, a pedantic air surrounded him, so calling him an old man was not out of place in the least. He entered with a scroll in hand, and when opened, it unrolled long and far across the floor. He then started lecturing them on the rules of the Lan Clan just like that, his grip on the scroll firm. The boys present all turned ashen as they listened.

Wei Wuxian was bored, his eyes flickering all over, and they eventually flickered back to Lan Wangji's side profile. Seeing how the boy appeared genuinely focused and stern, he was astonished in spite of himself.

How does he manage to pay such serious attention to something so boring?!

Suddenly, up at the front, Lan Qiren threw the scroll down on the floor and sneered. "This is all engraved onto the stone wall, but as no one read it, it seems I must now repeat each rule one by one. Let us see if there will be anyone else using ignorance as an excuse for their transgressions. Seeing as there are those who are still inattentive despite this explanation—very good. I will lecture on something else."

Although his words applied to everyone in the Orchid Room, Wei Wuxian had a hunch this was a warning targeted at him.

Sure enough, Lan Qiren called out, "Wei Ying."

"Present," Wei Wuxian answered.

"Let me ask you. Are yao, demons, ghosts, and monsters the same thing?"

Wei Wuxian replied with a grin, "No."

"How are they not? How are they differentiated?"

"Yao are formed from nonhuman living beings. Demons are formed from living humans. Ghosts are formed from deceased humans. Monsters are formed from nonhuman deceased."

"Yao and monsters are easily confused. Give an example of their difference."

"Easy." Wei Wuxian pointed at the lush, green tree outside the Orchid Room. "For example, a living tree, should it breathe in the air of scholarship, could cultivate over the span of a century into a spirit and form its own consciousness—and also develop a taste for causing mischief for the living. Such is a yao. Then I take up an axe and cut the tree down, leaving a dead tree stump, and that stump cultivates into a spirit. Such is a monster."

"What was the profession of the founder of the Nie Clan of Qinghe?"

"Butcher."

"The family insignia of the Jin Clan of Lanling is the white peony. What variety of white peony is it?"

"Sparks Amidst Snow."

"Who was the first within the cultivation world to focus on strengthening the clan and weakening the sect?"

"The founder of the Wen Clan of Qishan, Wen Mao."

He answered fluently and without hesitation while the others listened with trepidation. While they felt relieved, they also prayed that he would never be stumped. Please, let him absolutely continue answering like this, so Lan Qiren wouldn't have the chance to pick someone else.

However, Lan Qiren said, "As a disciple of the Jiang Clan of Yunmeng, you should be so familiar with all this information that you can recite it without issue. There should be no pride taken in answering correctly. Let me ask you something else. There is an executioner who executed hundreds while alive. His parents and wife are alive and well. He was murdered in town, his corpse lying in open air for seven days, brewing resentment. He now haunts and perpetrates violence. What is to be done?"

This time, Wei Wuxian didn't immediately respond. The others thought he was stumped and began to fidget in their seats.

Lan Qiren berated, "What are you all looking at him for? Everyone, think. Do not consult your books."

The students hastily removed the books they were about to frantically flip through and were stumped as well. Murdered in town, a corpse in the open air for seven days—it was the very definition of a major malicious ghost, a great fierce corpse, super difficult to handle. They prayed Old Man Lan would skip them for this question.

Seeing how Wei Wuxian hadn't come up with an answer after a while, only looking contemplative, Lan Qiren said, "Wangji, tell him what is to be done."

Lan Wangji did not look in Wei Wuxian's direction but only nodded in respect. He then responded in a colorless tone:

"First, deliverance; second, suppression; third, obliteration.

"Confer with his family and endeavor to learn how to fulfill his dying wish; one must absolve him of his obsession in order to ensure he is released. If the attempt proves futile, then one must suppress him with decision and with force. If his crimes are excessively heinous and his resentment still does not disperse, his existence cannot be tolerated; in this case he must be eradicated. In discharging duty, cultivators must heed this ordering without error."

The class heaved a long sigh, inwardly thanking the heavens and the earth. Thank goodness the old man had picked Lan Wangji. If their turn had come, they would've missed some points or gotten the order wrong.

Lan Qiren nodded, pleased. "Not a word amiss." After a pause, he added, "Should it be cultivation or conduct, one must always build such solid foundations. If one is proud and arrogant, unruly and divergent simply because of a false reputation earned from defeating simple mountain spirits, then it invites nothing but future humiliation."

Wei Wuxian quirked his brows and cast a glance at Lan Wangji's profile. *So this old man really is targeting me. Calling his prized pupil to come to class was nothing more than an attempt to show me up.*

"I have a question," he said.

"Speak," Lan Qiren said.

Wei Wuxian said, "Although 'deliverance' is the first step, deliverance is often impossible. 'Fulfill his wish, absolve his attachment' is easier said than done. If his wish is for a new set of clothes, then sure. But if it's to kill an entire family for revenge, then what is to be done?"

Lan Wangji repeated, "Deliverance is supplemented by suppression as required. Obliterate when necessary."

Wei Wuxian smiled at the response. "What a waste of resources." After a pause, he continued, "It wasn't that I didn't know the answer, I was just thinking of a fourth option."

"I have never heard of any fourth option," Lan Qiren said.

"This executioner died a horrible death, so him transforming into a fierce corpse is inevitable," Wei Wuxian said. "Since he executed hundreds whilst alive, why not dig up the graves of those hundreds? Awaken their resentment, fuse their skulls, and have them fight the fierce corpse…"

Lan Wangji finally turned his head to look at him. His expression remained impassive, yet his brows were slightly knit. Lan Qiren was shaking so hard even his goatee was trembling.

He shouted, "Such ignorance!"

Everyone within the Orchid Room was stunned, and Lan Qiren shot to his feet.

"The purpose of exorcism is deliverance! Not only do you pay no thought to the deliverance methods, you want to awaken resentful energy? You are reversing the proper order of things, disregarding ethics!"

Wei Wuxian argued, "Some creatures are impossible to deliver anyway, so why not make use of them? When Yu the Great was taming the waters, he already knew blockage was an unwise plan and that redirection was the way. Suppression is a form of blockage, so isn't that an unwise method?"

Lan Qiren hurled a book at him and he ducked, continuing his nonsense without batting an eye.

"Spiritual qi is energy. Resentment is also energy. Spiritual qi is stored within the dantian and can be used for great feats, so why can't resentful qi be used the same way?"

Lan Qiren hurled another book his way and exclaimed sharply, "Then let me ask you! How will you guarantee all this resentful qi will remain under your control and not harm others?!"

Wei Wuxian ducked as he answered, "Haven't thought that far yet!"

CHAPTER 4: THE ELEGANT FLIRT

Lan Qiren was outraged. "If you had, then the cultivation world would have no place for you. Get out!"

Wei Wuxian couldn't have been happier to oblige and quickly got the hell out.

He sauntered aimlessly about the Cloud Recesses, spending half the day playing in the greenery. When class was dismissed, it took a while before they found him on top of a wall. Wei Wuxian was sitting atop the black tiles by the head of the wall with a sprig of grass dangling from his lips, his face resting in his right hand. He had one leg propped up while the other hung down, swaying lightly. The people down below pointed at him.

"Wei-xiong! You're amazing! He told you to get out and you actually left! Ha ha ha ha…"

"He couldn't wrap his head around what happened for the longest time after you left, his face was so sour!"

Still with the grass in his mouth, Wei Wuxian shouted down in response, "I answered his questions and got out when he told me to, what more does he want from me?"

Nie Huaisang chimed in, "Why does it seem that Old Man Lan is particularly strict with you? Calling you out in front of everyone to scold?"

Jiang Cheng humphed. "Serves him right. What's with those answers? All that nonsense is okay to say at home, whatever, but to say it in front of Lan Qiren? He's asking for it."

Wei Wuxian replied, "He won't like me either way, so I might as well say what I want. Besides, it's not like I called him names. I only gave honest answers, that's all."

Nie Huaisang contemplated this. Then envy began to surface on his face. "What Wei-xiong said is actually very interesting. Obtaining spiritual qi requires cultivating and laboriously forming a golden core. Who knows how long that'll take for someone like me? Any aptitude I have seems like it got chewed on by dogs in my mother's womb. But resentful qi... That's abundantly produced by all those nefarious creatures out there. If it could be put to use, how nice would that be?"

The golden core was a core formed within the body of a cultivator once they had cultivated to a certain level, and its purpose was to store and generate spiritual power. Once a core formed, one's cultivation power would skyrocket and would only become greater and greater the more one cultivated, surmounting the highest peaks. Without a core, one was considered to be an unqualified cultivator. If a prominent clan's juniors formed their cores too late, it would be too great an embarrassment to speak of. Nie Huaisang wasn't the least bit ashamed, however, and Wei Wuxian also laughed in response.

"Right? It'd be a waste not to use it."

"Enough," Jiang Cheng warned. "You can talk about it all you want, but don't actually go down those deviant paths."

Wei Wuxian laughed. "Why would I leave the grand avenue under the sun to walk the single-planked bridge in the shadows? If it's that easy to walk it, someone would've done so already. Relax, he's asking his questions, and I'm just answering them. Hey, you guys coming? Come hunt pheasants with me before curfew starts."

Jiang Cheng scolded, "What pheasants? Where did you see pheasants here?! Go transcribe *The Righteousness Collection*. Lan Qiren told me to tell you to copy the 'Highest Justice' chapter three times so you can learn what ethics and natural law are all about."

The Righteousness Collection was the Lan family precepts. Their family precepts were so numerous that Lan Qiren had edited and

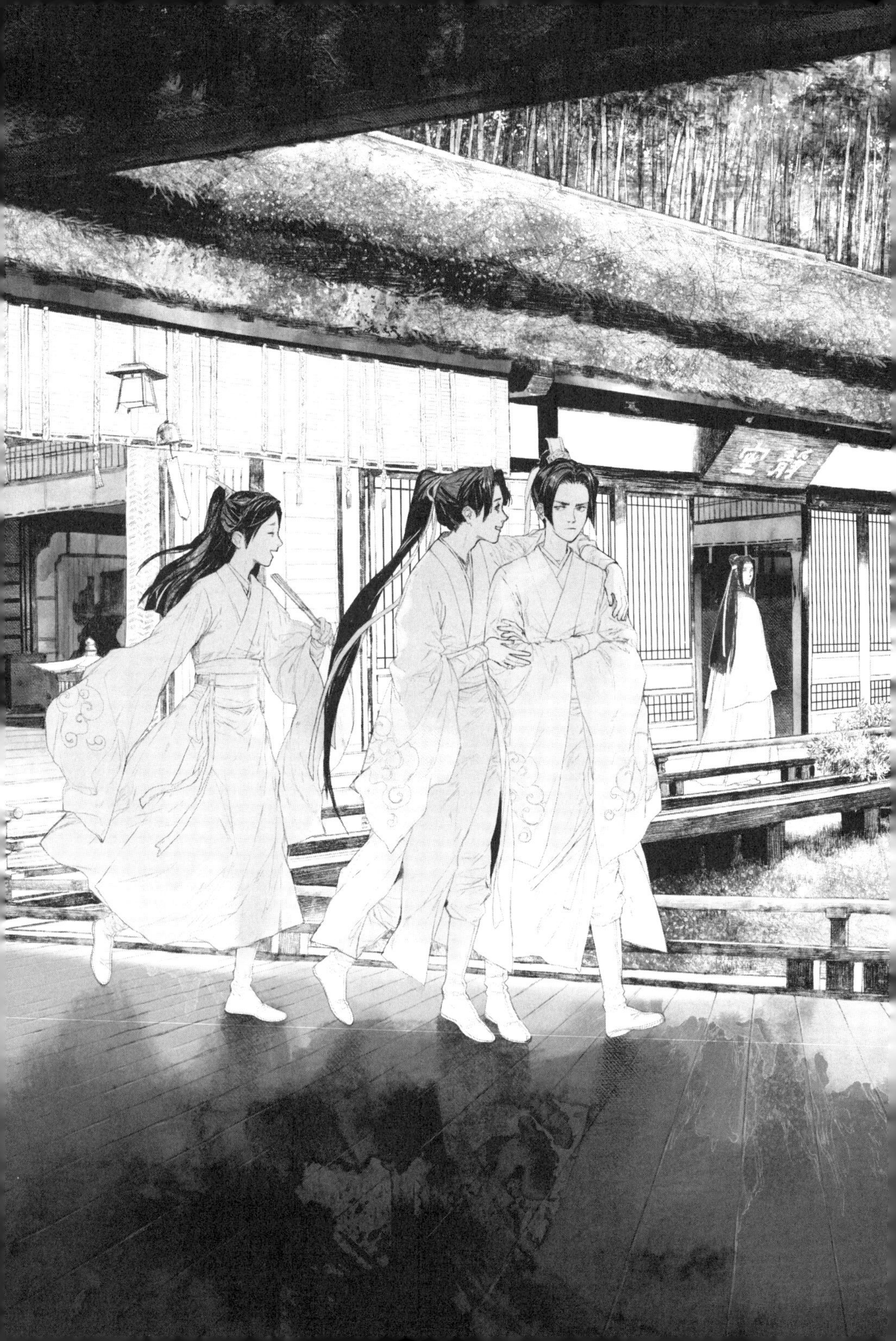
静室

assembled them into a thick collection, and the "Highest Justice" and "Standard Etiquette" chapters took up most of the work.

Wei Wuxian spat out the sprig of grass in his mouth, dusted off his boots, and said, "Copy three times? I'll ascend after the first time. I'm not a Lan, and I don't plan on marrying into the Lans, so what do I need to copy their family precepts for? I refuse."

Nie Huaisang quickly said, "I'll copy it for you!"

"There's always something fishy about someone being so helpful out of nowhere," Wei Wuxian said. "Go on, tell me. What do you need from me?"

"You see, Wei-xiong," Nie Huaisang explained. "Old Man Lan has a bad habit. He…"

He abruptly stopped mid-sentence. He cleared his throat, opened his fan, and shrank to the side. Wei Wuxian knew something was up, and when he looked around—sure enough, Lan Wangji was standing a distance away under a lush, ancient tree. With Bichen carried on his back, he was watching the group from afar. He was graceful and elegant, as if he himself were a tree of jade, mottled with the shadows of the leaves and the sun's rays. And yet his gaze was exceptionally unfriendly. Meeting his glare was akin to plunging into an icy cellar. Everyone knew they'd been a little too loud shouting back and forth earlier, and it was probably that commotion that had drawn him over, so they very consciously shut up.

Wei Wuxian, however, jumped down and went over to call after him, "Wangji-xiong!"

Lan Wangji turned and left immediately, but Wei Wuxian chased after him excitedly, shouting.

"Wangji-xiong, wait for me!"

That white robe and its airy sashes flashed behind the tree and instantly disappeared without a trace, a clear indication that Lan

Wangji did not want to converse with him. Having been met only with his retreating figure, Wei Wuxian felt snubbed and turned back to the others to accuse him.

"He ignored me."

"Yeah," Nie Huaisang replied. "Looks like he really doesn't like you, Wei-xiong. Lan Wangji usually… No, he's never this rude."

"He hates me already? I was gonna apologize."

Jiang Cheng said sardonically, "*Now* you're apologizing? Too late! Just like his shufu, he probably thinks you're completely evil, a bad apple. He won't care to give you the time of day."

Wei Wuxian didn't care. He chuckled aloud. "He can ignore me all he wants. It's not like he's even *that* pretty."

But then when he thought about it, yes, the boy was indeed that pretty. So he nonchalantly tossed that pouty feeling to the back of his mind.

Three days later, Wei Wuxian finally became intimately familiar with Lan Qiren's bad habits.

Lan Qiren's lectures were excessively and incomparably long, and everything had to be tested or written out from memory alone. The changes of cultivation clans throughout the generations, the division of power, distinguished cultivators and famous quotes, the clan pedigree…

Attending these lectures was like listening to the incomprehensible scripture of heaven, and writing from memory was like slavery. Nie Huaisang helped Wei Wuxian copy "Highest Justice" twice, and before the exam, he begged him for aid.

"Please, I beg you, Wei-xiong. This is my third year attending school at Gusu. If I get another Yi evaluation, my older brother really will break my legs! Differentiating between all the direct bloodlines, the collateral bloodlines, head family or branch family—juniors from prominent clans like us can't even get our *own* relatives straight! Any relatives twice removed, we just call them aunts and uncles or whatever. Who has the extra brain power to memorize someone else's family?!"

During the exam, all the little cheat sheets flying about were intercepted by the sudden appearance of Lan Wangji, who also caught the troublemaking ringleaders. Lan Qiren was outraged and sent letters to every major clan to lodge complaints with profound bitterness. Although this gang of juniors had been unable to sit still at first, at least no one had started anything, managing to keep their butts stuck to their calves. But once that Wei Ying had showed up, the brats who previously hadn't dared to act out were all encouraged to mischief—venturing out at night, drinking alcohol, doing as they pleased. The trend of delinquency grew as time went by. This Wei Ying really was as he had expected—the largest threat to humanity!

Jiang Fengmian responded: "Ying has always been thus. Thank you, Lan-xiansheng, for taking the trouble to discipline him."

And so Wei Wuxian was punished again.

He didn't care at first. It was just book copying, right? He never lacked for people willing to help. Yet unexpectedly, this time, Nie Huaisang said, "Wei-xiong, I'd really love to help, but I can't. Good luck holding out on your own."

"What?" Wei Wuxian said.

"Old..." Nie Huaisang paused and then continued on, "Lan-xiansheng said this time, you'll have to copy 'Highest Justice' and 'Standard Etiquette' at the same time."

"Standard Etiquette" was the most tedious chapter of the twelve in the Lan Clan precepts, referencing classics, lousy and long and amazingly replete with uncommon words to boot. One would lose

CHAPTER 4: THE ELEGANT FLIRT

all interest in life after copying it once. Copy it ten times and you'd ascend on the spot.

Nie Huaisang added, "He also said that no one is allowed to hang around you for the duration of the punishment, and no one is allowed to help you copy it out."

Wei Wuxian was amazed. "How would he know if I got help with copying or not? What, is he gonna get someone to supervise me or something?"

"Correct," Jiang Cheng said.

"...What?"

Jiang Cheng said, "He said you will not be permitted to go out. Every day, you are only to go straight to the Lan Library Pavilion to copy the book, and you'll reflect on yourself against the wall for a month while you're at it. Of course, there'll be someone watching you. As for who it is, there's no need for me to elaborate, is there?"

Inside the Library Pavilion...

A verdant mat, a wooden desk. Two dishes of candles, two people. On one end, one sat poised and proper. On the other, Wei Wuxian had copied a dozen pages of "Standard Etiquette" and his head was swimming. Feeling bored, he abandoned the brush for a breath of fresh air and peered over to the opposite side.

Back at Yunmeng, there had been plenty of girls at the Jiang household envious that he would attend the same school as Lan Wangji, saying that the Lan clan of Gusu produced beautiful men every generation, and the Twin Jades, the two Lan brothers, were particularly exceptional. Wei Wuxian hadn't initially had the chance to scrutinize Lan Wangji's full face properly, but now that he had, he let his thoughts fly.

He is fairly pretty. His face has nothing to pick on. I just really want those girls to come see for themselves that, if you constantly wear a profoundly bitter scowl like you just lost your parents, you can't be saved no matter how pretty you are.

Lan Wangji was transcribing anew the ancient books that had been stored in the Lan Library Pavilion for ages, but which were too inconvenient to bring out to show outsiders. His brushstrokes were unhurried and deliberate, the writing proportioned and its character clean.

Wei Wuxian blurted praise in spite of himself, "Beautiful writing! Best of the best."

Lan Wangji remained unmoved.

Wei Wuxian seldom kept his mouth closed for such a long expanse of time. He was going crazy. He thought, *This guy is so dull. If I sit here with him for hours a day for an entire month, won't that kill me?*

Having thought this, he couldn't help but lean forward a bit.

Wei Wuxian was very good at finding ways to amuse himself, and he was especially an expert in finding joy amidst suffering. Since there was nothing else to play with, he could only play with Lan Wangji.

"Wangji-xiong," he said.

Lan Wangji steadfastly stood his ground.

Wei Wuxian tried again, "Wangji."

It fell on deaf ears.

Wei Wuxian continued, "Lan Wangji."

Wei Wuxian persisted, "Lan Zhan!"

Lan Wangji finally paused in his writing and looked up with a cold gaze. Wei Wuxian dodged back, raising his hands in defense.

"Don't look at me like that. I only called you by your birth name because you won't answer to Wangji. If you're not happy about it, you can call me by my birth name too."

"Put your legs down," Lan Wangji said.

Wei Wuxian's sitting posture was extremely improper, with his body slouched and his legs propped up. Seeing that he'd finally been able to tease Lan Wangji into talking, he was secretly delighted, like he'd seen the bright moon at last after waiting for the clouds to part. He obediently put his legs down but leaned forward in the process without realizing it, his arms pressing down on the desk, still in an unmannerly sitting position.

He asked sternly, "Lan Zhan, I've a question for you. Do you really hate me?"

Lan Wangji lowered his eyes, his lashes casting light shadows over his jade-like cheeks.

Wei Wuxian said promptly, "Oh, don't. Ignoring me after a few words... I want to offer you an apology, to say sorry. Look at me."

After a pause, he continued, "Won't look at me? Fine, then I'll go ahead. It was my fault that night. I was wrong. I shouldn't have scaled the wall, I shouldn't have drunk the booze, I shouldn't have fought you. But I swear I wasn't trying to provoke you on purpose! I really just didn't look at your family's rules. The family precepts of the Jiang clan are all passed around by word of mouth; none of it is written down. I never would've done any of that otherwise."

Never would've drunk an entire jug of Emperor's Smile in front of you. I'd have tucked it in my robes and snuck it back to my room to enjoy. I'd drink it every day, I'd share it with everyone, and we'd all have our fill.

Wei Wuxian continued, "Besides, let's be reasonable here. Who was the one to start that fight? You. If you hadn't made the first move, we could've talked properly and cleared up that little misunderstanding. But if someone attacks me, I have to fight back. You can't blame me for that. Lan Zhan, are you listening? Look at me.

Lan-gongzi?" He snapped his fingers. "Lan-er-gege, c'mon, grant me some face. Look at me."

Without lifting his eyes at all, Lan Wangji said, "Transcribe it all an additional time."

Wei Wuxian instantly slumped to the ground. "Don't be like that. I said I was sorry~!"

Lan Wangji exposed him heartlessly. "You are not remorseful in the least."

Wei Wuxian said, without any dignity, "I'm sorry, I'm sorry, I'm sorry, I'm sorry, I'm sorry, I'm sorry, I'm sorry. I can say it as many times as you like; I can even kneel and say it."

Lan Wangji put down his brush. Wei Wuxian thought he had finally had enough and was going to punch him, but just as he was about to flash him a silly grin, he suddenly realized his upper and lower lips were glued together, and he could laugh no more.

His expression dropped drastically, and he struggled to speak. "Mmph? Mmph, mmph, mmph!"

Lan Wangji closed his eyes and let out a small sigh. When he opened his eyes anew, he was tranquil once more, picking up his brush as if nothing had happened. Wei Wuxian had already heard of how abominable the Lan silencing spell was, but he had refused to believe the heresy that it could actually silence him. Yet after doing all he could, scratching his lips until they were red, he still couldn't open his mouth no matter what. And so he pulled out a sheet of paper, his brush flying over it rapidly before he tossed the note over.

Lan Wangji cast a glance at it and said, "Frivolous."

Then he rolled the paper into a ball and tossed it. Wei Wuxian rolled on his mat in a fit of anger, then crawled up and scribbled out another one, slapping it down in front of Lan Wangji. It was once again rolled into a ball and tossed out.

This silence spell lasted until he finished copying. When he came to the Library Pavilion the next day, the paper balls strewn all over the floor from the day before had been all cleared away.

Wei Wuxian had always been someone who'd forget the pain once the wound was healed. He'd suffered at the hands of the silence spell the very day before, and after sitting for two quarters of an hour, he was restless again. It only took a few brashly spoken words before he was silenced once more. Since he couldn't talk, he doodled all over the papers and shoved them over to Lan Wangji's side of the table, where they were all rolled into balls and tossed to the ground. Three days passed in this way.

Having been silenced repeatedly thus, upon the last day of this wall reflection, Lan Wangji thought there was something off about Wei Wuxian.

During his stay at Gusu, he had left his sword all over the place. Never once was he seen carrying it. Yet today, he had brought it and placed it next to the desk. What was more, instead of launching into his usual routine of endlessly annoying and harassing Lan Wangji, he did not utter a single word but took up the brush as soon as he sat down. He was so obedient, it was peculiar.

Lan Wangji had no reason to cast the silence spell. He took another look at him, and then another, as if he couldn't believe Wei Wuxian had all of a sudden decided to settle down. Sure enough, Wei Wuxian didn't sit for long before he started acting up again. He sent a sheet of paper over, gesturing for him to look.

Lan Wangji thought it would just be more nonsensical, frivolous words, but something made him glance at it. It was a portrait. The subject was sitting prim and proper, reading silently by the window, the expression and demeanor remarkably realistic. It was him.

Wei Wuxian saw he hadn't moved his eyes away from the paper and curled his lips, quirking his brows at him. He winked. There was no need for words; his meaning was plain as day: *Doesn't it look like you? Is it good?*

Lan Wangji said unhurriedly, "To waste time doodling instead of copying the text; I believe your punishment will never end."

Wei Wuxian blew at the still-wet ink on the portrait and replied nonchalantly, "I already finished, so I'm not coming tomorrow!"

Lan Wangji's long, slender fingers seemed to falter for a second over the yellowed scrolls before flipping to the next page, surprisingly not silencing him. Seeing how his tricks didn't work, Wei Wuxian lightly tossed the drawing his way.

"For you."

The drawing landed on the mat, but Lan Wangji showed no signs of taking it. In the past few days, Wei Wuxian had written to curse him, to curry favor, to admit fault, to beg for mercy, to scribble out more random drawings. The papers were all treated the same way, so he was used to it and didn't mind.

Suddenly, he said, "I forgot, there's something I gotta add for you."

He then picked up the paper and a brush, adding a few strokes. He looked at the drawing, then at the real person, and then fell to the ground laughing. Lan Wangji placed his book down and cast the paper a glance. As it turned out, Wei Wuxian had added a flower next to his ear in the drawing.

His lips seemed to have twitched. Wei Wuxian crawled upright and cut in first, "'Frivolous,' right? I know you were gonna say frivolous. Can you switch it up? Maybe add a word or two?"

Lan Wangji said coldly, "Exceedingly frivolous."

Wei Wuxian clapped. "Added a word as expected, thank you!"

Lan Wangji withdrew his gaze and picked up the book he'd

placed on the desk earlier, flipping it open anew. He had only taken a brief look before he threw it away as if he'd been burnt by fire.

What he'd been reading before was a Buddhist sutra. When he opened the book and glanced at it just now, his vision was assaulted by naked, entangled figures, revolting to the eyes. The volume he had been reading at first had been swapped with erotica, with a cover to disguise it as a sutra.

He didn't need a brain in his head to guess who had done this good and generous deed. It had to be a certain *someone* who had done it while he was distracted by the drawing. Not to mention Wei Wuxian had no intention of pretending otherwise at all and was laughing uproariously while slapping the table.

"HA HA HA HA HA HA HA HA HA HA HA HA HA!"

That book was thrown to the ground as Lan Wangji instantly retreated to the corner of the Library Pavilion like he was avoiding a venomous creature. He roared in extreme outrage, "WEI YING—!"

Wei Wuxian was laughing so hard he was practically rolling underneath the desk; arduously did he finally raise his hand. "Here! I'm here!"

Lan Wangji swiftly drew Bichen. Wei Wuxian had never seen him so flustered in the time they had known each other.

He hastily grabbed his own sword, flashed three parts of the blade out of the sheath, and reminded him, "Manners! Lan-er-gongzi! Watch your manners! I've brought a sword today too. If we start fighting, what's going to happen to your family's Library Pavilion?!"

He had already anticipated that Lan Wangji would be shamed into anger, so he had brought a sword for self-defense, in case Lan Wangji accidentally stabbed him to death in his rage. Lan Wangji pointed at him with his sword, those light-colored eyes practically shooting flames.

"What kind of person are you?!"

"What else can I be?" Wei Wuxian replied, "A man!"

"Shameless!" Lan Wangji denounced scathingly.

"Do you need to feel shame over something like this? Don't tell me you've never seen that sort of thing. I don't believe it," Wei Wuxian said.

Lan Wangji's biggest disadvantage was not knowing how to curse. After needing a good moment to contain himself, he finally waved his sword at Wei Wuxian with a face of frozen frost.

"Go out. We will fight."

Wei Wuxian shook his head repeatedly, pretending to be cute and obedient. "Nope, no fighting. Didn't you know, Lan-gongzi? The Cloud Recesses prohibits private fights."

He was about to pick up the discarded book when Lan Wangji rushed over and took it. Wei Wuxian quickly guessed that he planned on using the book as evidence to report him.

So he intentionally asked, "What are you so grabby for? I thought you weren't gonna look at it? You want to now? You don't have to be so aggressive if you do, you know. I borrowed it specifically to share with you. Now that you've seen my erotica, you're my friend. We can keep sharing. There's even more…"

Lan Wangji was completely pale, now, as he enunciated each of these words: "I. Will. Not. Look. At. It."

Wei Wuxian continued to twist the truth. "Why are you grabbing for it if you're not gonna look? Keeping it for yourself? That won't do—I borrowed it from someone else. When you're done, I have to return it… Hey, hey, hey, stay where you are. If you come too close, I'll get nervous. We can talk. You're not thinking of handing that in, are you? Who will you hand it to? Old… To your shufu? Lan-er-gongzi, is that something that can be shown to the clan elders?

He'll definitely suspect you've already peeked at it yourself. You're so thin-faced, won't you die of embarrassment...?"

Lan Wangji's spiritual power poured into his right hand and the book was ripped into thousands of shreds that whirled into the air and then fluttered down. Seeing that he had successfully destroyed the evidence, Wei Wuxian relaxed and pretended to feel regret.

"What a waste!" He plucked a piece of the shredded paper from his hair and held it up to show Lan Wangji, who had gone pale with anger. "Lan Zhan, you're good at everything, but that habit of yours of throwing things around is awful. Look at yourself. How many paper balls have you tossed on the floor in the past few days? And now you're bored with paper balls, so you're ripping up paper for fun? Clean up after yourself, yeah? I'm not gonna help you."

Of course, he never had helped to begin with.

Lan Wangji tried to endure it, but in the end, he could not. He shouted angrily, "Get lost!"

"Damnit, Lan Zhan," Wei Wuxian said. "They all say you're a shining man of virtue, light of this world, that you have the best manners. Turns out that's only half true. The Cloud Recesses prohibits clamor, did you know that? And you actually told me to get lost. Is this the first time you've ever said something like that...?"

Lan Wangji brandished his sword and lunged. Wei Wuxian quickly hopped onto the windowsill.

"I'll get lost. I'm excellent at getting lost. No need to see me off!"

When he jumped down from the Library Pavilion, he laughed boisterously like a lunatic as he charged headlong into the forest. There was already a group waiting for him there.

Nie Huaisang asked, "How did it go? Did he see it? What was his reaction?"

"His reaction?" Wei Wuxian said. "Heh! Didn't you guys hear how loud he yelled just now?"

Nie Huaisang was full of admiration. "We heard! He told you to get lost! Wei-xiong, this is the first time I've heard Lan Wangji tell anyone to 'get lost'! How did you do it?"

Wei Wuxian preened triumphantly at his success. "There is much to celebrate. I helped him break that rule today. You all saw it, right? The self-restraint and discipline that the world praises Lan-er-gongzi for collapses before me."

Jiang Cheng glowered and scolded, "What nonsense! What's there to be so proud of?! Is it such an honor to have people tell you to get lost? What an embarrassment for our family!"

Wei Wuxian said, "I was gonna apologize, but he kept ignoring me. He'd already silenced me for so many days, so what if I teased him a little? Too bad about that prized erotica of yours, Huaisang-xiong... I hadn't even finished reading it yet. It was so spectacular! Lan Zhan really doesn't get it. He got all upset when I showed it to him. What a waste of that face of his."

"It's not too much of a loss!" Nie Huaisang said. "There's plenty more where that came from."

Jiang Cheng sneered. "You've thoroughly offended both Lan Wangji and Lan Qiren now. Get ready to die tomorrow! No one will collect your corpse for you."

Wei Wuxian waved him off and then hooked his arm around Jiang Cheng's shoulders. "Who cares? I'll tease him a bit more before I go. You've already collected my corpse so many times. Once more won't hurt."

Jiang Cheng struck out with a kick. "Away with you! Next time you do something like this, don't let me know! And don't tell me to come watch either!"

CHAPTER 4: THE ELEGANT FLIRT

In order to prevent the ol' stick-in-the-mud and the li'l stick-in-the-mud from attacking him in the middle of the night and hauling him out of bed for punishment, Wei Wuxian slept hugging his sword the entire night. Who would've thought that all would be peaceful until the next day? It was then that Nie Huaisang came to find him, elated.

"Wei-xiong, you really have the best of luck. The old man went to attend the symposium hosted by my family at Qinghe. We don't have class for the next few days!"

The old one was gone, leaving the little one. And he was a piece of cake to handle! Wei Wuxian scrambled out of bed, tugging on his boots.

He said happily, "Well, doesn't fortune smile down on me today? Auspicious clouds above tell me that heaven's got my back."

On the side, Jiang Cheng was wiping his sword with the utmost care while he rained on his parade. "You still won't escape punishment when he comes back."

"Why worry about what happens to us after we die? Let's just live freely while we're all still alive. I refuse to believe I can't find a couple li'l pheasants on this Lan mountain."

The three strolled out, arms around each other's shoulders. As they passed by the Cloud Recesses' reception hall, the Elegance Room, Wei Wuxian suddenly chuckled and stopped in his tracks.

He said, amazed, "Two li'l sticks-in—...Lan Zhans!"

A number of people emerged from the Elegance Room, but the ones leading the group were two young men. Their faces were of sculpted ice and refined jade, and they were clad in attire as white as snow. Even the tassels swaying from the hilts of the swords on their backs danced airily in the wind. It was only their demeanor and expressions that told of the difference between them. Wei Wuxian could immediately tell the one with the stiff face was Lan Wangji. This meant the gentle-looking one must be the other Twin Jade of the Lan clan: sobriquet Zewu-jun, courtesy name Lan Xichen.

When Lan Wangji spotted Wei Wuxian, his brows furrowed. He was practically shooting him a death glare, as if he'd be corrupted if he looked at him for a second longer. He moved his eyes to gaze into the far distance. Lan Xichen, on the other hand, smiled.

"And you two are?"

Jiang Cheng gestured in courtesy. "Jiang Wanyin of Yunmeng."

Wei Wuxian gestured in courtesy as well. "Wei Wuxian of Yunmeng."

Lan Xichen returned the greeting. Nie Huaisang squeaked, his voice soft as a mosquito's.

"Xichen-gege."

Lan Xichen said, "Huaisang, I have recently returned from Qinghe. Your older brother was asking after your studies. How go things? Will you be able to pass this year?"

"For the most part, yes…" Nie Huaisang was like a wilted squash after frost, looking pleadingly at Wei Wuxian.

Wei Wuxian grinned widely. "Zewu-jun, where are you off to?"

"To exterminate evil water ghosts," Lan Xichen replied. "We are short on capable hands, so I returned to find Wangji."

Lan Wangji said coldly, "Xiongzhang, no need to speak overmuch on the matter. Time is of the essence—let us depart."

Wei Wuxian quickly stopped him. "Hold on, hold on, hold on, I know how to catch water ghosts. Zewu-jun, why don't you bring us along?"

Lan Xichen smiled but did not speak, and Lan Wangji said, "It is against the rules."

"How is that against the rules?" Wei Wuxian demanded. "We're always catching water ghosts back at Yunmeng. Besides, it's not like there's school these next few days."

Yunmeng was replete with lakes and other bodies of water, teeming with water ghosts, so the Jiang clansmen truly were experts in this area. Jiang Cheng also wanted to regain the considerable amount of face the Jiang Clan of Yunmeng had lost during their stay at the Lan sect, so he chimed in.

"That's right. Zewu-jun, we can definitely help."

"Unnecessary. The Lan Clan of Gusu can also—"

Lan Wangji hadn't finished when Lan Xichen said with a smile, "That may not be a bad idea. Thank you in advance. Go make your preparations, and we will depart together. Will Huaisang join us?"

Although Nie Huaisang wanted to go with the party, the sight of Lan Xichen reminded him of his older brother and guilt seized him, so he didn't dare lark around.

"I'll pass; I'll go back and review my studies…"

This studious posturing was done in the hopes that next time, Lan Xichen would say more good things about him in front of his older brother. As for Wei Wuxian and Jiang Cheng, they returned to their rooms to make preparations.

Lan Wangji watched their retreating backs with a puzzled frown. "Xiongzhang, why bring them? Joking and larking about is unsuitable during spirit extermination."

Lan Xichen replied, "Sect Leader Jiang's chief disciple and his only son both have a fair reputation in Yunmeng. They may not only know how to joke and lark about."

Lan Wangji did not comment, but his face was written with a certain sentiment that could have said *"I beg to differ."*

Lan Xichen added, "Besides, were you not amenable to the offer of his company?"

Lan Wangji was dumbfounded.

Lan Xichen explained, "I only agreed because I saw you looked like you might want Sect Leader Jiang's eldest disciple to come with us."

Before the Elegance Room, the silence was like frozen ice.

It was a good moment before Lan Wangji said arduously, "Nothing of the sort."

He wished to defend himself further, but Wei Wuxian and Jiang Cheng had already returned speedily, their swords on their backs. Thus, Lan Wangji had no choice but to remain silent, and the group mounted their swords and took off.

◇ ◈ ◇

The place haunted by the water ghosts was called Caiyi Town, and it was more than ten kilometers away from the Cloud Recesses.

Caiyi Town was woven through with scores of waterways. It could have been said that the little city was covered with a dense net formed of tangled rivers, or perhaps it was that the densely packed local houses along the shores were what covered the cobweb-like waterways. The truth of it was unclear. Lined by the little houses with white walls and gray-tiled roofs, the riverways were crowded with boats filled with men and women, and baskets upon baskets. Blooming bouquets, fresh vegetables and fruits, bamboo crafts and cakes, tofu and tea, and fine silk; all sorts of teeming trade bustled along the riverway.

Gusu was situated in Jiangnan, and the lilting local dialect was soft and sweet to the ear. Two of the boats crashed head-on, toppling several jugs of sticky rice liquor, but even the resulting argument between the two boatmen sounded like the chirping of birds. There were many lakes in Yunmeng, but such small water towns were few and far between. Wei Wuxian watched curiously, then took out some money to buy two jugs of the sticky rice liquor, passing one to Jiang Cheng.

"The way the Gusu people speak is so kittenish. How is that arguing? They should see how people of Yunmeng fight, it'll terrify them… Lan Zhan, what are you looking at me for? I didn't get you one, but it's not because I'm stingy. People of your clan aren't allowed to drink, right?"

Without further ado, the group boarded dozens of little sampans, poling toward where the water ghosts were gathering. The locals crowding either shore gradually lessened in number, and the riverways also became still and quiet. Wei Wuxian and Jiang Cheng each took over a sampan and were racing to see who could go faster while listening to the arrangements concerning the local evil water ghosts.

This riverway led to a vast lake, called Biling Lake. For decades, there had never been any hauntings by water ghosts at Caiyi Town. In recent months, however, there had been many who fell into the water in this riverway as well as in Biling Lake, and cargo ships would randomly sink. Many days ago, Lan Xichen had set up an array to cast a net. He'd thought he would capture a few ghosts on this first attempt. Who could've imagined that he would catch over a dozen instead? Once the faces of those corpses were washed and the bodies brought to the nearby towns for inspection, a surprising number of them remained unclaimed. None of the locals knew them. When the array was set again just yesterday, plenty more had been captured.

Wei Wuxian commented, "It doesn't really appear to be the case that they drowned elsewhere and were washed down here by the currents. Water ghosts are a territorial sort. They usually only recognize one body of water: the one where they drowned. Very seldom do they leave it."

Lan Xichen nodded. "Correct. Which is why I feel this is no trivial matter and had Wangji come, in case something unpredictable happens."

Wei Wuxian said, "Zewu-jun, water ghosts are all super intelligent. If we take our time poling around like this, won't the search take forever? What if they all hide at the bottom of the lake and we can't find them?"

Lan Wangji said, "We stop only when they are found. It is our duty."

"So we use nets?" Wei Wuxian asked.

"Correct," Lan Xichen said. "Could the Jiang Clan of Yunmeng have other methods?"

Wei Wuxian smiled but didn't answer. The Jiang Clan of Yunmeng also employed nets, of course, but he had always simply jumped into the river and hauled the water ghosts ashore because he was good at swimming. But that was definitely too dangerous a method for him to use in front of the Lans, lest it reach Lan Qiren's ears and get him chewed out again.

He changed the subject. "It'd be good if there were something like fish bait that could lure the water ghosts to us on their own. Or something that could pinpoint their positions, like a compass."

"Keep your head down and watch the water. Focus on your target. You and your wild imagination again," Jiang Cheng said.

"Cultivation and flying swords used to be nothing but someone's wild imagination too!" Wei Wuxian argued.

He looked down. Coincidentally, he could see the bottom of the sampan that Lan Wangji was riding. An idea hit him, and he called out.

"Lan Zhan, look at me!"

Lan Wangji was on guard and concentrating, so he looked to him in reflex when he heard the call. But all he saw was Wei Wuxian slash the water with his bamboo pole, sending a wave of water splashing over. Lan Wangji tipped his toes and leapt lightly onto another sampan, dodging the splash.

Upset that Wei Wuxian really had come just to horse around, he gritted his teeth. "Frivolous!"

However, Wei Wuxian gave a kick to the side of the sampan he had been standing on. With a flick of his pole, the boat flipped upside down, revealing the bottom. And to the planks of that bottom, there clung three bloated-faced and ghastly pale water ghosts!

The closest sect disciples immediately suppressed them. Lan Xichen smiled.

"Wei-gongzi, how did you know they were on the bottom of the sampan?"

Wei Wuxian knocked on the side of the sampan. "Easy! The boat draft was wrong. He was the only one on the sampan just then, yet the load draft was heavier than the weight of two people. So there had to be something clinging to the bottom."

"Experienced as expected," Lan Xichen commended.

Wei Wuxian gently stirred the water with his pole. The little sampan sped up, and he slid in next to Lan Wangji.

With the two sampans side by side, he said, "Lan Zhan, I wasn't trying to splash you on purpose earlier. Water ghosts are shrewd, so if I said something first, they would've run away if they heard me. Hey, don't ignore me. C'mon, look at me, Lan-er-gongzi."

Lan Wangji condescended to cast him a glance. "Why have you come?"

Wei Wuxian replied sincerely, "To offer an apology. It was my fault last night, I was wrong."

Lan Wangji's face was faintly dark, probably because he hadn't forgotten exactly how Wei Wuxian had last offered him an "apology."

Despite knowing the answer, Wei Wuxian asked, "Why do you look so upset? Don't worry, I'm really here to help today."

Jiang Cheng couldn't watch this anymore and piped up, "If you're helping, then stop talking and get over here!"

One of the sect disciples shouted, "The net has moved!"

Sure enough, the ropes of the net abruptly started jerking. Wei Wuxian instantly perked up.

"It's here, it's here!"

Long hair, thick as fine black silk, swirled near the dozens of little boats, and pair after pair of ghastly white hands clawed at the sides of the sampans. Lan Wangji twisted his hand back to draw his sword. Bichen was unsheathed, and the motion cleanly sliced off a dozen wrists on the left side of the boat, leaving only the hands, their fingers still deeply dug into the wood. Just as he was going for the right side, a red glare flashed past him and Wei Wuxian was already sheathing his sword.

The strange movement in the water ceased, and the net calmed once more. Wei Wuxian's move had been extremely fast, but Lan Wangji had still seen that it was a top-grade spiritual sword he was carrying.

He asked respectfully, "What is the name of your sword?"

"Whatever," Wei Wuxian replied.

Lan Wangji stared at him. Wei Wuxian thought he hadn't heard properly and repeated himself.

"Whatever."

Lan Wangji frowned and rejected the answer. "That sword has a spirit. It is disrespectful to call it whatever."

Wei Wuxian sighed. "Think outside the box, won't you? I'm not telling you to call it whatever, I'm saying the name of my sword *is* the word 'whatever.' 'Suibian.' Here, you see?"

He passed over his sword to show Lan Wangji the characters engraved on it. Within the engravings upon the hilt were the carvings of two ancient characters, and what they spelled was the word "Suibian."

Lan Wangji was at a loss for words.

Wei Wuxian considerately explained, "You don't have to say anything. I know. You must be wondering why I gave it that name? Everyone asks if there's a special meaning to it. To be honest, though, there isn't. It's just that when Jiang-shushu was bestowing the sword upon me, he asked me what I wanted to call it. I thought of over twenty names at the time and wasn't happy with any of them, so I thought, why don't I let Jiang-shushu give it a name instead? So I responded with 'whatever'! Who would've figured that when the sword was forged and came out of the kiln, that would be the word on it? Jiang-shushu said, 'Since that's the case, let the sword be called Suibian.' It's not actually such a bad name, don't you think?"

At last, Lan Wangji squeezed a word out through the cracks of his teeth: "...Absurd!"

Wei Wuxian slung the sword over his shoulder. "You're too boring. The name is so much fun. It fools uptight people like you every single time, ha ha!"

Just then, within the jade-green lake, a long black shadow circled around the sampans and flashed past. Jiang Cheng had just finished cutting down the water ghosts on his side and was still scanning around to see if there were any left when he saw that black shadow.

He immediately shouted, "It's come again!"

Several sect disciples pushed over with nets to pursue the black shadow in the water. Then another cry came from the other side, "There're more here too!"

Over on the other side, another vast black shadow sped past. Many sampans sped after it with nets, yet nothing was captured.

"That's weird," Wei Wuxian commented. "The shape of the shadow doesn't appear to be human. And it's constantly changing form, suddenly long, suddenly short, from big to small... Lan Zhan, on the side of your boat!"

On Lan Wangji's back, Bichen answered the call. It pierced the water and, a moment later, shot out of the river with a shrill shriek, drawing a rainbow streak. However, it had speared nothing.

He gripped the sword, watching the water fixedly. Just as he was about to speak, the sword of a sect disciple nearby also flew out of its sheath, lunging toward a long black shadow swimming past in the river.

However, once his sword entered the water, it never resurfaced. He prompted repeatedly with the sword hand seal to summon it back, yet nothing emerged from the depths. It was as if his sword had been swallowed by the lake and disappeared without a trace. This sect disciple, a boy about the same age as Wei Wuxian and company, blanched at the loss of his sword, turning paler by the minute.

One of the older sect disciples nearby spoke up, "Su She, why would you act on your own initiative and urge your sword to enter the water? And before even finding out what's in there..."

Though somewhat flustered, Su She still appeared composed enough. "I saw er-gongzi had also sent his sword into the water..."

He realized before he finished just how foolish he sounded. No one could compare to either Lan Wangji or the sword Bichen. Lan Wangji could send his sword into the water when the enemy was still unknown and emerge unscathed, but others might not be able to say the same. Su She's pale face flushed with a tinge of embarrassment, as if he had suffered some sort of humiliation, and he stole a glimpse at Lan Wangji. Lan Wangji didn't look at him, however. He was staring intently at the water. A second later, Bichen flew out of its sheath once more.

This time, the sword did not stab into the water. Instead, the tip flicked and lifted a black shadow that was leaping past. With a splash, a wet, black lump crashed onto the deck. Wei Wuxian stood on his toes and peeked. It was a robe.

Wei Wuxian laughed so hard he almost fell headfirst into the river. "Lan Zhan, you're amazing! This is the first time I've seen a water ghost's robe get pulled off during a hunt."

Lan Wangji concentrated on inspecting to see whether there was anything wrong with Bichen, seeming to have made up his mind not to converse with him.

Jiang Cheng piped up, "Shut up, you. It wasn't a water ghost swimming past below just now, only a robe!"

Of course, Wei Wuxian saw the same, but he couldn't *not* tease Lan Wangji. "The thing slinking about was this robe? No wonder the nets couldn't catch it and the swords couldn't pierce it. Its shape keeps changing. But a mere article of clothing can't possibly swallow a spiritual sword, so there must be something else in the water."

At this time, the boats had already drifted to the heart of Biling Lake. The lake was extremely deep and profoundly dark in its shade of green. Suddenly, Lan Wangji raised his head slightly.

"We must go back immediately."

"Why?" Lan Xichen asked.

"The creature intentionally lured us to the lake's heart," Lan Wangji replied.

Just as he finished, everyone felt their boats dip violently.

Water rapidly flooded into the boats, and Wei Wuxian suddenly realized that the lake water of Biling Lake was no longer dark green but closer to black. Near the center of the lake, a humongous maelstrom had formed without their notice. Dozens of the boats were spinning in that maelstrom, submerging as they spun, as if they were about to be swallowed by a giant mouth!

The clanging of blades being unsheathed rang all around as the party began to mount their swords. Wei Wuxian had already risen into the air, bowing his head as he looked down. However, he saw that the boat deck of sect disciple Su She, who had sent his sword into the water, had already been swallowed by Biling Lake. The water was over his knees. He appeared fully panicked yet did not utter any cries for help, perhaps because he was too terrified. Without hesitation, Wei Wuxian bent down and reached out, seizing his wrist and dragging him up.

With an extra person, the sword beneath his feet unexpectedly dipped, yet it continued to rise. However, it didn't climb for long before a sudden huge tug from Su She's side almost pulled Wei Wuxian off the sword.

The bottom half of Su She's body was already submerged within the black maelstrom, and it was whirling faster and faster, his body also sinking deeper and deeper, almost as if there was something lurking underwater hugging his legs and dragging him down. Jiang Cheng, mounted on his Sandu, had risen to over sixty meters in the sky above the surface of the lake, quite unconcerned. When he looked down, he charged back downward, quite upset.

"What are you up to now?!"

The suction from within Biling Lake was growing progressively more powerful. While Wei Wuxian's sword excelled in dexterity and agility, a lack of strength just happened to be its weakness, and it was forcefully pulled to lower and lower altitudes until it was close to the surface of the lake.

CHAPTER 4: THE ELEGANT FLIRT

Wei Wuxian steadied himself while yanking on Su She with both hands, shouting, "Somebody come help! If I can't get him up, I'm gonna have to let go!"

Suddenly, Wei Wuxian felt a tightening on his back collar and he was lifted into the air. He twisted his head around and saw Lan Wangji had him single-handedly held up by the back collar. While Lan Wangji only gazed impassively in another direction, he was supporting the weight of three people all by himself. Even as he fought against the unknown creature in the lake, they were still steadily rising higher into the air.

Jiang Cheng was a little astonished. *Had I rushed to grab Wei Wuxian earlier, I probably wouldn't have been able to rise so quickly and so steadily on Sandu. Lan Wangji is only around the same age as me...*

Right then, Wei Wuxian said, "Lan Zhan, the strength of your sword is pretty powerful, huh? Thank you, thank you, but why are you grabbing me by the collar? Can't you just hold on to me? It's very uncomfy like this. I'll give you my hand, just drag me."

"I do not touch others," Lan Wangji said coldly.

"Who's this 'others'? We're so well acquainted now," Wei Wuxian said.

"We are not," Lan Wangji said.

Wei Wuxian pretended to be hurt. "Why are you like this..."

Jiang Cheng really couldn't stand it anymore and yelled, "WHY ARE *YOU* LIKE THIS?! When you're being dangled in midair by your collar, maybe talk a little less?!"

The group speedily retreated from Biling Lake on their swords and landed back on shore. Lan Wangji loosened his right hand's grip on Wei Wuxian's collar and composedly turned around to face Lan Xichen.

"It is the Waterborne Abyss."

Lan Xichen shook his head. "That makes things difficult, then."

Wei Wuxian and Jiang Cheng understood the moment the name "Waterborne Abyss" was dropped. The most terrifying thing in Biling Lake and this riverway wasn't some water ghost but the flowing current within.

Some rivers or lakes, due to terrain or currents, often capsized boats or drowned the living. As time went on, the water body itself would nurture a certain temper, not unlike a spoiled little miss who refused to go anywhere without extravagant clothes and gourmet food. Every so often, a cargo ship would capsize, or the living would drown as sacrifices to it. If there weren't any sacrifices, then it would seek out and create trouble to seize them on its own.

The people local to Caiyi Town were expert swimmers and rarely experienced tragedies such as sunken boats or drownings, so it was impossible for a Waterborne Abyss to be nurtured nearby. Since the Waterborne Abyss had appeared here, there was only one possible explanation: it had been *driven* here from elsewhere.

Once a Waterborne Abyss was formed, the entire water body would transform into a monster that was extremely difficult to exterminate. Unless the water was drained completely, unless everything and everyone beneath the depths was salvaged, and unless they were able to expose the riverbed to the light of the sun for several years—but that was practically an impossible task. However, there was a method that could temporarily alleviate the problem, albeit at the expense of others. That method was to drive it to another body of water to have it cause havoc elsewhere.

"Were there any areas disturbed by the Waterborne Abyss recently?" Lan Wangji asked.

Lan Xichen pointed to the sky.

He wasn't pointing at anything else—he was pointing at the sun. Wei Wuxian and Jiang Chen exchanged a look, understanding dawning on them. The Wen Clan of Qishan.

Within the cultivation world were countless prominent clans both big and small, littered throughout the land like stars. However, there was a colossus that towered absolutely above them all, and that was the Wen Clan of Qishan.

The family insignia of the Wen Clan was the sun, symbolizing "Contend the sun's glory; commensurate the sun's longevity." Their cultivation residence occupied an immense area, comparable to that of a city, and word had it that night did not fall within its walls. Thus, it was called "Nightless Sky" and also known as the Nightless Immortal Capital. The clan was called a colossus because no matter the metric—its number of disciples, its power, its claims to land, its spiritual devices—it was head and shoulders above the rest, and none could compete. Quite a number of cultivators thought it the greatest of honors to be a guest cultivator of the Wen Clan. And based on the Wen Clan's usual standards of conduct, it was extremely likely the Waterborne Abyss of Caiyi Town had been driven here by them.

Although the origin of the water spirit was now known, everyone fell silent.

If this was the doing of the Wen Clan, then it would be pointless. No matter how much they were accused or condemned, the clan would not admit to it to begin with and would offer no reparations regardless.

A sect disciple complained indignantly, "Their clan driving the Waterborne Abyss here is going to cause serious trouble for Caiyi Town. If the Waterborne Abyss grows and invades the waterways of the town, so many people's livelihoods will be at the whim of a monster. It's really so…"

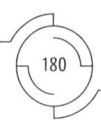

To have others' messes discarded on their doorstep…the Lan Clan of Gusu would surely face endless trouble going forward. Lan Xichen sighed.

"It's fine, it's fine. Let's return to town."

They boarded new boats at the harbor and poled toward the more densely populated part of town. After passing under the arch bridge, the boats entered the waterways, and Wei Wuxian started acting up again.

He tossed his bamboo pole and set one foot onto the side of the boat, checking to see if he had any hair out of place by using the water as his mirror. He acted not a bit like he had just fought a number of water ghosts and barely escaped from the mouth of a Waterborne Abyss. Calm and easygoing, he sent flirtatious looks to both sides of the shore.

"Jiejie, how much for half a kilo of loquats?"

He was extremely youthful and brightly handsome, glowing with such exuberance that he exemplified the frivolous peach blossoms that flowed away down the river.[5] A woman tipped her bamboo hat and smiled brightly.

"Li'l laddie, no need for ya to pay. How's about I give it to ya free?"

The Wu dialect was soft and supple, refreshing and sweet. Melodic sentiment trilled from the speaker's lips while the listener's ears were filled with honey. Wei Wuxian cupped his hands in courtesy.

"Of course I'd want them if they're a gift from jiejie!"

The woman reached into her basket. Out came flying a perfectly round, golden loquat. "No need for that kinda courtesy, it's for that handsome face a' yours!"

The boats moved fast. When two met, they instantly swept past each other. Wei Wuxian spun and caught the fruit perfectly, laughing.

---

5 *Reference to a verse from Tang poet Du Fu's Man Xin. Peach blossoms symbolized love.*

"Jiejie is the more beautiful one!"

While he boasted and flirted on the side, Lan Wangji did not spare him a glance, appearing entirely noble in character and sterling in integrity. Pleased with himself, Wei Wuxian tossed the loquat in his hand in the air, then pointed at Lan Wangji all of a sudden.

"Jiejie, do you ladies think he's handsome?"

Lan Wangji had never expected he'd be dragged into this. Just as he was at a loss for how to respond, the women on the river all shouted in unison: "EVEN MORE HANDSOME!" There even seemed to be snickering from men mixed in there.

"Who will gift him one too, then?" Wei Wuxian asked. "If you only give me one and not him, I'm scared he'll turn into a big ol' sourpuss over it when we get back!"

Chirping laughter tittered along the entire river. Another woman came poling over.

"Okay, okay, okay, we'll gift ya two. Take mine. Catch, li'l laddie!"

With a second loquat captured in hand, Wei Wuxian shouted, "Jiejie is both beautiful and kind. Next time I'm here, I'll buy an entire basket!"

The woman's voice was clear and sonorous, and she was spunkier than the first. She pointed at Lan Wangji. "Tell him to come too. Come buy the loquats together!"

Wei Wuxian brought the loquat to the level of Lan Wangji's eyes. Lan Wangji continued to stare squarely at the boat's bow.

"Take it away."

And so Wei Wuxian took it away. "I knew you wouldn't want it. So I wasn't gonna give it to you in the first place. Jiang Cheng, catch!"

It just so happened that Jiang Cheng was speeding past on another little boat, and he caught the loquat with a single hand. A smile appeared on his face, but then he immediately humphed.

"Were you strutting around, flirting with everything in sight again?"

Wei Wuxian preened. "Get outta here!" Then he turned his head and asked, "Lan Zhan, you're from Gusu. You know how to speak the dialect, right? Teach me, how do you tell someone off in the Gusu dialect?"

Lan Wangji threw him a single word, "frivolous," then boarded a different boat. Wei Wuxian hadn't really expected him to answer in the first place. He just thought the kittenish local dialect was incredibly fun and that Lan Wangji must've spoken it since he was young, so he was having fun teasing him. He tossed back a gulp of the sticky rice liquor. Then, with the round, black, shiny little jug dangling from his fingers, he picked up the bamboo pole and lunged over to fight Jiang Cheng.

Lan Wangji, on the other hand, stood side by side with Lan Xichen. This time, both wore similar expressions, each appearing laden with thoughts as they contemplated how to handle the Waterborne Abyss—and how to inform the mayor of Caiyi Town of the many follow-up arrangements to be made.

A heavily loaded cargo boat approached them from the boat's front, laden with baskets upon baskets heavy with golden loquats. Lan Wangji glanced at it and continued to look squarely to the front.

Lan Xichen, however, said, "Shall we buy a basket of loquats, if you want to try some?"

"..." Lan Wangji swept his sleeve and turned. "I do not!"

Then he boarded a different boat, again.

Wei Wuxian bought a bunch of random trinkets in Caiyi Town to bring back to the Cloud Recesses, and those souvenirs were all divvied up among the other clan disciples. Since Lan Qiren had gone to Qinghe, there were no classes, and the youths let themselves loose to the extreme. They swarmed into Wei Wuxian and Jiang Cheng's room to sprawl out on the floor, eating and drinking, arm-wrestling, dice-rolling, and picture-book-flipping all through the nights. One night, Wei Wuxian lost a dice roll and was sent to scale the wall and go down the mountain to buy Emperor's Smile. This time, everyone was finally able to get their fill of the gourmet liquor.

Yet unexpectedly, before day even broke the next morning, when the floor of the room was still strewn with bodies all sleeping like the dead, someone suddenly opened the door.

The sound alerted a few people. Still bleary-eyed, they saw Lan Wangji standing at the door with a face as frigid as ice and instantly jolted awake. Nie Huaisang pushed crazily at Wei Wuxian, who was sleeping with his head on the ground and his body twisted above him.

"Wei-xiong! Wei-xiong!"

After several shoves, Wei Wuxian asked blearily, "Who? Who else wants to go?! Jiang Cheng? Well, let's go then—like I'm scared of you!"

Jiang Cheng had drunk too much the night before and his head was still pounding. With his eyes closed, still lying on the ground, he grabbed the first thing his hand touched and hurled it in the direction of Wei Wuxian's voice.

"Shut up!"

That thing crashed onto Wei Wuxian's chest, flapping as pages flipped. Nie Huaisang looked to see that what Jiang Cheng had thrown at Wei Wuxian was one of his treasured, out-of-print erotica illustration books. When he looked up again and saw Lan Wangji's frigid gaze, he felt like his soul was going to leave his body. Wei Wuxian grumbled, hugging that book, and passed out again. Lan Wangji entered the room, seized Wei Wuxian by the back collar, picked him up, and hauled him out the door.

Wei Wuxian was dragged thusly for a while, then stared blearily for a moment before finally becoming somewhat awake. He twisted his neck back.

"Lan Zhan, what are you doing?"

Lan Wangji didn't say a single word, dragging him onward without pause, and Wei Wuxian woke up some more. The other sleeping corpses also jolted awake, one by one. When Jiang Cheng saw Wei Wuxian had been caught by Lan Wangji again, he rushed out.

"What's going on? What are you doing?"

Lan Wangji looked back, and enunciated each word: "Collecting punishment."

Jiang Cheng's mind was still slowed by drink and sleep. Only now did he remember the mess strewn on the ground in the room. Recalling the countless Cloud Recesses rules they had broken last night, his face froze.

Lan Wangji dragged Wei Wuxian to the ancestral hall of the Lan Clan of Gusu, where a number of older Lan sect disciples waited quietly. There were a total of eight of them, four of whom held incredibly long sandalwood ferules in their hands. The ferules were densely carved with squared words, the very image of austerity. Seeing that Lan Wangji had dragged the penitent over, two immediately approached and firmly pushed Wei Wuxian down.

Wei Wuxian half-knelt on the ground, unable to struggle, and asked, "Lan Zhan, you're going to punish me?"

Lan Wangji only stared at him coldly, unspeaking.

"I won't concede," Wei Wuxian said.

Just then, the other youths, who were mostly awake now, also came rushing over, but they were blocked outside the ancestral hall, unable to enter. They were anxious and helpless, and—when they saw those ferules—also scared speechless. However, Lan Wangji lifted the hem of his white robe and also knelt next to Wei Wuxian.

Wei Wuxian was greatly shocked at this sight and struggled to get up, but Lan Wangji shouted, "Strike!"

Wei Wuxian gaped and quickly exclaimed, "Wait, wait, wait, wait, I concede, I concede, Lan Zhan, I was wrong…*ah*!"

Their palms and the backs of their legs were beaten by the ferules over a hundred times. Lan Wangji did not require anyone to hold him down; his back remained straight as a brush from the start, kneeling in proper posture. Wei Wuxian, on the other hand, howled and wailed without reservation, and the disciples frowned as they watched, feeling their own flesh ache too. After the beating was over, Lan Wangji quietly stood up, bowed to the sect disciples inside the ancestral hall, then immediately left, showing no sign of having been wounded. Wei Wuxian was the complete opposite. After he was carried out of the ancestral hall on Jiang Cheng's back, he whined nonstop the whole way.

The youths surrounded the two of them like bees and buzzed, "Wei-xiong, what happened, exactly?"

"Lan Zhan wants to punish you, whatever, but why did he take a beating too?"

Wei Wuxian was draped on Jiang Cheng's back, sighing and gasping. "*Haah!* What a miscalculation! It's such a long story!"

"Cut your nonsense! What exactly did you do?!"

"I didn't do anything!" Wei Wuxian protested. "I went down to buy Emperor's Smile after losing at dice last night, right?"

"…Don't tell me you ran into him again," Jiang Cheng said.

"You got it," Wei Wuxian said. "Don't know what's with my luck, but when I scaled the wall with Emperor's Smile, he caught me red-handed again. I suspect he really is keeping an eye on me every day…"

"You think everyone has as much free time as you? And then?" Jiang Cheng asked.

"And then I still greeted him," Wei Wuxian replied. "I said, 'Lan Zhan! What a coincidence, it's you again!' But of course, he ignored me again and came striking with his hand without so much as a word. I said, 'C'mon, why do this?' He said, 'Should guests violate curfew too many times, they will have to collect punishment at the Lan ancestral hall.' So I said, 'There's only two of us here; if you don't say anything, and I don't say anything, then no one would know I broke curfew, am I right? I promise that there'll be no next time. We're so well acquainted now, can't you grant me some face and let me off easy?'"

Everyone grimaced.

Wei Wuxian continued, "In the end, he told me that we're not well acquainted, and he lunged at me with his sword without holding back at all. So I had to put the Emperor's Smile aside and parry him. He used his fists and palms too. He was coming at me so hard, I couldn't get rid of him at all! In the end, I got really tired of the chase, so I asked, 'You sure you won't let me go? You won't let me go?!' But he still said, 'Collect your punishment!'"

The youths had their hearts in their throats listening to the story, and Wei Wuxian was exultant in his retelling. Completely forgetting he was still on Jiang Cheng's back, he gave Jiang Cheng's shoulder a forceful slap.

"I said, 'Sure!' And then I stopped dodging, pounced, and grabbed on to him, and then we both fell outside the Cloud Recesses' wall!"

"..."

"And so the two of us both fell outside the boundary of the Cloud Recesses!" Wei Wuxian said. "That fall had me seeing stars, I tell ya."

Nie Huaisang was already blank. "...He didn't break free?"

"Oh, he tried," Wei Wuxian replied. "But I had him locked in real good with all four of my limbs. He couldn't have broken free even if he wanted to, and he had no way of getting away from my body. He went stiff as a board. I said, 'How's that, Lan Zhan? Now you're outside the Cloud Recesses too. You and I have both violated curfew—don't go and be strict on others but not on yourself, yeah? If you punish me, then you have to punish yourself too. Everyone's equal, how's that?'

"He looked ghastly after he got up," Wei Wuxian said. "I sat next to him and said, 'Don't worry, I won't tell anyone else. Only you, me, the heavens and the earth know about this.' Then he left without a word. Who knew he'd pull something like that this morning… Jiang Cheng, walk slower, you're gonna throw me off."

Not only did Jiang Cheng want to throw Wei Wuxian off, but he practically wanted to bash his head into the ground to create a human crater. "So fussy even though I'm carrying you!"

"I didn't tell you to carry me," Wei Wuxian reasoned.

Jiang Cheng flew into a rage. "If I didn't carry you, I think you'd hang out at their ancestral hall all day, rolling around on the floor. I can't afford this embarrassment! Lan Wangji took fifty more strikes than you, but he walked away on his own, and you're not embarrassed, pretending to be an invalid? I don't want to carry you anymore. Get the hell off!"

"No, I'm wounded," Wei Wuxian said.

The group were jostling about on the white-stoned path when they just so happened to run into a white-clad man passing through with a book in his hand and stopped in surprise.

Lan Xichen smiled. "What's happened?"

Jiang Cheng felt incredibly awkward and didn't know how to answer, but Nie Huaisang rushed to respond.

"Xichen-ge, Wei-xiong was punished with over a hundred strikes from the ferule. Do you have any medicine for injuries?"

The one in charge of punishment in the Cloud Recesses was Lan Wangji. Plus, Wei Wuxian had been lamenting and wailing to those who were escorting him; his injuries seemed serious. Thus, Lan Xichen immediately came over.

"Wangji administered the punishment? Wei-gongzi cannot walk anymore? What exactly happened?"

Jiang Cheng was of course too sheepish to say it was because of something Wei Wuxian had done. And when they got down to it, it was the whole group that had egged on Wei Wuxian to go buy liquor, so the punishment should've justly fallen upon them all.

He could only reply, "It's nothing, it's nothing, nothing that outrageous! He can walk. Wei Wuxian, get down now!"

"I can't walk," Wei Wuxian said. He extended his astoundingly swollen red palm, complaining to Lan Xichen, "Zewu-jun, your little brother is so harsh."

Lan Xichen looked over his palm and said, "Ah, this punishment was indeed a little too severe. I'm afraid it will take several days to heal, or perhaps more."

Jiang Cheng hadn't realized the beatings were that severe. He exclaimed in alarm, "What? Several days? His legs and his back were also beaten… How can Lan Wangji be like this?!"

The last part had carried an unconscious tone of displeasure, and Wei Wuxian had already secretly given him a pat before he'd realized it. Lan Xichen, however, did not mind. He smiled.

"But it is fine. Medication won't be necessary. Wei-gongzi, let me tell you of a remedy that will have you recovered within hours."

◊◈◊

Nighttime, The Cloud Recesses, Cold Spring.

CHAPTER 4: THE ELEGANT FLIRT

Lan Wangji was soaking in the icy spring waters with his eyes closed, refreshing his spirit, when a voice suddenly whispered into his ear.

"Lan Zhan."

"..."

Lan Wangji's eyes snapped open. Sure enough, Wei Wuxian was lounging upon the moss-green rock by the cold spring, grinning at him with his head tilted.

Lan Wangji blurted out, "How did you get in?!"

Wei Wuxian languidly crawled to his feet and replied as he untied his sash, "Zewu-jun let me in."

"What are you doing?" Lan Wangji demanded.

Wei Wuxian kicked off his boots and spoke while undressing, littering the ground with clothes. "I'm already stripping and you're asking what I'm doing? They say your clan's cold spring, besides calming the spirit for cultivation purposes, has the ability to heal external injuries. So, your gege told me to come and soak with you. But it's so sneaky of you to come recuperate alone. Ack, it really is cold, hissss—"

He entered the spring, and the bone-bitingly freezing spring water had him flailing about. Lan Wangji speedily pulled away.

"I have come for cultivation, not for recuperation... Stop thrashing!"

"But it's so cold, so cooold..." Wei Wuxian complained.

He wasn't trying to intentionally exaggerate this time; it was indeed difficult for outsiders to adapt to the Lans' cold spring so quickly. It felt as though stopping for even a moment would see his blood freezing and his limbs turning to ice, so he had to keep flopping about in the water in the hopes that moving around would warm him. Lan Wangji had planned on meditating properly here, but Wei Wuxian's flopping about had gotten him splashed with a face full of water, the droplets slipping down along his long lashes and ebony locks.

Unable to endure this any longer, he exclaimed, "Do not move!"

He reached out as he spoke, pressing a hand down on Wei Wuxian's shoulder.

Wei Wuxian instantly felt warmth surge from where their bodies touched. Feeling a little better, he unconsciously moved in his direction. Lan Wangji tensed.

"What?"

"Nothing," Wei Wuxian said innocently. "It feels warmer on your side."

Lan Wangji kept an arm firmly between them to maintain distance and stated sternly, "That is untrue."

Wei Wuxian had wanted to shuffle closer and get chummy to loosen him up, but when he couldn't and was snubbed, he still wasn't upset. He snuck a glance at Lan Wangji's hands and back. His injuries hadn't yet faded, as Wei Wuxian had expected, so he really hadn't come here for recuperation.

Wei Wuxian said earnestly, "Lan Zhan, I really am so in awe of you. You really turned yourself in for punishment too when it came to it, without letting yourself off easy in the slightest. I'm speechless."

Lan Wangji shuttered his eyes anew, still and silent.

Wei Wuxian added, "It's true. I've never seen anyone be so serious and really mean what they say. I could definitely never reach your level; you're amazing."

Lan Wangji still ignored him.

After getting used to the chill, Wei Wuxian started swimming around the cold spring. After swimming for a while, he still couldn't resist wading over to Lan Wangji.

"Lan Zhan, can't you tell what I meant by all that chatter?"

"No," Lan Wangji replied.

"You can't?" Wei Wuxian said. "I was complimenting you, tryin' to get chummy!"

Lan Wangji gave him a look. "What do you want?"

"Lan Zhan, let's be friends, yeah? We're so well acquainted now."

"We are not," Lan Wangji said.

Wei Wuxian slapped the water. "It's no fun if you're like this. Really, there's a lot of benefits to being my friend."

"For example?"

Wei Wuxian swam to the side of the pond and leaned back on the moss-green rock, laying his arm over it.

"I'm always very loyal to my friends, for example. Any newly obtained erotica, I will definitely show to you first... Heyyyy, come back! It's nothing if you don't want to look. Have you been to Yunmeng? Yunmeng is a lot of fun, and Yunmeng's food is good too. I don't know if this is a Gusu problem or a Cloud Recesses problem, but your food is awful. If you come hang out at the Lotus Pier, you can eat a lot of good food. I'll take you to pick lotus seed pods and water chestnuts. Lan Zhan, will you come?"

"No," Lan Wangji said.

"C'mon, don't keep issuing rejections with negative words. It sounds so cold," Wei Wuxian said. "Girls won't like hearing it. The girls in Yunmeng are particularly pretty, a different kind of beautiful from Gusu girls."

He winked at Lan Wangji with his left eye and asked again, pleased. "You really won't come?"

Lan Wangji paused for a moment, but still started to say, "No..."

Wei Wuxian said, "Rejecting me like this, without giving me a single bit of face. Aren't you worried that when I leave, I'll take your clothes away too?"

"GET LOST!!!"

Since Lan Qiren's return from Qinghe, he hadn't banished Wei Wuxian to the library to copy the Lan precepts, only giving him a severe scolding in front of everyone instead. Leaving out all the various allusions to the classics and simplifying it, the gist of the scolding was probably that he had never seen such an unruly, impossible, shameless person. Please get lost. Right now. As far as you can. Don't go near the other students, and especially do not corrupt his favorite student, Lan Wangji.

While he was yelling, Wei Wuxian listened gleefully with a grin, not the least bit embarrassed or angry. The moment Lan Qiren left, Wei Wuxian sat down and turned to Jiang Cheng.

"He's only telling me to get lost now—don't you think that's a little too late? Telling me that only after I've already corrupted everyone. Too late!"

◇ ◈ ◇

The Waterborne Abyss at Caiyi Town presented a major problem for the Lan Clan of Gusu. This thing couldn't be eradicated, nor could the Lan family be like the Wen Clan and drive it elsewhere. Over the years, the head of the Lan family had spent most of his time in secluded cultivation, so instead, Lan Qiren was expending all of his energy on the matter. Lectures became shorter and shorter, meaning Wei Wuxian was more and more often taking the others out gallivanting on the mountain.

On this day, he was once again swarmed by seven or eight youths to go out. As they passed by the Lan Library Pavilion, he took a glance up. Through the light-concealing yulan magnolia branches, he could see Lan Wangji sitting there alone by the window.

Nie Huaisang wondered, "Is he looking our way? He shouldn't be; we weren't that loud. So what's with that look in his eyes?"

CHAPTER 4: THE ELEGANT FLIRT

"Probably thinking about how to find fault in us," Wei Wuxian said.

"Wrong," Jiang Cheng said. "Not 'us,' it's 'you.' The only one he's watching is you."

"Heh, just wait. Watch how I'll put him in his place when I get back."

"Didn't you complain that he's too dull, that he's boring?" Jiang Cheng said. "So stop teasing him. Pulling a tiger's whiskers, breaking ground where Taisui presides[6]—you're just asking for it, every day."

"Wrong," Wei Wuxian said. "It's precisely because a grown, living person could be so incredibly boring that he's super interesting."

It was nearly noon before they returned to the Cloud Recesses. Lan Wangji sat poised at his desk, organizing the stack of papers he had just written, when he heard a light creaking sound from the window lattice. When he looked up, someone had hopped in from outside the window.

Wei Wuxian had climbed up the yulan magnolia branches outside the Library Pavilion. He exclaimed exultantly, "Lan Zhan, I'm back! How about it? There hasn't been any script-copying for days—did you miss me?"

Lan Wangji was like an old monk entering deep meditation, seeing all as nothing. He was even somewhat numb as he continued to sort his little pile of book scrolls. Wei Wuxian purposely twisted the meaning of his silence and continued on.

"You don't even have to say anything. I know you must've missed me, or why would you have been watching me from the window earlier?"

Lan Wangji immediately cast him a glance, his eyes filled with soundless condemnation. Wei Wuxian sat down on the window.

"Look at you, baited within two words. You're too easy to hook. So easily upset."

---

6 Both these idioms essentially mean "challenging or defying the almighty."

"Leave," Lan Wangji demanded.

"If I don't, are you gonna throw me out?"

Judging by Lan Wangji's expression, Wei Wuxian suspected if he said one more word, Lan Wangji really would abandon what was left of his restraint and nail him dead on the windowsill.

He quickly said, "C'mon, don't be so scary! I came to ask for forgiveness with a gift."

Lan Wangji rejected it without hesitation: "I do not want it."

"Are you sure?" Wei Wuxian asked.

Seeing Lan Wangji's eyes grow guarded, he pulled two rabbits from his robes like he was performing a magic trick. He gripped them by the ears like he was holding two chubby, round snowballs. Said snowballs were randomly flicking their feet. He delivered them to Lan Wangji.

"This place of yours is weird too. No pheasants, but lots of wild bunnies, and they're not afraid of people. What do you think? They're chubby, right? Want them?"

Lan Wangji watched him, unmoved.

"Fine. If you don't want them, then I'll give them to someone else. Food's been bland these days," Wei Wuxian said.

Hearing the last part, Lan Wangji said, "Stop."

Wei Wuxian shrugged. "It's not like I left."

"Who are you giving them to?" Lan Wangji demanded.

"To whoever roasts rabbit best," Wei Wuxian answered.

"Within the boundaries of the Cloud Recesses, killing is prohibited. That is the third rule on the Wall of Discipline," Lan Wangji said.

"Fine, then. I'll go down the mountain, have the rabbits killed outside the boundary, and bring the meat back up for roasting after. You don't want them anyway, what do you care?"

"...Give them to me," Lan Wangji said haltingly.

Wei Wuxian started snickering, sitting on the windowsill. "Now you want them? Look at you, always acting like this."

The two rabbits were both plump and round, like two fluffy snowballs. One had eyes like a dead fish, languidly laying unmoving on its stomach on the ground. Its pink, triangular mouth moved lazily as it chewed lettuce. The other hopped up and down nonstop as if it had swallowed a fighting cricket pill, crawling and rolling all over its companion, wriggling and bouncing about incessantly. Wei Wuxian tossed them some more lettuce he had plucked from who knew where and suddenly called out.

"Lan Zhan. Lan Zhan!"

That active rabbit had stepped on Lan Wangji's inkstone earlier, leaving a black ink pawprint on his desk; Lan Wangji didn't know what to do. He'd just pulled out a sheet of paper, contemplating with great seriousness how to wipe off the ink and planned on ignoring him. But hearing the urgency in his voice, he thought something was the matter.

"What is it?"

"Look how they're laying on top of each other, do you think they're..."

"They are both male!" Lan Wangji exclaimed.

"Male? Well, that's weird," Wei Wuxian said. He picked them up by the ears again to check, then confirmed. "They're indeed male, oh well. I didn't finish what I was saying. What are you being all stern for? What were you thinking about? Speaking of, I caught those two rabbits and didn't even pay attention to whether they're male or female, and yet you actually went and saw their..."

Lan Wangji finally bodily threw him out of the Library Pavilion.

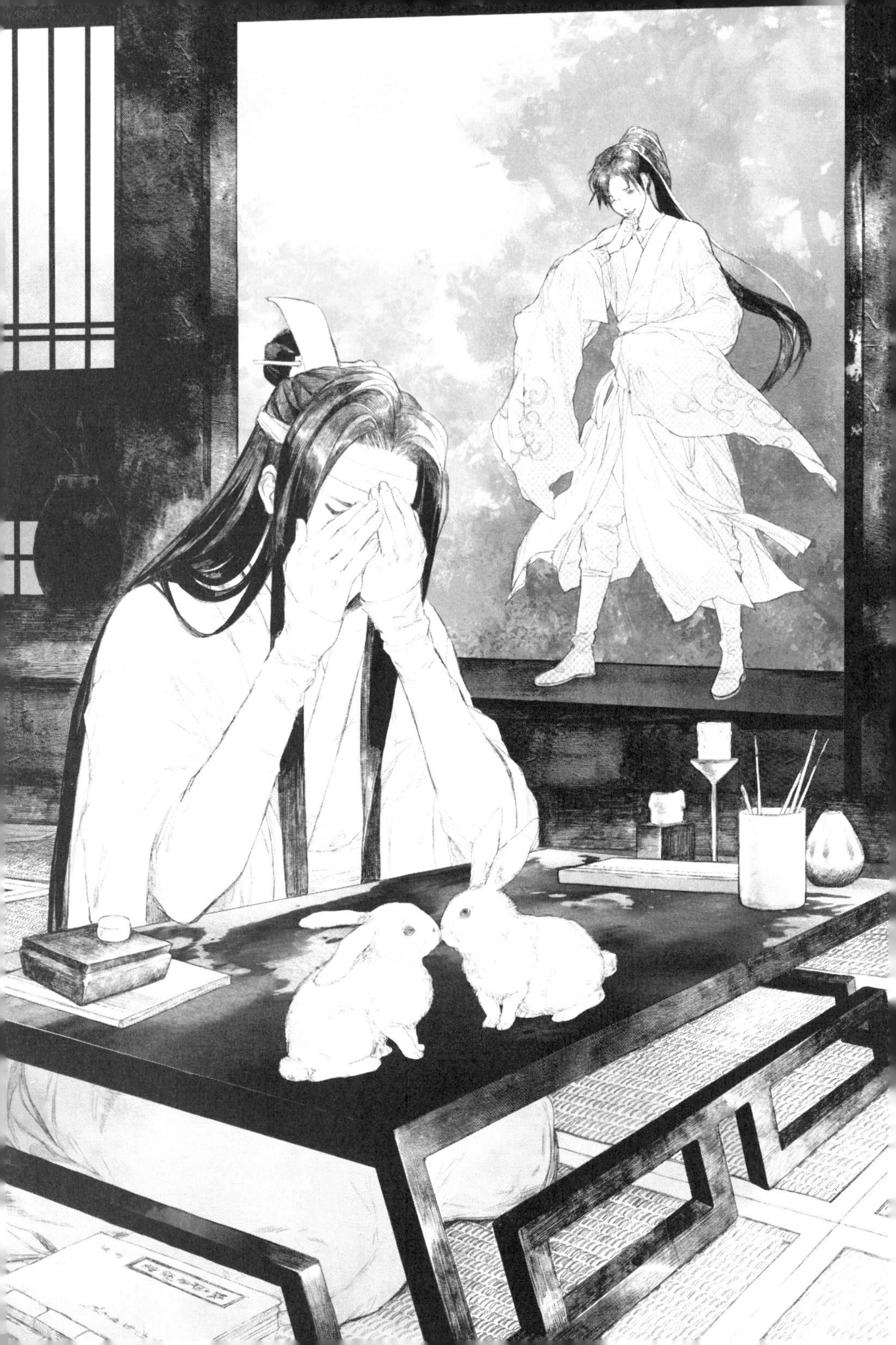

CHAPTER 4: THE ELEGANT FLIRT

Wei Wuxian laughed while plummeting through the air. "HA HA HA HA HA HA HA HA HA HA HA HA HA HA HA!"

Lan Wangji slammed the window shut with a loud bang, then collapsed next to his desk. He scanned the room, strewn with a mess of papers, inked pawprints, and two white rabbits rolling around with lettuce leaves. He closed his eyes, covering his ears.

The rustling yulan magnolia branches veiled the window and shut out the outside. But no matter how hard Lan Wangji fought it, Wei Wuxian's spirited and boisterous laughter could not be so easily shut out.

◊◈◊

The next day, Lan Wangji finally stopped coming to class.

Wei Wuxian's seat had changed three times. He had originally sat next to Jiang Cheng, but Jiang Cheng was actually attentive in class, and in order to perform well to gain some pride for the Jiang Clan of Yunmeng, he had moved to the first row. That spot was too conspicuous and would not have allowed Wei Wuxian to mess around, so he had abandoned Jiang Cheng and moved behind Lan Wangji.

While Lan Qiren gave lectures up front, Lan Wangji's upright sitting posture was like that of an ironclad wall, so Wei Wuxian was either sleeping to his heart's content or doodling wildly on paper. Other than the risk that the paper balls he'd throw at others would occasionally be caught by Lan Wangji's sudden hand, this seat was perfect in every aspect. However, Lan Qiren later noticed this scheme and swapped the two of them. Since then, whenever Wei Wuxian's posture slacked, he could sense two icy, piercing eyes nailed into his back, and Lan Qiren would shoot ferocious glares at him as well. It was an extreme pain to be monitored at all times by the old one up front and the little one behind.

After the erotica and rabbit-couplet incidents, Lan Qiren had determined Wei Wuxian to be a vat of ink-black dye. Terrified his favorite student would be stained or influenced by being so near him, he quickly stopped Lan Wangji from coming to class anymore. And so Wei Wuxian returned to his old spot, and things remained settled for a good half-month.

Unfortunately, the good days never lasted long for someone like Wei Wuxian. Within the Cloud Recesses, there was a long, windowed wall. For every seven steps, there was a window with carved fretwork, and every carving was different: there was the playing of the qin upon high mountains, there was soaring through the air on swords, there was the killing of yao and beasts. Lan Qiren had explained that every window on the wall was engraved with a story of a Lan ancestor. The oldest among the carvings, as well as the most famous, depicted four scenes from the life of the founding father of the Lan clan, Lan An.

This founder had been born in a temple. Innately intelligent, he grew up amidst the murmur of Buddhist sutras and became an eminent monk known far and wide from a young age. At his crowning age, he returned to secular life with the "Lan" of "Qielan"—Sanskrit for "Monastery"—as his surname and became a musician. On his path of cultivation, he met in Gusu the "fated one" he had sought. The two became cultivation partners and went on to form the foundation of the Lan family. When his partner passed, he returned to the temple and ended his life. The four windows were named thus: "The Monastery," "Music Study," "Cultivation Partners," and "Return to Nothingness."

Finally, after so long, there was something interesting being taught. Although Lan Qiren made it sound like some dry, tedious annal, Wei Wuxian absorbed the information. After class was dismissed, he laughed.

"So the founding father of the Lan was a monk; no surprise there. To enter the secular world for the sake of one person—*should you leave, I too shall leave, this life shall not remain in the world*—with such a character for a founder; how did he give birth to such unromantic descendants?"

No one else had imagined that the infamously old-fashioned Lan family would have such a founder either, and they got into a discussion over it. As they talked, the topic veered off to cultivation partners, and they began exchanging their thoughts on their ideal match, commenting on the girls of various reputable sects.

Then someone asked, "Zixuan-xiong, who do you think is the best girl?"

When Wei Wuxian and Jiang Cheng heard this, they both looked to a youth sitting in the front row of the Orchid Room.

This youth was proud and handsome with a cinnabar dot between his brows, and his collars, cuffs, and sashes were all embroidered with the white peony Sparks Amidst Snow. This was the little young master the Jin Clan of Lanling had sent, Jin Zixuan.

Someone else answered, "Don't bother asking Zixuan-xiong that. He already has a fiancée, so the answer is surely his fiancée."

Having heard the word "fiancée," Jin Zixuan seemed to purse his lips, looking a little unhappy. The disciple who first asked the question wasn't one to take hints and was still buoyantly curious.

"For real? Which family is she from? She must be shockingly smart and beautiful, right?!"

Jin Zixuan arched his brows. "No need to bring this up again."

Wei Wuxian suddenly cut in, "What do you mean, no need to bring it up again?"

Everyone in the Orchid Room looked at him, surprised. Wei Wuxian had always been a happy-go-lucky soul; even when scolded or punished, he never got genuinely angry. Yet now the hostility on his face was apparent. Furthermore, Jiang Cheng didn't chide Wei Wuxian for seeking trouble like he usually did, but sat next to him looking quite upset.

Jin Zixuan said haughtily, "Is it so hard to understand what 'don't bring it up again' means?"

Wei Wuxian sneered. "The words aren't, but is there something about my shijie that dissatisfies you? That's what I'm finding hard to understand here."

The others whispered among themselves. After some words were exchanged, they finally understood what was going on. Turned out, Jin Zixuan's words earlier had unintentionally prodded a huge hornet's nest: Jin Zixuan's fiancée was indeed Jiang Yanli from the Jiang Clan of Yunmeng.

Jiang Yanli was Jiang Fengmian's eldest daughter and Jiang Cheng's elder blood sister. She had a moderate temper, nothing exceptional—steady in speech, but nothing memorable. Her looks were above average, but her talents were nothing astounding. When you compared the beauty of the girls of various clans, she couldn't help but be overshadowed.

She was the exact opposite of her fiancé, Jin Zixuan. He was Jin Guangshan's only legitimate son and was outstanding in both looks and talent. In terms of Jiang Yanli's own qualifications, she indeed wouldn't normally have been a match for him. In fact, she would have had no right to compete with the other girls of prominent clans at all. The reason Jiang Yanli had been able to become betrothed to

Jin Zixuan was because her mother was of the Yu Clan of Meishan, a clan friendly with the clan from which Jin Zixuan's mother hailed. These two madams had grown up together and shared a strong friendship.

The Jin clan was proud and haughty, a trait Jin Zixuan had inherited completely. With extremely high expectations for a partner, he had long since been dissatisfied with this engagement. Not only was he dissatisfied with the candidate, he was even more so that his mother had decided his marriage entirely on her own. Inwardly, he'd become more and more resentful of the whole situation. Having been presented with the chance today, he could take it, use it, and throw a fit.

Jin Zixuan demanded back, "Why don't you ask what, exactly, should satisfy me about her?"

Jiang Cheng shot to his feet.

Wei Wuxian pushed Jiang Cheng back and stood in front of him, sneering. "And you think you're that amazing yourself? Where did you get the confidence to be so choosy?!"

Because of his engagement, Jin Zixuan didn't hold a high opinion of the Jiang Clan of Yunmeng. He'd also long since looked askance at Wei Wuxian's behavior. Besides, he prided himself on being singularly exceptional among these juniors—never had he been degraded like this before.

He blurted, "If she's dissatisfied, tell her to cancel this engagement! Either way, I don't care for your precious shijie. If you do, why don't *you* go ask her father for her hand?! Doesn't he treat you more dearly than his own son?"

The last comment made Jiang Cheng's gaze freeze. Wei Wuxian was beside himself with rage, lunging with a raised fist. Although Jin Zixuan had expected the attack, he didn't expect Wei Wuxian to be so fast, and the punch landed before he was done talking. Instantly, half of his face was numb. Without another word, he immediately fought back.

This fight alarmed two major clans. Jiang Fengmian and Jin Guangshan arrived in Gusu the very same day, from Yunmeng and Lanling respectively.

After seeing the two kneeling in punishment, the two heads of the families went to Lan Qiren for a round of severe scolding, both wiping sweat from their foreheads afterward. After exchanging greetings, Jiang Fengmian raised the subject of canceling the engagement.

He said to Jin Guangshan, "It was A-Li's mother who was adamant about this engagement in the first place; I do not agree with it. From the looks of things, neither party is happy with the arrangement, so let's not force things."

Jin Guangshan was astonished and somewhat doubtful. No matter what, to cancel an engagement with another prominent clan was not a good thing at the end of the day.

He said, "What do children know? Let them throw their tantrums. Fengmian-xiong, you and I can very well ignore them."

"Jin-xiong, although we can arrange their marriage, we cannot carry it out on their behalf," Jiang Fengmian said. "They are the ones who will be spending their lives together, after all."

This marriage had never been Jin Guangshan's original intention. If he had wanted to arrange a marriage with a prominent family to bolster his power, the Jiang Clan of Yunmeng wasn't the only, nor the best, choice. It was just that he never dared to disobey Madam Jin, was all. But since the head of the Jiang family had raised the subject voluntarily, why keep pestering him? The Jin family was the groom's side and thus didn't have as many concerns as the bride's. Besides, Jin Zixuan had always been displeased with Jiang Yanli as his fiancée. Jin Guangshan knew this.

After much consideration, Jin Guangshan boldly agreed to the cancellation.

At this time, Wei Wuxian was still unaware of what he had destroyed. He was kneeling on the cobblestone path that Lan Qiren had designated when Jiang Cheng approached from afar.

He said sarcastically, "Well, well, you're kneeling all honest-like."

Wei Wuxian gloated, "You know I kneel all the time. But a pampered guy like Jin Zixuan must never have knelt before. If it doesn't make him cry for his mommy and daddy, I won't be named Wei."

Jiang Cheng hung his head for a moment, then said dryly, "Father is here."

"Shijie didn't come, did she?" Wei Wuxian asked.

"Why would she? To watch how you embarrassed her?" Jiang Cheng said. "If she came, would she not have already been by to keep you company or deliver medicine?"

Wei Wuxian heaved a sigh. "…It would've been nice if shijie had come. Thank goodness you didn't get dragged into this."

"I was going to," Jiang Cheng said. "If you hadn't pushed me away, the other half of Jin Zixuan's face would be done for too."

"Best not," Wei Wuxian said. "The asymmetry makes him look uglier. I heard he particularly treasures that face of his. Like some peacock. I wonder how he feels right now, staring at himself in a mirror? Ha ha ha ha…"

He pounded the ground and laughed.

Wei Wuxian then added, "Actually, I should've let you fight while I stood and spectated. That way, Jiang-shushu might not have had to come. But it can't be helped—I couldn't resist!"

Jiang Cheng humphed and said softly, "You wish."

Wei Wuxian had said what he said offhandedly, but inwardly, Jiang Cheng felt complicated. He knew deep down that it wasn't a lie. Jiang Fengmian had never once rushed to another clan within a day over any of Jiang Cheng's own affairs, whether they be good or bad, major or minor.

Never.

Wei Wuxian saw him looking glum and thought he was still feeling upset over something Jin Zixuan had said. He said, "Go on, you don't have to keep me company. If Lan Wangji comes again, you'll be caught. If you're free, go gawk at how dumb Jin Zixuan looks while kneeling."

Jiang Cheng was slightly surprised. "Lan Wangji? Why would he come? He still dares to come see you?"

"Yeah," Wei Wuxian said. "I think it's mighty courageous of him to dare to come see me too. It's probably just that his shufu told him to make sure I'm kneeling properly, though."

Jiang Cheng instinctively felt a sense of foreboding. "Then were you kneeling properly at the time?"

"I was at the time," Wei Wuxian replied. "But once he walked away for a bit, I picked up a branch and started digging a hole nearby. It's that mound right next to your feet; there's an anthill there. It took me a while to find it. When he looked back and saw me with slumped shoulders, he must've thought I was crying or something, because he came over to ask after me. You should've seen his face when he saw that anthill."

"...I think you best get the hell back to Yunmeng!" Jiang Cheng said. "I think he never wants to see you ever again."

And so, that very night, Wei Wuxian packed up and went the hell back to Yunmeng with Jiang Fengmian.

5
The Sunny Pair

WEI WUXIAN had lain there like that on his stomach the entire night. The first half of the night was spent wondering what exactly had happened to Lan Wangji, and it wasn't until the second half that he finally fell into a bleary sleep. Early the next morning, when he opened his eyes, Lan Wangji had already gone without a trace. He himself was laid out properly on the bed, both his hands placed by his sides, arranged into a mannerly and respectable pose.

Wei Wuxian threw off the blanket covering him and tangled the fingers of his right hand in his hair. An unexplainable, absurd, and horrifying feeling plagued his mind, and it could not be dispersed.

Just then, there were two soft knocks on the wooden door to the Tranquility Room. Lan Sizhui's voice came from the other side.

"Mo-gongzi? Are you awake?"

"What are you calling me so early for?!" Wei Wuxian answered.

"E-early? But it's already si time?" Lan Sizhui replied.

The Lans all rose at mao and rested at hai, extremely regular. Wei Wuxian rose at si and rested at chou, also very regular—and later than the Lan family by exactly four hours. He had lain on his stomach for half the night and his back was aching, so he answered honestly.

"I can't get up."

"Uh, what's wrong with you now?" Lan Sizhui asked.

"What's wrong with me? Your sect's Hanguang-jun made me sleep with him, that's what!" Wei Wuxian exclaimed.

Lan Jingyi's truculent voice sounded out, "If you won't stop that nonsense of yours, I won't forgive you. Come out!"

Wei Wuxian cried out, aggrieved, "It's true! He forced me to sleep with him all night long! I'm not coming out, I'm too ashamed!"

The juniors looked at each other in dismay. Others were not to enter Hanguang-jun's living quarters. They didn't know whether to laugh or cry, but they had no way of going in directly to haul the man out.

Lan Jingyi yelled angrily, "How shameless! Hanguang-jun isn't a cut-sleeve! Him? Sleeping with you?! If *you* weren't the one forcing yourself on *him*, he'd thank the heavens. Get up! Take that donkey of yours away and control it a little, it's so noisy!"

Having heard his steed mentioned, Wei Wuxian quickly rolled out of bed. "What did you do to my Little Apple?! Don't touch it, it throws tantrums, and its kicks are something fierce."

"What little apple?" Lan Jingyi questioned.

"My donkey!" Wei Wuxian said, emerging from the Tranquility Room.

He shooed the juniors until they took him to his steed. They led him to a green pasture where, sure enough, the spotted donkey was braying nonstop, incredibly loud. The reason it was braying was because it wanted to graze, but the pasture had over a dozen round white fluffballs crowding about, keeping it from eating.

Wei Wuxian was delighted. "So many rabbits! Come, come, come, skewer and roast them!"

Lan Jingyi was going to explode. "*Killing is prohibited in the Cloud Recesses!* Shut that donkey up quickly; the morning study groups came to ask so many times already! Keep this up and we'll get lectured to death."

Wei Wuxian fed it the apple from his breakfast, and sure enough, once the spotted donkey started chomping on the fruit, it no longer cared to bray, instead filling the air with crunching as it ground its lips. Wei Wuxian stroked the back of its neck, scheming about the juniors' jade travel tokens. He pointed at the round white balls of rabbits.

"Can we really not roast them? Would I get kicked out of the mountain if I did?"

Lan Jingyi was greatly alarmed and hastily opened his arms, blocking him. "They're kept by Hanguang-jun—we only help watch them occasionally. Don't you dare!"

Wei Wuxian almost fell to the ground laughing when he heard this, thinking, *Jeez, this guy! He rejected the rabbits back when I tried to give them to him, and now he's secretly raised a whole horde. Don't want them? Who's he kidding? Good gods help me, he actually secretly likes those fluffy little white things, right?! That stiff-faced Hanguang-jun, holding a rabbit, oh gods, I just can't...*

But then he remembered how he had spent the previous night lying on top of Lan Wangji, and he suddenly couldn't laugh anymore.

Just then, tolling bells sounded from the west side of the Cloud Recesses.

The sound of this bell was vastly different from the bell that marked the hours. It was hurried and intense, as if a madman who had lost his mind was pounding it. Lan Jingyi and Lan Sizhui's faces fell drastically, and not bothering to joke around with him any longer, they ran off, leaving him. Wei Wuxian knew something was wrong and quickly followed after them.

The sound of the bell had come from one of the corner watchtowers.

This watchtower was called the "Nether Room," and its walls had been fabricated from special material and sealed with spells. It was a building the Lans used for summoning souls. When the bell atop this corner watchtower started tolling wildly, it meant only one thing: whoever was conducting a soul-summoning ritual inside had met with an accident.

Outside the corner watchtower, more and more Lan juniors and sect disciples had gathered, but none dared recklessly enter. The entrance to the Nether Room was a set of pitch-black wooden doors that were firmly locked, and they could only be opened from the inside. Not only would it be difficult to break in from the outside, but it would also violate the rules. To have accidents happen during a soul-summoning ritual was a terrifying thing. No one knew what might come from the summoning, or what would happen should they recklessly enter. Furthermore, there had never been any failures in soul-summoning since the establishment of the Nether Room, which made this even more distressing.

Wei Wuxian noticed Lan Wangji didn't show up and felt a sense of foreboding. If Lan Wangji was still in the Cloud Recesses, he should've come immediately when he heard the alarm bells go off. Unless…

Suddenly, the black doors burst open with a bang, and a white-clad sect disciple came stumbling out. His steps were unsteady, and the moment he charged out, he rolled off the stairs. The doors to the Nether Room closed on their own immediately after, slamming shut like they had been angered.

The others hurried to help the sect disciple up, but when he stood, he immediately slumped down again. His face streaming with uncontrollable tears, he clutched at whoever he could.

"It shouldn't have…it shouldn't have been summoned…"

Wei Wuxian seized his hand and demanded darkly, "What creature's soul are you guys summoning? Who else is in there? Where's Hanguang-jun?!"

This sect disciple seemed to have difficulty breathing. He opened his mouth. "Hanguang-jun, told me to run…"

Before he finished, bright red blood gushed from his nose and his mouth. Wei Wuxian shoved the person into Lan Sizhui's arms. The roughly made bamboo flute was still stuck on his waist. He ran up the many-layered stairs in a mere few strides, then kicked the doors to the Nether Room and shouted bitingly:

"OPEN!"

The grand doors of the Nether Room opened abruptly, like they were laughing maniacally. Wei Wuxian swiftly ducked inside, and the grand doors closed immediately after him. Shocked, the sect disciples quickly rushed over too, but no matter how hard they tried, the doors would not budge. One of the guest cultivators pounded on the door in both shock and fury.

He blurted out, "Who exactly was that?!"

Lan Sizhui was carrying the sect disciple. He said, his teeth clenched, "Come give me a hand first, he's bleeding from his apertures!"

The moment Wei Wuxian entered the Nether Room, he could sense an oppressive black energy assault his face.

This black energy seemed to be a combination of resentment, anger, and madness. It was almost visible to the eye, and within its entrapment, the pressure caused a dull pain in his chest. The Nether Room was over ten meters in length and width, and a few people lay slumped and unconscious in the four corners of the room. Within the array formation in the center of the room there stood the object of the soul-summoning.

Only an arm. There was nothing else. It was the one brought back from the Mo Manor!

It stood upright like a stick. Its stump was planted in the ground while four of its fingers were clenched into a fist. The index finger pointed to the sky, appearing to point at someone in rage. The endless stream of black energy that filled the room seemed to be emitting from the arm.

Those who participated in the soul-summoning ritual had all either run away or collapsed. Only upon the presiding host seat in the east corner was there one who sat upright and proper: Lan Wangji.

An old guqin was laid out next to him. His hand wasn't on the strings, yet they vibrated and strummed continuously on their own. At first, he seemed to be deep in thought, or perhaps he was focused on listening to something. Only when he noticed an intruder did he look up.

Lan Wangji appeared unperturbed. Wei Wuxian couldn't tell what he was thinking. Lan Qiren, who had assumed a position in the array, had already collapsed. Just like that sect disciple who had run out of the Nether Room, he was bleeding from his apertures and thoroughly unconscious. Wei Wuxian took over his position, swiftly stepping into the west seat. He pulled out the bamboo flute at his waist, raising it to his lips, matching Lan Wangji from the opposite end.

That night at the Mo Manor, Wei Wuxian had perturbed the creature with his whistling before Lan Wangji struck it with guqin notes from afar, suppressing the arm because the two had unintentionally joined forces. Lan Wangji met his eyes, understood, and raised his right hand. A series of notes strummed forth, and Wei Wuxian immediately joined his flute in harmony.

The song they played was called "Evocation." Using the corpse, a part of the corpse, or a beloved item of the deceased as the medium, the soul of the dead would come forth at the sound of the music. Usually, only a segment was needed before the soul would appear within the array. Yet though the two were almost done playing, still nothing heeded their call.

Veins popped along the body of the arm. It seemed to be angered, and the oppressive feeling in the air became even thicker. If it had been someone else guarding the west side, they would have collapsed from the pressure by now, as unable to escape the same bloody end as Lan Qiren. Inwardly, Wei Wuxian was alarmed. The idea that his duet of "Evocation" with Lan Wangji still couldn't call forth the soul of the deceased was practically impossible. Unless… unless the soul of this deceased was split along with its corpse!

It appeared that this good buddy was just a mite more tragic than him. Back then, although Wei Wuxian's corpse had been ripped apart, at the very least his soul still remained intact.

Since "Evocation" was ineffective, Lan Wangji altered the melody that his fingers plucked and began playing a different song.

This song was serene and peaceful, vastly different from the eerie, interrogative melody from earlier. It was entitled "Rest." Both these songs were widespread and renowned within the cultivation world. It wasn't suspicious for the average person to know the tunes, so Wei Wuxian very naturally joined in.

The name of the Yiling Patriarch's ghostly flute was Chenqing, and its mighty reputation was spread far and wide. At this moment, he joined in chorus using a bamboo flute and purposely played with ample errors: lacking breath, incredibly discordant to the ears. Lan Wangji had probably never played a duet with anyone so awful. After a while, finally unable to continue to play as if nothing was the matter, Lan Wangji looked up at him with an expressionless face.

With his thick skin, Wei Wuxian pretended not to notice, letting the melody go further and further off-tune. Just as he was about to continue playing, something bizarre suddenly occurred behind him. He turned his head to look and was instantly taken aback. Lan Qiren, who had already lost consciousness, was surprisingly sitting upright. His face bleeding and smoking from all apertures, his goatee, his voice, and even the finger that was pointing at Wei Wuxian all shook as he cried hoarsely with all his might.

"STOP PLAYING! GET OUT! GET OUT NOW! DO NOT..."

He didn't finish his instructions regarding what not to do before he spat a mouthful of blood and collapsed once more, sinking into oblivion anew.

Lan Wangji commented, "..."

Wei Wuxian gaped.

He knew what came after Lan Qiren's "do not": Do not play anymore! Do not play a duet! Do not defile his beloved student Wangji's music!

Their guqin and flute duet had actually forcibly roused Lan Qiren from anger alone, then forcibly knocked him out from anger alone, which made it apparent just how awful Wei Wuxian sounded...

But, even so, the arm still slowly drooped from the combined suppression of the flute and the guqin. Wei Wuxian, feeling no shame whatsoever, thought, *If it sounds bad, it sounds bad. As long as it's effective.*

The last note of the strings came to a stop, and instantly, the doors of the Nether Room sprang open, sunlight spilling in. It was probably because the alarm bell atop the corner watchtower had stopped that all the juniors and sect disciples who gathered outside the Nether Room came rushing in. All of a sudden, everyone was calling "Hanguang-jun!"

Lan Wangji pressed his hand on the strings, stopping the lingering sound of the resonance, then stood up to go check on Lan Qiren's pulse. With him taking the lead, the others quickly calmed down. Several of the elders laid flat the ones inside the Nether Room who were bleeding, carrying out medical treatment. While they applied acupuncture needles and administered medicine, another group of sect disciples came carrying a bronze bell with plans of trapping that arm inside it. While the scene was busy, everything was orderly and no one clamored nor made noise.

Someone asked, concerned, "Hanguang-jun, neither the medicinal pills nor needles work. What should be done?"

Lan Wangji still had three fingers placed on Lan Qiren's pulse, silent, brows furrowed. Lan Qiren had conducted innumerable soul-summoning rituals involving no shortage of malicious ghosts and fierce spirits, but even he'd been injured by the backlash of resentful energy. It said much about just how dreadful the resentment of this ghost arm was. Resentment in a league practically never seen before.

Wei Wuxian stuck the bamboo flute back on his waist and crouched down next to that bronze bell, stroking the golden characters engraved upon it. He was just thinking when he suddenly noticed Lan Sizhui's downcast expression.

"What's wrong?"

Lan Sizhui already knew he was no ordinary person. He said softly, somewhat hesitantly, "Just feeling a little guilty, that's all."

"Guilty about what?" Wei Wuxian asked.

"That ghost arm was coming for *us*," Lan Sizhui said.

Wei Wuxian smiled. "And how do you know that?"

"Different grades of spirit-attraction flags have different ways to draw them up, and different powers. The flags we drew back at the Mo Estate only had a working radius of two and a half kilometers, but that ghost arm was heavy with killing intent and consumed flesh and blood. If it had been within the working perimeters from the start, with its level of aggression, the Mo Estate would've been flowing with blood already. But it only appeared after we arrived…which means it must've been thrown into that location intentionally, at that precise time, by someone with malicious intent."

"You've learned your lessons well. That's a pretty good analysis," Wei Wuxian said.

Lan Sizhui hung his head. "If that was the case, then we will probably…have to take responsibility…for the lives lost at the Mo Estate. And now, even Lan-xiansheng and the others got mixed up in things, falling unconscious like this…"

After a brief moment of silence, Wei Wuxian patted his shoulder. "The one who should take responsibility isn't you guys, but whoever unleashed the ghost arm. There are some things in this world that can't be controlled."

On the other end, Lan Wangji withdrew his hand, and the Lan family members quickly asked after Lan Qiren.

"Hanguang-jun, how is he?"

Lan Wangji replied, "Trace the origins."

"That's right, trace the origins," Wei Wuxian said. "Naturally, once we find the complete corpse of this ghost arm and make clear its identity, there'll be a way to save them."

Although Lan Jingyi already knew Wei Wuxian was definitely not a lunatic, he still couldn't help speaking to him in a berating tone. "You make it sound so easy. Its soul won't heed summoning, and after all this chaos, where do we even go looking?"

"The northwest," Lan Wangji said.

Lan Sizhui asked curiously, "The northwest? Why the northwest, Hanguang-jun?"

"Didn't it already point the way for you all to see?" Wei Wuxian said.

Lan Jingyi was confused. "Point the way for us? Who? Hanguang-jun didn't point at anything?"

"*It* did," Wei Wuxian said.

Only then did the group discover that what he meant was the ghost arm!

That arm was firmly pointing in a particular direction. Someone tried changing its position, but it resolutely turned back around, returning to the original direction. No one had ever witnessed such a situation before, and all were stunned.

Lan Jingyi stammered, "It? What…what is it pointing at?!"

"What else could it be pointing at?" Wei Wuxian said. "It's either the rest of its body parts or the perp who left it like this."

Having heard this, the youths who had just so happened to be standing in the northwest quickly scurried away. Lan Wangji glanced at Wei Wuxian, then slowly rose to his feet. He turned to the sect disciples.

"Settle shufu properly."

The disciples nodded. "Yessir! Will you be descending the mountain, then?"

As Lan Wangji gave a light nod, Wei Wuxian had already snuck behind him, vocally talking to himself, sounding very pleased.

"Good, good, good, now we can finally go down the mountain and elope!"

The group grimaced, and the older sect disciples were especially horrified, but the few youths were more or less used to it now. There was only Lan Qiren on the ground whose face seemed to have twitched subconsciously.

A thought came to all of them: *Maybe if that person talks a bit more, Lan-xiansheng will be angered awake again...*

◇◈◇

When leaders of prominent cultivation clans joined Night Hunts, there was often great fanfare with ample pomp. However, Lan Wangji had always preferred coming and going alone. In addition, this arm was evil and strange, and it could easily harm others should there be the slightest carelessness. And so he brought neither clan juniors nor sect disciples with him—only Wei Wuxian. The watch kept on him was keener than ever.

At first, Wei Wuxian wanted to sneak off when they descended the mountain for investigation, but the end result of his many attempts at escape en route all involved getting dragged back by the collar by Lan Wangji. He changed tactics and tried very hard to stick and cling to Lan Wangji, especially at night. He'd climb into Lan Wangji's bed come hell or high water, hoping Lan Wangji would quickly strike him away with his sword in disgust. But no matter the fits he threw, Lan Wangji was still and unmoved. Every time Wei Wuxian burrowed into his blankets, he'd give Wei Wuxian a gentle tap, petrifying him. Then he would tuck Wei Wuxian into another set of blankets and arrange him into a proper sleeping position until morning. Wei Wuxian fell for it multiple times, and every time he'd wake up groaning with a sore back and weak legs.

He couldn't help but think, *This guy's so much less interesting now that he's grown. When I teased him in the past, he knew how to be shy, and hilariously so too. Now, not only is he completely unaffected, but he's even learned to retaliate. Absolutely ridiculous!*

Following the direction indicated by the left arm, the two headed northwest. They had to play a duet of "Rest" every day to temporarily pacify the arm's anger and killing intent. As they neared the area of Qinghe, the pointing gesture the arm had maintained for a long time suddenly changed. It withdrew its fingers and clenched them into a fist.

This meant that what this hand was pointing at was nearby.

They visited various places as they journeyed and finally came to a small city in Qinghe. It was the middle of the day, and the streets were full of people coming and going, lively and bustling. Wei Wuxian kicked and stomped as he followed behind Lan Wangji. Suddenly, a sharp scent of rouge and powder hit them in the face.

Having gotten used to Lan Wangji's light, refreshing scent of sandalwood, after this smell assaulted him, Wei Wuxian blurted out, "What do you sell? What's this smell?"

The scent came from a scammy-looking quack doctor dressed in a Daoist robe. He had a chest carried on his back and was selling little trinkets to passersby. When he saw someone was making inquiries, he was delighted.

"I sell everything! Rouge, powder, exquisite and cheap. Won't gongzi take a look?"

"Sure, I'll take a look," Wei Wuxian said.

"For your wife at home?" the doc asked.

Wei Wuxian smiled. "For myself."

"..." The doc's smile froze, and the thought crossed his mind: *You playin' me?!*

Before he could blow up, another man came back halfway and said expressionlessly, "Do not play around if you are not going to buy."

This man was exceptionally handsome and refined. His robes and forehead ribbon were whiter than snow, his eyes were pale in hue, and a longsword hung at his waist. The doctor was a fake cultivator.

He had some half-baked knowledge of the prominent cultivation clans and, recognizing the insignia of the Lan Clan of Gusu, didn't dare to act rashly. He tugged on the straps of his chest and ran off.

Wei Wuxian called after him, "What are you running for? I was really gonna buy some!"

"Do you have the money?" Lan Wangji asked.

Wei Wuxian replied, "Well, gimme some, then."

As he said this, he reached into Lan Wangji's robes. He hadn't expected to dig out anything at first, but after feeling around for a bit, he really did manage to pull out an exquisite and heavy little money pouch.

This didn't look like anything Lan Wangji would carry on his person at all, but after so many days, there were more than one or two things about him that perplexed Wei Wuxian. Unbothered by the odd sight, he grabbed the money pouch and walked away. Sure enough, Lan Wangji let him take it without a single word of complaint. If Wei Wuxian hadn't thought he knew a little bit about Lan Wangji's character and insistence on purity—and with Hanguang-jun's terrifyingly impeccable reputation on top of that—he would almost have suspected there was some sort of romantic entanglement between Lan Wangji and Mo Xuanyu.

How else could Lan Wangji still endure it, when he'd been this insufferable?!

After having walked a stretch, Wei Wuxian unconsciously looked back. Lan Wangji was left way behind, still standing in the same spot, watching him.

Wei Wuxian unconsciously slowed down.

For some reason, he vaguely felt that maybe he shouldn't be walking this fast, and that maybe he shouldn't leave Lan Wangji behind like this.

Just then, someone called out next to him: "The Yiling Patriarch, five pennies a sheet, ten for three!"

Wei Wuxian blurted out, "Who?!"

He hurried over to see who it was that was selling him, and it was indeed the fake-cultivator quack doctor from earlier. The man had packed up the poor-quality cosmetics and changed to a stack of posters, painted with devils looking as fierce and savage as threshold guardians, ferocious deities that guarded entryways.

He rattled on, "Five pennies a sheet, ten for three, it's a good price, no cheat! Three sheets are perfect. One for the main entrance, one for the main hall, and the last one at the head of the bed. Heavily ominous, thick with wickedness, fight evil with evil, fight poison with poison. No nefarious creatures will dare come close, guaranteed!"

"What is this bull?!" Wei Wuxian exclaimed. "If it really is that effective, why are you selling a sheet for five pennies?!"

"You again? If you're not buying, then leave," the doc said. "If you want to spend fifty pennies to buy one, I won't stop you."

Wei Wuxian flipped through the stack of "Portrait of the Yiling Patriarch, the Vanquisher of Evil." He really could not tolerate the idea that this green-faced, teeth-baring burly man with bulging eyes and popped veins was himself.

He argued with the power of logic. "Wei Wuxian was renowned as a beautiful man. What the heck is this drawing?! Don't just draw whatever if you've never seen the man himself before—it's misleading."

That doc was just about to speak when Wei Wuxian suddenly felt a threatening wind behind him. He swiftly dodged, but the quack doctor was sent flying and crashed into someone else's pinwheel stall. Some people helped him to his feet while others helped pick up the mess, it was a flurry of chaos.

The doc had wanted to swear at first, but when he saw the one who had kicked him was a little young master decked in shimmering gold all over—obviously either wealthy or noble—his courage was cut in half. Then, when he saw it was the white peony Sparks Amidst Snow embroidered on the young master's chest, he lost his confidence completely. But he still refused to be kicked for no good reason, so he complained meekly.

"Why did you kick me?"

That little young master was indeed Jin Ling. He said coldly with his arms crossed, "Kick you? Anyone who dares mention the name 'Wei Wuxian' in front of me should kneel and thank their lucky stars that I didn't kill them. You were hollering and making a heck of a racket on the streets too. You were asking for it!"

Wei Wuxian had never expected Jin Ling to appear in this place—and never imagined he'd act so bossy too.

He thought to himself, *What is going on with this child's temper? So hot-headed and belligerent—arrogant, spoiled, and looking down on everyone. He's thoroughly inherited everything bad about his uncle and father, and nothing good from his mother. If I don't knock him down a couple notches, he'll be at a huge disadvantage in the future.*

Seeing how Jin Ling didn't appear to have spent all of his anger and was walking threateningly toward the man on the ground, Wei Wuxian interrupted him.

"Jin Ling!"

That doctor didn't dare to make a sound, but his eyes were beaming with a thousand thanks. Sure enough, Jin Ling turned to Wei Wuxian.

He said disdainfully, "You haven't run away yet? Just as well."

Wei Wuxian laughed. "Gee, I wonder who it was last time that got pinned to the ground, unable to get up?"

Jin Ling scoffed and blew a short whistle. Wei Wuxian didn't understand what that meant at first, but a brief moment later, the sound of a heavy panting beast could be heard in the distance.

When he turned his head to look, a black-haired spirit dog half the size of a man emerged from around the street corner, running straight for him. The alarmed screams down the long street came closer and closer, louder and louder:

"A VICIOUS DOG ON THE LOOSE!"

Wei Wuxian's face abruptly changed color, and he bolted.

An embarrassing tale to tell, but for all his presumptuous claims of being invincible, the Yiling Patriarch was actually scared of dogs. It couldn't be helped. When he was younger, before he was found by Jiang Fengmian, he had lived on the streets and often had no choice but to steal food from the mouths of vicious hounds. He had suffered greatly and plentifully from all the biting, tearing, and chasing, and gradually become terrified of all canines, big or small. Jiang Cheng had often laughed at him for that. Not only was this embarrassing to tell, but not many believed it either, so it wasn't a widely known fact.

Wei Wuxian was practically scared witless. A tall, graceful white figure entered his vision all of a sudden, and he quickly let out a distressed cry.

"LAN ZHAN, SAVE ME!"

When Jin Ling saw Lan Wangji after giving chase, his face drained of color. *Why is that lunatic with him again?!*

Lan Wangji was a stern, taciturn man. Those of his generation within the cultivation world often felt trepidation at the sight of him, never mind the juniors. His power of intimidation was equal to or more than that of Lan Qiren, back in his era. That dog of Jin Ling's was no ordinary dog. It had been strictly trained and was exceptionally intelligent. It also seemed to know that it could not behave atrociously in front of this man, so it howled a few times before hiding behind Jin Ling with its tail between its legs.

This black-haired spirit dog was a rare breed that Jin Guangyao had gifted Jin Ling. Ordinarily, when people heard it was a gift from Lianfang-zun, no one would dare affront it. Unfortunately, Lan Wangji was no ordinary person. He didn't care whose gift it was. The one who let the dog loose would be punished as was fit, severely and without leniency. Jin Ling had been caught letting the dog loose in the streets and caught giving chase, and his heart sank.

He thought inwardly, *I'm dead. He'll have the spirit dog I worked so hard to train killed, then teach me a harsh lesson!*

Yet who would've believed the sight of Wei Wuxian shoving himself under Lan Wangji's arm, drilling around to his back, and desperately trying to climb up this tall and graceful pole; it would be best if he could reach the sky. With Wei Wuxian's arms encircling him, Lan Wangji seemed to have frozen solid. Using this chance, Jin Ling blew another two short whistles and fled with his black-haired spirit dog.

On the ground next to them, that doctor struggled to his feet. He said, still feeling lingering fear, "Public morality is declining by the day; the descendants of prominent clans are awful, just awful!"

Wei Wuxian listened to the barking of the dog disappear into the distance, then also emerged from behind Lan Wangji's back, agreeing with his hands folded behind him like nothing had happened.

"Indeed, public morality is declining by the day; nothing is what it used to be."

That doc now saw him as his savior and quickly agreed. To demonstrate his gratitude, he tossed the stack of "Portrait of the Yiling Patriarch, the Vanquisher of Evil" posters into Wei Wuxian's hands like a hot potato.

"Brother, thanks so much for earlier! Take this as my thanks; if you sell them at a discount, three pennies a sheet, you can make a profit of at least three hundred."

Lan Wangji glanced at the burly man with the green face and bared teeth and gave no comment. Wei Wuxian didn't know whether to laugh or cry at how his value was getting marked down cheaper and cheaper.

"Is this your thank-you gift? If you really wanna thank me, draw him better-looking... Stop, don't go, I've something to ask. While doing business here, have you heard of any strange occurrences? Or seen anything odd?"

"Strange occurrences? You've asked the right person," the doc said. "This humble one has resided here for a long time, and people call me the Know-It-All of Qinghe. What strange occurrences are you talking about?"

Wei Wuxian replied, "For example, hauntings, strange cases of dismembered corpses, clan annihilation tragedies, and so on."

"Not here," the doc said. "But if you go onward for two to three kilometers, there's a mountain ridge there called the Xinglu Ridge. I suggest you not go."

"Why not?" Wei Wuxian asked.

"The Xinglu Ridge is also nicknamed the 'Man-Eating Ridge.' What do you think?" the doc answered.

"Oh yeah? It's haunted by man-eating monsters, is it?" Wei Wuxian asked.

He had heard similar rumors at least a thousand times and had personally exterminated said things at least a hundred times, so it couldn't be helped that he found the idea mundane.

The doctor said dramatically, "That's right! They say in that forest lies a 'Man-Eating Fortress,' and there are man-eating monsters living in there. Any intruder will be devoured so completely that not even crumbs will be left of their bones. Not a single man shall be spared, without exception! Scary, right?"

No wonder Jin Ling had showed up here. He'd failed to nab the soul-eating Heavenly Maiden of Mount Dafan, so he had to be targeting the monsters of Xinglu Ridge this time.

Wei Wuxian replied, "So scary! But if not even bone crumbs are left and no one's been spared, how do you know intruders are eaten?"

The doctor was briefly speechless, then said, "Of course, it's because someone's witnessed it."

"But didn't you just say that intruders are devoured so completely that not even bone crumbs remain, without exception? Who's the one talking, then? I wonder who's so amazing that they could witness such a scene and still come out alive to tell the tale?" Wei Wuxian commented in admiration.

"...That's what the rumors say. How should I know?" the doctor said.

Wei Wuxian continued to prod, "Then do you know the total count of people who have been devoured at Xinglu Ridge? When they were devoured? Their ages? Male or female? Their names? Where they were from?"

"I don't know," the doctor said.

"'The Know-It-All of Qinghe,' hmm?" Wei Wuxian snidely jabbed.

The doctor angrily slung on his basket pack. "Rumors never cover that kinda stuff in the first place!"

Wei Wuxian laughed cheekily. "No, no, no, no, don't go, c'mon. Let me ask one more question. Xinglu Ridge is still within the borders of Qinghe, right? Isn't Qinghe the domain of the Nie family? If there really are man-eating monsters roaming about Xinglu Ridge, are they really not doing anything about it?"

Unexpectedly, the doctor didn't answer with "I don't know" this time. Instead, contempt flashed on his face.

"The Nie family? If it were the Nie family of the past, of course they wouldn't remain uninvolved. The rumor would hardly be two days old before they'd resolutely raid the evil thing's lair in no time at all. But isn't the current Nie family head—heh heh—that 'Head-Shaker'?"

The head of the Nie Clan of Qinghe had been Chifeng-zun, courtesy name Nie Mingjue. He took control of the Nie family before he came of age upon the death of his father, the former family head, who had been vexed to death by the head of the Wen Clan of Qishan, Wen Ruohan. Nie Mingjue's approach was principled and unyielding, and he was sworn brothers with Zewu-jun (that is, Lan Xichen) and Lianfang-zun (that is, Jin Guangyao). After the Sunshot Campaign, under his rule, there was a time when the Nie family almost matched the Jin Clan of Lanling in power and influence. However, he had suffered a qi deviation during training and died publicly and violently, with blood bursting from his body. The one who succeeded him to the position of family head would have been his little brother, Nie Huaisang.

Wei Wuxian asked, "So why is he called the 'Head-Shaker'?"

"You don't know the story?" the doctor asked. "That Nie family head…if he doesn't know the answer, he won't bother to say anything, and if he does know the answer, he won't dare to say anything. If you press him too hard, force him too hard, he'll just keep shaking his head, crying 'I don't know, I don't know, I really don't know!' and beg you to let him off the hook. Doesn't that make him a Head-Shaker?"

Wei Wuxian and Nie Huaisang had been classmates, so he could say a thing or two about the man. Nie Huaisang wasn't a bad person, and it wasn't that he wasn't smart—he just had zero inclination to apply himself academically. All of his smarts were spent elsewhere: in painting fans, catching feathered friends, skipping class, and loafing around. His capacity for cultivation was indeed amazingly poor, and it was only with great difficulty that he'd managed to form a golden core, eight or nine years after juniors of other clans of the same generation. Whilst alive, Nie Mingjue had often been anxious about his little brother's lack of progress and been extremely strict in disciplining him. Nonetheless, Nie Huaisang remained hopeless.

Now that his older brother was no longer around to shield him from storms and provide guidance, the Nie Clan of Qinghe was declining under Nie Huaisang's leadership—and rapidly. Once he came of age, and especially since he had become the family head, Nie Huaisang was often seen running around in a terrible tizzy over the various matters he had no idea how to handle, begging others for help wherever he could find anyone willing. His older brother's two younger sworn brothers were his favorite resources on this matter: today he'd be complaining tearfully to Jin Guangyao, tomorrow he'd go sniffling and stammering for assistance at the Cloud Recesses. It was by relying on the support of two great clan leaders of the Lans and Jins that he was able to, with immense difficulty, keep the position of family head. While it wouldn't be courteous to say so out loud, whenever Nie Huaisang was mentioned, the same phrase was written clearly on everyone's faces: good-for-nothing trash.

Thinking back on everything that happened in the past, one couldn't help but sigh.

After getting the information on Xinglu Ridge, Wei Wuxian still patronized the doctor's business. He bought two boxes of rouge and powder, hugging his purchases to him as he returned to Lan Wangji's side, the latter still showing no intention of asking for the return of his money pouch. Without a word, they headed in the direction that the doctor pointed.

A vast fir forest enveloped Xinglu Ridge. Wide, open paths wound through the lush green foliage. They traveled for a while and didn't run into anything unusual, but the two had had no great expectations as such in the first place. Walking through this place was only a precaution. If a terrifying local rumor actually had any truth to it, then the circulating talk would at least have a few substantial facts. When the soul-eating Heavenly Maiden of Mount Dafan was haunting its area, there were clear hard facts that had been easily sniffed out: where the victims' families lived, the victims' names—not even the nickname of A-Yan's fiancé could have been concealed. But if there were no details at all about the victims, and no information about the incidents aside from vague hemming and hawing, then it was most likely nothing but sensational and spurious hearsay.

Over an hour later, after the aforementioned untold hardships, they finally ran into some trouble. Ahead of them were seven or eight figures, wobbling as they approached. Their eyes were rolled back, their clothing was ragged, and they looked as if they'd collapse if struck by the weakest breeze. Judging by their unimaginable slowness, this was a row of walking corpses that could not be any lower in level.

Walking corpses like these were only good for getting bullied by their own kind. If they ran into a living human possessing even the slightest bit of strength, a single kick could topple an entire row of them; if they ran into a child who could run even slightly fast, they'd be left in the dust in an instant. Even if one was unlucky in the extreme and somehow got caught, letting them suck a couple breaths of yang energy wouldn't be fatal. So aside from their extremely ugly looks and horrid stench, they were no threat at all. When advanced cultivators ran into them during Night Hunts, they were ignored in most cases and left for junior disciples to deal with. When one went out hunting tigers and leopards, there was no point in pursuing mice—or such was the logic.

When Wei Wuxian saw them walking over, he knew this was going to be bad news. He bowed his head, retreating behind Lan Wangji. Sure enough, when this queue of wobbly walking corpses came within twenty meters of them, the moment they saw Wei Wuxian, they immediately turned around and wobbled on back from whence they came in terror, their legs moving threefold faster and more efficiently than when they had first surrounded them.

Wei Wuxian rubbed his temples. He then whirled around and said, his voice trembling with terrible fear, "Heavens, Hanguang-jun, you're so amazing! The moment they saw you, they ran away in fear! Ha ha."

Lan Wangji was speechless in response.

Wei Wuxian nudged him, laughing. "Come on, come on, let's get out of here; I'm not seeing any other monsters. Amazing how the locals can talk this place up. Some cowardly walking corpses, and they become monsters that swallow even bones. The 'Man-Eating' Fortress must be fabricated too. We've wasted our time!"

Lan Wangji only moved after he was pushed a couple of times. Before Wei Wuxian could follow, from the far distance of the fir forest, there came the crazed howling of a dog.

The color of Wei Wuxian's face violently changed. He ducked behind Lan Wangji in a matter of seconds, hugging his waist and crouching down, shrinking into a ball.

"...It is distant, still. Why are you hiding?" Lan Wangji said.

"H-h-h-h-h-hide first. Where is it? WHERE IS IT?!" Wei Wuxian stuttered.

Lan Wangji listened intently for a moment, then replied, "It is that black-haired spirit dog belonging to Jin Ling."

The moment Wei Wuxian heard Jin Ling mentioned, he stood up, but then immediately crouched back down at the sound of the howling.

Lan Wangji said, "Such crazed howls from a spirit hound. It must have encountered something."

Wei Wuxian groaned miserably, then arduously stood up on two shaking legs. "Th-th-th-th-th-th-then, let's go check it out!"

Lan Wangji didn't budge.

Wei Wuxian urged, "Hanguang-jun, move, go on! What'll I do if you don't?!"

After a moment of silence, Lan Wangji finally said, "You…let go, first."

The two dragged and pulled, stumbled and floundered as they followed the sound of the howling. They circled twice within the forest of fir, and yet the howling black-haired spirit dog seemed to elude them: now it was nearby, then it was far away. Having listened to the howls for so long, Wei Wuxian finally got somewhat used to them—or at the very least, he was no longer stuttering.

"There's a maze array here?"

This maze array was clearly a man-made effort. He'd just declared the Xinglu Ridge rumors to be nothing but baseless hearsay, but now things were getting interesting.

The black-haired spirit dog had been howling for half an incense time, but it was still invigorated. After the duo broke through the maze array, they followed its sound. Not long after, the contours of ghastly stone bunkers began to surface from the depths of the fir forest.

The fortress was comprised of stone bunkers built with grayish-white stones, and green vines and fallen leaves crawled over every surface. Every bunker was constructed in a peculiar half-dome shape. It was as if there were a number of large bowls overturned on the ground.

Stone bunkers like these actually existed on Xinglu Ridge! It appeared the rumors were not simply empty gossip. However, it was difficult to say whether this really was a "Man-Eating Fortress" or just what creatures lurked inside.

Jin Ling's black-haired spirit dog was running around in circles outside this group of stone bunkers, sometimes growling threateningly, sometimes barking loudly and viciously. When it saw Lan Wangji approach, although it backed away a bit in fear, it didn't flee. Instead, it barked at them even louder, then looked to the stone fortress. Anxious and agitated, its front paws dug at the earth so hard that mud was splattering.

Wei Wuxian was in agony hiding behind Lan Wangji. "Why isn't it leaving...? Where's its master? Why is its master gone?!"

Since they first heard the dog's howls, they had not heard a single sound from Jin Ling, not even a cry for help. He must've been the one to bring the black-haired spirit dog here, and he must also have been the one to break the maze array. And yet it was as if a living person had vanished, just like that.

"Let us go in and check," Lan Wangji said.

"How? There's no door," Wei Wuxian said.

There really was no door. The gray-whitish stone blocks were tightly sealed together, without any room for doors or windows. The black-haired spirit dog howled and jumped, seeming to want to bite the corner of Lan Wangji's sleeve but not daring to. So, it went around him to bite Wei Wuxian's hem instead, dragging him out.

Wei Wuxian's soul was about to leave his body. He reached out to Lan Wangji with both hands.

"Lan Zhan…Lan Zhan, Lan Zhan…Lan ZHAN, LAN ZHAN, LAN ZHAN!!!"

The black-haired dog dragged Wei Wuxian, Wei Wuxian dragged Lan Wangji, and thus did the dog drag the two men a good halfway around to the back of the stone fortress. Surprisingly, there was a hole there, about the size of a grown man. On the ground was scattered debris; the hole had obviously been violently blown out by a spiritual device just recently. It was pitch-black inside the hole and nothing was quite visible, but there seemed to be a subtle, faint red light. The black-haired spirit dog slackened its jaw and started barking incessantly toward the hole, then wagged its tail crazily at the other two.

Needless to say, it must've been Jin Ling who had forcefully broken into this stone bunker, and he had likely met with an accident once he went in.

Bichen unsheathed itself by half, its blade emitting an icy blue shimmer, illuminating the pitch-black road ahead. Lan Wangji bent down and entered first. Wei Wuxian, about to completely lose it because of the dog, quickly dashed after him, almost crashing into him. Lan Wangji took his hand to steady him, and whether in reproach or exasperation, he shook his head.

It was obvious that the black-haired spirit dog wanted to join them. It tried to charge inside, but it seemed to be blocked by some kind of force and couldn't break through the barrier no matter how hard it pushed. And so it had no choice but to sit down in front of the hole, its tail wagging ever harder. Wei Wuxian was so overjoyed he was practically ready to kneel. He pulled his hand back, taking a few steps deeper inside. The icy blue light of the sword brightened the surrounding blackness into a cold white.

The trees of Xinglu Ridge were tall, the woods deep—quite the chilly place. And yet the interior of this stone fortress was even more so. Wei Wuxian had entered the forest with lightly layered clothing, and the chilly wind swished through the openings at his cuffs and collar, drying the cold sweat from the dog-related fright earlier. The light at the opening had long disappeared like a candlelight extinguished. The deeper they went, the more spacious it became, and the darker it grew.

The ceiling of the stone bunker was round, and when Wei Wuxian kicked a pebble by his foot, he could hear a light echo. He finally could endure no longer and stopped, pressing his right hand against his temple, his brows slightly furrowed.

Lan Wangji looked back. "What is it?"

"…So noisy," Wei Wuxian said.

Within the stone bunker, it was deathly still and soundless, as silent as a grave. Just so, as it greatly resembled a grave in the first place.

But at this very moment, Wei Wuxian's ears told him that they were at the epicenter of a cacophony of noise.

The noise came from all directions. Front, back, left, right, above the head, below the feet. It was like a vast ocean of whispers, rustling and faint, hee hee ha ha. There were men and women, old and young, big and small. Wei Wuxian could even hear some odd phrases here and there, but they were fleeting, and he couldn't catch any of the exact words.

It really was too noisy.

Wei Wuxian kept one hand on his temple while the other went to dig out a palm-sized Compass of Ill Winds from the qiankun pouch. The needle of the Compass of Ill Winds quivered and faltered, spinning around twice, then spinning faster and faster. Soon, it started spinning crazily!

CHAPTER 5: THE SUNNY PAIR

Previously at Mount Dafan, it had already been bizarre that the Compass of Ill Winds couldn't point out a direction. But this time it actually started spinning on its own, without stopping for a single moment. This was even more perplexing than when the needle wasn't moving at all.

That foreboding feeling in Wei Wuxian's mind was growing stronger and stronger. He shouted out loud, "JIN LING!"

The two had already walked for a while within the stone bunker, but they still hadn't seen any trace of the living. Wei Wuxian called out a few times, and there was no response. The first few stone chambers were completely empty, but when they reached a deeper area, they came upon a stone chamber with a pitch-black coffin set in the center of the room.

The coffin's placement was incredibly conspicuous. Despite how suspicious it looked, the entirety of its body was leaden black, the shape of it exceptionally beautiful. Wei Wuxian found it particularly endearing. He liked it and couldn't resist giving it a pat. The quality of the wood was superior, and the resonance of the pat was a solid *toc-toc*.

He praised, "A good coffin."

Lan Wangji and Wei Wuxian stood on either side and exchanged a look, then both reached out at the same time and opened the coffin lid.

The moment the coffin lid was opened, the clamoring noise around them suddenly increased exponentially, drowning Wei Wuxian's hearing like an incoming tide. Before this, it had already felt as though they were being spied on by countless eyes—the owners of those eyes secretly monitoring them, discussing their every word and action—and in seeing them move to open the coffin, their agitation flared. Wei Wuxian thought of a dozen possibilities.

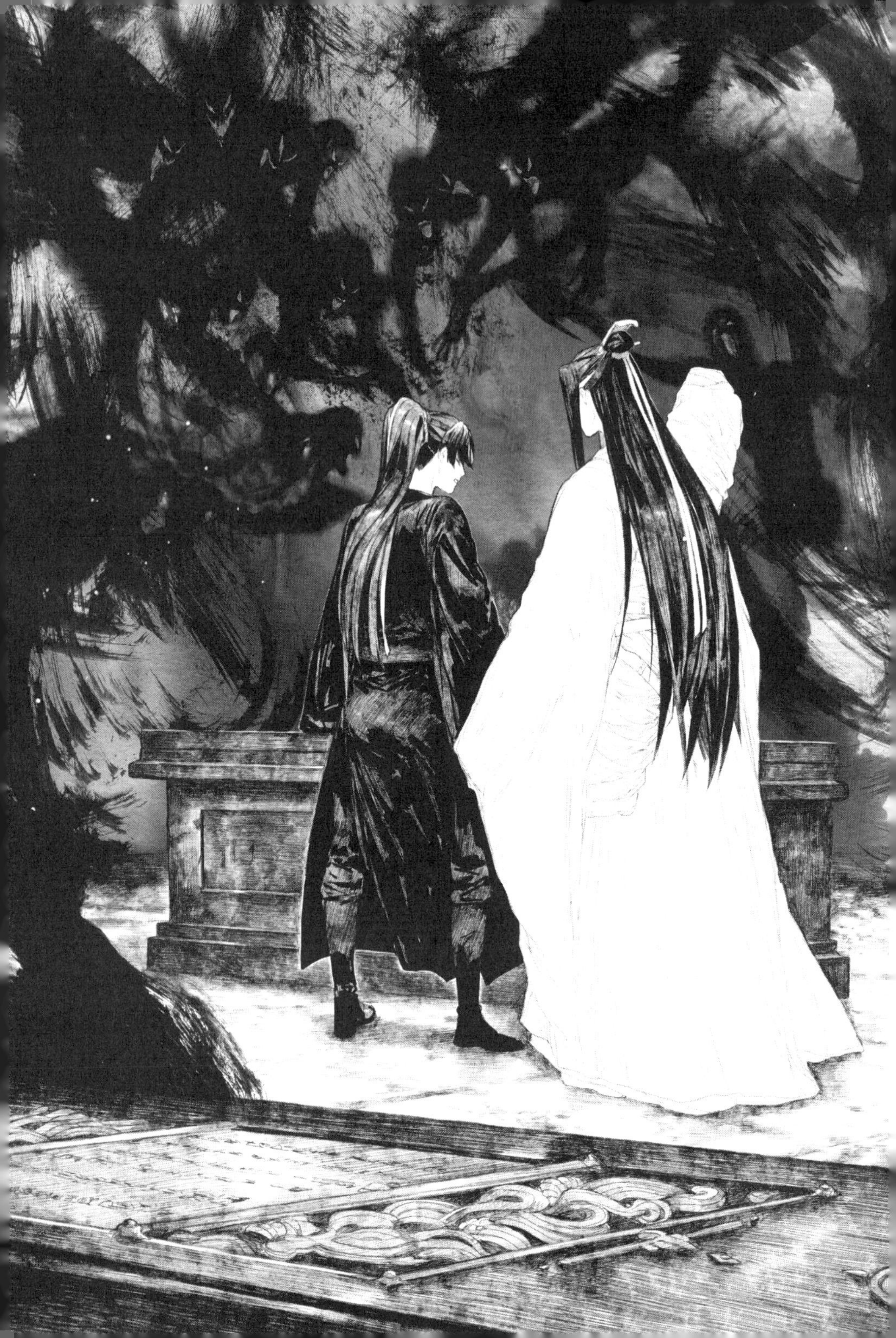

CHAPTER 5: THE SUNNY PAIR

He was already prepared to deal with rancid smells assaulting his nose, demonic claws suddenly lunging forth, venomous waters spraying, poisonous gas diffusing, assault by resentful spirits, and so on. Though of course, he hoped for the possibility he'd see Jin Ling the most of all these.

However, nothing happened. Absolutely nothing.

It was, surprisingly, an empty coffin.

Wei Wuxian was somewhat surprised, then a little disappointed that Jin Ling wasn't trapped in there. Lan Wangji edged closer, and Bichen unsheathed itself several centimeters. Its icy light shimmered and illuminated the bottom of the coffin. Only then did he notice something. It wasn't that there was nothing inside but rather that the object was much smaller than the corpse he had expected, and it was hidden in the deepest depths of the coffin.

Within the coffin there lay a long saber.

This saber had no sheath, and the hilt was forged in gold; it looked to have quite a heft to it. The body of the saber was long and slender, the blade bright as snow. Pillowed on a layer of red cloth at the bottom of the coffin, the blade reflected that blood-like color. Its killing aura was ominous.

The coffin gave rest not to a corpse but a saber. There was truly not a single normal thing about this row of stone bunkers at Xinglu Ridge. Every step they took led them to more strangeness.

The two closed the coffin lid and continued their travels deeper inside. There were several more stone chambers where they discovered the same kind of coffin. Judging by the condition of the wood, they spanned years of age, but the constant among them all was that within each coffin was a long saber laid to rest.

They had reached the very last room, and there was still no sign of Jin Ling. Wei Wuxian closed the last coffin lid, feeling slightly uneasy.

Lan Wangji observed his frown and his silence. After a moment of deliberation, he placed his guqin atop the coffin. He raised his hands, and a string of notes flowed from his fingers.

He only played a short segment before he withdrew his right hand from the guqin and then stared intently at the strings that were still vibrating.

Suddenly, the strings convulsed and played a note on their own.

"'Inquiry'?" Wei Wuxian asked.

"Inquiry" was a famous song composed by the forebears of the Lan Clan of Gusu. It was different from "Evocation" in that it was used in circumstances when the identity of the deceased was unknown and there was no medium. One who wished to pose an inquiry made it known through the guqin's melody, and with "Inquiry" serving as the conduit, the answer of the deceased would be transformed into notes and plucked upon the strings.

When the strings moved on their own, it meant Lan Wangji had successfully gained an audience with one of the deceased within this stone bunker. Next, both parties would engage in a duet of question and answer through the language of the guqin.

Guqin language was a unique and secret cipher of the Lan Clan of Gusu. Although Wei Wuxian had dabbled in many subjects, there were nevertheless things he could not wrap his head around, and guqin language was one of these.

He said softly, "Hanguang-jun, ask them for me: What is this place? What's it for? Who built it?"

Lan Wangji was proficient in guqin language, and without needing to think, he strummed a few clear notes. A moment later, the strings played on their own a few times more.

Wei Wuxian quickly asked, "What'd it say?"

"Do not know," Lan Wangji replied.

"Huh?"

Lan Wangji explained unhurriedly, "It said, 'Do not know.'"

"..."

Wei Wuxian stared at him and suddenly recalled a certain conversation regarding "whatever" many years ago. He rubbed his nose, feeling miffed.

Look at how much Lan Zhan's grown. He's even learned how to talk back to me now.

The first question was unsuccessful, so Lan Wangji played another verse. The strings responded again, and it was still the same two clanging notes from before. This time, Wei Wuxian understood the answer as "do not know" again.

He pressed him, "What did you ask?"

"Cause of death," Lan Wangji replied.

Wei Wuxian said, "If they were blindsided by it, then it certainly is possible for them not to know their own cause of death. Why don't you ask if they know who killed them?"

Lan Wangji raised his hands and strummed the strings once more. However, the response was still the two clanging notes: "Do not know."

An imprisoned soul who did not know what this place was, did not know their own cause of death, and did not know who killed them. This was the first time Wei Wuxian had met such a clueless deceased.

His mind turned, and he said, "Then switch the questions to something else. Ask them if they're a man or a woman. They have to know that at least?"

Lan Wangji played accordingly. After he withdrew his hands, a different string flicked with force.

Lan Wangji translated, "Man."

"Finally, something they know," Wei Wuxian commented. "Continue. Ask if there's a boy about fifteen years old who came here?"

The answer: "Yes."

Wei Wuxian then asked, "Where is he now?"

The strings paused for a moment before giving the answer.

Wei Wuxian quickly asked, "What did he say?"

Lan Wangji turned solemn. "He said, 'Right here.'"

Wei Wuxian was stunned into silence.

"Here" should have meant this stone bunker, but they had searched the whole place and hadn't seen Jin Ling.

Wei Wuxian said, "He can't lie, can he?"

"He cannot, when I am here," Lan Wangji replied.

This was true: the inquirer was Hanguang-jun, and under his control, the spirit could not lie and had no choice but to answer honestly. Wei Wuxian searched, turning the stone chamber inside out to see if there were any mechanisms or secret passageways he'd missed. Lan Wangji contemplated briefly, then inquired two verses more. After he received the answer, his face changed a little.

Seeing this, Wei Wuxian quickly asked, "What did you ask now?"

"His age, his origin," Lan Wangji replied.

Both questions were probing for the spirit's identity, and Wei Wuxian knew he must've gotten an unusual answer.

"And?"

"Fifteen, from Lanling," Lan Wangji said.

Wei Wuxian's face drastically changed too.

The soul "Inquiry" had invited was Jin Ling's?!

He quickly stopped to listen intently. He couldn't be sure, but in the overwhelming clamor, it seemed he really could faintly hear Jin Ling's weak cries.

Lan Wangji continued the discussion. Wei Wuxian knew he must be inquiring about the specific spot, and he stared at the strings, waiting for Jin Ling's answer.

This time, the response was fairly long. Once Lan Wangji finished listening, he turned to Wei Wuxian.

"From where you are, face southwestward and listen to the sound of the strings. Move one step forward with every note. Once the sound ceases, he will be before you."

Without a word, Wei Wuxian turned to the southwest. Behind him came several strums, so he took seven steps. However, there still was nothing in front of him.

The strings still plucked, but the intervals between the notes were growing longer and longer, and he was thus also walking slower and slower. Another step, two steps, three steps…

He walked six steps before the sound of the guqin finally fell silent, and the strings no longer strummed.

And yet, what was before him was only a wall.

This wall was built from grayish-white stone bricks, and every block was seamlessly stacked. Wei Wuxian turned around.

"…He's inside the wall?!"

Bichen was unsheathed and four streams of blue light swept past, carving overlapping lines that resembled the character for "well"[7] neatly onto the wall. The two rushed up and started tearing apart the bricks, and after removing several of them, a large swath of black earth was revealed.

So there were two layers to the walls of this stone bunker, and between the two layers of stone bricks there was a vein of earth. Wei Wuxian dug out a large dirt clod with his bare hands, and in the blackish mud there was a human face with its eyes tightly shut.

---

7   The Chinese character for "well" is 井.

It was the missing Jin Ling!

Jin Ling's face was sunken inside the earth, and the moment it was revealed, air rushed into his mouth and nose. Instantly, he started gasping with vigor. Seeing he was alive, Wei Wuxian was finally able to relax. Jin Ling's life really had been hanging by a thread. If not, "Inquiry" wouldn't have caught his soul as it was about to leave his body. Thankfully he hadn't been buried inside the wall for too long. If they had delayed for another quarter of an hour, he would've suffocated to death.

The two hurriedly dug him out of the wall. Who would've thought they'd pull out mud along with the carrot? The moment Jin Ling emerged from the earth, the longsword on his back hooked out something else too.

An arm decayed to nothing but eerie white bones!

Lan Wangji laid Jin Ling down on the ground and felt for his pulse to administer aid. Wei Wuxian, on the other hand, picked up Bichen's sheath and skillfully prodded and dug along the bone arm. Not long after, a complete skeleton appeared before him.

This skeleton was in the same position that they'd found Jin Ling: buried inside the wall, still standing. The ghastly white bones were a stark contrast to the pitch-black mud, piercing to the eyes. Wei Wuxian dug through the earth and tore off another few bricks, and sure enough, after rooting about, he discovered another set of bones nearby.

This set hadn't rotted completely just yet—there was still flesh attached to the bones and even some disheveled ebony hair on the skull. The ragged clothes were cherry-red. Evidently, this was a woman. She wasn't standing, though. Her posture was bent at the waist, and the reason she was bending likely involved the third set of corpse bones, curled up near her legs.

CHAPTER 5: THE SUNNY PAIR

Wei Wuxian didn't dig any further.

He backed up a few steps. The clamoring noise in his ears was tempestuous and insolent like the tides. He could practically be certain now: the thick walls of this stone fortress were stuffed full of corpses. Above the head, below the feet, southeast, northwest; standing, sitting, lying, crouching...

What exactly was this place?!

6
The Malevolent

RIGHT THEN, the unconscious Jin Ling suddenly sat up.

In front of the other two, he staggeringly crawled to his feet with eyes still closed. Wei Wuxian wanted to see exactly what he was going to do, so he didn't move. He saw Jin Ling slowly bypass him, then lift his leg and step into the wall anew, exactly where he had just been buried. He laid his hands by his sides. Even his posture was exactly the same as before.

Wei Wuxian yanked him out of the wall again, both amused and weirded out. Just as he was going to tell Lan Wangji that they shouldn't stick around, a sudden angry barking from the distance made him jolt. Ever since they had gone inside, the black-haired spirit dog had been obediently sitting outside the hole, wagging its tail. It was at once pitiful and anxious as it waited for them to bring its master back out, so it didn't make any more noise. Yet now it was roaring even more viciously than before.

"Something is amiss outside the bunker," Lan Wangji said.

He reached out to help support Jin Ling, but Wei Wuxian rushed to carry the boy on his back.

"Let's go out and see!"

The two swiftly went back the way they'd come. As they bent down and exited the hole, they saw that the black-haired spirit dog had its back facing them and was growling in a particular direction.

Wei Wuxian braced himself and tried to go over, but he just couldn't bear to listen to that sound and unconsciously backed up a number of steps. But the dog only had to turn its head and notice he was carrying Jin Ling before it came dashing over. Wei Wuxian wailed, but just as he was about to throw Jin Ling off his back, Lan Wangji sidestepped and blocked the dog.

The black-haired spirit dog immediately halted, then dropped its tail. It didn't pant, because there was something dangling from its jaws. Lan Wangji went over, bent down, and took out a piece of cloth from between its teeth. He returned to pass it to Wei Wuxian to see—it seemed to be a piece of a robe's hem. There must've been someone who was spying or wandering nearby, and the person must've acted suspiciously. Otherwise, the black-haired spirit dog wouldn't have barked with such animosity.

Wei Wuxian said, "They're not far away, chase after them!"

However, Lan Wangji said, "No need. I know who it is."

"Me too," Wei Wuxian said. "The same people who spread the Xinglu Ridge rumors, unleashed the walking corpses, set up the maze array, and built the stone fortress. And those sabers. But if we don't catch them now, it'll be hard to track them down later."

"I will give chase. You and Jin Ling?" Lan Wangji asked.

"I'll take him down Xinglu Ridge and find a place in Qinghe to settle him. The place where we ran into that quack doctor, let's meet up there."

The exchange was extremely rushed, and Lan Wangji only paused for a moment.

But still, Wei Wuxian added, "Go on. Take any longer and they'll get away. I'll be there!"

At the "I'll be there," Lan Wangji gave him a deep look. Without another word, he turned to take his leave. The black-haired spirit dog instantly moved to pounce at him once more, and Wei Wuxian wailed immediately.

"Wait, wait, wait, wait! Take the dog with you! TAKE THE DOG!!!"

And so Lan Wangji had no choice but to turn back. He gave the black-haired spirit dog a domineering look, and it didn't dare disobey, whimpering pitifully as it followed behind Lan Wangji. As it went along, it still gazed back at Jin Ling every few steps. Wei Wuxian wiped his sweat, then glanced back at those eerily white stone bunkers, resettled Jin Ling on his back, and went straight down Xinglu Ridge.

It was near dusk by then. He carried an unconscious youth on his back, both of them covered in dirt and looking to be in quite a sorry state, and for this they attracted frequent looks from passersby on the road. Wei Wuxian returned to the street where Jin Ling had called his dog to chase him earlier that day and found an inn. He used the money he'd fished from Lan Wangji's person to buy two sets of new clothing and asked for a room. He pulled off Jin Ling's robes, wrinkly from being buried in the earth but with the embroidery of the Sparks Amidst Snow family insignia still clear upon them. However, as he proceeded to pull off his boots, he stopped abruptly.

On Jin Ling's calf, there seemed to be a patch of shadow. Wei Wuxian crouched down and rolled his pant leg up. In doing this, he discovered it wasn't a shadow but a bruise. This wasn't a bruise from an injury. Rather, it was the mark of an evil curse.

A curse mark was a special blemish that evil spirits left on their prey. When it appeared, it meant that the person had encountered something exceedingly wicked—and that something would definitely come back to claim its target. Perhaps it would bide its time and take ages to come calling, or perhaps it would come that very night. In milder cases, it would simply remove the marked limb. In serious cases, it simply took your life.

Jin Ling's entire leg had turned black, and that mark was still festering further upward. Wei Wuxian had never seen a curse mark with such a dense black color, nor one spreading across this wide of an area. The more he inspected, the more grave his expression became. He dropped Jin Ling's pant leg and undid Jin Ling's inner robe. Seeing his chest and abdomen areas were clear and that the curse mark hadn't yet spread that far, he sighed a breath of relief.

Right then, Jin Ling opened his eyes.

He was dazed for a good while, his body bare and exposed to the chilly breeze. Then, he suddenly snapped awake and scrambled upright in a hurry, his face flushing as he yelled.

"WH-WH-WH-WHAT ARE YOU DOING?!"

Wei Wuxian laughed. "Aiyoh, you're awake."

It seemed Jin Ling was greatly shaken. He grabbed his inner robes, shrinking into the corner of the bed.

"What were you gonna do?! Where are my clothes?! Where's my sword?! Where's my dog?!"

"I was just going to dress you," Wei Wuxian said.

His expression and tone of voice were as compassionate as that of an old grandma wanting to add warm layers for her little grandson. Jin Ling clung to the wall, his hair loose and disheveled.

"I'M NOT A CUT-SLEEVE!!!"

Wei Wuxian was delighted. "What a coincidence, I am!!!"

Jin Ling grabbed his sword from the side of the bed, looking very much like he was going to kill himself to protect his honor should Wei Wuxian come a step closer. Wei Wuxian had to expend real effort to stop laughing.

He said, hugging his belly, "What are you so scared for? It's just a joke! I worked so hard to dig you out of that wall, aren't you even going to say thanks?"

In the midst of all the kerfuffle, Jin Ling grabbed a fistful of his messy hair and smoothed it out to appear more presentable as he said angrily, "If not for that, the fact that y-y-you dared strip me—for that I-I-I would've killed you a million times!"

"Don't. Dying once was painful enough," Wei Wuxian said. "All right, all right, put the sword down."

Still in a mess of confusion, Jin Ling put his sword down as told.

During the "Inquiry" session, his living soul had left his body and he couldn't remember much of anything. Despite this, he did vaguely know that the person in front of him was the one who had dug him out and carried him the entire way down the mountain. After he'd gotten buried inside that wall, there had been a period of time when he was still conscious, and the fear and despair in his heart had entirely consumed him. He'd never imagined the one who'd break through that wall, who'd save him from his fear and despair, would be this man whom he'd detested at first sight. His face changed colors: paling and flushing, blushing and embarrassed. His thoughts were flurries in the air, floating without a place to land.

Suddenly, he noticed the sky outside the window was already darkening, the night scarcely scattered with stars, and was instantly alarmed at the sight. It just so happened that Wei Wuxian had bent down to pick up the new clothes scattered on the ground, so Jin Ling hopped off the bed, pulled on his boots, grabbed his outer robe, and ran out the door.

Wei Wuxian had thought he'd be mopey for at least a few hours after enduring such torture. Who could've known the youths were so full of energy? Jumping around perfectly fine again in the blink of an eye, running out and disappearing from sight in a flash. Remembering that dire-looking curse mark on his leg, Wei Wuxian quickly yelled after him.

"What are you running for?! Come back!"

Jin Ling kept sprinting as he draped his wrinkled and dirty family robe back on, yelling back, "Don't follow me!"

He was lithe and his legs long, and it took only a handful of strides for him to charge out of the inn. Wei Wuxian chased after him for a number of streets and was finally actually thrown off his trail.

After searching around, twilight was looming, and the crowds on the streets were dwindling. Wei Wuxian gritted his teeth.

"Outrageous. That child is absolutely outrageous!"

With no other choice, he was about to give up. Just then, the furious voice of a man came from ahead, at the end of the long street.

"I only scolded you a little, and you decided to run off and disappear. Are you a spoiled young mistress?! Your temper's getting worse by the day!"

Jiang Cheng!

Wei Wuxian quickly ducked into an alleyway. Soon after, Jin Ling's voice came as well.

"Didn't I already come back perfectly fine? Stop nagging me!"

So, Jin Ling didn't come to Qinghe alone. No wonder. Jiang Cheng was there to assist him last time at Mount Dafan, so why wouldn't he come this time? But judging by the state of things, the two had a fight at Qinghe Town, which was why Jin Ling had climbed Xinglu Ridge alone. He must've run off in such a rush earlier because Jiang Cheng had threatened to teach him a lesson if he didn't return by nightfall, or something along those lines.

"Perfectly fine?" Jiang Cheng scolded. "You look like you rolled in the gutters, and you're telling me 'perfectly fine'? Aren't you embarrassed, wearing your family's uniform like this?! Hurry back and change this instant! Say it right now: What did you run into today?"

Jin Ling replied, irritated, "I already said I didn't run into anything. I tripped and fell; this trek was a total waste of time. Ow!" he yowled. "Don't pinch me like that! I'm not three!"

Jiang Cheng berated him sharply, "Oh, so you think I can't manage you anymore?! Let me tell you, even when you're thirty, I can still pinch you. If you dare run off on your own without saying anything again, the whip will be ready!"

"It's precisely because I don't want anyone's help—that I don't want anyone managing me—that I went alone," Jin Ling protested.

Wei Wuxian thought, *Everything else aside, Jiang Cheng saying he has the temper of a spoiled young mistress really is right on the money.*

"And now?" Jiang Cheng demanded. "What did you catch? Where's the black-haired spirit dog your uncle gave you?"

Taken by Lan Zhan to who knows where, Wei Wuxian was just thinking, when at the other end of the alley there came familiar barking.

Wei Wuxian's face changed drastically. His legs moving on their own; he charged out like a nasty arrow was hot on his trail. The black-haired spirit dog dashed over from the other end of the alleyway, passed Wei Wuxian, and pounced on Jin Ling's legs, wagging its tail with great affection.

Since the dog had appeared, that meant Lan Wangji had most likely caught the spy that had been lurking near the stone bunkers and gone to their appointed meeting place. However, at this moment, Wei Wuxian didn't have the time to think about that.

His mad dash had just so happened to bring him in front of Jiang Cheng and Jin Ling, as well as a large group of Jiang Sect disciples.

Both parties froze for a moment, then Wei Wuxian silently turned on his heel to flee.

He hadn't run very far before he heard the sizzling sound of lightning, and a long purple electric current wrapped around his calf like a venomous snake. A paralyzing pain flowed through his body from top to bottom, then he was yanked back, instantly collapsing to the ground. After that, he felt the front of his chest tighten. Someone had picked him up by the back of his robes. With astonishing speed, Wei Wuxian reached to grab for his spirit-trapping pouch, but it was taken away from him before he could manage.

With him firmly in his grasp, Jiang Cheng took a few steps, walked to the nearest inn, and kicked open the door that was already half-shut.

The inn owner had just been about to close down for the night, but suddenly there was a handsome and ill-tempered man in noble and elegant dress kicking his door open and storming in. That same guest was dragging someone with him, looking very much like he was going to cut the person's stomach open right there, and the inn owner was scared mute. A sect disciple came over, explained the situation to him in low whispers, and stuffed up any further protests with money. The inn owner then quickly hid in the back hall. There was no need for instructions; the Jiang Clan disciples quickly spread out, surrounding the inn inside and out, guarding the place so tightly that not even a drop of water could trickle through.

Jin Ling stood on the side, looking like he wanted to speak, bewildered and uncertain.

Jiang Cheng barked at him fiercely, "I'll deal with you in a moment. Stand right there and don't move!"

Ever since he could remember, Jin Ling had never seen such an expression on Jiang Cheng's face before. This uncle of his, who from a young age had single-handedly led the reputable cultivation sect of the Jiang Clan of Yunmeng, had always been coldly stern and somber, and the words he spoke were merciless and unkind. And yet now, though he was desperately trying to suppress any unnecessary expression, his eyes still flashed with terrifying light.

That face was forever colored by pride, twisted by sneers, and veiled by gloom. But now, it was as though it had brightened. It was hard to tell whether he was gritting his teeth with bone-deep hatred or whether he was feral with joy.

"Lend me your dog," Jiang Cheng said.

Jin Ling snapped out of his shock and hesitated for a moment. Jiang Cheng's gaze, sharp as lightning, came sweeping over, and only then did Jin Ling whistle. The black-haired spirit dog scurried over in a few trots. Wei Wuxian was frozen stiff as an iron board and could only let the man drag him, stumbling along step by step.

Jiang Cheng found an empty room and threw Wei Wuxian inside. The door closed behind him. the black-haired dog had followed in behind, sitting by the entrance. Both of Wei Wuxian's eyes were glued to it, high on guard in case it came pouncing over. Reflecting on how he'd been so quickly apprehended, Wei Wuxian thought to himself that Jiang Cheng really did know him like the back of his hand.

As Wei Wuxian ruminated, Jiang Cheng slowly sat down by the table and poured himself a cup of tea.

The two were silent for a long while. The cup of tea was steaming. Without having drunk a single sip, Jiang Cheng suddenly and viciously hurled it to the ground.

The corner of Jiang Cheng's lip curled up slightly. "You...do you have nothing to say to me?"

Growing up together, Jiang Cheng had lost count of how many times he'd witnessed the pathetic way Wei Wuxian dashed madly from the jaws of dogs. It was fine if Wei Wuxian refused to admit it to others, but this was something Jiang Cheng knew so very well and nothing Wei Wuxian could talk his way out of. This was a test more difficult to pass than facing Zidian.

Wei Wuxian replied earnestly, "I don't know what to say to you."

Jiang Cheng said softly, "You won't repent, just as expected."

Their conversations, back then, were always filled with fleet-footed sarcasm. They were constantly trying to pull the rug out from under each other. So, Wei Wuxian replied without thinking.

"You haven't improved at all either."

Jiang Cheng laughed out of sheer anger. "Very good. Let us see, then, who's the one who hasn't improved in the least?"

He remained seated and unmoving at the table but gave a shout. At the sound, the black-haired spirit dog immediately stood at attention!

Being in the same room as this creature already had Wei Wuxian in a cold sweat. But seeing a vicious dog half the size of a grown man appearing inches in front him in an instant with its teeth bared, its ears perked and its eyes sharp, the sound of its low growling sounding by his ears—waves of numbness coursed through him from the bottoms of his feet to the top of his head. He didn't remember much, anymore, of his time wandering the streets homeless when he was younger. The only thing he did remember was the panic of being chased and the unbearable pain of the sharp teeth and claws of dogs digging into his flesh. The fear had been deeply planted in his heart back then and could not fade or be overcome, no matter what.

Suddenly, Jiang Cheng gave him a side-eye. "What's your name?"

Wei Wuxian's wits were so scrambled that he couldn't recall whether he said anyone's name right then. It wasn't until Jiang Cheng commanded the black-haired spirit dog to retreat that he arduously regained himself. After blanking for a moment, he wrenched his head back. Jiang Cheng, meanwhile, had left his seat. A horsewhip hung askew on his waist, and he rested his hand over it, bending down to regard Wei Wuxian's face. After a brief pause, he straightened up.

He said, "Speaking of, I forgot to ask you. Since when have you gotten along so well with Lan Wangji?"

Wei Wuxian instantly figured out whose name he had blurted unconsciously just now.

Jiang Cheng smiled darkly. "It really is curious, why he went to such lengths to protect you, that time at Mount Dafan."

He then quickly corrected himself.

"No. The one Lan Wangji was protecting might not have been you. After all, there is no way the Lan Clan of Gusu would forget what you and that loyal dog of yours have done. How could someone like him, so lauded for his manners and solemn righteousness, possibly tolerate you? Perhaps he shares some sort of relationship with this body you've stolen."

His words were harsh and cruel. Everything he said was backhanded praise, heavy with implication.

Wei Wuxian couldn't listen anymore. He said, "Watch your tongue."

"I never do. Did you forget that, perhaps?" Jiang Cheng said.

"I must have," Wei Wuxian said derisively.

Jiang Cheng snorted. "As if you're one to tell me to watch my tongue. Did you remember to watch *your* tongue with Jin Ling, back at Mount Dafan?"

Wei Wuxian's face instantly stiffened.

Jiang Cheng, having cornered him again, appeared to brighten up once more. He sneered. "'Didn't your mother teach you any manners?' What an excellent rebuke, so well said. The reason there's so much talk behind Jin Ling's back is all thanks to you. An elder of your eminence is apt to forget—you've forgotten the things you've said, forgotten the promises you've made. But don't you dare forget exactly how his parents died!"

Wei Wuxian's head shot up. "I didn't forget! I was only…"

But no matter how he tried, he came up short on how to continue after that "only."

"Only what? Are you tongue-tied? That's all right. You can return to Lotus Pier, kneel before my parents' altar, and take your time to think about what to say."

Wei Wuxian composed himself, his mind turning rapidly as he tried to think of a way to get out of this. Although he missed Lotus Pier desperately, the place he wanted to return to wasn't the Lotus Pier of today, which had changed beyond recognition!

Suddenly, there was the sound of urgent footfalls dashing close. The door banged with the sound of someone's slapping palms.

Jin Ling was calling from outside the room, "Jiujiu!"

Jiang Cheng raised his voice. "Didn't I tell you to stay where you were? What are you doing here?!"

"Jiujiu, I have something very important to tell you!" Jin Ling exclaimed.

"What is *so* important that you have to say it right now, instead of when I was scolding you earlier?" Jiang Cheng demanded.

Jin Ling retorted angrily, "It's because you kept scolding me earlier that I didn't say anything! Do you want to listen or not? If not, then I'm not going to tell you anymore!"

Jiang Cheng flung the door open, fuming. "Out with it, then scram!"

Jin Ling stepped inside the moment the wooden door opened. He had already changed into a new set of white uniform robes.

"I actually did run into something really troublesome today. I think I ran into Wen Ning!"

Jiang Cheng's brows knitted, and his hand was immediately on his sword. He looked murderous. "When? Where?!"

"This afternoon," Jin Ling said. "About five kilometers from here, there's a dilapidated house. I only went there because I heard there'd been unusual sightings. Who knew a fierce corpse was hidden inside?"

Jin Ling made it sound so real, but every word Wei Wuxian heard was a bald-faced lie. He knew better than anyone where Jin Ling had been earlier this afternoon. Besides, once Wen Ning went into hiding, unless Wei Wuxian summoned him directly, he would never allow a junior to discover his trail so easily.

"Why didn't you say so sooner?!" Jiang Cheng said.

"I wasn't sure," Jin Ling said. "The fierce corpse moved extremely fast; the moment I went over, it fled, and I only just caught a glimpse of its shadow before it got away. But back at Mount Dafan, I heard those chains that were on him, which was why I wondered if it might be him. If you didn't yell at me so much, I would've told you the moment I got back. And now if he's run off and you don't manage to catch him, you'll have to blame your own bad temper, not me."

He clearly wanted to poke his head in further, but Jiang Cheng angrily shut the door in his face with a bang.

He said through the door, "I'll deal with you later! Beat it!"

Jin Ling *oh*-ed, and the sound of his footsteps retreated into the distance. Seeing Jiang Cheng turn around, Wei Wuxian quickly screwed his face into a complicated expression as if he were losing color from alarm, as if panicked thoughts were racing through his mind. *"My secret's been found out! What to do? Wen Ning's been discovered!"*

Jin Ling was pretty clever. He knew Jiang Cheng hated Wen Ning to the very marrow of his bones and was able to lie to his face on the spot—and so smoothly too. Jiang Cheng had known the Yiling Patriarch often appeared together with the Ghost General to wreak havoc, and he already suspected that Wen Ning was nearby. On hearing Jin Ling's story, he believed it 60 percent. After Wei Wuxian's reaction, he believed another 20 percent. On top of that, he was engulfed with rage whenever he heard Wen Ning's name, his anger surging to his head, so he had no sense left in him to doubt. His chest was going to explode from fury. He raised the whip, lashing the ground right next to Wei Wuxian.

He spat hatefully, "You really do take that good, obedient dog of yours everywhere!"

"He's already a dead man, and I was dead once too. What more do you want from us?" Wei Wuxian asked.

Jiang Cheng pointed at him with the whip. "What more do I want? He can die a thousand times, ten thousand times, and my hatred will not be appeased! Since he didn't perish back then, very good! I will destroy him myself today. I will burn him to ashes—right now, right in front of you!"

He slammed the door in his wake, barking instructions to Jin Ling in the main hall.

"Watch the man in the room carefully. Don't believe anything he says—don't listen to anything he says! Don't let him utter a single sound. If he dares to whistle or play the flute, gag him. If you can't, cut off his hands or his tongue!"

Wei Wuxian knew Jiang Cheng said that purposely for him to hear, to threaten him to not try anything funny. And of course, not taking him along was guarding against Wei Wuxian seizing the opportunity to control Wen Ning. However, Jin Ling didn't sound worried in the least.

"I got it. It's not like I don't know how to watch someone. Jiujiu, what were you doing, locked in that room with that damn cut-sleeve? What'd he do now?"

Jiang Cheng replied, "That's none of your business. Remember to keep a good eye on him. If he disappears, so help me, I'll break your legs!"

He then demanded the general direction of his target and set off to pursue the nonexistent Wen Ning with half the disciples in tow.

After a brief wait, Jin Ling's arrogant voice issued a command. "You, go over there. You, go stand watch on the side. You guys, stand by the main entrance. I'm going to go in and have a talk with him."

The sect disciples didn't dare disobey and acknowledged the order. A short moment later, the door to the room was opened and Jin Ling's head poked in, his eyes shining with pride at his own cleverness. Wei Wuxian sat up, and Jin Ling raised a finger to his lips. He walked in lightly and placed his hand on Zidian, mumbling an incantation under his breath.

Zidian would only obey the command of one it acknowledged as a legitimate owner. Jiang Cheng must've instructed it to recognize Jin Ling as such, since the electrical current quiesced instantly. The whip transformed into a silver ring adorned with a purple crystal, which dropped into Jin Ling's fair-skinned palm.

Jin Ling whispered, "Go."

The sect disciples of the Jiang Clan of Yunmeng had been scattered everywhere at his haphazard orders, and making use of the disorder, the two tiptoed to make their escape by hopping out the window and scrambling up the wall. Once out of the inn, they bolted soundlessly. After running into the forest, Wei Wuxian heard an unusual sound behind him. When he looked back, he completely lost his mind with terror.

"Why is it following us too?! Tell it to go away!"

Jin Ling blew two short whistles. The black-haired spirit dog panted with its long lolling tongue, whined and flicked its pointy ears a few times, then turned around and ran off, looking depressed.

Jin Ling said derisively, "You're so useless. Fairy never bites anyone. It only looks ferocious, that's all. You see a spirit-dog that's undergone strict training and only bites evil creatures, and you take it for an average canine?"

"Hold up," Wei Wuxian said. "What did you call it?"

"Fairy. That's its name," Jin Ling replied.

"You gave a dog a name like that?!" Wei Wuxian was shocked.

Jin Ling replied with full confidence, "What's wrong with that? When it was little, it was called Little Fairy. I can't keep calling it that now that it's grown."

Wei Wuxian had to dispute this explanation. "No, no, no, that's not the issue—who taught you how to name pets?!"

But there was no doubt in Wei Wuxian's mind that it must've been his uncle. Jiang Cheng had also kept several puppies in the past, and they were all named something like "Jasmine," "Feifei," "Xiao-Ai,"[8] or other such wanton brothel names.

Jin Ling said, "Men don't bother with such trifling matters, so why are you nitpicking this?! All right?! Stop. After offending my uncle, you would've lost half your life for sure. Now that I'm letting you go, we're even."

"Do you know why your uncle apprehended me?" Wei Wuxian asked.

---

8 "Xiao-Ai" means "Little Love." "Fei" is the word for consort, and doubling a word in this makes it cutesy.

"Yeah. He suspects you're Wei Wuxian," Jin Ling said.

Wei Wuxian thought, *It's not "suspicion" this time. He's caught the right person.* Then he asked, "What about you? Aren't you suspicious?"

"It's not the first time my uncle has done something like this," Jin Ling said. "He would always rather catch the wrong person than let them go. But since Zidian couldn't whip out your soul, I've determined for now that you can't be him. Besides, that Wei guy isn't a cut-sleeve, but you still dared to harass…"

He didn't say to whom the harassment was directed, cutting off the topic with a violent shudder, then waving him off like he was shooing away the God of Misfortune.

"Either way, from today onward, you are no longer affiliated with the Jin Clan of Lanling! Don't come knocking on my family's door if you're gonna be all nutty! Otherwise, I won't let you off easy!"

Jin Ling turned to leave after he'd said his piece. However, after taking a few steps, he turned his head back.

"What are you standing around for? Are you waiting for my uncle to come and catch you? Let me make this clear—don't think I'll be grateful to you just because you saved me, and don't expect me to say anything sappy either."

Wei Wuxian strode over with his hands clasped behind his back. "Young man, sometimes in life, there are a few sappy things one must say."

"What?" Jin Ling asked.

"'Thank you' and 'I'm sorry,'" Wei Wuxian replied.

Jin Ling clicked his tongue. "Well, I refuse. What're you gonna do about it?"

"There'll come a day when you'll say them through tears," Wei Wuxian said.

Jin Ling scoffed, and Wei Wuxian suddenly said it himself.

"I'm sorry."

Jin Ling was taken aback. "What?"

"What I said to you back at Mount Dafan. I'm sorry," Wei Wuxian said.

It wasn't the first time Jin Ling had heard the accusation "Mother didn't teach you manners," but no one had ever apologized so earnestly before. To be hit right in the face with a "sorry" left him not knowing what to feel, and surprisingly, he became altogether uncomfortable.

He waved wildly and humphed. "It's nothing. It's not like you're the first person to say that anyway. It's true I don't have a mother. But I'm not any less than anyone just because of that! In any case, I'm gonna make everyone see clearly that I'm much stronger than all of you!"

Wei Wuxian smiled and was about to speak when his face suddenly changed colors.

He exclaimed, stunned, "Jiang Cheng? You!"

Jin Ling had stolen Zidian and released the man. He was already feeling jumpy. The moment he heard that name, he spun around in a hurry, and Wei Wuxian took the chance to hand-chop his neck.

He laid Jin Ling down on the ground and rolled up his trouser cuff to inspect the curse mark on his leg. He tried a few methods, but none made the mark fade. Knowing this to be a troublesome affliction, he let out a sigh a moment later.

While he couldn't dissolve the curse mark, he could transfer it onto his own body.

It was a while before Jin Ling slowly came to. He felt his neck, where a slight pain still lingered. He was so angry he leapt up and pulled his sword on the spot.

"You actually hit me! Not even my uncle has hit me before!"

Wei Wuxian was shocked. "Really? Didn't he always say he was going to break your legs?"

"He's all talk!" Jin Ling exclaimed furiously. "You damn cut-sleeve, what are you up to, I…"

Wei Wuxian hugged his head and cried at a target behind Jin Ling. "Ah! Hanguang-jun!"

Jin Ling was more scared of Lan Wangji than he was of his uncle, since his uncle was family but Hanguang-jun was not. Stricken, he turned and fled, yelling as he ran.

"You damn cut-sleeve! Cursed lunatic! I'll remember this! We're not done!"

Wei Wuxian was laughing so hard at his retreat that he couldn't breathe. Once Jin Ling was gone, he felt a dull tickle in his chest. He coughed for a bit before slowly reining in his laughter. Only then did he have the time to think upon other things.

Wei Wuxian had been nine years old when Jiang Fengmian carried him home.

The memories he had of that time were mostly blurry by now, but Jin Ling's mother Jiang Yanli remembered and had told him of it.

She'd said that when her father learned of the death of Wei Wuxian's parents, Jiang Fengmian had been determined to search for the child his old friends had left behind. He searched for a long time before finally finding that child in the Yiling area. The first time he set eyes on the child, he was kneeling on the ground, eating fruit peels that others had thrown away.

Winters and springs in Yiling were very cold. This child's clothing was threadbare, with the knees worn to tatters, and he clumsily balanced on his toes in two different shoes, neither one the right size. Although he was deeply immersed in rummaging for fruit peels, when Jiang Fengmian called out to him, he still remembered his name had a "Ying" in it and looked up. His cheeks were red and cracked from the cold, but he still wore a smile.

Jiang Yanli said he had been born with a smiling face, a natural smiling fortune. No sadness would be taken to heart, and he could be cheerful under any circumstances. It made him sound like a simpleton, but it was a good thing.

Jiang Fengmian fed Wei Wuxian a mere piece of melon, and that was enough for him to let Jiang Fengmian take him back. Jiang Cheng had been only eight or nine at the time and kept several puppies as pets at Lotus Pier. Jiang Fengmian noticed Wei Wuxian was terrified of dogs, so he softly instructed Jiang Cheng to give those puppies away. Jiang Cheng was very unwilling to do so and threw a tantrum, complete with hurling things, furious glares, and tearful, hysterical outbursts. However, in the end, the dogs were still sent away.

Although he harbored animosity toward Wei Wuxian because of this for a long time, after the two grew close, they henceforth became a true disaster duo that wreaked havoc wherever they went. When they ran into dogs after this, Jiang Cheng was always the one chasing them off for (and laughing unreservedly at) the boy who leapt up to the top of the trees to avoid them.

Wei Wuxian slowly walked to the place where he and Lan Wangji had agreed to meet. There were barely any lights and no one on the streets at night. He didn't need to look around: that white-clad form was standing at the end of the long street, his head hanging slightly, unmoving.

Wei Wuxian hadn't yet called out in greeting when Lan Wangji already looked up, spotting him. After their eyes met for a moment, he stalked over with a grim face.

CHAPTER 6: THE MALEVOLENT

Wei Wuxian unconsciously took a step back for some reason. He could almost see the blood turning Lan Wangji's eyes red. He had to say...Lan Wangji was looking mighty scary.

Yet unexpectedly, with just that step back, he stumbled and looked almost as if he was going to fall. Lan Wangji's face changed, and he dashed over, firmly gripping Wei Wuxian's wrist just like he had back at Mount Dafan, steadying him. He bent one knee to the ground, reaching to check his leg.

Wei Wuxian was quite shocked. He quickly said, "Don't, don't, don't, Hanguang-jun, you don't have to do that."

Lan Wangji looked up slightly, his light-colored eyes gazing at him. Then he lowered his head and continued to roll up his trouser leg. Wei Wuxian's hand was still in his clutches. He couldn't get away, and so he could only look up to the sky.

His leg was completely covered with the bruising black curse mark.

Lan Wangji stared at it for a good moment before he said, greatly embittered at the sight, "I was only gone for a few hours."

Wei Wuxian shrugged. "Several hours is a long time. Anything can happen. Come now, come now, you may rise."

He pulled Lan Wangji to his feet and continued.

"It's only a normal curse mark. When the evil spirit comes to seek me out, I'll just smash it to bits. Of course, Hanguang-jun, you'll have to help me. If you don't, I won't be able to handle it. Did you catch that person? Was it him? Where is he?"

Lan Wangji moved his gaze to the shop sign of an inn down the street, and Wei Wuxian said, "Let's resolve the matter of the stone fortress first."

Then he headed toward that inn. He hadn't noticed it before, but now felt his legs were a bit numb, probably from getting shocked by

Zidian. Thankfully, Jiang Cheng knew to control Zidian's power and didn't completely turn him into a charred, electric-sparking corpse.

Lan Wangji, standing behind him, suddenly called out, "Wei Ying."

Wei Wuxian faltered for a moment, then quickly responded like he hadn't heard that name. "What is it?"

"That was transferred from Jin Ling?" Lan Wangji asked.

It wasn't truly a question but a statement.

Wei Wuxian didn't comment, and Lan Wangji continued, "You ran into Jiang Wanyin."

On top of the curse mark were marks left by Zidian, so this wasn't difficult to deduce. Wei Wuxian spun around.

"As long as we both live in this world, we'll meet sooner or later."

"Stop. Don't go," Lan Wangji said.

"Why? Are you going to carry me?" Wei Wuxian said.

"…" Lan Wangji gazed at him quietly, and the smile hanging off of Wei Wuxian's lips froze. A foreboding shadow arose in his mind.

If this was the Lan Wangji of the past, he would've been stumped by the joke, put on a cold face, and left—or ignored him completely. But the Lan Wangji of now…it really was hard to say how he would react. Sure enough, when Lan Wangji heard him, he moved in front of Wei Wuxian and seemed to really be bending at the knees, lowering himself to carry him on his back. Wei Wuxian was stunned once again.

He quickly said, "Hold on, wait, I was just joking. I just got zapped by Zidian a couple times, that's all. It's not like my legs are broken. A full-grown man needing to be carried on someone's back is too unsightly."

"Is it unsightly?" Lan Wangji asked.

"Is it not?" Wei Wuxian countered.

After a moment of silence, Lan Wangji said, "But you've also carried me on your back before."

"Really? How come I don't remember?" Wei Wuxian said.

Lan Wangji replied impassively, "You never remember these things."

"Everyone says my memory's bad. Fine. It is what it is. Either way, that's a no."

"You really don't want to?" Lan Wangji pushed.

Wei Wuxian refused categorically. "No."

The two stared at each other in stalemate for a moment. Then suddenly, one of Lan Wangji's arms circled around his back. He bent forward slightly while the other hand swept beneath the crooks of Wei Wuxian's knees.

Wei Wuxian was smaller and lighter in build, so he was easily swept up, his body held in midair by a pair of strong arms. Wei Wuxian had never expected this to be the end result of his "no." Whether in his past or present life, this was the very first time he'd been treated this way by anyone.

He cried in alarm, "Lan Zhan!!!"

Lan Wangji, with Wei Wuxian in his arms, walked very steadily and answered very steadily. "You said not to carry you on my back."

"But I didn't say to carry me like this!" Wei Wuxian protested.

Thankfully, night had already fallen and there was no one on the streets, so it wasn't too embarrassing at least. Wei Wuxian wasn't a thin-skinned individual, so after being carried for a few steps, he relaxed. He batted at the sashes on Lan Wangji's chest and then laughed as he moved his hands as if to pull them apart.

"You wanna see who's more thick-skinned, right?"

Wei Wuxian was awash in that refreshing scent of sandalwood. Lan Wangji didn't look at him, his eyes staring straight ahead, unmoved. Ever that incomparably upright, incomparably serious, indifferent face. Seeing how his words were falling on deaf ears, Wei Wuxian thought as he continued to play with the sashes,

Can't believe Lan Zhan is actually so vindictive. He wants to get revenge for every little thing I teased him with in the past, dousing my fun with that cold water of his. What progress. Not only did his cultivation improve—so did his thick skin.

"Lan Zhan, did you already know it was me back at Mount Dafan?" Wei Wuxian asked.

"Mn," Lan Wangji replied.

"How?" Wei Wuxian was curious.

Lan Wangji lowered his eyes, "You want to know?"

"Yes." Wei Wuxian said affirmatively.

"You told me yourself," Lan Wangji said.

"Me? Because of Jin Ling? Because I summoned Wen Ning? It can't be any of that, can it?" Wei Wuxian wondered.

A ripple seemed to stir the pool of Lan Wangji's eyes. However, this barely noticeable disturbance soon faded, and they immediately returned to deep, clear waters.

He said sternly, "Think for yourself."

"It's because I can't that I'm asking you," Wei Wuxian complained.

This time, however, no matter how much he questioned, Lan Wangji kept his mouth shut and stopped responding. He entered the inn with Wei Wuxian in his arms, and aside from the clerk at the counter of the main hall who spat out his water, the other onlookers didn't act like anything was outrageous.

They came to the door of their room and Wei Wuxian said, "All right, we're here, you can put me down now. You don't have the hands to open…"

Before he finished, Lan Wangji performed an extremely indecorous act. This was perhaps the most boorish thing he'd ever done in his life.

With Wei Wuxian in his arms, he kicked the door open.

The two doors of the room sprang open, and the jittery person sitting inside immediately cried out.

"Hanguang-jun, I don't know, I don't know…"

After seeing the way the two outside the door had made their entrance, he arduously finished, dumbstruck.

"…I really don't know."

Truly the Head-Shaker.

It was as though Lan Wangji hadn't seen him. He carried Wei Wuxian inside, placing him on the mat. Nie Huaisang looked aghast and immediately opened his folding fan, blocking his own face. Wei Wuxian sized him up through that folding fan. This former classmate of his hadn't changed much over the years. He had been the same back then as he was now. He had a refined, scholarly face, yet always wore a submissive expression that made him look like an easy target for bullying into compliance. His outfit was tasteful, simple but remarkable; he must've spent a lot of time putting it together. Rather than the leader of a sect, he more resembled the idle rich. Even in dragon robes, he wouldn't have had the air of a crown prince. Even bearing a long saber, he had not the air of a cultivation leader.

He obstinately refused to admit to anything, so Lan Wangji set down the piece of fabric the black-haired spirit dog had torn off. Nie Huaisang tried to cover the part of his sleeve that was missing.

"I just happened to pass by, I really don't know anything," he said dolefully.

Wei Wuxian said, "Let me speak then, since you don't know. Try and see if you know something after you've listened."

Nie Huaisang hemmed and hawed, not knowing how to respond, so Wei Wuxian continued.

"There's talk of a 'Man-Eating Ridge' and a 'Man-Eating Fortress' in the Qinghe Xinglu Ridge area, but there weren't any real victims, so it was only a rumor. This rumor would cause regular folks to stay away from Xinglu Ridge; its real purpose is a line of defense. And that's only the first line.

"Where there is one, there are two. The second line of defense is the walking corpses at Xinglu Ridge. Even if there are normal folks who aren't afraid of the Man-Eating Fortress rumor and trespass up the ridge, or happen to enter the ridge by accident, they would flee at the sight of the walking dead. However, those walking corpses are few in number and weak in strength, so they can't cause any real damage.

"The third line of defense is the maze array near the stone bunkers. The first two defenses were to guard against normal people while this one guards against cultivators. However, its effect is limited to normal cultivators. As for cultivators equipped with spiritual devices or spirit hounds, or those who specialize in destroying maze arrays, or distinguished persons of Hanguang-jun's level, this line of defense is easily unraveled.

"Three lines of defense were erected for the purpose of hiding that stone fortress on Xinglu Ridge from discovery. It's more than evident who constructed that stone fortress. This is the domain of the Nie Clan of Qinghe. Other than the Nie family, there is no one who could so easily set down three defense checkpoints in Qinghe. Besides, you just happened to appear near the stone fortress and left evidence behind.

"What is the purpose of the Nie Clan of Qinghe constructing a Man-Eating Fortress on Xinglu Ridge? Where did the corpses inside the walls come from? Were they devoured? Sect Leader Nie, if you don't explain everything clearly today, when this gets out later, the cultivation world will all be knocking on your door for answers. When that time comes, even if you want to speak, no one will listen. Nor will they believe you."

Giving up, Nie Huaisang finally replied hopelessly, "That's not a Man-Eating Fortress at all. That…that's my family's ancestral grave!"

"Ancestral grave?" Wei Wuxian asked. "Whose family has an ancestral grave that buries blades and not bodies?"

Nie Huaisang said with a long face, "Hanguang-jun, before I say anything—will you promise that for the sake of our families' friendship, and the fact that my older brother and your older brother were sworn brothers, that no matter what I say, you…and the gentleman next to you, will absolutely not tell? And if this gets exposed in the future, please also help defend me and stand as witnesses. You have always been a man of your word. As long as you promise, I will believe you."

"As you wish," Lan Wangji said.

"You said it's not a man-eating fortress. Then has it devoured anyone?"

Nie Huaisang gritted his teeth and answered honestly, "Yes."

"Whoa…" Wei Wuxian breathed.

Nie Huaisang immediately added, "But it was only the once! The primary fault didn't lie with our family, and besides, it was decades ago! The story of the Man-Eating Fortress of Xinglu Ridge started back then. I…I only fanned the flames and exaggerated the rumors severalfold, that's all."

"Please elaborate," Lan Wangji said.

He sat there, the threat beneath those well-mannered words palpable. Nie Huaisang began his slow and reluctant explanation.

He said, "Hanguang-jun, you know our Nie family is different from the other prominent cultivation clans. Since our founding father was a butcher, the other clans all wield spiritual swords while our clan wields sabers."

This was a widely known fact, not a secret whatsoever. Even the insignia of the Nie Clan of Qinghe was the savage head of a beast that looked both like a hound and a wild boar.

Nie Huaisang continued, "Our cultivation method is different from the other clans, and with our founding father's butcher background…bloodshed was inevitable. The sabers wielded by our clan leaders throughout history have always been extremely heavy with resentment and killing aura. Almost every clan leader has suffered a qi deviation and died a violent death. Their characters were also irascible, and those sabers have a lot to do with it."

Take Nie Huaisang's older brother, Nie Mingjue, for example. This young cultivation leader was sworn brothers with Lan Xichen and Jin Guangyao. Chifeng-zun was decisive and resolute, dignified, and magnanimous; Zewu-jun was gentle like jade, noble and pure in character; and Lianfang-zun smooth and resourceful, sharp-witted and intelligent. The three took an oath of sworn brotherhood during the Sunshot Campaign. Each had their own praiseworthy deeds and were later venerated as the Three Zun by the cultivation world. However, in the prime of his life, Nie Mingjue's qi deviated during an important symposium and he died violently, his body bursting with blood. Many attendees of the symposium that day were injured while he was in the throes of madness. His dignified name, built up over a lifetime, fallen to such disgrace.

Nie Huaisang must've been thinking of his older brother, for he looked downcast. He continued, "While the clan leaders were still alive, the agitation of their sabers could be suppressed by their masters. However, once the masters were dead, they had no one to control them, so they would turn murderous."

Wei Wuxian arched his brow. "Well, that's hitting a bit close to the demonic cultivation path."

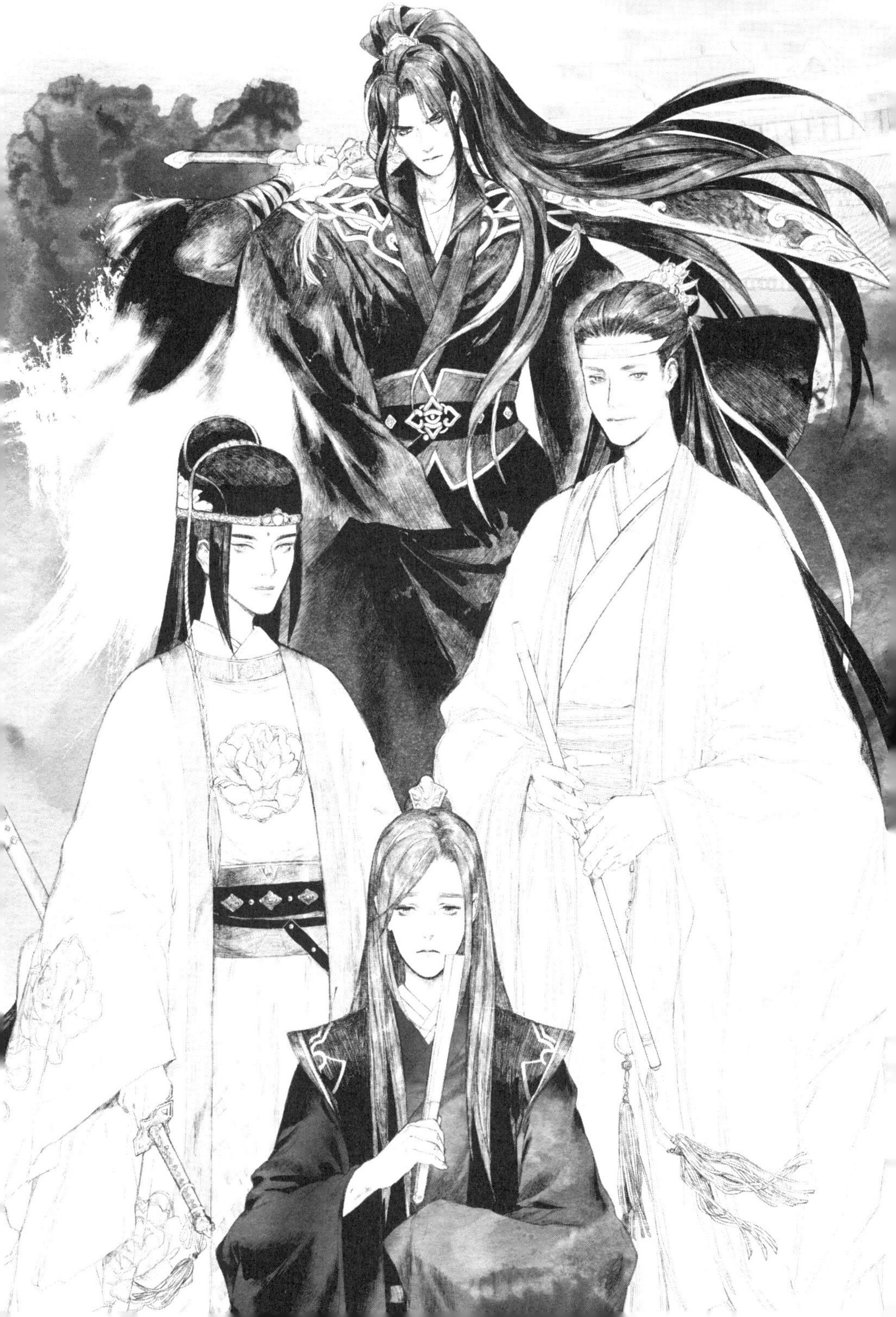

Nie Huaisang quickly explained, "It's different! The demonic path is called as such because it consumes human lives. But my family's sabers aren't after people—rather, they're after all nefarious beings such as resentful ghosts and belligerent spirits. They spend their entire lives exterminating those creatures, so if there's nothing for them to eradicate, they will stir up trouble themselves and cause unrest in the family. The spirit of a saber recognizes only one master, never to be handled by another. We descendants can't melt them down because one, it's disrespectful to their forebears, and two, melting doesn't necessarily solve this problem."

"Oh lord," Wei Wuxian commented.

"Aren't they just so?" Nie Huaisang said. "Sabers that followed their ancestral masters in hacking through obstacles and following their path of cultivation—they are lords in their own right."

He continued, "With advancements in cultivation through the generations, this problem grew more serious with time. Until the sixth clan leader of my family came up with a solution."

"Build this Man-Eating Fortress?" Wei Wuxian asked.

"No, no—although it's related, that wasn't thought of at first," Nie Huaisang answered. "This is what the sixth clan leader did. He built two coffins for his father's and his grandfather's sabers and dug a tomb. Nothing precious was placed inside the tomb. Instead, hundreds of corpses about to turn fierce were installed inside."

Lan Wangji creased his brows, and Nie Huaisang immediately interrupted in fright.

"Hanguang-jun, let me explain! Those corpses weren't killed by my family! They were arduously sought out and collected from all over! Many were bought at a hefty price. The sixth clan leader said, 'If those saber spirits want to fight evil, then we will give them evil to fight.' Burying those corpses about to change alongside the coffins housing the blades—it was to make burial offerings to the saber spirits. The saber spirits would suppress the transformation of those corpses, and at the same time, those corpses could mollify the saber spirits' yearning and madness. It would retain the current status quo, and they would balance each other. It was this method that allowed for generations of peace for us descendants to come."

"Then why was the stone fortress constructed afterward?" Wei Wuxian asked. "Why bury the bodies inside the walls? And you said it devoured someone?"

Nie Huaisang replied, "Those questions are actually one and the same. I guess you could say it…devoured someone. But it wasn't intentional!!! It was a saber tomb our sixth clan leader constructed, and it was built in a very common style of graves at the time, with the generations after simply following suit. But over fifty years ago, this grave was invaded by a band of graverobbers."

"Oh," Wei Wuxian said, thinking, *Well, that really is breaking ground where Taisui lies.*

"Tomb construction is such a huge ordeal; word gets out no matter how prudent and low-profile you try to be," Nie Huaisang said. "That band of graverobbers probably asked around and heard there was a grand tomb on Xinglu Ridge. They marked this target and came prepared. There were a couple of genuinely able cultivators who actually managed to decipher the position, break the maze array, and find our clan's saber tomb. They dug a hole and went down, entering the grave. Those in that profession have seen plenty of corpses, so they weren't afraid of the dead inside. But while they ransacked the place looking for gold and treasure, they were breathing right next to the bodies. Every single one of them were young and strong males, full of yang energy. You must understand, there were corpses about to transform lying in there!

"It's easy to imagine what happened next. Over a dozen corpses turned fierce on the spot. But that band of graverobbers were very capable and gutsy, and very well equipped at that; they actually managed to kill all the transformed walking corpses. After a vigorous fight, with body parts strewn everywhere, they finally realized this was a perilous place and were preparing to leave. It was when they were retreating that they were devoured!

"The number of corpses installed in the tomb is strictly controlled—not one more, not one less. Just enough to balance the saber spirits. But those graverobbers went in and caused havoc. If they'd only activated the corpses' transformation, it would've been all right. After they left, the saber spirits would energize and suppress them. But they just had to batter the bodies to pieces. Suddenly, there was a deficit of over a dozen bodies. In order to maintain enough fierce corpses to restrict the saber spirits, the saber tomb…had no choice… but to automatically seal the tomb completely, forcefully trapping them inside and having that group fill in the vacancies they had themselves created…

"With the destruction of the saber tomb, the clan leader at the time began to seek other methods. He selected another plot of land on Xinglu Ridge, and instead of building another tomb as a replacement, a Saber Offerings Hall was constructed. In order to prevent another visit by graverobbers, the bodies were hidden inside the walls to deceive others.

"This Saber Offerings Hall is thus the 'Man-Eating Fortress' in the rumors. Those graverobbers came to Qinghe disguised as hunters. When they never returned from Xinglu Ridge and there were no bones to be found, word began to spread that they were devoured by monsters on the ridge. Later, the stone fortress was erected, but before the new maze array was set up, someone saw it by accident in passing. Thankfully, none of the bunkers had doors, so he couldn't enter. But after descending the ridge, he told everyone he met that there was a creepy white fortress on the ridge, and that must be where the man-eating monsters reside. Our clan thought it'd be good to aggrandize the rumors so no one would dare go close to that area. So we embellished the story and created the 'Man-Eating Fortress' tale. But it really can eat people!"

From his sleeve, Nie Huaisang took out a handkerchief and a white pebble the size of a garlic head. The handkerchief was to wipe away his sweat, but he passed the white pebble over.

"You two can take a look at this."

Wei Wuxian took the white pebble to examine it. He discovered something white between the powder. It appeared to be…a human finger bone.

It was clear in his mind now. After Nie Huaisang wiped his sweat, he continued.

"As for that…little Jin-gongzi…I don't know how he managed to blow a hole in the wall. That he could do so to such a thick wall means he must've carried plenty of spiritual devices with him, but that's not the point… I mean to say, the place he blew up just so happened to be the earliest of the Saber Offerings Halls constructed on Xinglu Ridge. At the time, the idea of using two layered walls with earth in between—to separate the yang energy and prevent easy corpse transformation—hadn't been formulated, and bodies were put directly into the plaster. So, when little Jin-gongzi blew open a hole, he didn't notice he'd actually blown up a skeleton buried inside the walls. Soon after he entered, he was sucked into the walls of the stone bunker to replace the body he had blown up… I check on Xinglu Ridge regularly, and when I went today, that's what I saw. I had just picked up a rock and then there was a dog chasing after me.

Hahhh... The Saber Offerings Hall is pretty much the same as our ancestral grave, I really..."

The more Nie Huaisang spoke, the sadder he became.

"Generally, cultivators know this is my clan's domain, so they don't conduct Night Hunts in the Qinghe area. Who knew..."

Who knew he'd be so unlucky that first there was Jin Ling, disregarding the rules and setting his eyes on Xinglu Ridge? And then Lan Wangji and Wei Wuxian, who came on the directions of the ghost arm?

He said, "Hanguang-jun, and this gentleman...I've said everything. Please absolutely do not let this out. Otherwise..."

Otherwise—because the Nie Clan of Qinghe was already pretty much half dead at this point, if something like this got out, Nie Huaisang would become a condemned sinner in the history books and be too ashamed to face his ancestors when he entered those graves himself. No wonder he would rather be a secret laughingstock among the cultivation world than diligently cultivate, never mind wielding a saber. Should his cultivation come to fruition, he would become more irascible by the day and end up like his older brother and all those that had come before him: berserk and dying alongside a saber that would curse the world after his death. Rather than cause unrest in the clan, having zero accomplishments was the better choice.

This was a problem without a solution. The Nie clan had forged this path since its founding generation, so would its descendants have to denounce the path and foundation established by their forebears? The prominent cultivation clans all had their unique specialties. Just as the Lan Clan of Gusu was adept in music, the saber spirits of the Nie Clan of Qinghe were fierce and tough; their power was so mighty and destructive precisely because the skill required to master it was in a league of its own. If they were to abandon the discipline of their ancestors to start anew, to find a new path, who knew how many years that would take? Success would not be guaranteed. Not to mention, Nie Huaisang would never dare defect from the Nie clan to cultivate a different path. Thus, he had no choice but to be useless.

If he hadn't been a clan leader and could spend his life playing around and painting fans like he had back at the Cloud Recesses, he would definitely have been much more at ease than he was now. But since his older brother had passed away, no matter how much his abilities fell short of his aspirations, he had no choice but to shoulder the clan's heavy burden and stumblingly march forward.

After Nie Huaisang left, exhorting and pleading their silence all the way, Wei Wuxian zoned out for a while. Then suddenly, he noticed Lan Wangji walking over and bending one knee to the ground in front of him, rolling up his trouser leg seriously.

He quickly said, "Wait, again?"

"Expel this curse mark first," Lan Wangji said.

Within a day, Hanguang-jun had kneeled in front of him in this position on several occasions. While the other party was exceedingly serious, Wei Wuxian couldn't bear to watch such a scene.

"Lemme do it myself."

He quickly pulled up his trouser leg and saw the curse mark had spread to the entirety of his calf, climbing past his knee and crawling up the thigh.

Wei Wuxian glanced at it and said casually, "It's all the way up my inner thigh, now."

Lan Wangji twisted his head away and didn't respond. Wei Wuxian was puzzled.

"Lan Zhan?"

Lan Wangji turned his head back at the call, but his eyes were still dodging about. Seeing this, Wei Wuxian blinked. He felt like playing a trick on him, for some reason. Just as he was about to tease the man, however, there was suddenly a cracking sound from the table.

They both rose to their feet to look and saw the teacups and teapot were shattered on the ground. An evil-sealing qiankun pouch was lying among the white porcelain fragments and the spilled tea. The surface of the bag was pulsing as if something was trapped inside, desperate to get out.

Although this evil-sealing qiankun pouch appeared to only be the size of a palm, it possessed magical storage powers and was sewn inside and out with complicated spells to reinforce the multiple layers of the seal. Lan Wangji had originally sealed the arm inside the bag and weighed it down with the teacup on the table, but seeing it so agitated now finally reminded them it was time to play "Rest." If they didn't temporarily appease it every night with a song, then no matter how strong the evil-sealing qiankun pouch's subduing powers might be, it would not confine the ghost arm on its own.

Wei Wuxian reached for the flute at his waist but came up empty. He looked around, and as it turned out, the bamboo flute was already in Lan Wangji's hand. He had his head slightly bowed and carved at the bamboo flute in concentration for a while before handing it back. When Wei Wuxian took it back and looked at it, the tone holes and other little details were much cleaner and more exquisite after his mending.

"Play properly," Lan Wangji said.

Recalling the duet they'd played that was so horrible it had angered Lan Qiren awake before making him spit blood and faint once more, Wei Wuxian almost fell to the ground laughing. He thought, *Must've been hard for him to have tolerated my playing for so long.*

He stopped playing dumb about it and very seriously placed the bamboo flute to his lips. Unexpectedly, he had only played a couple of notes when the qiankun pouch instantly swelled many times over all of a sudden, standing up!

Wei Wuxian scoffed and played a cracked note. "What, is it so used to the ugly melody that if I play better, it doesn't like it anymore?"

As if in response, the evil-sealing qiankun pouch shot toward Wei Wuxian. The notes under Lan Wangji's fingers swerved, and with a sweep across the guqin, all seven strings strummed in unison, letting out an angry roar akin to a landslide. At this admonishment from the guqin, the evil-sealing qiankun pouch collapsed once more. Wei Wuxian continued playing like nothing had happened, and the tension that had stiffened Lan Wangji's wrists softened. He followed the melody of "Rest," and the sound turned tranquil and leisurely as they harmonized.

After the session was over, the evil-sealing qiankun pouch finally shrank back to its normal size and lay there, quiet and unmoving. Wei Wuxian stuck his flute back on his waist.

"It was never this agitated the past few days. It seems to have been triggered by something."

Lan Wangji inclined his head in agreement and turned to him. "And it is something on your person."

Wei Wuxian immediately looked down to inspect himself. There was only one thing that had been added to his person today—the curse mark transferred from Jin Ling. And that was something left on Jin Ling by the stone fortress of Xinglu Ridge. Did the strength of the ghost arm's reaction to the mark mean…

Wei Wuxian reasoned aloud, "Meaning, inside the walls of the Nie Saber Offerings Hall, there might be a part of its body?"

Early the next day, the two departed together to return to Xinglu Ridge.

Nie Huaisang, caught red-handed the day before, had given up the whole unsavory inside story. He had called together all the trusted sect disciples in the clan to come clean up the mess left by the intruders. When Wei Wuxian and Lan Wangji approached, he had just gotten people to refill the hole Wei Wuxian had dug Jin Ling out of, patching it up with a brand-new corpse. He wiped at his sweat as he watched the white bricks laid layer by layer. Yet unexpectedly, he looked back and his legs went weak.

He smiled apologetically. "Hanguang-jun…and this gentleman…"

Wei Wuxian cupped his hands and smiled. "Sect Leader Nie. Building walls, are you?"

Nie Huaisang had wiped his sweat so much with that handkerchief that he was going to wipe off a layer of skin at this point. "Yes, yes, yes…"

Wei Wuxian said, very sympathetically and with a little bit of shyness, "Sorry, but we might need to trouble you to rebuild again in a bit."

Nie Huaisang replied, "Yes, yes, yes… Huh?! Wait!"

Before he finished, Bichen was unsheathed. Nie Huaisang had to watch helplessly as the brick wall he had just rebuilt was cracked once more.

It was always easier to destroy than to build. Wei Wuxian tore the bricks down with insane speed, who knew how many times faster than they had been laying them. Nie Huaisang trembled, gripping his folding fan, aggrieved tears threatening to stream from his eyes. And yet Hanguang-jun was just standing there, without any sign or gesture, so Nie Huaisang didn't dare say anything. Lan Wangji gave him a succinct explanation of their reasons, and Nie Huaisang immediately pointed to the heavens and the earth to swear.

"No! There definitely aren't any! The corpses used in my clan's Saber Offerings Hall are all complete, there's definitely no male corpse missing an arm. If you don't believe me, I'll tear everything down to prove my innocence, but after that, everything needs to be repaired immediately without delay—this is my family's ancestral grave, you know..."

A number of the Nie sect disciples joined in, and with others doing the work, Wei Wuxian retreated, standing by the side to wait for the result. An hour later, more than half the bricks of the wall where Jin Ling had been buried were dismantled. Of the sect disciples, some pulled on face masks while others swallowed special red pills to prevent their breath and human qi from activating fierce corpse transformation. In the black dirt, sometimes a pale arm would be revealed, sometimes a leg with popped veins. There was also a mass of tangled and grimy black hair.

Every male corpse was roughly cleaned and placed flat in an orderly manner on the ground. Some of these corpses were already degraded to white bones, some were still in the process of rotting, and some were still very fresh. There were all sorts—but all of them had all of their limbs intact. They did not uncover a male corpse missing a left arm.

Nie Huaisang asked cautiously, "We only need to tear down this wall, right? Do we need to take down more? There's no need to, right?"

It was indeed enough. The curse mark on Jin Ling's body was extremely dark in color, so the creature who left it must've been buried very close to him at the time. It would definitely not have gone beyond the perimeter of this wall. Wei Wuxian crouched down by the row of corpses and pondered deeply.

Lan Wangji suggested, "Retrieve the evil-sealing qiankun pouch?"

It wasn't a bad idea to retrieve the left arm from the evil-sealing qiankun pouch to have it conduct the identification on its own. But if it came too close to the other parts of its body, they couldn't guarantee that wouldn't make it grow excited, thereby resulting in a more dangerous situation. And this location was incredibly unique, heavy with yin energy, which made the danger all the greater. This was why they'd prudently chosen to come during the day.

Wei Wuxian shook his head and pondered, *Could this arm be a woman's? No, I can tell from a look whether it was a man or a woman's arm... Then, could its master have three arms?!*

He was just amusing himself with this thought when Lan Wangji spoke up.

"The leg."

With that mention, Wei Wuxian finally remembered that he'd actually neglected the fact that the curse mark had been restricted to his leg.

He quickly exclaimed, "Pants off! Pants off!"

Nie Huaisang was immensely alarmed. "Why would you say such a shameful thing in front of Hanguang-jun?!"

"What's there to be shy about? We're all men here," Wei Wuxian said. "Give me a hand. Help me take the pants off the corpses. This doesn't concern the female bodies, just the male ones!"

He flashed his demonic claws, reaching for the trouser waists of the corpses on the ground. Nie Huaisang could never have expected this. He had only just told the whole sordid story the day before, and today he had to strip the corpses of their trousers inside his ancestors' Saber Offerings Hall. Male corpses, at that! He would definitely get a big ol' slap in the face from every single one of his ancestors when he himself died and entered the ground, he felt. Slapped silly until he was born crippled in his next life. Tears streamed uncontrollably down his face.

Thankfully, Lan Wangji stopped Wei Wuxian in the act. However, just as Nie Huaisang was going to praise him with an *"as expected of Hanguang-jun,"* he heard:

"Let me."

"You?" Wei Wuxian asked. "*You're* gonna do this?"

The corners of Lan Wangji's brows seemed to be faintly twitching like he was enduring something, and he repeated, "Do not touch them. Let me."

Of all the shocks Nie Huaisang had received today, this was the strongest.

Of course, Lan Wangji didn't actually remove the trousers of those corpses with his hands. He merely used Bichen's sword qi to lightly slash their clothing, revealing the skin underneath. Some didn't even need to have their clothes slashed, since they were already tattered.

It didn't take long before he said, "Found it."

The group quickly went over to see. The corpse next to Lan Wangji's white boots had, upon his thighs, a very faint threaded circle. The thin, flesh-colored stitches were dense and cramped. There was a subtle difference in the skin color above and below the threaded circle. It was obvious the legs and upper body of this corpse did not belong to the same person.

Those two legs were stitched on!

Nie Huaisang gaped.

Wei Wuxian asked, "Who is responsible for picking the corpses used for the Nie saber offerings?"

Nie Huaisang was in a confused daze. "Usually, it's the clan leader themselves who picks and stores the bodies while they're still alive. My older brother passed early and didn't have enough, so I helped him pick some… As long as the facial features and limbs were all intact, I'd keep the body. I don't know about the other ones…"

He definitely wouldn't know who'd snuck that corpse in, even if they asked him directly. The suspects were countless in number, ranging from the ones who'd provided the bodies to the internal personnel of the Nie Clan of Qinghe. They would probably have to find every single body part and put the pieces and the soul back together before they figured out what was going on.

It took great effort to remove the legs from the half-bodied male corpse. Wei Wuxian tucked them into a new evil-sealing qiankun pouch.

He said to Lan Wangji, "Looks like this good brother was dismembered by five horses, eh. Not only was the body divided, but the limbs were thrown everywhere—one there, one here. What measure of hatred could've prompted this? Let's pray he's not cut into too many pieces."

Although Nie Huaisang still said "see you next time" when they bid farewell, judging by the terror on his face, he probably never wanted to see them again in this lifetime. The two left Xinglu Ridge and returned to the inn, a safer place, before they took out the three limbs for a more detailed examination. Sure enough, the legs and the left arm had the same skin color. If they were placed near one another, it produced an intense reaction, causing them to shake nonstop, like they wanted to be rejoined. Unfortunately, the body's torso was missing, so that couldn't be done. But they definitely belonged to the same person.

Besides the few facts they managed to determine—that this was a man of large build with long and slender limbs, strong and healthy in body and soul, and possessing exceptional cultivation—nothing else was known. It was a bewildering mystery. Thankfully, the ghost arm quickly pointed out the next destination: southwest.

Following its direction, Wei Wuxian and Lan Wangji arrived at the city of Yueyang.

7
The Morning Dew

ONCE IN THE CITY, the two walked side by side among the bustling crowd.

Suddenly, Lan Wangji asked, "How is the curse mark?"

Wei Wuxian replied, "Jin Ling was buried too close to our good buddy at the time, so he got stained by quite a bit of resentment. It's faded a little but not entirely. We'll probably have to find the complete corpse, or at the very least the head, before I can think of a way to get rid of it once and for all. But it's not an issue."

"Good buddy" was the fellow who had been dismembered. Since they didn't know his identity, Wei Wuxian had suggested they call him "good buddy." Lan Wangji didn't say anything, but he didn't object either, so it was technically a silent agreement. Of course, he never used that term of address himself.

Lan Wangji asked, "How little is a little?"

Wei Wuxian gestured a measurement with his hands and replied, "A little is a little. How do I explain it? Do you want me to strip to show you?"

Lan Wangji's brows twitched slightly, seeming to really be concerned that he would strip on the street. He said flatly, "Strip after we return."

Wei Wuxian laughed, then spun around and walked backward for a bit. Before, in order to escape as soon as possible, he'd tried very hard to make himself unlikable. He'd done plenty of embarrassing things, feigning madness and acting like an idiot. Now that his identity had been exposed, anyone else would have wanted to dig a hole to hide in out of embarrassment once they thought back on all the things they'd done. But Wei Wuxian had always been someone with thick skin, so he still acted like nothing was the matter. That being said, someone with the slightest bit of shame would never do something like climb into someone else's bed in the middle of the night, forcibly try to get into the same bathtub, demand to know if he was pretty after putting on makeup, or other such weird antics.

But he pretended not to remember anything, so naturally, Lan Wangji wasn't going to voluntarily mention it either. The two had been acting as if nothing had happened, meaning today was the first time since then that he'd made such a joke.

After he was done laughing, Wei Wuxian composed himself.

"Hanguang-jun, do you think the same group that threw our good buddy's arm into the Mo Manor to attack your clan's juniors was also the one who sewed his legs onto another corpse before burying the whole thing in the wall?"

In both the past and present, he had always called Lan Wangji by his birth name in his own head. But recently, he'd gotten used to using his venerated sobriquet every day. Besides, using this form of address carried a certain flavor he'd developed a taste for; it pretended to be serious, yet had an odd sense of silliness. So, he continued to use the name outside half-jokingly.

"Two groups," Lan Wangji replied.

"So we're of basically the same mind," Wei Wuxian said. "Going to all the trouble of sewing the legs onto another corpse and then hiding them in a wall, clearly not wanting the limbs to be discovered… If that's the case, then the left arm wouldn't have been purposely thrown out to attack the disciples of the Lan Clan of Gusu, since that would for sure attract attention and investigation. One took great pains to hide the limbs away. The other struck rashly, fearing the limbs *wouldn't* be discovered. The two groups couldn't be one and the same."

He'd said everything there was to say. There didn't seem to be anything left for Lan Wangji to add, but still, he *mn*-ed in response.

Wei Wuxian spun back around and talked as he walked. "The legs-hider knew about the Nie Clan of Qinghe's Saber Offerings Hall customs, while the left-arm-tosser knew the movements of the Lan Clan of Gusu. The two parties are not simple. The mystery thickens."

"One step at a time," Lan Wangji said.

"How did you recognize me?" Wei Wuxian asked.

"Think for yourself," Lan Wangji replied.

They went back and forth, questioning and answering without pause. Wei Wuxian had originally wanted to catch Lan Wangji by surprise and tempt out a blurted response to his question, but the attempt had been a failure. He wasn't discouraged, though, and rapidly swerved the topic to something else.

"I've never come to Yueyang before. In the past, I always got other people to hunt for information. Let me slack off a little and trouble you to do the work this time. Will Hanguang-jun mind?"

Lan Wangji immediately turned to leave, and Wei Wuxian quickly called after him.

"Stop. Hanguang-jun, may I ask where you're going?"

Lan Wangji looked back. "To the cultivation clan that is stationed in this area."

Wei Wuxian tugged on the tassel of his sword and reeled him back in. "What are you doing, knocking on their door? This is their domain. Even if they know anything, they won't tell you—either because they can't handle it and want to cover that up because it's humiliating, or because they'd adamantly refuse to let outsiders stick their noses in. Esteemed Hanguang-jun, it's not that I'm trying to discredit you, but you really can't work right without me, huh? It'd be a miracle if you managed to get any information, the way you hunt for it."

What he said was a little blunt, but in Lan Wangji's gaze, beneath his eyelashes, there was nothing but softness.

He answered quietly, "Mn."

Wei Wuxian laughed. "What's with the 'mn'? 'Mn'-ing to this too?"

His mind was delighted at the opportunity to tease: *Only knowing how to say "mn"...he IS still dull!*

"How should information be sought?" Lan Wangji asked.

Wei Wuxian pointed in a direction. "By going there, of course~!"

The place he pointed at was a long, wide street. Along the sides of the street hung showy store signs of various sizes—bright, incredibly eye-catching red cloths wafting in the wind. Every store had their doors wide open and round, black jugs displayed outside. There were waiters carrying trays of small wine cups, slapping their chests and recommending brews.

The wafting, fragrant scent of strong spirits filled the street. It was no wonder Wei Wuxian had found himself walking slower and slower earlier. When they reached the intersection, he came to a complete stop and pulled Lan Wangji to a stop too.

Wei Wuxian said seriously, "The waiters in places like these are usually young and sharp-witted, fast and efficient. And since there are many customers every day, talk runs rampant. Word of strange occurrences never escapes their eyes and ears."

Lan Wangji *mn*-ed and didn't disagree, but a certain assumption was already written on his face: *You clearly only want to drink.*

Wei Wuxian pretended he couldn't read his expression. He yanked on Lan Wangji's sword tassel and stepped into the tavern district with eyes beaming. Immediately several waiters from different taverns approached, surrounding him, each more enthusiastic than the next.

"Try a taste? It's the locally famous He Family Brew!"

"Try this one, gongzi, tasting is free. If you enjoy it, then please come patronize our humble shop."

"This liquor doesn't smell strong, but the aftereffect is sure to satisfy you!"

"If you can still stand after drinking this, I'll change my surname to yours!"

Having heard this, Wei Wuxian exclaimed, "Great!"

He took the bowl of liquor the waiter was holding and tossed it back, then grinned and showed him the empty bottom of the bowl.

"Changing to my surname?"

Surprisingly, the waiter didn't cower. Instead, he held his head high and spoke with more gusto. "I meant, drink an entire jug!"

"Then give me...three jugs," Wei Wuxian said.

The waiter was overjoyed and rushed back into the tavern. Wei Wuxian turned to Lan Wangji to explain himself.

"It's business. We help their establishment first, then talk after. It's easier to open mouths after all that's taken care of."

Lan Wangji paid the bill.

The two entered the tavern. There were wooden tables and chairs installed inside for guests to rest and chat while they drank. There was another waiter inside who perceived Lan Wangji's dress and demeanor to be shockingly divine and didn't dare to receive him poorly, so he gathered his strength and scrubbed the furniture hard before he dared direct them to their seats. Two jugs sat next to Wei Wuxian's feet while another was held in his hand. He bantered a bit with the waiter, getting chummy with him, before cutting to the chase: were there any strange happenings in the area?

The waiter was a talkative one too, so he rubbed his hands together and asked, "What sort of strange happenings?"

"Haunted houses, abandoned graves, dismembered corpses, that kinda thing."

The waiter darted his eyes between the two of them and said, "I see… What do you guys do? You and him?"

"Haven't you already guessed?" Wei Wuxian said.

The waiter said with understanding, "True enough. It's easy to guess. You two must be some kinda prominent cultivators who can fly around riding clouds and whatnot, right? Particularly the one beside you, sir. Usually, I never see anyone so…so…"

Wei Wuxian grinned. "So beautiful."

The waiter laughed aloud. "Listen to you, sir, this gongzi is gonna be displeased. Strange happenings, right? There have been some. But the news ain't current—it's from about a decade ago. If you head in that direction and walk for about another couple of kilometers after leaving the city, you'll see a rather beautifully built mansion. Dunno if the establishment plaque is still there, but that place is the Chang residence."

"What's wrong with that mansion?" Wei Wuxian asked.

"A terrible case of clan extermination!" the waiter said. "You're asking for strange happenings, sir, so of course I'm picking the strangest of the strange. The entire family died, and I hear they were all terrified to death!"

Lan Wangji appeared thoughtful at hearing this, like he was remembering something. Wei Wuxian paid no attention to him and continued to press for more information.

"Is there a cultivation clan stationed in this area?"

To be able to terrify an entire family to death—it had to be the work of extremely cruel, terrifying malicious ghosts or belligerent spirits. Not every family had inescapable, unspeakable difficulties like the Nie Clan of Qinghe. Normal cultivation clans wouldn't tolerate such creatures lurking in their territory.

The waiter replied, "There is. Why wouldn't there be?"

"How did they handle the case, then?" Wei Wuxian asked.

"Handle?" The waiter slung the rag over his shoulder and sat down too, spilling in all seriousness the burden he'd been holding back. "Gongzi, do you know the name of the cultivation clan that was stationed in Yueyang? It's Chang. The family that died is them! They all died, so who's left to handle anything?"

The Chang family that had been exterminated was the cultivation clan that was stationed here?!

Wei Wuxian had never heard of any Chang Clan of Yueyang, so they must not have been a prominent clan of any repute. But to have an entire clan be exterminated was definitely a shockingly huge event. Not a trifling matter at all.

He hurriedly asked, "How was the Chang family exterminated?"

The waiter replied, "This is all hearsay, yeah? That Chang family... One night, there suddenly came the sound of banging on the door, and it was coming from inside the residence."

"Banging?" Wei Wuxian asked.

"That's right! The banging was so loud, it shocked the heavens. There was yelling and crying coming from inside, like everyone was locked in and couldn't get out. That's just too strange, ain't it? The door was barred from the inside, so if people inside wanna get out, just remove the bar! Why slap the door? It's not like anyone outside can do anything. Besides, if you can't get out through the door, don't you know how to hop over the wall?

"The people outside were griping. Everyone in this area knew the Chang family was an amazing clan of the cultivation sort. Their family head—I think his name was Chang Ping—had a sword that could fly, and he could stand on it and soar about! If something really did happen in there that the family themselves couldn't handle, wouldn't regular folks be seeking death if they approached? So no one put up a ladder or hopped the wall to check inside. That went on for an entire night. The wailing grew softer and softer. The next day, when the sun came out, the entrance to the Chang residence opened by itself.

"The entire household—men and women, about a dozen masters and over fifty servants—were sitting or sprawled out, foaming at the mouth. They had all been terrified to death."

The tavern owner looked over and yelled, "*You're* dead! What're you doing, chattering about the cursed dead of the past and not working?"

"Another five jugs," Wei Wuxian said.

Lan Wangji paid enough for ten, and the owner's face immediately split into a wide smile.

He instructed the waiter, "Keep the guests in good company; don't go anywhere!"

"Continue the story," Wei Wuxian said.

With no more fear of disturbance, the waiter thus gave all he had in telling the tale with all the drama it warranted.

"Ever since then—for a long time after!—if passersby were to travel in the dark of night near the Chang residence, they would hear banging on the door coming from the inside! Just think. They were the ones riding clouds, cultivating, and exterminating monsters. They'd seen plenty of evil before, and yet they were still terrified to death. How horrifying is that? If you walk the night road too often, sooner or later, you'll run into ghosts. Even after they were buried, you could still hear the sound of banging in their coffins! Though they say that the family head Chang Ping was out at the time, so he escaped disaster…"

"Didn't you say the entire family died?" Wei Wuxian asked.

"Relax, I was just gettin' to it," the waiter assured. "They did all die. I said 'escaped disaster,' and that was temporary too. A couple of years later, that master Chang Ping still died. And this time, the death was even more terrifying. It was death by lingchi—with a sword! You don't need me to explain what death by lingchi is, right? It's when ya take a knife or a sword and slice up a person, cut them three thousand and six hundred times until the flesh is all sliced off, leaving only the bones…"

Of course Wei Wuxian knew what lingchi was. If a book were to be written entitled *A Thousand Ways to Die Violently*, no one would be more qualified than him to author it. He raised his hand.

"I get it. Then, buddy, do you know the reason why the Chang family was exterminated?"

The waiter replied, "I heard it was a setup by another cultivation sect. There's no doubt about that, though! Otherwise, how could a group of live folks, live cultivator folks no less, not be able to escape? They must've been trapped inside by something…or someone."

The tavern owner, afraid the topic would dampen their good time, had thus brought them two small plates of peanuts and melon seeds. Wei Wuxian nodded his thanks, then munched on the melon seeds as he continued his questions.

"Did anyone ever find out just what that something or someone was?"

The waiter laughed. "Ain't that a funny joke, gongzi. We're just some nobodies trying to make a living—what do we know of the affairs of a bunch of lords who fly around in the sky all day? You're all cultivators, sir, so you should know better than me. I only heard some gossip about how they offended someone they shouldn't have. In any case, since then, all the evil things around here were left running amok with no one to beat them back. Alas."

Wei Wuxian wondered, "Someone he shouldn't have offended?"

"That's right, that's right." The waiter ate a couple of peanuts. "All the grudges and grievances of all those cultivation clans or sects or whatever are so complicated. I figure the Chang family must've gotten targeted by other cultivators. Murdering for treasure is a common thing, right? That's what the storytellers always say. And that's what's written in legends and romances, to boot. Although I don't exactly know who it was, it seems it was related to an infamous evil overlord."

Wei Wuxian smiled as he brought the liquor bowl to his lips, side-eyeing the waiter. "Let me guess. You're gonna say you don't know who this evil overlord is, right?"

The waiter laughed. "Wrong, sir! This I know. I think it was some old pa...oh, patriarch, Yiling Patriarch!"

Wei Wuxian choked and *pfft*-ed, letting out a stream of bubbles in the liquor bowl. "What?"

Him again?!

The waiter said with conviction, "Yes, that's right! Surname Wei. I think he's called Wei Wuqian.[9] When others mention him, they always sound both hateful and scared!"

"..."

Wei Wuxian reviewed the facts in his head and finally confirmed two things: one, he had never visited Yueyang before, and two, none of the people he'd killed were done in through lingchi. This was an

---

9 "Wuqian" means "no money."

absurd accusation. He twisted his head to look questioningly at Lan Wangji, seeming to want an explanation from him.

Lan Wangji, who had been waiting for this look, said, "Let us go."

Wei Wuxian immediately understood: Lan Wangji had something to say about this, and it would be unsuitable to say in front of others at the tavern. He rose to his feet.

"Let's go, then. The bill…the bill is paid, right? Little buddy, we're gonna stash the liquor we bought here with you. Once we're done with our business, we'll come back to finish it off." He added, half-jokingly, "Don't cheat me, eh."

The waiter, who had already polished off over half the plate of peanuts by himself, protested, "We would never! This shop cheats neither children nor the elderly. You just leave the liquor here, sir, no worries. We won't close our doors until you two are back. Hey, hey, gongzi, are you two heading to the Chang residence now? Wow, that's amazing. I'm a local, and I haven't even gone yet! I only dare to sneak peeks from a distance. Are you two gonna go inside? What do you plan on doing?"

Wei Wuxian replied, "We are also going to just sneak a peek. From a distance."

This young waiter was quick-witted and very much a natural at socializing, so now that they'd been chatting for a bit, he no longer took Wei Wuxian for a stranger. He shuffled over, wanting to put his arm around his shoulders.

"Is this profession hard work? Do you two make a lot of money? You must, right?! It's so respectable. Hey, can I ask something? Is it hard to enter the trade? I…"

He was just babbling on, but then abruptly shut up as if stricken with fear, peeping off to the side. He asked in a low whisper, "Gongzi, the gentleman next to you…what's he glaring at me for?"

Wei Wuxian looked over, following his gaze, just in time to see Lan Wangji twist his head away and rise to his feet to leave the tavern.

He said, "Oh. Him, huh. That friend of mine was raised in a strict household. He detests seeing anyone with their arms around each other in front of him. Isn't that a little weird?"

The waiter sulkily removed his arm as he whispered, "It is. Look at the way he's glaring, you'd think I was putting my arm around his wife…"

Lan Wangji's sharp hearing meant it was impossible he hadn't heard that, even though the words were whispered. It did make one wonder what his thoughts were on the matter. Wei Wuxian was holding back his laughter so desperately that he was about to sustain an internal injury. He quickly turned to the waiter.

"I finished a jug."

"Huh?" the waiter replied.

Wei Wuxian pointed at himself. "Still standing."

Only then did the young waiter remember that he had said, *"I'll change my surname to yours."* He quickly exclaimed, "Ooh…ooh, oh! That's…amazing! I'm not tryin' to boast, but you're the first one I've seen that could still stand upright and speak without your tongue tangling up after finishing a jug. What's your surname, sir?"

Wei Wuxian replied, "I'm…"

Then he remembered how the waiter had said "Wei Wuqian" earlier, and the corners of his lips twitched.

He calmly continued, "Surnamed Lan."

The waiter was a thick-skinned one too. He announced loudly, without skipping a beat, "Yes, from today onward, I am surnamed Lan!"

Beneath the bright red sign that invited guests inside, it seemed that Lan Wangji's stride faltered, just for a moment. Wei Wuxian was smirking slyly. He strode over with his hands folded behind his back, then patted Lan Wangji's shoulder.

"Many thanks to Hanguang-jun for the kindness of paying the bill. I got the waiter to name himself after you."

After leaving the city, the two headed in the direction that the waiter had pointed. As the number of travelers thinned, the woods thickened.

Wei Wuxian asked, "Why didn't you let me keep grilling him with questions earlier?"

Lan Wangji replied, "Details of the Chang Clan of Yueyang case have suddenly returned to me. I know of the rumors, and thus there was no longer a need to ask."

"Before you tell me, let me ask you something," Wei Wuxian said. "Just confirm this for me now. Um…the Chang family extermination wasn't my doing, right?"

Even putting aside the fact that he had already been dead ten years ago and his soul had been well behaved as heck, there was no way he'd forget charging up to some clan's doorstep and annihilating the whole family!

"It was not you," Lan Wangji confirmed.

"I see," Wei Wuxian said.

He felt like he'd been transported back to that particular time in his life when everyone had yelled for him to be beaten, a time when he'd lived worse than a gutter rat. He had been blamed for every bad deed, and people had dumped buckets of crap on him as and when they pleased. If the little grandson of the old lord grandpa next door lost weight from refusing to eat, even that could be blamed on him—surely the boy was just too horrified by the stories of the Yiling Patriarch's terrible massacres with the Ghost General.

Yet unexpectedly, Lan Wangji added, "You did not kill them, but it is related to you."

"What's the connection?" Wei Wuxian asked.

"There are two," Lan Wangji said. "First, there is a character implicated in this case who was linked to your mother."

Wei Wuxian paused in his step. He didn't know how to feel, nor did he know what face to make.

He asked, hesitantly, "My mother?"

Wei Wuxian was the son of a family servant of the Jiang Clan of Yunmeng, Wei Changze, and his mother had been the wandering cultivator Cangse-sanren. Jiang Fengmian and his wife had been well acquainted with his parents, but Jiang Fengmian had very rarely reminisced aloud regarding his old friends, and Jiang Fengmian's wife Yu Ziyuan had never spoken well of them to him—honestly, things had been pretty good if she didn't whip him or tell him to scram, or kneel in the ancestral hall, or stay away from Jiang Cheng. Many of the stories he'd heard about his parents were told to him by others, so he actually didn't know much more than anyone else.

Lan Wangji also stopped, then turned around to meet his gaze. "Have you ever heard of one named Xiao Xingchen?"

Wei Wuxian thought for a moment, then replied, "No."

"'No' is correct," Lan Wangji said. "It was twelve years ago when this man emerged from the mountain and achieved fame. And now there are none who speak of him."

Twelve years ago happened to be the year right after the Siege of the Yiling Burial Mounds, so they had just missed each other.

Wei Wuxian asked, "Which mountain was it, and who was his teacher?"

Lan Wangji replied, "The mountain is unknown. Xiao Xingchen studied the way of the dao under the tutelage of Baoshan-sanren."

CHAPTER 7: THE MORNING DEW

Now Wei Wuxian understood why Lan Wangji had said that this man was linked to his mother. He said, "That means this Xiao Xingchen was technically my mother's martial brother, huh?"

Cangse-sanren had also come from Baoshan-sanren's school.

This Baoshan-sanren was a hermit cultivator who lived hidden away from the secular world. Apparently, she was a cultivator of the same generation as Wen Mao and Lan An. Other celebrities of that generation had long since dissipated in both body and soul. Only Baoshan-sanren still walked the earth. If that really was true, then she should be many hundreds of years old, which proved she was in possession of incredible cultivation. In the years ruled by those of her generation, with Wen Mao as leader, clans had flourished while sects declined. Leading factions of cultivation authority that were bound by blood ties sprouted like bamboo shoots in the spring. Any cultivator with a lick of fame founded their own sect, and yet this master chose to retreat to a mountain hermitage. Her cultivator name was Baoshan, meaning "to embrace the mountains." Which mountain was it that she embraced? No one knew. But it was precisely because no one knew that it was called a hermitic retreat—if she could be easily found, it wouldn't have been considered so.

This elder led a hermitic life upon an unknown immortal mountain. She often secretly picked up orphans and brought them up the mountain, taking them in as her disciples. However, every disciple had to swear an oath: focus only on cultivation in this life. Never descend the mountain, never enter the secular world. If they did, no matter the reason, they would never be allowed to return. They would have to survive on their own and train in hardship within the secular world, never again to have any ties with their one-time school.

People said Baoshan-sanren was worthy to be called an enlightened master, and this rule of hers truly demonstrated great foresight.

Over hundreds of years, she only had three disciples leave the mountain: Yanling-daoren, Cangse-sanren, and Xiao Xingchen. Three disciples, not one of whom had come to a good end.

Wei Wuxian had known from a young age what the end had been for the first two disciples, so there was no need to listen to those tales again. So, what Lan Wangji succinctly told him was the story of the deeds of that last disciple—Wei Wuxian's mother's younger martial brother.

When Xiao Xingchen emerged from the mountain, he was seventeen. Although Lan Wangji had never met him in person, he had heard from others of the man's noble bearing.

At the time, it had only been a few years since the end of the Sunshot Campaign, and the Siege of the Yiling Burial Mounds had just concluded. The great clans dominated and were recruiting for talent all over the place, all to serve their own purposes. Xiao Xingchen emerged from the mountains with the desire to save the common world. Immensely skilled and taught by a true master, he charged the mountain in his first Night Hunt with his one Daoist whisk, his one longsword, and his one lone person, and claimed first place—winning fame in one battle.

At the sight of this young cultivator who was pure in character and accomplished in cultivation, the cultivation clans all felt great admiration. They all sent invitations to him, but Xiao Xingchen courteously declined each one, making it clear that he did not wish to affiliate with any clans at all. Instead, together with his most intimate friend, he was determinedly set on establishing a brand-new sect that did not emphasize blood ties.

Xiao Xingchen's character was as soft as pampas grass, but his heart was as strong as a rock—gentle on the outside, steadfast on the inside, and spurning contamination by corrupt forces. At the time, if a difficult matter arose, any and all would rush to seek help from him first and foremost. Furthermore, he never rejected anyone, so opinion of him was extremely high.

The obliteration of the Chang Clan of Yueyang happened right around then.

One fateful day, the family head of the Chang Clan of Yueyang took a few family members with him to attend a Night Hunt. Over half a month later, he suddenly received the awful news during his travels and hurried home. After the period of mourning, it was discovered upon further investigation that someone had maliciously destroyed the protection array of the home, allowing the entry of a band of cruel and belligerent evil spirits. Beyond that, everything was a mystery.

Normally, few people paid heed to the tragedies of such small clans. But this situation was unique. The Sunshot Campaign had long since ended, and the Siege of the Burial Mounds was just over. On the surface, the state of the world could have been said to be somewhat peaceful. But to have such an incident happen so out of the blue, immediately caused huge waves among the cultivation clans. There were many alarmists spreading the rumor that the Yiling Patriarch Wei Wuxian had returned to the world for revenge—however, there was never any evidence of that, and no way of catching the murderers. Of course, Xiao Xingchen could not remain indifferent to this case. He voluntarily took it on right then and there to seek the truth for Chang Ping.

The name of the murderer was Xue Yang.

This Xue Yang was younger than Xiao Xingchen, a boy through and through. However, his odious temperament was not hampered by his young age. At fifteen, he was already a major thug known far and wide in the Kui Prefecture area. His smile was sweet, his methods vicious, and his personality cruel. In Kui Prefecture, everyone's face would change colors at the mention of Xue Yang's name. He grew up on the streets as an urchin and seemed to have a grudge against Chang Ping's father, which he had nurtured for many years. It was revenge, among other reasons, that prompted him to commit this violent crime.

After Xiao Xingchen had figured out the truth, he crossed three provinces and caught Xue Yang, who was still freewheeling about and brawling with others, and quite self-satisfied. At that time, the Jin Clan of Lanling was holding a symposium at their residential mansion, Golden Carp Tower, and all the major clans were present to debate and discuss Daoism. There, Xiao Xingchen dragged Xue Yang forward for all to see. The whole story was explained in detail and severe punishment was pleaded for.

Xiao Xingchen had laid down every piece of evidence clearly. Most of the clans had no objections. Only one clan opposed him vehemently, and that was the Jin Clan of Lanling.

"Objecting under those circumstances would risk universal condemnation," said Wei Wuxian. "Could Xue Yang have been a favorite of Jin Guangshan?"

"A guest cultivator," Lan Wangji replied.

"He was their guest cultivator?" Wei Wuxian asked. "The Jin Clan of Lanling should've ranked as one of the four major clans by then, right? Why invite a little thug to be a guest cultivator?"

"This is the second connection," Lan Wangji said.

He stared intently at Wei Wuxian's eyes and continued, slowly, "It was because of the Yin Tiger Tally."

Wei Wuxian's heart violently lurched.

He was definitely no stranger to the name "Yin Tiger Tally." On the contrary, no one was more familiar.

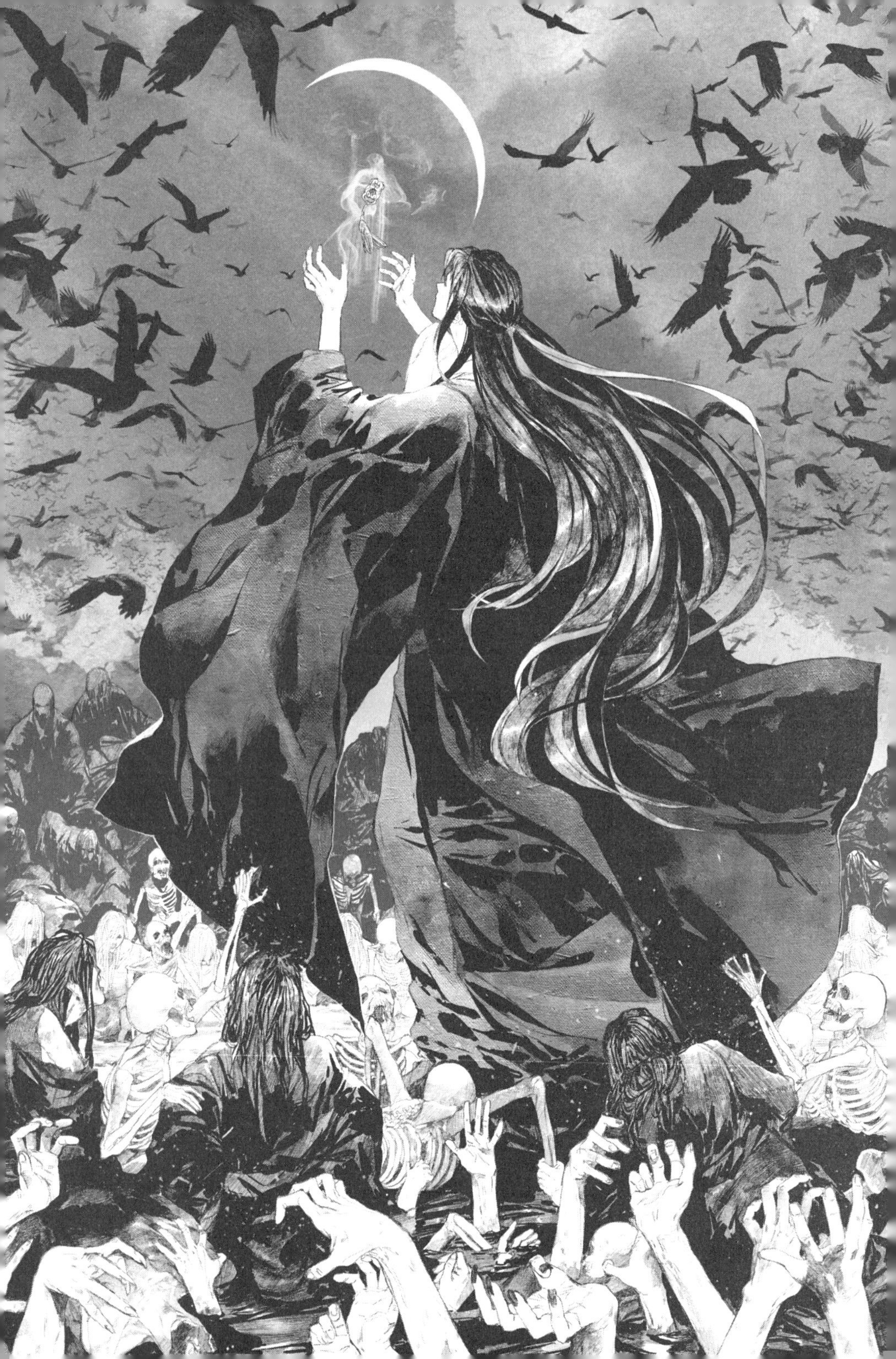

Of all the spiritual weapons he had refined while alive, it was the most terrifying, and at the same time, the most desired by all.

The function of a tiger tally was to command. As the name implied, those who possessed the Yin Tiger Tally possessed commanding power over corpses, ghosts, and belligerent spirits of all sorts, forcing their obedience.

Back when Wei Wuxian had first created it, he hadn't thought too much about it. Using his primordial spirit alone to control the corpse puppets and belligerent spirits made it inevitable that there'd be times when he got tired. He recalled having seen a rare iron spirit in the stomach of a yao beast once, and so he had retrieved it, refined it, and forged a tiger tally.

Wei Wuxian had only used that tiger tally once after it was forged. He had instantly realized it was bad news.

The power of the Yin Tiger Tally was far stronger and more terrifying than he had expected. He had originally wanted to use it simply as a supplement, but unexpectedly, its power showed the faint potential to overwhelm its own creator. Moreover, the thing didn't recognize any one master. If someone got their hands on it, no matter who that person was—good or bad, friend or foe—it would be theirs to use.

The disaster had already been born into the world. It wasn't that Wei Wuxian had never thought of destroying it, but forging the tiger tally had been no easy task and destroying it would have been just as difficult, demanding all his energy and time. Besides, he had already vaguely sensed that he was in a bad situation. Sooner or later, everyone would be after his life. The Yin Tiger Tally served as an immense force of deterrence. People wouldn't dare target him incautiously while he had this spiritual weapon, so he kept it as temporary protection. All he did was split the tiger tally into two so that its powers could only be activated when assembled, thus making it so it would never be used unless absolutely necessary.

He had only ever used it twice, and each time, blood had flowed like rivers. The first time had been during the Sunshot Campaign. After using it the second time, he finally made up his mind and thoroughly destroyed half of the tally. Before he could destroy the other half, the Burial Mounds were besieged. Whatever came after that, well, it had no longer been within his means to care.

Wei Wuxian was confident enough to provide commentary on his own creations, and on this topic, he was quite sure that even if the clan that had snatched the remaining piece placed it on an altar to worship every day, with offerings of tall incense and frequent prostration, the only remaining half of the Yin Tiger Tally was no more than mere scrap iron. However, Lan Wangji revealed something shocking: this Xue Yang appeared to have been able to reverse engineer the other half of the Yin Tiger Tally!

Xue Yang had been very young but also unusually smart, as well as an incredibly perverse heretic. The Jin Clan of Lanling discovered that he actually could roughly piece together the other half of the Yin Tiger Tally based on the half left behind. Although the duration of use for the assembled, restored item was not long, nor was its power as strong as the original, it could already produce incredibly terrifying results.

Wei Wuxian understood now. "The Jin Clan of Lanling still needed Xue Yang to continue the restoration of the Yin Tiger Tally, so they had to shield him."

Maybe the reason Xue Yang had annihilated the Chang clan hadn't entirely been to avenge wrongs committed against him while an impoverished urchin. Maybe he had used the lives of this family to test the power of the restored Yin Tiger Tally!

No wonder the rumors had connected Wei Wuxian with the clan extermination case. He could practically imagine how those cultivators had gritted their teeth. *"That Wei Wuxian! If he hadn't made such a thing, there wouldn't be so many disasters in the human world!!!"*

In any case, back to the events at Golden Carp Tower.

The Jin Clan of Lanling was determined to shield Xue Yang, yet Xiao Xingchen would not yield to persuasion or coercion. The two were stuck in a stalemate, and this finally alerted Chifeng-zun—that is, Nie Mingjue—who had not attended this particular symposium. He was called upon to fly over from elsewhere and hurry to make an appearance.

Although Nie Mingjue was of a younger generation than Jin Guangshan, he possessed a stern character. He refused to tolerate, refused to appease, and after a severe scolding, Jin Guangshan was too embarrassed to speak and lost a great deal of face. Nie Mingjue, ever violent in temper, drew his saber on the spot and was ready to execute Xue Yang. Even when his sworn younger brother Lianfang-zun—that is, Jin Guangyao—went up to smooth things over, he was furiously told to leave and viciously berated until he hid behind Lan Xichen, not daring to utter one more word. Finally, the Jin Clan of Lanling had no choice but to concede.

Ever since he'd been dragged to the Golden Carp Tower by Xiao Xingchen, Xue Yang had been without fear the entire time, knowing he had a strong backing. Even when Nie Mingjue's saber had pressed against his neck, he was still grinning happily.

Before he was carried away, he said quite warmly to Xiao Xingchen, "Daozhang, don't you forget me. Just you wait and see."

Having listened thus far, Wei Wuxian knew that "wait and see" was a certain promise to make Xiao Xingchen pay an incomparably excruciating price.

As deserving of their name, the Jin Clan of Lanling was the most thick-skinned of the clans. Although they agreed to get rid of Xue Yang in front of all the clans at the Golden Carp Tower, the moment Nie Mingjue was out of sight, they swiftly locked Xue Yang in the dungeons and changed the verdict to imprisonment, never to be released. Once Nie Mingjue learned of this, he was outraged. He exerted pressure on them once more, but the Jin Clan of Lanling dragged their feet and refused to give that person over, no matter what. The other clans all watched this spectacle from the sidelines with their arms crossed.

Who would've thought that, not long after, Nie Mingjue would suffer qi deviation and die? He had cultivated faster than any of the previous Nie clan leaders before him but also died sooner than any of them.

With the most difficult man gone, the Jin Clan of Lanling grew ever more unscrupulous as they brewed more crooked ideas. Jin Guangshan began thinking of ways to pull Xue Yang out of jail to continue the restoration of the Yin Tiger Tally and the research into its secrets.

However, this was still ultimately a dishonorable affair. It wouldn't do to pull a criminal who murdered an entire clan out of jail without a proper cause.

Thus, they turned their eyes to Chang Ping.

They coerced and tempted him, harassing him nonstop until finally, the Jin Clan of Lanling successfully persuaded Chang Ping to change his story. He withdrew all the grievances he had stated before and announced publicly that the clan extermination case had nothing to do with Xue Yang.

Having heard the news, Xiao Xingchen went knocking to demand answers. Chang Ping, full of resignation, said to him, "Other than ceding, what else could I have done? If I can't endure this, the rest of my family will have no way of living. Many thanks, Daozhang, but…please don't help me anymore. If you help me again now, you would be harming me. I don't want the Chang Clan of Yueyang to end just yet."

And thus was the tiger released back to the mountain.

Wei Wuxian fell into a deep silence.

If he were Chang Ping, it wouldn't matter whether the Jin Clan of Lanling was a prominent clan who abused their power and could deceive the world as they willed. It wouldn't matter who promised him a future of glory and luxury—he would never give in. On the contrary, he would personally visit the dungeons at night and cut Xue Yang into pieces alive, then summon his spirit back to do it again, over and over, until the boy wished he'd never been born into this world.

However, not everyone shared the urge to drag an opponent down along with them. There were still several Chang family members alive, and Chang Ping himself was still young, with no wives or children. He had only just started on the path of cultivation. He had to carefully weigh his options, no matter whether it was the lives of his remaining family, or his future and cultivation being threatened.

After all, Wei Wuxian wasn't Chang Ping. He couldn't be outraged on his behalf, nor could he help him bear his fear and endure this torture of both body and mind.

After Xue Yang was released, he carried out his revenge, as expected—except he didn't enact revenge on Xiao Xingchen.

Xiao Xingchen had emerged into the world alone and only made one good friend after descending the mountain. This friend, known as Song Lan, was also a reputable Daoist at the time—aloof, proud, and highly regarded. The two had both wanted to establish a sect that focused on shared ideals rather than nepotism. They could have been considered the best of friends, and they shared the same aspirations and interests. People of their time described them in such words: "Xiao Xingchen, bright moon, cool breeze, ever-distant; Song Zichen, dauntlessly scorns the snow and frost."

And so, Xue Yang decided to target his attack here. He reused the same tricks to thoroughly annihilate Baixue Temple, the place where Song Lan had grown up and studied. In addition to that, he hatched and successfully carried out a plot to blind Song Lan's eyes with caustic powder.

This time, he was experienced in clan annihilation. He was exceptionally efficient in the act, leaving no clues behind. While everyone knew it was definitely him, what was the use in knowing? There was no evidence. Jin Guangshan was purposely shielding him, and on top of that, Chifeng-zun of the thunderous temper had passed away. Shockingly, there was no one else who could do anything about him.

Having listened to this point, Wei Wuxian suddenly found it a little odd. Although Lan Wangji seemed indifferent to worldly matters and too uncaring to meddle, based on Wei Wuxian's past understanding of him, he abhorred evil no less keenly than Nie Huaisang's older brother. The Jin Clan of Lanling's actions had been less than savory back then, and Lan Wangji never hesitated to speak out. Even now, he rarely attended their clan's symposiums and was completely unsupportive. Two consecutive, odious incidents of murder would've been the talk of the town back then. Lan Wangji would not have sat back quietly. So how come he hadn't brought Xue Yang under control?

Just as he was about to ask, he remembered the discipline whip scars on Lan Wangji's back.

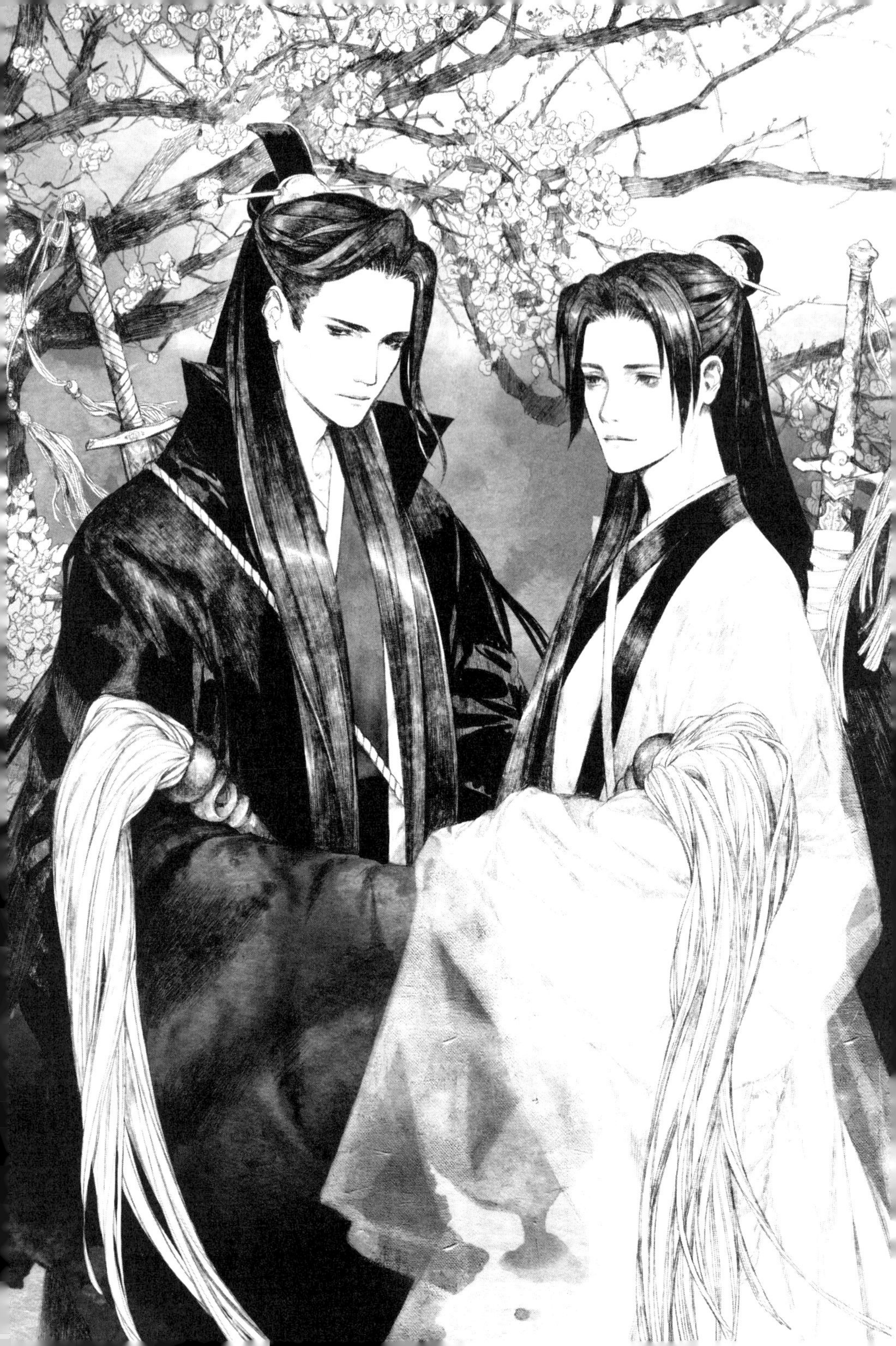

CHAPTER 7: THE MORNING DEW

One lash from the discipline whip was deadly enough. There must have been a period of many years when Lan Wangji was forbidden to step outside the clan's walls, if he had committed a grave crime that resulted in so many lashes. These incidents had probably happened when Lan Wangji was being punished, or when he was nursing his wounds. No wonder he only said he had "heard rumors."

Those scars really bothered Wei Wuxian, for some reason, but it wasn't his place to ask directly, so the feeling would have to be suppressed for the time being.

He asked, "So what happened to Xiao Xingchen-daozhang after that?"

After that, of course the curtains could only drop dismally on this play. In the past, Xiao Xingchen had bid farewell to his master and left the mountain, vowing to never return. He took his promises very seriously. But Song Lan was blinded and had suffered further grave injuries, and so he broke his own vow. Carrying Song Lan on his back, he returned to Baoshan-sanren's hermitage to beg his master to save his good friend.

In consideration of their past relationship as master and disciple, Baoshan-sanren accepted his request. Xiao Xingchen thus descended the mountain again, and his whereabouts had remained unknown ever since.

Another year passed before Song Lan also emerged from the mountain. The people of the world were astonished to find his once thoroughly blinded eyes could see light anew. But the truth was this: it wasn't that Baoshan-sanren's healing abilities were godly, but that Xiao Xingchen…had dug out his own eyes and gifted them to Song Lan, who had only been caught up in this mess because of him.

Song Lan had wanted to seek revenge against Xue Yang, at first. But by then, Jin Guangshan had already passed away. Jin Guangyao had inherited control of the Jin Clan of Lanling and risen to the position of Cultivation Chief. To prove that this would be the dawning of a new regime, the moment he ascended the stage, he got rid of Xue Yang and never spoke of the Yin Tiger Tally's restoration again. In the hopes of restoring his clan's damaged reputation, he implemented all sorts of restorative and reassuring measures to push any rumors down.

Song Lan pursued the lingering traces of his good friend of times past. At first, one still heard talk of where he had gone. However, as time passed, there were no more words to be heard. Since the Chang Clan of Yueyang was also a small, unknown family, many things about this whole affair gradually returned to dust.

After listening to this long, long story, Wei Wuxian let out a quiet sigh, a sense of regret and sympathy sprouting in him.

To end like this over something that originally had nothing to do with him. That truly is... Had Xiao Xingchen been born a few years earlier, or if I had died a few years later, then things wouldn't have turned out this way. If I were alive, I wouldn't have ignored something like this. I would've made friends with such a character!

He then immediately felt both amused and annoyed at the same time. He mocked his own words, thinking, *I would've taken care of it, huh? How? If I were still alive then, the Chang clan extermination case probably wouldn't even have gotten an investigation—they'd just blame it all on me and be done with it. If Xiao Xingchen-daozhang saw me on the road, and I tried to get chummy with him, he'd most likely have given me a round of whacking with his whisk, ha ha.*

They had already walked past the Chang residence and come to a cemetery nearby. Wei Wuxian saw the word "Chang" in dark red on the ceremonial gateway.

"How did Chang Ping die afterward? Who was the one who killed his surviving family with lingchi?"

CHAPTER 7: THE MORNING DEW

Lan Wangji hadn't yet answered when, through the blue-tinged colors of dusk, there came the *bang-bang-bang* sound of a door being slapped. At least, the sound *resembled* a door being slapped. But at the same time, it wasn't. It was forceful and panicked, without a moment of pause. It also sounded dull, like it was separated from their ears by a layer of something.

The two both froze.

There were over fifty members in the Chang Clan of Yueyang. And presently, they were lying in their coffins, banging on the lids from the inside. They were banging wildly, just like the night when they had been terrified to death—but no one would ever answer and open that door for them.

This was what the tavern waiter had spoken of—the sound of coffins banging, coming from the Chang family graves!

But the tavern waiter had also said the hauntings took place ten years ago and had long since stopped. So why had the banging just so happened to start again the moment they arrived?

Wei Wuxian and Lan Wangji restrained their breathing at the same time and noiselessly slunk closer. Once they were leaning behind the pillar of the ceremonial gateway, they both saw that at the center of the cemetery, among the tombstones, there appeared to be a hole. It was an extremely deep hole, and next to it were mounds of dirt that appeared to have been recently piled there. A soft sound came from inside the hole.

Someone was digging graves.

The two quietly held their breath and watched intently, waiting for the person inside the hole to come out on their own. Not half an incense time later, two figures leapt lightly up from the open grave.

Luckily, both Wei Wuxian and Lan Wangji had good enough eyesight that they were able to tell it was two individuals—the two were firmly attached to one another like conjoined babies, with one carrying the other on their back. They were also dressed entirely in black, so it was extremely difficult to discern details.

The one who'd leapt up stood there with their back to them, long-armed and long-legged. The one carried on their back, however, had their head and limbs drooping, with no sign of life. But that was how it should have been. Since it had been dug out of a grave, it had to be a corpse. Thus, lifeless was normal.

Just as Wei Wuxian was thinking this, the gravedigger whipped their head around and saw them.

The person's face was shrouded in a thick, black haze—their facial features and appearance couldn't be discerned at all!

Wei Wuxian knew the person must've cast some sort of strange spell to conceal their face. Lan Wangji had already brandished Bichen, swept into the cemetery and crossed swords. The gravedigger reacted extremely fast. When they saw the blue glare of Bichen's attack, they made a hand seal and summoned their own streaking sword glare. However, this sword glare was the same as their face, all wound up with a rolling black haze so its color and aura couldn't be discerned. With a body carried on their back, the gravedigger was forced to fight in an odd posture. The two sword glares clashed multiple times before Lan Wangji called Bichen back. He gripped it in hand, a layer of frost rapidly overtaking his expression.

Wei Wuxian knew why his expression had turned so piercingly cold. It was because even an outsider like him could easily tell from the exchange of attacks just now that this gravedigger was extraordinarily familiar with Lan Wangji's sword technique!

Lan Wangji did not speak a word as the power of Bichen's thrusts grew ever stronger, the will of his sword akin to the force of mountains toppling and seas overturning. The gravedigger was forced back again and again. Seeming to know they were no match against Lan Wangji while carrying a body on their back, and that they would be captured if this fight continued, they suddenly pulled a dark blue talisman from around their waist.

A transportation talisman!

Such talismans could send a person five hundred kilometers away in an instant. But they also exhausted an immense amount of spiritual power, and the caster would need ample rest to regain their strength. Those without such power couldn't use them, which was why they were not in wide use despite being high-grade items.

Wei Wuxian saw the person was going to escape. He hurriedly struck out twice with his palm, then bent one knee, smashing a fist on the ground.

The power of this punch penetrated through layer after layer of earth, reaching the deepest part of the soil and piercing through the thick coffin lids. It stimulated the deceased trapped within to a near crazed state. There was the sound of cracking, then four bloody arms sprouted from the ground, forcefully seizing the left and right legs of the gravedigger!

The gravedigger was unperturbed. They poured spiritual power into their legs, shocking off the four corpse arms and sending them flying. Wei Wuxian pulled out his bamboo flute, and a sharp, piercing melody ripped open the falling night. Two skulls broke through the ground, their bodies shortly following. They crawled up the length of the gravedigger's leg, entangling their body like snakes, their mouths wide open and ready to bite down on their neck and arms.

The gravedigger snorted disdainfully, as if saying *"nothing but petty tricks."* Spiritual power coursed through their body again. But this time, after sending out the shock wave of spiritual power, they jerked at the realization that they'd been had.

They had sent the corpse on their back flying as well!

Wei Wuxian laughed maniacally, slapping a tombstone. Lan Wangji, on the other hand, seized the limp corpse with one hand while the other lunged with Bichen. When the gravedigger saw the thing they'd just dug out had been snatched by another, they didn't dare stick around. They couldn't beat Lan Wangji in a one-on-one fight, never mind with an additional troublemaker on the side causing mischief. They whipped the transportation talisman to the ground at their feet. There was a huge boom, blue flames rolled toward the sky, and their figure vanished within.

Wei Wuxian already knew that the gravedigger had a transportation talisman, and that they'd find an opportunity to escape even if they caught them. The corpse they'd unearthed was already a clue, so he didn't consider this a total loss. He walked over to Lan Wangji.

"Let's see who they dug out."

He was slightly taken aback once he saw. The head of the corpse was, surprisingly, already bludgeoned. The gaping wound didn't show any blood or brains, but rather, wads and wads of cotton that were already slightly blackened.

Wei Wuxian yanked, and the head came off easily. Dangling the exquisitely made fake head, he said, "What the heck is this? There's a fake corpse made of cotton and rags buried in the Chang family cemetery?"

Only then did Lan Wangji take the corpse. He weighed it in his hand and realized there was something odd afoot.

"It is not all fake."

Wei Wuxian felt the corpse all over and discovered its four limbs were limp, but the chest and abdomen area were hard and solid to the touch. He ripped the clothes off to see, and sure enough, the torso was real, but the other parts were all fake.

The head and four limbs made of cotton must've been used to "deceive" this torso, to make it think it was still attached to its master. Judging by the skin color and where the left shoulder had fractured, this was the torso of their good buddy, which they had been seeking. The gravedigger just now had actually come to dig it out.

Wei Wuxian rose to his feet. "It seems the corpse-hider has already taken notice of our investigation into this case. They were afraid we'd dig up the torso, so they came to transfer it. We arrived just in the nick of time and ran into them, ha ha. But..." His tone took a turn. "Why was that smoke-mask so familiar with your clan's sword technique?"

It was evident Lan Wangji was pondering the same thing as well, as the layer of frost on his face had not yet fully subsided.

Wei Wuxian said, "That person's cultivation sure was strong. Strong enough that they could withstand the exhaustion of using a transportation talisman. They'd also cast a spell on both their face and sword. I can understand casting spells on your face; you don't want people finding you out, duh. But an unknown cultivator would have no need to cast concealment spells on their sword—unless their sword has a bit of a reputation within the cultivation world, and it's famous enough that people could recognize the sword glare. In that case, they'd have no choice but to conceal it, since they'd be exposed the moment they brandished their sword."

Wei Wuxian then asked cautiously, "Hanguang-jun, when you were crossing swords with him earlier, did you think they were someone you're very familiar with?"

Anything more specific than that would be discourteous to say. For example, Lan Xichen. Or Lan Qiren.

Lan Wangji replied with certainty, "No."

Wei Wuxian had full confidence in Lan Wangji's answer. He did not think Lan Wangji was someone who'd conceal the truth or someone who couldn't face the truth. Since he said no, then it must be so. He did not like to lie either. The way Wei Wuxian saw it, Lan Wangji would sooner cast the silencing spell on himself than lie. So Wei Wuxian immediately crossed off those two as suspects.

"Then that makes things even more complicated."

Lan Wangji packed the torso into a different double-layered evil-sealing qiankun pouch and put it away properly. The two made a few rounds around the area, then leisurely rounded back to the tavern district.

The waiter had indeed kept his word. Most of the other taverns on this street were closed, but their sign was still up, the lights still on. The waiter was outside hugging a giant bowl, digging into his food, and when he saw them, he exclaimed in delight.

"You're back! Whaddya think? We always keep our word, eh! Did sirs see anything?"

Wei Wuxian answered a few of his queries with a smile as he and Lan Wangji went to sit back at the same spot they had taken during the day. The table and the floor around his feet were piled with liquor jugs as he said, "Oh yeah, where were we? That grave-digging guy who jumped out all of a sudden interrupted us. I still don't know how Chang Ping died."

Thus, Lan Wangji continued to succinctly and flatly tell the rest of the tale without embellishment.

Xue Yang, Xiao Xingchen, and Song Lan had gone one by one, whether missing or dead. One day, many years after this case was uncovered, Chang Ping and his remaining family members were found dead from lingchi overnight. What was more, Chang Ping's eyes were also dug out.

This time, no one could figure out who the murderer was. After all, everyone involved with the original case had already disappeared. However, there was one thing that was certain after examining the wounds. The sword that had inflicted lingchi had been the one wielded by Xiao Xingchen, Shuanghua.

Wei Wuxian paused in raising the bowl of liquor to his lips, dumbfounded at this turn of events.

"Lingchi with Xiao Xingchen's sword? Then was the culprit truly him?"

"Inconclusive, as Xiao Xingchen remains missing," Lan Wangji replied.

"If the living person himself can't be found, has soul-summoning been attempted?" Wei Wuxian asked.

"Yes," Lan Wangji replied. "It was unfruitful."

Unfruitful. Then either he hadn't died, or he'd died and his soul had dispersed. As an expert in this field, Wei Wuxian expressed his opinions on this matter.

"Lemme tell you, soul-summoning isn't that absolute. The time and place must be exactly right, and mistakes can happen. I bet there're a lot of people who thought that was Xiao Xingchen's revenge, right? What about you, Hanguang-jun? What do you think?"

Lan Wangji shook his head slowly and said, "I will not comment without knowing the full story."

Wei Wuxian greatly admired his attitude and principles in handling matters. He smiled happily, taking a sip of liquor.

He then heard Lan Wangji ask, "What are your views?"

Wei Wuxian replied, "Lingchi is a form of torture. Punishment is precisely its nature. And with his eyes dug out on top of that, it's very hard not to associate it with Xiao Xingchen's deal with his own eyes, so it can't be helped if people assume the incident is Xiao Xingchen's revenge. But..."

He contemplated for a second to find the right words.

"I don't believe that, from the very beginning, Xiao Xingchen stepped forward to interfere in this matter for the sake of gaining Chang Ping's gratitude. I..."

He hadn't decided what would follow that "I" before that waiter very attentively brought over two small plates of peanuts. Wei Wuxian was interrupted, but just as well, since he didn't need to continue anymore. He looked up at Lan Wangji and smiled.

"Hanguang-jun, why are you looking at me like that? 'I' nothing. I don't know the whole story either, so I also won't comment. You're very right. No one should presumptuously judge anything before understanding the inside story and the sequence of events. I only wanted five jugs, but you bought me another extra five—I probably won't be able to finish all this myself. How about it, drink with me? We're not in the Cloud Recesses, so it's not against the rules, right?"

He was prepared to be rejected at first, yet unexpectedly, Lan Wangji said, "Let's."

Wei Wuxian *tsk tsk*-ed. "Hanguang-jun, you've really changed. In the past when I drank a tiny jug in front of you, you were super mean, trying to throw me over the wall and hitting me too. And now you're even hiding Emperor's Smile in your own room, drinking in secret."

Lan Wangji fixed his sleeves and said quietly, "I did not touch a single jug of Emperor's Smile."

Wei Wuxian teased, "Why are you hiding the jugs, then? Keeping them for me? Fine, fine. You didn't touch them. I believe you, all right? I won't mention it anymore. Come. I absolutely have to see just how many cups it'll take for a Lan descendant, an abstainer from drink, to collapse."

He poured a bowl for Lan Wangji, who took it and downed it without hesitation. Wei Wuxian got inexplicably excited, staring at his face to see when the man would start flushing. Yet unexpectedly, he stared for a long time, and neither the colors nor the expression on Lan Wangji's face changed in the slightest. Those light-colored pupils gazed at him very calmly—there was no change at all!

Wei Wuxian felt mightily disappointed. But just when he was about to egg the man on to drink another bowl, Lan Wangji's brows suddenly knitted. He lightly rubbed between his brows. A moment later, with one hand propping up his forehead, he closed his eyes.

…He fell asleep?

…He fell asleep!

Normally, after drinking liquor, one should first become drunk and *then* fall asleep. How could Lan Wangji skip the drunk step and go directly to sleep?!

What he wanted to see was the "drunk" part!

Wei Wuxian waved his hand at Lan Wangji, who looked stern and upright even in slumber, and clapped next to his ear. No answer.

The man was surprisingly a one-bowl lightweight.

Wei Wuxian had never expected such a situation. He slapped his own leg, contemplated for a moment, then circled his right arm around Lan Wangji's shoulders and carried the man out of the little tavern, dragging and pulling all the way.

He was already infinitely used to fishing things out from Lan Wangji's person, so he took out the money pouch and found them two rooms at an inn. He dropped Lan Wangji off in one of those rooms—removing his boots and tucking him into bed—and went out while it was still night.

Wei Wuxian made his way to a remote place outside the city, where he took out the bamboo flute on his waist, pressed it to his lips, and played a segment of a melody. After that, he waited quietly.

These past several days, Wei Wuxian and Lan Wangji had been together day in and day out, with no time alone. So, he had been unable to summon Wen Ning. Aside from the fact that he'd been trying to hide his identity before, there was another reason.

There were lives from the Lan Clan of Gusu that had been lost at Wen Ning's hands. Even if Lan Wangji treated him very well, Wei Wuxian couldn't just summon Wen Ning in front of him. Or rather, it was precisely because Lan Wangji was so good to him that Wei Wuxian felt too embarrassed to summon Wen Ning. No matter how thick-skinned he might be, this wasn't something to be shameless about.

When his mind came back around, there was already an ominous clinking sound drifting to his ears. The figure of Wen Ning, his head hung low, surfaced beneath the shadows of the city wall ahead.

He was dressed entirely in black, melting into the darkness around him. Only those pupilless eyes were glaringly white. Savagely white.

Wei Wuxian folded his hands behind his back and slowly circled the man. Wen Ning shifted, seeming to want to circle along behind him in his steps, and Wei Wuxian stated aloud, "Stand properly."

And so he behaved and stopped moving. That delicate, handsome face looked even more dejected.

"Hand," Wei Wuxian said.

Wen Ning extended his right hand and Wei Wuxian caught his wrist, raising it up to closely inspect the iron cuffs and chains.

Those were not normal chains. When Wen Ning went berserk, he was extremely violent. He could wring steel into mud. There was no way he would have intentionally allowed these chains to drag along behind him. These were probably a set of restraints specifically fabricated to shackle Wen Ning.

Bones crushed to ashes?

Even the remnant piece of the Yin Tiger Tally was being painstakingly restored. Of course certain clans would also be drooling over the Ghost General. How could they bear to have him crushed to ashes?

Wei Wuxian sneered and stood next to Wen Ning. After some thought, he reached out and started slowly kneading around in his hair.

The one who kept and locked up Wen Ning must have forbidden him from thinking on his own. For him to obey the command of another, Wen Ning's consciousness needed to be destroyed. Which meant there had to be something planted inside his brain. Sure enough, after kneading a few times, Wei Wuxian pressed on a hard little spot in a certain acupoint on the right side of his head. He put his other hand on the matching place on the left side of Wen Ning's head, and there was the same hard little object. It seemed to be something like the head of a nail.

Wei Wuxian pinched the ends of both nails at the same time. Moving slowly, he pulled two long, black nails from Wen Ning's skull.

These two black nails were several centimeters long, their thickness that of a red string that strung jade pendants, and they were buried deep inside Wen Ning's skull. The instant the nails were out, Wen Ning's features trembled lightly, and a layer of something like black blood vessels spiderwebbed within the white of his eyes. He appeared to be enduring the pain with immense effort.

He was clearly a dead man, yet he could still feel such a thing as "pain."

The nails were carved with intricate and complex patterns. Their origins must've been extraordinary, and the skill of the one who had created them might have been considerable. If Wei Wuxian wanted Wen Ning to recover, he would have to wait for some time. Wei Wuxian tucked the nails away, then looked down at the iron chains around Wen Ning's wrists and ankles. *Dragging those clink-clanking things around with him all the time won't do. I'll have to find a spiritual sword to cut them off.*

The first one that came to mind was, of course, Lan Wangji's Bichen. Although taking a Lan's sword to help Wen Ning cut off those chains didn't feel quite right, that was the spiritual sword he could most easily take, and he couldn't possibly leave Wen Ning like this, dragging around such a burden.

Wei Wuxian thought, *How's this? I will go back to the inn right now. If Lan Zhan is awake, I won't borrow the sword. If Lan Zhan is still asleep, then I'll borrow Bichen for a bit.*

With his mind made up, he turned right around. Unexpectedly, Lan Wangji was standing right behind him.

Wei Wuxian's emotions were in a jumbled state after summoning Wen Ning, so it couldn't be helped that he wasn't sharp and alert. As for Lan Wangji, if he hadn't wanted anyone to notice his arrival; that was a simple feat for him to accomplish. So the moment Wei Wuxian looked back, he saw beneath the moonlight that icy face that was ever colder. His heart stopped for a second, and he was very slightly startled.

He didn't know how long Lan Wangji had been there or whether he had heard all that he'd done and said. If Lan Wangji hadn't been drunk all along, but had followed behind him all the way, then this situation was even more awkward. Not mentioning a word regarding Wen Ning in front of him, but coming out to summon Wen Ning surreptitiously and sneakily the moment the man was asleep… It really was awkward.

Lan Wangji had his arms crossed with the sword Bichen hugged between them, his expression extremely cold. Wei Wuxian had never seen him so obviously upset, so he felt he had to speak first, to give an explanation and ease the mood.

"Ahem, Hanguang-jun."

Lan Wangji didn't respond.

Wei Wuxian stood in front of Wen Ning and stared back at Lan Wangji. He rubbed his chin. For some reason, a powerful sense of guilt enveloped him.

At last, Lan Wangji dropped the hand holding Bichen and took a couple steps forward. Wei Wuxian saw him lunge straight for Wen Ning with his sword and thought he was going to slay him. His mind spun rapidly. *Crap. Was Lan Zhan pretending to be drunk just to wait for me to come out and summon Wen Ning so he could slay him? That'd make sense—who really drops at one bowl?*

He tried, "Hanguang-jun, let me explain…"

Pah! Lan Wangji slapped Wen Ning.

The sound of this slap was loud and crisp, but the attack didn't hold any real power. Wen Ning only stumbled back a number of steps from the strike, swayed once, then steadied himself before he stood properly once more, looking completely at a loss.

Though Wen Ning's temper wasn't as explosive and easily provoked in his current state as it had been when he used to go berserk in the past, it wasn't that much better now. A sword hadn't even poked him on the night when he was surrounded at Mount Dafan and he'd sent the attackers flying, going as far as picking one of them up by the neck to choke them. If Wei Wuxian hadn't stopped him, he would've strangled every single person present. But now Lan Wangji had just slapped him, and he still had his head down, looking like he didn't dare to retaliate. Wei Wuxian thought this somewhat odd, but he was more relieved. If Wen Ning struck back and these two started fighting, it wouldn't be easy to make peace.

Presently, Lan Wangji seemed to think this slap wasn't quite enough to express his ire. He shoved Wen Ning with one hand and pushed him meters away.

He very unhappily said to Wen Ning, "Go away."

Wei Wuxian finally noticed something was off.

Lan Wangji's two moves, whether they were action or speech, were both very…childish.

After pushing Wen Ning far enough away, Lan Wangji seemed to finally be satisfied. He turned around and walked back, stopping beside Wei Wuxian.

Wei Wuxian stared at him, studying every detail.

There was nothing unusual about Lan Wangji's face or expression. In fact, he was even more solemn than usual, more serious, more flawless. His forehead ribbon was fastened extremely properly in place, his face unflushed, his breath unhurried, walking with wind beneath his feet, steady and firm. From the way he looked, he was still the same stern and proper, calm and collected, distinguished cultivator Hanguang-jun.

But when he looked down, he noticed Lan Wangji's boots were on the wrong feet.

Before he had come out, he had helped Lan Wangji remove his boots and tossed them by the bedside. And now Lan Wangji's left boot was on his right foot, and his right boot on his left.

Hanguang-jun, born of a prominent clan, who regarded grace and etiquette so highly, would never come out in public dressed like this.

Wei Wuxian ventured, "Hanguang-jun, how many fingers is this?"

He held up two fingers. Lan Wangji didn't respond but solemnly reached out with both hands, one left, one right, and earnestly held those two fingers.

Pah. With that motion, Bichen was dropped to the ground by its master.

"…"

This was definitely not the normal Lan Zhan!

"Hanguang-jun, are you drunk?" Wei Wuxian asked.

"No," Lan Wangji replied.

Drunk people never admitted that they were drunk. Wei Wuxian pulled his fingers back, but Lan Wangji maintained his hold, still absorbed in his slack fists. Wei Wuxian watched him speechlessly. Standing in the cold night breeze, he looked up at the moon.

Other people slept after they got drunk, but Lan Wangji slept first and *then* was drunk. And when he was inebriated, he looked no different from usual, so it was difficult to tell.

Wei Wuxian had had countless drinking buddies way back when, and he'd seen hundreds if not thousands of instances of bizarre drunken buffoonery. Some bawled aloud, some giggled endlessly, some lost it and made a scene, some passed out right on the streets, some lamented and wished for death, and some mewled weeping accusations of "Why don't you want me anymore?" This was his first time seeing Lan Wangji's type: quiet, composed, upstanding in appearance, but incomparably weird in action.

The corners of his lips twitched, and he forced back his desire to laugh. He picked up Bichen, which had been dropped to the ground, and slung it behind his back. "All right, come with me, let's go back."

He couldn't leave Lan Wangji running around outside in this state, gosh. Heaven knew what else he'd do.

Fortunately, Lan Wangji seemed very obliging, now that he was drunk. He inclined his head in a quite well-mannered motion and started walking with him. If anyone was to pass by, they would believe they were seeing two good friends roaming the night in deep conversation and would praise such elegant behavior.

Behind them, Wen Ning quietly caught up. Wei Wuxian was just about to say something to him when Lan Wangji whipped around and struck out with another enraged smack. This time, he slapped Wen Ning's head askew, bowing it even lower. Even though the muscles of his face were stiff from rigor mortis and he had no facial expression whatsoever, his white eyes displaying no emotion to speak of, it was possible to tell that he looked very aggrieved. Wei Wuxian didn't know whether to cry or laugh as he pulled Lan Wangji's arm back.

"What are you hitting him for?!"

Lan Wangji spoke in a threatening tone that he would never have used if sober. "Go away!"

Wei Wuxian knew you couldn't oppose drunk people. He quickly said, "Okay, okay, okay, we'll do what you want. I'll make him go away."

Then he pulled out the bamboo flute. However, before the flute made it to his lips, Lan Wangji snatched it over.

He stated, "You are not allowed to play for him."

Wei Wuxian teased, "Why are you so bossy, huh?"

Lan Wangji repeated unhappily, "You are not allowed to play for him!"

Wei Wuxian realized something. The drunk often had much to say, and since Lan Wangji didn't normally like speaking, after he had too much to drink, he would repeat the same sentence over and over. He thought that since Lan Wangji disliked the sight of the wicked arts, he probably didn't like him controlling Wen Ning with the flute.

He would have to smooth his ruffled fur a bit, and thus, he promised, "All right. I will only play for you, is that okay?"

Lan Wangji gave a satisfied "mn," but he was still fiddling with the flute in his hands and appeared to have no intent to give it back to him yet.

So Wei Wuxian had no choice but to blow two whistles instead. He said to Wen Ning, "Keep on hiding yourself. Do it properly and don't let anyone discover you."

Wen Ning looked like he really wanted to follow along, but since he had received the order and was afraid Lan Wangji would slap him further, he very slowly turned around and, dragging his feet, clinking and clanking, walked away somewhat dejectedly.

Wei Wuxian turned to Lan Wangji. "Lan Zhan, how come your face doesn't even turn a tiny bit red when you're drunk?"

Since Lan Wangji looked way too normal—even more normal than Wei Wuxian—he couldn't help but speak to him in a normal tone. Yet unexpectedly, when Lan Wangji heard him, he suddenly reached out, hugged Wei Wuxian's shoulders, and yanked him into his arms.

Caught off guard, Wei Wuxian crashed headfirst into his chest.

He was still dizzy when Lan Wangji's voice came from above. "Listen to the heartbeat."

"What?"

Lan Wangji said, "The face doesn't show it. Listen to the heartbeat."

As he spoke, his chest vibrated with a low sound, his heart beating constant and strong. *Thump-thump, thump-thump.* It was a little on the fast side. Wei Wuxian understood and pulled his head back.

"I can't tell from your face, so I have to figure it out by listening to your heartbeat?"

"Mn," Lan Wangji honestly replied.

Wei Wuxian hugged his belly as he laughed.

Could Lan Wangji's skin be so thick that not even a blush could surface? He didn't look to be the type!

An inebriated Lan Wangji was so surprisingly honest. And compared to his normal self, his actions and speech were...much more unrestrained!

It was so rare to see such an honest and frank Lan Wangji, so to tell Wei Wuxian to stay courteous, without playing a little prank? ...Yeah, right!

He rushed Lan Wangji back to the inn. Once they entered the room, Wei Wuxian pushed Lan Wangji onto the bed, then removed that mismatched pair of boots. Considering Lan Wangji likely didn't know how to wash his own face right now, Wei Wuxian removed Lan Wangji's forehead ribbon and fetched a bucket of hot water and a cloth. He wrung the cloth dry and folded it into a square, then gently wiped his face.

During the process, Lan Wangji did not make any protests but obediently allowed his own face to be squished around. When the cloth washed near his eyes, he'd squint, but otherwise, he kept staring at Wei Wuxian without blinking once. Wei Wuxian was brewing all sorts of mischief in his mind, and seeing his clear, innocent eyes, he couldn't resist giving the underside of Lan Wangji's chin a light scratch with his finger, chuckling as he did.

"What're you looking at me for? Am I good-looking?"

Wei Wuxian happened to be done with washing now, so he didn't wait for Lan Wangji to respond before tossing the cloth back into the water bucket.

"Your face is washed. Do you want to drink some water?"

There was no response behind him. When he turned to look, Lan Wangji had the water bucket in his hands and had already dunked his face.

Wei Wuxian, greatly alarmed, hurriedly snatched the bucket back, putting it aside. "I didn't tell you to drink *that* water!"

Lan Wangji lifted his head, looking impassive as drops of clear water rolled down his chin, wetting his front collar. Wei Wuxian watched him, his mind filled with mixed emotions, not knowing what to say.

...So did he drink the water or not? Lan Zhan best not remember anything when he sobers up, or he'll be too ashamed to face anyone for the rest of his life.

Wei Wuxian used his sleeve to wipe the droplets dripping off Lan Wangji's chin, then put his arm around his shoulders. "Hanguang-jun, are you gonna do whatever I tell you to right now?"

"Mn," Lan Wangji said.

"You'll answer anything I ask of you?"

"Mn."

Wei Wuxian pushed a knee onto the bed and crooked a smile. "Well, then. Let me ask you: have you ever snuck a sip of the Emperor's Smile you hid in your room?"

"No."

"Do you like rabbits?"

"Yes."

"Have you ever violated the rules?"

"Yes."

"Do you have someone you like?"

"Yes."

Wei Wuxian pulled his punches with his questions, since he didn't actually plan on prying into Lan Wangji's private business.

He was simply ensuring that the man was indeed going to answer every one of his questions.

He continued, "What do you think of Jiang Cheng?"

A frown. "Humph."

"What about Wen Ning?"

Clearly disinterested. "Heh."

Wei Wuxian pointed at himself with a wide, happy grin. "What about this one?"

"Mine," Lan Wangji answered.

"..."

Lan Wangji gazed intently at him and repeated, impeccably, clearly, emphasizing the word, "Mine."

Wei Wuxian suddenly got it.

He took off Bichen and thought, *I pointed at myself just now, but Lan Zhan probably misunderstood "this one" as Bichen on my back.*

Having thought this, he got off the bed and walked around the room from left to right, from east to west, with Bichen in hand. Sure enough, Lan Wangji's eyes also closely followed him wherever he went. So very candid, so very open, so very direct, so very naked.

Wei Wuxian was practically going weak-kneed from that gaze, which was as fervent as fire. He raised Bichen before Lan Wangji's eyes.

"Want it?"

"I do," Lan Wangji replied.

He seemed to think that wasn't enough to demonstrate his desire, so he seized the hand that was holding Bichen, his light-colored eyes gazing directly at Wei Wuxian. He breathed a soft sigh, then pronounced each word with force as he repeated himself.

"...I do."

Wei Wuxian knew full well the man was a drunken mess, knew

what he said wasn't directed at him, but still those two words struck him so hard his arm went weak, as did his legs.

He thought, *Honestly, this Lan Zhan…what a terrifying man he would be if he were this honest and enthusiastic toward a girl!*

Wei Wuxian regained his composure and asked, "How did you recognize me? Why are you helping me?"

Lan Wangji moved his lips softly, and Wei Wuxian moved closer, ready to hear the answer. Yet unexpectedly, Lan Wangji suddenly changed expression and shoved, pushing Wei Wuxian down on the bed.

Candlelight was extinguished with a sweep of his hand, and Bichen was once again dropped to the ground by its master.

The push made Wei Wuxian see stars. He thought perhaps Lan Wangji had sobered up. He called out, "Lan Zhan?!"

A certain familiar spot on the small of his back was tapped, and he felt sore and numb all over, unable to move, just like the first night he'd spent at the Cloud Recesses. Lan Wangji withdrew his hand and lay down right next to him. He covered both of them with the blanket and tucked the corner around Wei Wuxian carefully and thoroughly.

"It is hai time. Rest."

As it turned out, it was that terrifying Lan routine at work.

Wei Wuxian's question session was cut short. He stared at the ceiling of the bedroom. "Can we not chat and rest at the same time?"

"No," Lan Wangji said.

…Well, all right. There would always be another chance to get Lan Wangji drunk. He'd get his answer sooner or later.

"Lan Zhan, undo this. I rented two rooms, we don't have to squish together in the same bed," Wei Wuxian said.

After a moment of silence, Lan Wangji reached over and groped under the blanket, then slowly started undoing Wei Wuxian's sash.

Wei Wuxian shouted, "It's fine! I'm good! I didn't mean that kind of undo!!! Mn!!! Okay! I'll lie here, I'm sleeping!!!"

Within the darkness, it was deathly still.

Wei Wuxian was silent for a while before he spoke again, "I finally understand why your family banned liquor. One-bowl lightweight, and an awful drunk too. If every Lan is like you when they're drunk, liquor deserves to be prohibited. Whoever drinks gets a beating."

Lan Wangji had his eyes closed. He raised his hand to cover Wei Wuxian's mouth.

"Shh," he hushed.

Wei Wuxian's fit of annoyance was stuck between his chest and his teeth, unable to be expelled, unable to be dispelled.

Ever since he'd returned, it seemed like every time he'd wanted to tease Lan Wangji like he had in the past had ultimately become his own undoing.

That shouldn't be!! Where had he gone wrong?!

This time, Wei Wuxian did not shut his eyes the entire night. He stayed awake, firmly hanging on until just before mao time, and when he felt that numbing, aching limpness had passed and his limbs could move once more, he calmly and unhurriedly stripped off his top robe under the blanket and tossed it out of bed.

Then, he pulled on Lan Wangji's sash and forcefully tugged his top robe down by half. At first, he'd wanted to completely strip him too, but halfway through the act, he was slightly startled to see the brand under Lan Wangji's collarbone. His hands unconsciously stopped. Remembering the discipline whip scars on his back as well, Wei Wuxian knew that this wasn't right. He was about to immediately pull Lan Wangji's clothes back into place, but in that momentary delay, Lan Wangji seemed to have felt a chill. He shifted slightly, with furrowed brows, and then slowly opened his eyes.

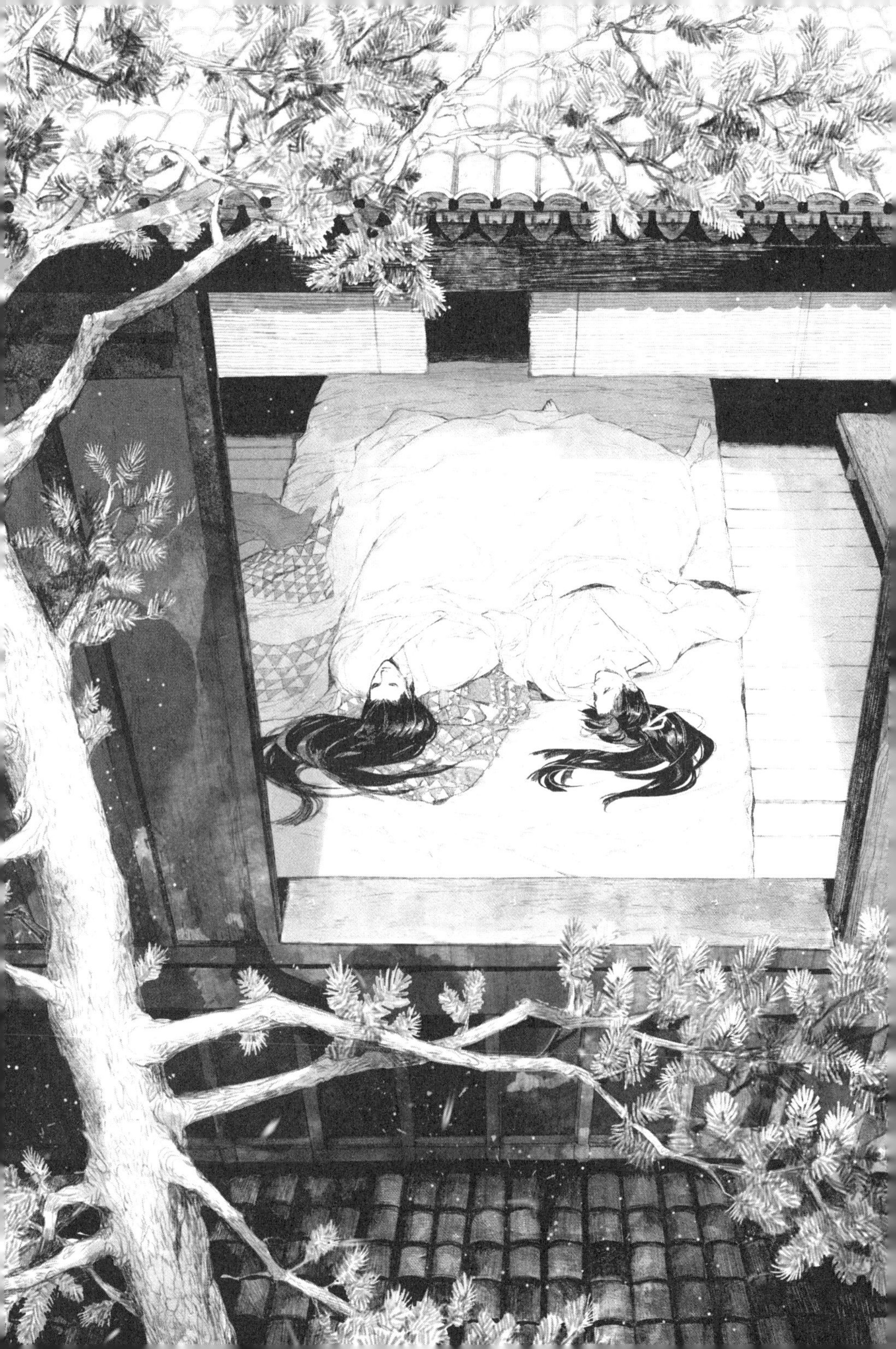

The moment his eyes opened, he tumbled off the bed.

The elegant Hanguang-jun couldn't be blamed for his entirely inelegant overreaction. No man would have a thought in his head for elegance when, after a night of drunkenness, they awoke half-naked in bed with another naked man, both of them pressed tightly together skin-to-skin under the same blankets.

Wei Wuxian used the blanket to half-cover his chest, revealing his smooth and bare shoulders.

Lan Wangji gaped. "You…"

Wei Wuxian answered nasally, "Hmm?"

Lan Wangji said, "Last night, I…"

Wei Wuxian winked and propped up his cheek with one hand, smirking wickedly. "Hanguang-jun, you were so bold last night~!"

"…"

"Do you not remember anything from yesterday evening?" Wei Wuxian asked.

Looked like he really didn't; Lan Wangji's face had paled to the color of snow.

It was good that he didn't. If Lan Wangji remembered that Wei Wuxian had snuck out last night to summon Wen Ning and started asking questions, it would be bad if Wei Wuxian lied, and bad if he told the truth too.

After his many failed dalliances and many instances of shooting himself in the foot, Wei Wuxian had finally recovered his past might for once, and he struck back at Lan Wangji. Although he was tempted to chase after more victories, he also still wanted to trick Lan Wangji into drinking more for his own petty amusement. So, he couldn't afford to have the man traumatized and on his guard from here onward.

Quitting while he was ahead, Wei Wuxian peeled back the

blanket to show his trousers in proper order and his yet-to-be-removed boots.

"What an honorable man! Hanguang-jun, I only stripped our clothes for a joke. You remain pure and unsullied, don't worry!"

Lan Wangji was still frozen on the spot, but before he could manage to say anything, the sound of shattering dishware came from the center of the room.

The sound was not foreign. This was the second time they had heard it. The evil-sealing qiankun pouch pinned on the table was agitated again and had toppled the teapot and teacups. It was more violent this time, with all three pouches going off at once. One of them had been a drunken mess the night before, and the other had been getting tossed about by said mess, so naturally, they had put the duet at the back of their minds.

Wei Wuxian was worried that Lan Wangji might accidentally stab him to death on the bed in a moment of impulse born of his immense shock. He hurriedly said, "Work. Come, come, let's get down to work first."

He grabbed a robe and draped it on, scrambling out of bed, and reached out for Lan Wangji, who had just risen to his feet. He had meant to pull him up, but his gesture looked like he was going to rip off his clothing. Lan Wangji hadn't recovered yet from his scare and took a step back. Something tripped him, and he wobbled in place. When he looked down, he realized it was the sword Bichen, which had lain there the entire night.

By now, the rope that tied the pouch had already been worked loose, and a ghastly white arm had crawled halfway out of the opening of the tiny qiankun pouch. Wei Wuxian reached into Lan Wangji's half-opened robes and fished around, digging out a flute.

"Hanguang-jun, c'mon, don't be scared. I wasn't gonna do anything to you. I was only taking back the flute you took from me last night. I need it back," he said, and even very thoughtfully helped him pull the robe over his shoulders and tie the sash.

Lan Wangji stared at him with a complicated look, looking like he really wanted to ask the details of what had happened the night before, after he'd gotten drunk. But attending to business was a habitual priority, so he forced himself to endure it. He composed his expression and took out his seven-stringed guqin. Three evil-sealing qiankun pouches: one sealed the left arm, one sealed the two legs, and one sealed the torso. Those three body parts could already constitute most of a body. They affected each other, their resentment increasing exponentially and becoming more troublesome than before. The two of them played "Rest" three times before the agitation gradually ceased.

Wei Wuxian put away the flute and was just about to clean up the corpse parts strewn on the ground when he suddenly went "oh?"

He said, "Our good buddy trained pretty good, eh?"

The sash of the funeral garb worn by the torso had come loose, the collar tugged askew to reveal the solid and powerful body of a man: his shoulders broad, his waist thin, his abs defined, strong but not exaggerated. It was a manly body innumerable men dreamed of having themselves. Wei Wuxian checked it out every which way and couldn't resist giving those abs a slap or two.

"Hanguang-jun, look at him. If he were alive, and I gave him a smack, it'd probably rebound and smack me right back. How in the world did he train to manage those results?"

The tips of Lan Wangji's brows seemed to twist. He didn't speak. Unexpectedly, Wei Wuxian slapped it twice more, and Lan Wangji finally, expressionlessly, took the evil-sealing qiankun pouch and

CHAPTER 7: THE MORNING DEW

silently began to seal the corpse. Wei Wuxian hastened to get out of the way. A moment later, Lan Wangji had resealed all the body parts and even tied a bunch of dead knots around the pouch. Wei Wuxian didn't think anything strange of it. He looked down at himself to inspect the shape of his current body, raised his brows, then tied his sash properly and appeared to don an air of decency once more.

He glanced to see that Lan Wangji had put away the qiankun pouches and was unwittingly casting looks his way, his eyes seemingly full of a certain hesitation to speak.

Wei Wuxian purposely broached the subject. "Hanguang-jun, why are you looking at me like that? Still worrying? Trust me, I really didn't do anything to you last night. Of course, you didn't do anything to me either."

Lan Wangji hesitated for a moment. Then, seeming to have made up his mind about something, he asked quietly, "Last night, other than taking the flute, what…"

"What? What else did you do, right?" Wei Wuxian said. "Not much, you just talked a lot."

Lan Wangji's snow-white throat bobbed once. "…Talked about what?"

"Nothing much," Wei Wuxian replied. "Just, mmn, for example, you really like…"

Lan Wangji's eyes stiffened.

"Really like rabbits," Wei Wuxian finished.

"…"

Lan Wangji closed his eyes and turned his head away. Wei Wuxian very thoughtfully consoled him.

"It's fine! Rabbits are so cute—who doesn't like them? I like them too. To *eat*, ha ha ha ha ha ha! Come on now, Hanguang-jun. You drank so much last night…uh, well, not that much, actually, but you were so drunk last night, you probably don't feel that great this morning. Go wash your face, drink some water, then sit for a bit longer. We'll depart after you feel better. The direction it pointed to this time is south, partially to the west. I'll go down and buy breakfast, so I'll leave you alone."

He was just leaving when Lan Wangji called out coldly, "Wait."

Wei Wuxian looked back. "What?"

Lan Wangji stared at him fixedly for a good while before he asked, at last, "Do you have money?"

Wei Wuxian smiled. "Yes! Don't I know where you put your money? I'll bring you breakfast too, 'kay? Take your time, Hanguang-jun, no rush."

He exited the room, closed the door, and stood in the hallway hugging his belly, laughing soundlessly for a good while.

Lan Wangji seemed to have been dealt a heavy blow. He locked himself in the room for a very long time, and while waiting for him, Wei Wuxian leisurely descended the stairs and went out of the inn, strolling around on the streets and buying some random food items. He sat on the steps, his eyes scrunched up into crescents as he ate, enjoying the sun. After a while, a group of thirteen- or fourteen-year-old children ran past on the street.

The child leading in the front ran fast as the wind, and his hand was yanking a long string. At the end of the string was a kite, flying neither high nor low, bobbing up and down as it did. The children behind had toy bows and arrows, and they shouted as they chased that kite, shooting miniature arrows at it.

Wei Wuxian had loved playing this game in the past. Archery was a mandatory art studied by every clan junior, but they didn't usually like shooting properly at normal targets. Besides shooting nefarious beings during Night Hunts, they enjoyed shooting kites like this.

CHAPTER 7: THE MORNING DEW

Everyone got a kite; whoever could fly it the highest, farthest, and shoot the most on mark was the winner. This game had been popular only among the younger juniors of various cultivation clans, but when the trend got out, children from ordinary families had liked it a lot too. Of course, their little arrows paled in comparison to the power packed in those wielded by privileged and proficient clan juniors.

Back when Wei Wuxian was at the Lotus Pier and played kite-shooting with the Jiang juniors, he'd won first place many times. Jiang Cheng, on the other hand, was always second; either his kite flew too far, and the arrows couldn't reach, or he'd shoot his kite, but it hadn't flown as far as Wei Wuxian's. The two of them had a kite a whole size larger than everyone else's, constructed in the shape of a flying yao beast, with dazzling, extravagant colors, a mouth open in a howl, and several pointy tails drooping down to roil with the winds. Seen from afar, the kite was extraordinarily vibrant and vivacious, not savage so much as charming and adorable. The spine of this kite had been personally constructed by Jiang Fengmian before being passed off to Jiang Yanli to paint it for the two of them, so every time they took it out to compete, they'd always felt a sense of pride.

Having remembered this, the corners of Wei Wuxian's lips curled lightly, and he unconsciously looked up to see what the kites those children were flying looked like. All he saw was a big, round shape, completely gold. He wondered, *What is that thing? A pancake? Or some monster I don't know of?*

Just then, a gust of wind blew past. The kite wasn't flying very high in the first place, and not in an open, spacious area, so it fell immediately when the wind hit. One of the children called out, "Gah, the sun's fallen down!"

Wei Wuxian instantly understood. This group of children was most likely playing a game that mimicked the Sunshot Campaign.

This was Yueyang. Back when the Wen Clan of Qishan was at the peak of its prominence, they had lorded over everyone and everywhere, and Yueyang was technically not too far from Qishan. The locals must've suffered profoundly at their hands, either from rampaging yao beasts they hadn't locked up properly or by being abused and humiliated by the domineering cultivators of their clan. After the Sunshot Campaign, the Wen Clan was crushed by the combined might of the other clans, their century-old foundation collapsing in an instant. Many places near the Qishan area all happily engaged in pastimes that celebrated the annihilation of the Wen Clan, going as far as transforming such pastimes into cherished traditions. This game was probably one such tradition.

The children stopped the chase and gathered around, looking very troubled. They started discussing the situation at hand.

"What do we do? The sun hasn't been shot yet, and it dropped on its own. Who will be the big boss now?"

Someone raised their hand. "It's gonna be me, of course! I'm Jin Guangyao! The Wen family's big villain was killed by me!"

Wei Wuxian sat there on the steps in front of the inn, watching with relish.

In games like this one, the now infinitely glorious Cultivation Chief Lianfang-zun was, of course, the most popular character. Although his background was too embarrassing to speak of, that was precisely why the higher he climbed, the more admirable he grew. During the Sunshot Campaign, he spent years as a spy, and took to the role like a fish released into water. He had the entire Wen Clan of Qishan fooled both inside and out, and they ran around in circles, unknowingly betraying their own secrets. After the Sunshot

Campaign, he curried favor by every means possible, using his quick and clever wit in thousands of ways until finally he sat in the position of Cultivation Chief, the head of the cultivation world. Such a life was worthy of being called legendary. If Wei Wuxian was the one playing, he'd want to try being Jin Guangyao once too. Picking this kid to be the big boss made a lot of sense!

Another child objected, "I'm Nie Mingjue, I've won the most battles, and I've taken the biggest number of captives. I should be the big boss!"

"Jin Guangyao" said, "But I'm Cultivation Chief."

"Nie Mingjue" waved his fist. "So what? You're still my san-di. Don't you still have to run away with your tail between your legs at the sight of me?"

"Jin Guangyao" was indeed very cooperative, very into the act. He hunched his shoulders and ran off.

Another one said, "You short-lived devil."

To have chosen a certain cultivation leader naturally meant the child in question probably looked up to and liked said cultivator. "Nie Mingjue" got mad.

"Jin Zixuan, you died sooner than me, you're even more short-lived!"

"Jin Zixuan" refused to yield. "So what if I'm short-lived? I'm ranked third!"

"That third place was only for looks!"

Just then, one of the kids seemed to tire of running and standing. He shuffled to the steps, sat down next to Wei Wuxian, waved, and said like a good ol' peacekeeper, "Okay, okay, stop fighting. I'm the Yiling Patriarch, I'm the most powerful. I suppose I can maaaaaybe be the big boss."

Wei Wuxian was speechless. "..."

He looked down. Sure enough, this kid had a tiny, thin wooden stick stuck at his waist. This was probably Chenqing.

Only a small child would be simple enough not to fuss about good and bad, and only care about rating things by strength—and therefore condescend to be the Yiling Patriarch for a bit.

Another one countered, "No, I'm Sandu Shengshou, *I'm* the most powerful one."

"Yiling Patriarch" said, very understandingly, "Oh, Jiang Cheng. Can you match me in anything? Haven't you lost to me every time? Where did you get the face to say you're the most powerful? Aren't you embarrassed?"

"Jiang Cheng" retorted, "Humph. I can't match you? Don't you remember how you died?"

That shallow smile on Wei Wuxian's lips instantly dispersed.

It was like being jabbed by an extremely poisonous little needle without warning. A slight, stabbing pain suddenly flared all over his body.

The "Yiling Patriarch" next to him clapped. "Lookit me! Chenqing in my left hand, the tiger tally in my right, plus a Ghost General—I'm invincible! Ha ha ha ha…"

He raised a stick with his left hand and a rock with his right, then laughed maniacally.

"Where's Wen Ning? Come out!"

A small child raised his hand among the crowd and said meekly, "I'm here…um…I wanna say…since it's during the Sunshot Campaign, I haven't died yet…"

Wei Wuxian felt he had to step in now.

He spoke up, "Cultivation leaders, may I ask a question?"

No adult had ever intervened when this group of children played this game before. And it wasn't even to scold but to pose a serious

CHAPTER 7: THE MORNING DEW

question. "Yiling Patriarch" looked at him in wonder and caution. "What's your question?"

"How come there's no one from the Lan Clan of Gusu?" Wei Wuxian asked.

"There is."

"Where?"

"Yiling Patriarch" pointed at a child who had not spoken a single word throughout. "That one's him."

Wei Wuxian looked. Sure enough, that child was very delicately handsome, obviously solidly on the path to becoming an attractive young man. On his smooth forehead was fastened a white rope, a substitute for the forehead ribbon.

Wei Wuxian asked, "Who's he?"

"Yiling Patriarch" pursed his lips disdainfully, then said, "Lan Wangji!"

...All right. This group of children had truly captured the essence. One certainly should keep their mouth shut and not speak when playing Lan Wangji!

The corners of Wei Wuxian's lips curled up anew all of a sudden. That extremely poisonous little needle was pulled out and tossed to an unknown corner, and the stabbing pain was all swept away in an instant.

Wei Wuxian mumbled to himself, "Well, ain't that strange. How can such a dull person always make me so happy?"

When Lan Wangji finally came downstairs, he saw Wei Wuxian sitting on the steps with a bunch of kids sitting next to him and sharing meat buns. Wei Wuxian ate his bun as he directed two little kids pressed back-to-back in front of him.

"...Right now, the ones in front of you are millions of Wen cultivators, every single one of them fully decked out in military gear, and they have surrounded you in an impenetrable circle. Look sharp—that's right, just like that. Good. Lan Wangji, pay attention. You're not your usual self right now, you're covered in blood! You're very heavy with killing intent! Your eyes are fierce! Wei Wuxian, get closer to him, do you know how to spin your flute? Let's see it. Spin it with one hand. Do it more nonchalantly, do you understand what that means? Come here, lemme teach you."

"Wei Wuxian" *oh*-ed and passed the thin little stick over to him. Wei Wuxian expertly twirled "Chenqing" with two fingers, and the group of kids crowded over in a flash, exclaiming aloud in awe.

Lan Wangji commented, "..."

He approached silently. When Wei Wuxian saw him come over, he dusted off the dirt on his bum and bid farewell to the children. It took great effort for him to stand, and as they went, he laughed the entire way as if he'd been poisoned with something strange.

Lan Wangji commented, "..."

"Ha ha ha ha ha ha, sorry, Hanguang-jun, I already shared the breakfast I bought for you with them. Let's buy more later."

"Mn," Lan Wangji said.

"How was it? Weren't those two kids cute? The one with a rope tied around his head, guess who he's imitating? Ha ha ha ha..."

After a long moment of speechlessness, Lan Wangji finally couldn't hold back any longer. He asked, "What else did I do last night, exactly?"

It couldn't be that simple, otherwise why would Wei Wuxian still be laughing even now?!

Wei Wuxian waved him off. "Nothing, nothing, nothing. You didn't do anything, it was me who was being nonsensical, ha ha ha ha ha ha...all right, ahem, Hanguang-jun, I'm about to talk about serious business now."

"Speak," Lan Wangji said.

Wei Wuxian began, in all seriousness, "The coffin-banging at the Chang family cemetery had been still for ten years, but it suddenly started up again. This is definitely not a coincidence. There must be a cause."

"What do you think the cause is?" Lan Wangji asked.

"Good question. I think the cause is the torso being dug out," Wei Wuxian said.

"Mn," Lan Wangji said.

His thoughtful expression reminded Wei Wuxian of his serious face the previous night, when he had drunkenly held onto Wei Wuxian's two fingers. He painfully held back his laughter.

He said solemnly, "I was thinking—the dismemberment can't have been a simple act of revenge regarding a personal grudge but a malicious subduing spell. The one who dismembered the corpse intentionally selected places with unusual hauntings to settle the body parts."

"Fight poison with poison; maintain equilibrium through mutual checks and balances," Lan Wangji said.

"Correct," Wei Wuxian said. "So when that gravedigger dug out the torso yesterday, there was nothing to subdue the resentful spirits of the Chang family, and the coffin-banging started up again. The concept and method are the same as the Nie Saber Offerings Hall's, subduing the saber spirits and wall corpses. Perhaps it was mimicking the Nie family's Saber Offerings Hall from the start. It seems this individual is deeply connected with both the Nie Clan of Qinghe and the Lan Clan of Gusu. They're probably not just some nobody."

"There are not many such individuals," Lan Wangji said.

Wei Wuxian agreed, "Mn. Things are slowly coming to light. And, since the other party has started trying to move the corpse bits, that means he—or they—are starting to panic. They'll definitely make a move soon, so even if we don't go find them, they'll come knocking. With all the searching, they'll give themselves away sooner or later. Besides, our good buddy's arm will point the way for us. But we should probably move faster too. With only the right arm and a head left, we have to get to those before they do."

The two traveled southwestward. This time, the location the left hand had pointed to was Shudong, a place blanketed by thick fog.

And it was a ghost city that locals avoided at all cost.

THE STORY CONTINUES IN
Grandmaster of Demonic Cultivation
VOLUME 2

Grandmaster of Demonic Cultivation
MO DAO ZU SHI

Character & Name Guide

CHARACTER & NAME GUIDE

Characters

> The identity of certain characters may be a spoiler; use this guide with caution on your first read of the novel.
>
> Note on the given name translations: Chinese characters may have many different readings. Each reading here is just one out of several possible readings presented for your reference and should not be considered a definitive translation.

MAIN CHARACTERS

Wei Wuxian

BIRTH NAME: Wei Ying (魏婴 / Surname Wei, "Infant")

COURTESY NAME: Wei Wuxian (魏无羡 / Surname Wei, "Having no envy")

SOBRIQUET: Yiling Patriarch

WEAPON:

  Sword: Suiban (随便 / "Whatever")

  Hufu/Tiger Tally: Yin Tiger Tally (阴虎符)

INSTRUMENT:

  Dizi (side-blown flute): Chenqing (陈情 / "To explain one's situation in detail." This is a reference to a line in a collection of poems, *Chu Ci* [楚辞], by famous poet Qu Yuan)

  Unnamed dizi (side-blown flute)

In his previous life, Wei Wuxian was the feared Yiling Patriarch. He commanded an army of the living dead with his wicked flute Chenqing and laid waste to the cultivation world in an orgy of blood that eventually resulted in his death. Thirteen years later, a troubled young man sacrifices his soul to resurrect Wei Wuxian in his own body, hoping the terrible Yiling Patriarch will enact revenge on his behalf. Awakening confused and disoriented in this new body, Wei Wuxian stumbles forth into his second chance at life. Now, he must piece together the mystery surrounding his return—and face the lingering consequences of his last life, which continue to dog him even beyond death.

Wei Wuxian is mischievous and highly intelligent. He seems physically incapable of keeping his mouth shut; similarly, he just can't seem to stop himself from teasing people that catch his interest—with Lan Wangji being a perennial favorite target, even after thirteen years away from the land of the living.

Lan Wangji

BIRTH NAME: Lan Zhan (蓝湛 / "Blue," "Clear" or "Deep")

COURTESY NAME: Lan Wangji (蓝忘机 / "Blue," "Free of worldly concerns")

SOBRIQUET: Hanguang-jun (含光君 / "Light-bringer," honorific "-jun")

WEAPON: Sword: Bichen (避尘 / "Shunning worldly affairs")

INSTRUMENT: Guqin (zither): Wangji (忘机 / "Free of worldly concerns")

Lan Wangji's perfection as a cultivator is matched by none. Shunning petty politics and social prejudices, he appears wherever there is chaos to quell it with his sword Bichen, and evildoers quake in fear at the sound of strumming guqin strings. His remarkable grace and beauty have won him renown far and wide, even though his perpetual frown makes him look like a widower.

Lan Wangji is younger brother to the current Lan Sect leader,

Lan Xichen. He is stern, reserved, highly principled, and an avid fan of rabbits. While in his youth Lan Wangji was more easily ruffled by teasing, the ruffling these days seems harder to manage.

SUPPORTING CHARACTERS

Mo Xuanyu

COURTESY NAME: Mo Xuanyu (莫玄羽 / "Nothing" or "There is none who," "Mysterious" or "Black," "Feathers")

The young man who offered up his own body to bring Wei Wuxian back into the land of the living at a most horrible price: the obliteration of his own soul. He is one of the many illegitimate sons of Jin Guangshan. After he was expelled from the Jin Sect, the humiliation took a dreadful toll on his mind. He endured years of relentless abuse by the Mo household and eventually turned to demonic cultivation to exact revenge on those who tormented him. With his soul destroyed, Mo Xuanyu himself is now but a memory, and Wei Wuxian inhabits his body.

Lan Jingyi

COURTESY NAME: Lan Jingyi (蓝景仪 / "Blue," "Scenery," "Bearing" or "Appearance")

WEAPON: Unnamed sword

A junior disciple in the Lan Sect. He is close friends with Lan Sizhui, and appears to have a special kind of admiration for Lan Wangji. Although he was raised in such a strict sect, Lan Jingyi is distinctly un-Lan-like in his mannerisms, being loud, bluntly honest, and easily worked up into a tizzy. That being said, like any Lan, he is still very quick to spot and accuse instances of rule-breaking on the Cloud Recesses' premises.

Lan Sizhui

BIRTH NAME: Lan Yuan (蓝愿 / "Blue," "Wish")

COURTESY NAME: Lan Sizhui (蓝思追 / "Blue," "To remember and long for")

WEAPON: Unnamed sword

INSTRUMENT: Unnamed guqin

A junior disciple in the Lan Sect. He is close friends with Lan Jingyi and appears to have a special kind of admiration for Lan Wangji. Lan Sizhui is poised and quite mature for his age, and is a natural leader of his peers when the juniors are sent out on investigations. Although he was raised in such a strict sect, Lan Sizhui retains an air of warmth about him. He is kind, intuitive, and willing to see beyond surface appearances.

Jiang Cheng

BIRTH NAME: Jiang Cheng (江澄 / "River," "Clear")

COURTESY NAME: Jiang Wanyin (江晚吟 / "River," "Night," "Recitation")

SOBRIQUET: Sandu Shengshou (三毒圣手 / "Three Sufferings," a reference to the Buddhist three roots of suffering: greed, anger, and ignorance, "Sage Hand"

WEAPON:

Whip: Zidian (紫电 / "Purple," "Lightning")

Sword: Sandu (三毒 / "Three Sufferings")

Jiang Cheng is the leader of the Jiang Sect, and Jin Ling's maternal uncle. Known to be stern and unrelenting, he possesses a long-standing grudge against Wei Wuxian even after the latter's death. This is a far cry from the way things once were—Jiang Cheng and Wei Wuxian grew up together at Lotus Pier when the homeless and orphaned Wei Wuxian was taken in by Jiang Cheng's father, and were the closest of friends as well as martial siblings. However, after Wei Wuxian's rise as the Yiling Patriarch, their friendship ended alongside the many people who died at his hands…or so it seems.

Jin Ling

BIRTH NAME: Jin Ling (金凌 / "Gold," "Tower aloft")
COURTESY NAME: Jin Rulan (金如兰 / "Gold," "Like" or "As if," "Orchid")
WEAPON:
 Sword: Suihua (岁华 / "Passage of time"),
  previously owned by Jin Zixuan
 Fairy (spirit dog)
 Unnamed bow

The young heir to the Jin Clan and son of Jin Zixuan and Jiang Yanli. Jin Ling grew up a lonely child, bullied by his peers and overly doted on by his caretakers out of pity. Though Jin Ling remains quite spoiled and unmanageable in temperament, he strongly dislikes being looked down upon and seeks to prove himself as a cultivator. He is often seen squabbling with his maternal uncle and sometimes-caretaker Jiang Cheng, or hurling himself headlong into mortal peril alongside his loyal spirit dog Fairy.

Jin Guangshan

COURTESY NAME: Jin Guangshan (金光善 / "Gold," "Light and glory," "Kindness")

The former Jin Sect head and father to Jin Zixuan, Jin Guangyao, Mo Xuanyu, and many, many more. He was a womanizer who would abandon his lovers just as quickly as he would any children born of his dalliances. Despite this ravenous appetite, he only sired one child (Jin Zixuan) with his lawful wife. Under his rule, the Jin Sect was loathed by the cultivation world for its shameless abuses, corruption, and excess. Thankfully, he eventually died of exhaustion during an orgy and was succeeded by Jin Guangyao.

Jin Zixuan

COURTESY NAME: Jin Zixhuan (金子轩 / "Gold," common male prefix "Son," "Pavilion")

WEAPON: Sword: Suihua (岁华 / "Passage of time")

The Jin Clan heir and the only legitimate son of Jin Guangshan. He married Jiang Yanli and together they had a son, Jin Ling. He attended school at the Cloud Recesses in his youth and was classmates with Wei Wuxian, Jiang Cheng, and Nie Huaisang. Due to his status, his natural skill, and his good looks, Jin Zixuan was generally rather prideful and arrogant, and was disliked by his peers.

Jiang Yanli

BIRTH NAME: Jiang Yanli (江厌离 / "River," "To dislike separation")

WEAPON: Love, patience, soup

The eldest daughter of the Jiang Clan, older sister to Jiang Cheng, and older martial sister to Wei Wuxian. She is Jin Zixuan's wife and Jin Ling's mother, and is warmly remembered by Wei Wuxian as being unconditionally kind and caring.

Jin Guangyao

COURTESY NAME: Jin Guangyao (金光瑶 / "Gold," "Light and glory," "Jade")

SOBRIQUET: Lianfang-zun (敛芳尊 / "Hidden fragrance," honorific "-zun")

The current Jin Sect head. He is half-siblings with Jin Zixuan, Mo Xuanyu, and countless other children born of Jin Guangshan's wandering libido. He is also sworn brothers with Lan Xichen and Nie Mingjue, and together, they are known as the Three Zun. He is particularly close to Lan Xichen and frequently hosts him at Golden Carp Tower.

Jin Guangyao rose from humble circumstances and became not only the head of the Jin Sect but also the Cultivation Chief of the inter-sect alliance. His skill at politicking and networking is matched by none, and through restructuring and reparations he was able to largely make up for the damage done to the Jin Sect's reputation by his father's rule.

Nie Huaisang

COURTESY NAME: Nie Huaisang (聂怀桑 / "Whisper," "Cherish," "Mulberry")

SOBRIQUET: Head-Shaker (一问三不知 / "One Question, Three Don't-Knows")

WEAPON:

Unnamed saber (ostensibly)

Crying (actually)

The current Nie Sect head and Nie Mingjue's younger half-brother. When they were young, he attended school at the Cloud Recesses with Wei Wuxian and Jiang Cheng. Nie Huaisang is a dilettante dandy who possesses a passionate love of fashion and the arts, but unfortunately possesses no such innate genius for politics or management. He is frequently seen looking stricken and panicked, and largely relies on the compassion and assistance of his older brother's sworn brothers (Lan Xichen and Jin Guangyao) to keep the Nie Sect struggling along.

Nie Mingjue

COURTESY NAME: Nie Mingjue (聂明玦 / "Whisper," "Bright" or "Righteousness," "Jade ring")

SOBRIQUET: Chifeng-zun (赤锋尊 / "Crimson Blade," honorific "-zun")

WEAPON: Saber: Baxia (霸下 / "To be ruled by force," also the name of one of the mythical Dragon King's nine sons.)

The former Nie Sect head and Nie Huaisang's older half-brother. He is also sworn brothers with Lan Xichen and Jin Guangyao, and together they are known as the Three Zun. Nie Mingjue was a fierce man who was quick to use violence as a solution. He was unable to tolerate injustice or underhanded behavior, and was fearless in calling out even those in the highest seats of power. Unfortunately, his temperament eventually got the better of him, and he died at a young age from a qi deviation.

Lan Qiren

COURTESY NAME: Lan Qiren (蓝启仁 / "Blue," "Open" or "Awaken," "Benevolence")

WEAPON: Long lectures, closed-book exams

A Lan Clan elder and the paternal uncle of Lan Xichen and Lan Wangji. He is well known across the cultivation world as an exemplary (and extremely strict) teacher who consistently produces equally exemplary students. He loves his nephews deeply, and is clearly extremely proud of their accomplishments and skill as cultivators and gentlemen both. However, he does not exclude them from the prescribed clan punishments on the rare occasion that such things are warranted.

Lan Xichen

BIRTH NAME: Lan Huan (蓝涣 / "Blue," "Melt" or "Dissipate")

COURTESY NAME: Lan Xichen (蓝曦臣 / "Blue," "Sunlight," "Minister" or "Subject")

SOBRIQUET: Zewu-jun (泽芜 / "Moss-shaded pool," honorific "-jun")

WEAPON: Sword: Shuoyue (朔月 / "New moon")

INSTRUMENT: Xiao (end-blown flute): Liebing (裂冰 / "Cracked," "Ice")

The current Lan Sect head and Lan Wangji's elder brother. He is also sworn brothers with Jin Guangyao and Nie Mingjue, and together they are known as the Three Zun.

Lan Xichen possesses a warm and gentle personality, and can easily get along with anyone and everyone. He possesses the unique and curious ability to understand his reticent little brother at a glance. He is as calm and undisturbed as the shaded pool from which he takes his sobriquet and will lend an ear to anyone who approaches, whatever their social standing.

Song Lan

BIRTH NAME: Song Lan (宋岚 / Surname Song, "Mist")

COURTESY NAME: Song Zichen (宋子琛 / Surname Song, a common male name prefix "Son," "Gem" or "Jewel")

WEAPON: Sword: Fuxue (拂雪 / "To sweep away snow")

A Daoist cultivator and close friend of Xiao Xingchen. He was known to be quiet and stern, and dreamed of founding a sect by Xiao Xingchen's side.

Wen Ning

BIRTH NAME: Wen Ning (温宁 / "Mild" or "Warm," "Peaceful")
SOBRIQUET: Ghost General (鬼将军)
WEAPON: Fists, feet, and metal chains

A fierce corpse known as the Ghost General, thought to have been destroyed during the Siege of the Burial Mounds. One of the Yiling Patriarch's finest creations, Wen Ning retains his mind and personality. Coupled with the strength to crush steel to dust with his bare fists, it is no wonder that he was once Wei Wuxian's right-hand man.

Xiao Xingchen

COURTESY NAME: Xiao Xingchen (晓星尘 / "Dawn," "Stardust")
WEAPON: Sword: Shuanghua (霜华 / "Frost Flower," referring to the natural phenomenon when ice crystals form on long-stemmed plants)

A mysterious and once-highly regarded cultivator. He is close friends with Song Lan and dreamed of founding a sect with him. He lived on a remote mountaintop for most of his life, under the tutelage of his shizun, the immortal Baoshan-sanren. He descended the mountain to do good deeds for the common people of the world, and was well known for his skill and sense of justice. However, just as suddenly as he appeared, he disappeared, and has not been heard from since.

Xue Yang

BIRTH NAME: Xue Yang (薛洋 / Surname Xue, "Ocean")

On the surface, Xue Yang is a petty thug with a penchant for violence. Below the surface, he is still a petty thug with a penchant for violence, but with a strange knack for understanding the dark arts—a truly terrible combination.

Little Apple

WEAPON: Hooves, teeth, and raw fury

A spotted donkey that Wei Wuxian stole from Mo Manor as he made his escape after the ghost arm incident. Little Apple is imperious, hard to please, and very temperamental; however, it possesses a strong sense of justice and a heart brave enough to put even the most renown cultivators to shame. It also really loves apples. Little Apple's gender is never specified in the text.

Fairy

WEAPON: Claws, jaws, and the only brain in the room (usually)
INSTRUMENT: Woof!

Jin Ling's loyal spirit dog. As a spirit dog, Fairy possesses intelligence of a level above the average canine and can detect supernatural beings. Regarding the pup's name, "Fairy" could refer to the Chinese *xianzi* (仙子), a female celestial being, but it is also a common way to describe a woman with ethereal, otherworldly beauty. That being said, Fairy's gender is never specified in the text.

Locations

Mo Estate (莫家庄)

An estate a few days' walk from Mount Dafan. It is the location of Mo Manor and the home of Mo Xuanyu (and the rest of the Mo family).

Mount Dafan (大梵山)

A mountain a few days' walk from Mo Estate. The mountain resembles a Laughing Buddha statue, hence its name: "Big Brahma."

Fojiao Town (佛脚镇)

A tiny town at the base of Mount Dafan. Because Mount Dafan resembles a Buddha statue and the town is at its feet, Fojiao Town got its name: "Buddha Foot."

Shrine of the Heavenly Maiden (天女祠)

A temple on Mount Dafan. It houses a natural rock formation that resembles a dancing woman, dubbed by locals as the Heavenly Maiden. Over the years, locals started worshiping the rock formation as a wish-granting goddess, which allowed it to cultivate spiritual powers and gain rudimentary sentience.

Gusu (姑苏)

A city in the Jiangnan region. Jiangnan is famous for its rich, fertile land and its abundant agricultural goods. Its hazy, drizzling rainy weather and the soft sweet dialect make it a popular setting in Chinese romance literature.

Cloud Recesses (云深不知处)

The residence of the Lan Clan of Gusu, located on a remote mountaintop. The Cloud Recesses is a tranquil place constantly shrouded in mist. Beside the entrance there looms the Wall of Discipline, carved with the three thousand (later four thousand) rules of the Lan Clan.

The Cloud Recesses is home to the Library Pavilion where many rare and ancient texts are housed, the Tranquility Room where Lan Wangji resides, and the Orchid Room where Lan Qiren hosts lectures. There is also the Nether Room, a tower in which spirit-summoning rituals are performed, as well as a cold spring for bathing. On the back of the mountain is a secluded meadow where Lan Wangji keeps his pet rabbits.

The Cloud Recesses' name translates more literally to "Somewhere Hidden in Clouds" and is a reference to a line in the poem "Failing to Find the Hermit," by Jia Dao.

> *I asked the young disciple beneath the pine;*
> *"My master is gone to pick herbs," he answered.*
> *"Though within this mountain he is,*
> *The recesses of clouds hide his trail."*

Caiyi Town (彩衣镇)

A town about six miles from the Cloud Recesses. It adjoins Biling Lake and is built on dozens of connecting waterways, which are always lively with trade boats. The banks are lined with traders selling various fruits, crafts, and other goods.

Qinghe (清河)

A city in the Hebei region. Qinghe is the home territory of the Nie Clan and is where their residence is located.

Xinglu Ridge (行路岭)

A ridge near Qinghe. It is heavily forested and is rumored to be home to man-eating monsters.

Stone Bunkers (石堡 / 吃人堡)

Rumored to eat people, these strange bunkers (which look like overturned bowls) lie near Xinglu Ridge. They are in fact the ancestral tombs of the Nie Clan, but there's further strangeness afoot: the coffins entombed within contain not corpses but rather sabers.

Yueyang (栎阳)

A city in the Shaanxi region. It is near Qishan, the territory the Wen Sect once controlled. It was the home of the Chang Clan, until they were wiped out in a terrible massacre that claimed the lives of the whole family. It's said that if you venture near the cemetery, you can hear their spirits desperately banging their terrified fists on the lids of their coffins.

Other local attractions include the many taverns lining the streets that provide a scenic spot to enjoy regional brews, and inns that provide a convenient bed for you to sleep off the resulting hangover.

Name Guide

Courtesy Names

A courtesy name is given to an individual when they come of age. Traditionally, this was at the age of twenty during one's crowning ceremony, but it can also be presented when an elder or teacher deems the recipient worthy. Generally a male-only tradition, there is historical precedent for women adopting a courtesy name after marriage. Courtesy names were a tradition reserved for the upper class.

It was considered disrespectful for one's peers of the same generation to address someone by their birth name, especially in formal or written communication. Use of one's birth name was reserved for only elders, close friends, and spouses.

This practice is no longer used in modern China but is commonly seen in wuxia and xianxia media, as such, many characters have more than one name. Its implementation in novels is irregular and is often treated malleably for the sake of storytelling. For example, in *Grandmaster of Demonic Cultivation*, characters as young as fifteen years of age are referred to only by their courtesy names, while traditionally they would not have been permitted to use them until the age of twenty.

Diminutives, Nicknames, and Name Tags

XIAO-: A diminutive meaning "little." Always a prefix.
    EXAMPLE: Xiao-Pingguo (Little Apple)

-ER: A word for "son" or "child." Added to a name, it expresses affection. Similar to calling someone "Little" or "Sonny."

A-: Friendly diminutive. Always a prefix. Usually for monosyllabic names, or one syllable out of a two-syllable name.
    EXAMPLE: A-Qing, A-Yuan, A-Xian (For Wei Wuxian)

Doubling a syllable of a person's name can be a nickname, and has childish or cutesy connotations. For example: Xianxian (for Wei Wuxian, referring to himself).

FAMILY

DI: Younger brother or younger male friend. Can be used alone or as an honorific.

DIDI: Younger brother or a younger male friend. Casual.

XIAO-DI: Does not mean "little brother", and instead refers to one's lackey or subordinate, someone a leader took under their wings.

GE: Familiar way to refer to an older brother or older male friend, used by someone substantially younger or of lower status. Can be used alone or with the person's name.

GEGE: Familiar way to refer to an older brother or an older male friend, used by someone substantially younger or of lower status. Has a cutesier feel than "ge."

JIE: Older sister or older female friend. Can be used alone or as an honorific.

JIEJIE: Older sister or an unrelated older female friend. Casual.

JIUJIU: Uncle (maternal, biological).

MEI: Younger sister or younger female friend. Can be used alone or as an honorific.

MEIMEI: Younger sister or an unrelated younger female friend. Casual.

SHUFU: Uncle (paternal, biological) Formal address for one's father's younger brother.

SHUSHU: An affectionate version of "Shufu."

XIAOSHU: Little uncle.

XIONG: Older brother. Generally used as an honorific. Formal, but also used informally between male friends of equal status.
XIONGZHANG: Eldest brother or oldest male friend. Very formal.
XIANSHENG: "Husband" or "Mister" in modern usage; historical usage was broadly "teacher."

If multiple relatives in the same category are present (multiple older brothers, for example) everyone is assigned a number in order of birthdate, starting with the eldest as number one, the second oldest as number two, etc. These numbers are then used to differentiate one person from another. This goes for all of the categories above, whether it's siblings, cousins, aunts, uncles, and so on.

EXAMPLES:

If you have three older brothers, the oldest would be referred to as "da-ge," the second oldest "er-ge," and the third oldest "san-ge."

If you have two younger brothers you (as the oldest) would be number one. Your second-youngest brother would be "er-di," and the youngest of your two younger brothers would be "san-di."

Cultivation and Martial Arts

GENERAL

GONGZI: Young master of an affluent household
-JUN: A suffix meaning "lord."
-ZUN: A suffix meaning "esteemed, venerable." More respectful than "-jun."

SECTS

SHIDI: Younger martial brother. For junior male members of one's own sect.

SHIFU: Teacher/master. For one's master in one's own sect. Gender neutral. Mostly interchangeable with Shizun.

SHIJIE: Older martial sister. For senior female members of one's own sect.

SHIMEI: Younger martial sister. For junior female members of one's own sect.

SHINIANG: The wife of a shifu/shizun.

SHISHU: The younger martial brother of one's master.

SHIXIONG: Older martial brother. For senior male members of one's own sect.

SHIZUN: Honorific address (as opposed to shifu) of teacher/master.

Cultivators and Immortals

DAOREN: "Cultivator."

DAOZHANG: A polite address for cultivators. Equivalent to "Mr. Cultivator." Can be used alone as a title or attached to someone's name

   EXAMPLE: referring to Xiao Xingchen as "Daozhang" or "Xiao Xingchen-daozhang."

SANREN: "Scattered One." For cultivators/immortals who are not tied to a specific sect.

CHARACTER & NAME GUIDE

Pronunciation Guide

> Mandarin Chinese is the official state language of China. It is a tonal language, so correct pronunciation is vital to being understood! Below is a simplified guide on the pronunciation of select character names and terms from MXTX's series to help get you started.

Series Names

SCUM VILLAIN'S SELF-SAVING SYSTEM (REN ZHA FAN PAI ZI JIU XI TONG):
ren jaa faan pie zzh zioh she tone

GRANDMASTER OF DEMONIC CULTIVATION (MO DAO ZU SHI):
mwuh dow zoo shrr

HEAVEN OFFICIAL'S BLESSING (TIAN GUAN CI FU):
tee-yan gwen tsz fuu

Character Names

SHEN QINGQIU: Shhen Ching-cheeoh
LUO BINGHE: Loo-uh Bing-huhh
WEI WUXIAN: Way Woo-shee-ahn
LAN WANGJI: Lahn Wong-gee
XIE LIAN: Shee-yay Lee-yan
HUA CHENG: Hoo-wah Cch-yung

XIAO-: shee-ow
-ER: ahrr
A-: ah
GONGZI: gong-zzh

DAOZHANG: dow-jon
-JUN: june
DIDI: dee-dee
GEGE: guh-guh
JIEJIE: gee-ay-gee-ay
MEIMEI: may-may
-XIONG: shong

Terms

DANMEI: dann-may
WUXIA: woo-sheeah
XIANXIA: sheeyan-sheeah
QI: chee

General Consonants & Vowels

X: similar to English sh (**sh**eep)
Q: similar to English ch (**ch**arm)
C: similar to English ts (pan**ts**)
IU: yoh
UO: wuh
ZHI: jrr
CHI: chrr
SHI: shrr
RI: rrr

ZI: zzz
CI: tsz
SI: ssz
U: When u follows a y, j, q, or x, the sound is actually ü, pronounced like eee with your lips rounded like ooo. This applies for yu, yuan, jun, etc.

Grandmaster of Demonic Cultivation
MO DAO ZU SHI

Glossary

Glossary

> While not required reading, this glossary is intended to offer further context to the many concepts and terms utilized throughout this novel and provide a starting point for learning more about the rich Chinese culture from which these stories were written.

GENRES

Danmei

Danmei (耽美 / "indulgence in beauty") is a Chinese fiction genre focused on romanticized tales of love and attraction between men. It is analogous to the BL (boys' love) genre in Japanese media. The majority of well-known danmei writers are women writing for women, although all genders produce and enjoy the genre.

Wuxia

Wuxia (武侠 / "martial heroes") is one of the oldest Chinese literary genres and consists of tales of noble heroes fighting evil and injustice. It often follows martial artists, monks, or rogues, who live apart from the ruling government, which is often seen as useless or corrupt. These societal outcasts—both voluntary and not—settle disputes among themselves, adhering to their own moral codes over the governing law.

Characters in wuxia focus primarily on human concerns, such as political strife between factions and advancing their own personal sense of justice. True wuxia is low on magical or supernatural elements. To Western moviegoers, a well-known example is *Crouching Tiger, Hidden Dragon*.

Xianxia

Xianxia (仙侠 / "immortal heroes") is a genre related to wuxia that places more emphasis on the supernatural. Its characters often strive to become stronger, with the end goal of extending their life span or achieving immortality.

Xianxia heavily features Daoist themes, while cultivation and the pursuit of immortality are both genre requirements. If these are not the story's central focus, it is not xianxia. The Scum Villain's Self-Saving System, Grandmaster of Demonic Cultivation, and Heaven Official's Blessing are all considered part of both the danmei and xianxia genres.

Webnovels

Webnovels are novels serialized by chapter online, and the websites that host them are considered spaces for indie and amateur writers. Many novels, dramas, comics, and animated shows produced in China are based on popular webnovels.

Grandmaster of Demonic Cultivation was first serialized on the website *JJWXC*.

TERMINOLOGY

ARRAY: Area-of-effect magic circles. Anyone within the array falls under the effect of the array's associated spell(s).

ASCENSION: A Daoist concept, ascension refers to the process of a person gaining enlightenment through cultivation, whereupon they shed their mortal form and are removed from the corporeal world. In most xianxia, gods are distinct from immortals in that gods are conceived naturally and born divine, while immortals cannot attain godhood but can achieve great longevity.

BOWING: As is seen in other Asian cultures, standing bows are a traditional greeting and are also used when giving an apology. A deeper bow shows greater respect.

BUDDHISM: The central belief of Buddhism is that life is a cycle of suffering and rebirth, only to be escaped by reaching enlightenment (nirvana). Buddhists believe in karma, that a person's actions will influence their fortune in this life and future lives. The teachings of the Buddha are known as The Middle Way and emphasize a practice that is neither extreme asceticism nor extreme indulgence.

BODHISATTVA: A bodhisattva is a Buddhist who achieves enlightenment and, rather than release into nirvana, returns to show others the way.

CLANS: Cultivation clans are large blood-related families that share a surname. Clans are led by family elders, and while only family members can be leaders, disciples can join regardless of blood relation. They may eventually take on the family name, depending on whether the family chooses to offer it. This could be accomplished via adoption or marriage. Clans tend to have a signature cultivation or martial art that is passed down through generations along with ancestral magical artifacts and weapons.

Colors

WHITE: Death, mourning, purity. Used in funerals for both the deceased and mourners.

BLACK: Classy, scholarly. Considered masculine, representing the Heavens and the dao.

RED: Happiness, good luck. Used for weddings.

YELLOW/GOLD: Wealth and prosperity, and often reserved for the emperor.

BLUE/GREEN: Health, prosperity, and harmony.

PURPLE: Divinity and immortality.

CONFUCIANISM: Confucianism is a philosophy based on the teachings of Confucius. Its influence on all aspects of Chinese culture is incalculable. Confucius placed heavy importance on respect for one's elders and family, a concept broadly known as *xiao* (孝 / "filial piety"). The family structure is used in other contexts to urge similar behaviors, such as respect of a student towards a teacher, or people of a country towards their ruler.

CORES/GOLDEN CORES: The formation of a *jindan* (金丹 / "golden core") is a key step in any cultivator's journey to immortality. The Golden Core forms from and replaces the lower dantian, becoming an internal source of power for the cultivator. Golden Core formation is only accomplished after a great deal of intense training and qi cultivation.

Cultivators can detonate their Golden Core as a last-ditch move to take out a dangerous opponent, but this almost always kills the cultivator. A core's destruction or removal is permanent. It cannot be re-cultivated, as there is no longer a lower dantian to form it from. Its destruction also prevents the individual from ever being able to process or cultivate qi normally again.

COURTESY NAMES: A courtesy name is given to an individual when they come of age. (See Name Guide.)

CULTIVATORS/CULTIVATION: Cultivators are practitioners of spirituality and martial artists who seek to gain understanding of the will of the universe while also attaining personal strength and expanding their life span.

Cultivation is a long process marked by "stages." There are traditionally nine stages, but this is often simplified in fiction. Some common stages are noted below, though exact definitions of each stage may depend on the setting.

- Qi Condensation/Qi Refining (凝气/练气)
- Foundation Establishment (筑基)
- Core Formation/Golden Core (结丹/金丹)
- Nascent Soul (元婴)
- Deity Transformation (化神)
- Great Ascension (大乘)
- Heavenly Tribulation (渡劫)

CULTIVATION MANUAL: Cultivation manuals and sutras are common plot devices in xianxia/wuxia novels. They provide detailed instructions on a secret/advanced training technique, and are sought out by those who wish to advance their cultivation levels.

CURRENCY: The currency system during most dynasties was based on the exchange of silver and gold coinage. Weight was also used to measure denominations of money. An example is something being marked with a price of "one liang of silver."

CUT-SLEEVE: A term for a gay man. Comes from a tale about an emperor's love for, and relationship with, a male politician. The emperor was called to the morning assembly, but his lover was asleep on his sleeve. Rather than wake him, the emperor cut off his sleeve.

DANTIAN: *Dantian* (丹田 / "cinnabar field") refers to three regions in the body where qi is concentrated and refined. The Lower is located three finger widths below and two finger widths behind the navel. This is where a cultivator's golden core would be formed and is where the qi metabolism process begins and progresses upward. The Middle is located at the center of the chest, at level with the heart, while the Upper is located on the forehead, between the eyebrows.

DAOISM: Daoism is the philosophy of the *dao* (道 / "the way") Following the dao involves coming into harmony with the natural order of the universe, which makes someone a "true human," safe from external harm and who can affect the world without intentional action. Cultivation is a concept based on Daoist superstitions.

DEMONS: A race of immensely powerful and innately supernatural beings. They are almost always aligned with evil. Evil-aligned cultivators who seek power are said to follow the demonic cultivation path. Depending on the setting, evil-aligned cultivators may be able to transform into demons through demonic cultivation.

GLOSSARY

DISCIPLES: Clan and sect members are known as disciples. Disciples live on sect grounds and have a strict hierarchy based on skill and seniority. They are divided into Core, Inner, and Outer rankings, with Core being the highest. Higher-ranked disciples get better lodging and other resources.

When formally joining a sect or clan as a disciple or a student, the sect/clan becomes like the disciple's new family: teachers are parents and peers are siblings. Because of this, a betrayal or abandonment of one's sect/clan is considered a deep transgression of Confucian values of filial piety. This is also the origin of many of the honorifics and titles used for martial arts.

DIZI: A flute held horizontally. They are considered an instrument for commoners, as they are easy to craft from bamboo or wood.

ERHU: A two-stringed fiddle, played with a bow.

FACE: *Mianzi* (面子), generally translated as "face," is an important concept in Chinese society. It is a metaphor for a person's reputation and can be extended to further descriptive metaphors. For example, "having face" refers to having a good reputation, and "losing face" refers to having one's reputation hurt. Meanwhile, "giving face" means deferring to someone else to help improve their reputation, while "not wanting face" implies that a person is acting so poorly/shamelessly that they clearly don't care about their reputation at all. "Thin face" refers to someone easily embarrassed or prone to offense at perceived slights. Conversely, "thick face" refers to someone not easily embarrassed and immune to insults.

FAIRY/XIANZI: A term commonly used in novels to describe a woman possessing ethereal, heavenly beauty. *Xianzi* is the female counterpart to *xianren* ("immortal"), and is also used to describe celestials that have descended from heaven.

THE FIVE ELEMENTS: Also known as the *wuxing* (五行 / "Five Phases"). Rather than Western concepts of elemental magic, Chinese phases are more commonly used to describe the interactions and relationships between things. The phases can both beget and overcome each other.

Wood (木 / mu)
Fire (火 / huo)
Earth (土 / tu)
Metal (金 / jin)
Water (水 / shui)

FUNERALS: Daoist or Buddhist funerals generally last for forty-nine days. During the funeral ceremony, mourners can present the deceased with offerings of food, incense, and joss paper. If deceased ancestors have no patrilineal descendants to give them offerings, they may starve in the afterlife and become hungry ghosts. Wiping out a whole family is punishment for more than just the living.

After the funeral, the coffin is nailed shut and sealed with paper talismans to protect the body from evil spirits. The deceased is transported in a procession to their final resting place, often accompanied by loud music to scare off evil spirits. Cemeteries are often on hillsides; the higher a grave is located, the better the feng shui. The traditional mourning color is white.

GHOST: Ghosts (鬼) are the restless spirits of deceased sentient creatures. Ghosts produce yin energy and crave yang energy.

GUQIN: A seven-stringed zither, played by plucking with the fingers. Sometimes called a qin. It is fairly large and is meant to be laid flat on a surface or on one's lap while playing.

HAND GESTURES: The *baoquan* (抱拳 / "hold fist") is a martial arts salute where one places their closed right fist against their open left palm. The *gongshou* (拱手 / "arch hand") is a more generic salute not specific to martial artists, where one drapes their open left palm over their closed right fist. The orientation of both of these salutes is reversed for women. During funerals, the closed hand in both salutes switches, where men will use their left fist and women their right.

HAND SEALS: Refers to various hand and finger gestures used by cultivators to cast spells, or used while meditating. A cultivator may be able to control their sword remotely with a hand seal.

IMMORTAL-BINDING ROPES OR CABLES: Ropes, nets, and other restraints enchanted to withstand the power of an immortal or god. They can only be cut by high-powered spiritual items or weapons and often limit the abilities of those trapped by them.

INCENSE TIME: A common way to tell time in ancient China, referring to how long it takes for a single incense stick to burn. Standardized incense sticks were manufactured and calibrated for specific time measurements: a half hour, an hour, a day, etc. These were available to people of all social classes. When referenced in *Grandmaster of Demonic Cultivation*, a single incense time is usually about thirty minutes.

INEDIA: A common ability that allows an immortal to survive without mortal food or sleep by sustaining themselves on purer forms of energy based on Daoist fasting. Depending on the setting, immortals who have achieved inedia may be unable to tolerate mortal food, or they may be able to choose to eat when desired.

JADE: Jade is a culturally and spiritually important mineral in China. Its durability, beauty, and the ease with which it can be utilized for crafting both decorative and functional pieces alike has made it widely beloved since ancient times. The word might cause Westerners to think of green jade (the mineral jadeite), but Chinese texts are often referring to white jade (the mineral nephrite). This is the color referenced when a person's skin is described as "the color of jade."

JADE EMPEROR: In Daoist cosmology, the Jade Emperor (玉皇大帝) is the emperor of heaven, the chief of the heavenly court, and one of the highest ranked gods in the heavenly realm, lower only to the three primordial emanations. When one says "Oh god/lord" or "My heavens", it is usually referring to the Jade Emperor. In Heaven Official's Blessing, Jun Wu's role replaces that of the Jade Emperor.

JIUTIAN XUANNU: In Daoist cosmology, Jiutian Xuannu (九天玄女 / "Dark Lady of the Nine Heavens"), is the Goddess of War and protectress of a nation.

Numbers

TWO: Two (二 / "er") is considered a good number and is referenced in the common idiom "good things come in pairs." It is common practice to repeat characters in pairs for added effect.

THREE: Three (三 / "san") sounds like sheng (生 / "living") and also like san (散 / "separation").

FOUR: Four (四 / "si") sounds like si (死 / "death"). A very unlucky number.

SEVEN: Seven (七 / "qi") sounds like qi (齊 / "together"), making it a good number for love-related things. However, it also sounds like qi (欺 / "deception").

EIGHT: Eight (八 / "ba") sounds like fa (發 / "prosperity"), causing it to be considered a very lucky number.

NINE: Nine (九 / "jiu") is associated with matters surrounding the Emperor and Heaven, and is as such considered an auspicious number.

MXTX's work has subtle numerical theming around its love interests. In *Grandmaster of Demonic Cultivation*, her second book, Lan Wangji is frequently called Lan-er-gege ("second brother Lan") as a nickname by Wei Wuxian. In her third book, *Heaven Official's Blessing*, Hua Cheng is the third son of his family and gives the name San Lang ("third youth") when Xie Lian asks what to call him.

PEONY: Symbolizes wealth and power. Was considered the flower of the emperor.

PILLS AND ELIXIRS: Magic medicines that can heal wounds, improve cultivation, extend life, etc. In Chinese culture, these things are usually delivered in pill form. These pills are created in special kilns.

PRIMORDIAL SPIRIT: The essence of one's existence beyond the physical. The body perishes, the soul enters the karmic wheel, but the spirit that makes one unique is eternal.

QI: *Qi* (气) is the energy in all living things. There is both righteous qi and evil or poisonous qi.

Cultivators strive to cultivate qi by absorbing it from the natural world and refining it within themselves to improve their cultivation base. A cultivation base refers to the amount of qi a cultivator possesses or is able to possess. In xianxia, natural locations such as caves, mountains, or other secluded places with beautiful scenery are often rich in qi, and practicing there can allow a cultivator to make rapid progress in their cultivation.

Cultivators and other qi manipulators can utilize their life force in a variety of ways, including imbuing objects with it to transform them into lethal weapons or sending out blasts of energy to do powerful damage. Cultivators also refine their senses beyond normal human levels. For instance, they may cast out their spiritual sense to gain total awareness of everything in a region around them or to feel for potential danger.

QI CIRCULATION: The metabolic cycle of qi in the body, where it flows from the dantian to the meridians and back. This cycle purifies and refines qi, and good circulation is essential to cultivation. In xianxia, qi can be transferred from one person to another through physical contact and can heal someone who is wounded if the donor is trained in the art.

QI DEVIATION: A qi deviation (走火入魔 / "to catch fire and enter demonhood") occurs when one's cultivation base becomes unstable. Common causes include an unstable emotional state, practicing cultivation methods incorrectly, reckless use of forbidden or high-level arts, or succumbing to the influence of demons and devils.

Symptoms of qi deviation in fiction include panic, paranoia, sensory hallucinations, and death, whether by the qi deviation itself causing irreparable damage to the body or as a result of its symptoms such as leaping to one's death to escape a hallucination. Common treatments of qi deviation in fiction include relaxation (voluntary or forced by an external party), massage, meditation, or qi transfer from another individual.

QIANKUN: (乾坤 / "universe") Common tools used in wuxia and xianxia. The primary function of these magical items is to provide unlimited storage space. Examples include pouches, the sleeve of a robe, magical jewelry, a weapon, and more.

SECT: A cultivation sect is an organization of individuals united by their dedication to the practice of a particular method of cultivation or martial arts. A sect may have a signature style. Sects are led by a single leader, who is supported by senior sect members. They are not necessarily related by blood.

SEVEN APERTURES/QIQIAO: (七窍) The seven facial apertures: the two eyes, nose, mouth, tongue, and two ears. The essential qi of vital organs are said to connect to the seven apertures, and illness in the vital organs may cause symptoms there. People who are ill or seriously injured may be "bleeding from the seven apertures."

SHICHEN: Days were split into twelve intervals of two hours apiece called *shichen* (时辰 / "time"). Each of these shichen has an associated term. Pre-Han dynasty used semi-descriptive terms, but in Post-Han dynasty, the shichen were renamed to correspond to the twelve zodiac animals.

    ZI, MIDNIGHT: 11pm - 1am
    CHOU: 1am - 3am
    YIN: 3am - 5am
    MAO, SUNRISE: 5am - 7am
    CHEN: 7am - 9am
    SI: 9am - 11am
    WU, NOON: 11am - 1pm
    WEI: 1pm - 3pm
    SHEN: 3pm - 5pm
    YOU, SUNSET: 5pm - 7pm
    XU, DUSK: 7pm - 9pm
    HAI: 9pm - 11pm

SHIDI, SHIXIONG, SHIZUN, ETC.: Chinese titles and terms used to indicate a person's role or rank in relation to the speaker. Because of the robust nature of this naming system, and a lack of nuance in translating many to English, the original titles have been maintained. (See Name Guide for more information.)

THE SIX ARTS: Six disciplines that any well-bred gentleman in Ancient China was expected to be learned in. The Six Arts were: Rites, Music, Archery, Chariotry or Equestrianism, Calligraphy, and Mathematics.

SPIRIT-ATTRACTION FLAG: A banner or flag intended to guide spirits. Can be hung from a building or tree to mark a location or carried around on a staff.

SWORDS: A cultivator's sword is an important part of their cultivation practice. In many instances, swords are spiritually bound to their owner and may have been bestowed to them by their master, a family member, or obtained through a ritual. Cultivators in fiction are able to use their swords as transportation by standing atop the flat of the blade and riding it as it flies through the air. Skilled cultivators can summon their swords to fly into their hand, command the sword to fight on its own, or release energy attacks from the edge of the blade.

SWORD GLARE: *Jianguang* (剑光 / "sword light"), an energy attack released from a sword's edge.

SWORN BROTHERS/SISTERS/FAMILIES: In China, sworn brotherhood describes a binding social pact made by two or more unrelated individuals of the same gender. It can be entered into for social, political, and/or personal reasons and is not only limited to two participants; it can extend to an entire group. It was most common among men, but was not unheard of among women or between people of different genders.

The participants treat members of each other's families as their own and assist them in the ways an extended family would: providing mutual support and aid, support in political alliances, etc. Sworn siblinghood, where individuals will refer to themselves as brother or sister, is not to be confused with familial relations like blood siblings or adoption. It is sometimes used in Chinese media, particularly danmei, to imply romantic relationships that could otherwise be prone to censorship.

TALISMANS: Strips of paper with incantations written on them, often done so with cinnabar ink or blood. They can serve as seals or be used as one-time spells.

TIGER TALLY: A *hufu* (虎符 / "tiger tally"), was used by Ancient Chinese emperors to signal their approval to dispatch troops in battle. A hufu was in two parts: one in the possession of the emperor, and the other in the possession of a general in the field. To signal approval, the emperor would send his half of the hufu to the general. If the two sides matched, troops would advance.

WHISK: A whisk held by a cultivator is not a baking tool, but a Daoist symbol and martial arts weapon. Usually made of horsehair bound to a wooden stick, the whisk is based off a tool used to brush away flies without killing them, and is symbolically meant for wandering Daoist monks to brush away thoughts that would lure them back to secular life. Wudang Daoist Monks created a fighting style based on wielding it as a weapon.

YAO: Animals, plants, or objects that have gained spiritual consciousness due to prolonged absorption of qi. Especially high-level or long-lived yao are able to take on a human form. This concept is comparable to Japanese yokai, which is a loanword from the Chinese yao. Yao are not evil by nature, but often come into conflict with humans for various reasons, one being that the cores they develop can be harvested by human cultivators to increase their own abilities.

YIN ENERGY AND YANG ENERGY: Yin and yang is a concept in Chinese philosophy that describes the complementary interdependence of opposite/contrary forces. It can be applied to all forms of change and differences. Yang represents the sun, masculinity, and the living, while yin represents the shadows, femininity, and the dead, including spirits and ghosts. In fiction, imbalances between yin and yang energy can do serious harm to the body or act as the driving force for malevolent spirits seeking to replenish themselves of whichever they lack.

YU THE GREAT: (大) A legendary figure in ancient China (2123–2025 BC) who became widely known due to his success taming the Yellow River floods by way of dredging and redirecting flow. Tales say that in the many years of the water control project, he had passed by his home three times and each time turned away, resolved to only return when he succeeded. He was praised for his moral character and later established the Xia dynasty.